'It is extraordinary th[...]re acclaimed. While nove[...]k in publicity, his work [...]t over the past decade [...]f novels of harrowing [...]n brings Edric's unflinching and entirely unsentimental attention to the appalling things human beings perpetrate against each other . . . the first world war – or, to be more precise, its aftermath of trauma and mutilation – is his subject. The date is 1919 and the setting a Swiss spa where Elizabeth Mortlake, a young woman from Oxford, is holidaying with her widowed sister-in-law, Mary. Here they hope to begin to recuperate from their shared loss, during the war, of a brother and a husband. But it soon becomes apparent they could hardly have selected a location less favourable to forgetfulness and consolation . . . The emotional climate of this novel is as freezing as the late-autumn Switzerland Edric so atmospherically evokes. Eerily distanced and formal prose – icily hard, transparent, largely devoid of metaphor and entirely devoid of sentiment – communicates an appropriately numbed-seeming lack of warmth. True to its title, this is a work of bleak accomplishment'

PETER KEMP, *SUNDAY TIMES*

'At the book's heart there is a deep darkness in which sex and death are intermingled . . . *In Desolate Heaven* is like one of those dreams where you can come awake, then fall asleep and continue where you left off: it has that kind of coherence and necessity. Apart from its poetic power, it demonstrates the truth of Plato's perception that only the dead ever see the end of a war'

ROBERT NYE, *THE TIMES*

'Robert Edric has written of cruelty before, in his acclaimed novel about Tasmanian aborigines [*Elysium*], but this book is a wider revelation, of a continent insanely destroying itself and released, reeling, into "peace". It seems to me to be an individual and important book, pared down almost to poetry . . . The book is important because it sees war from a new geographical angle, with Switzerland, now in place as central Europe again, comforting itself with a sort of joyless lust. The mysterious English hero, Jameson, is a scholar and collector of rare books who has drifted into the pornography industry. He has money but not self-respect, does good, is kind and afraid for the doomed army captain, but there is no simple warmth or love. There is no simple love anywhere. Even the nuns are pretty reticent about the love of God . . . What makes this novel is Edric's extraordinary visual gift. He can take you immediately into the middle of the scene so that you can feel the great walls of ice, the blackness of mountain-shadowed water, the amazing skies; and see, as in a Tissot painting, the restaurants of icy linen, frail fires burning in the grates of high bedrooms, the beds slung with the pretty clothes of solitary women. You smell the wet, dark streets of the nasty little town. I would defy anyone not to sit down and read to the end of this glacial, painful book'

JANE GARDAM, *LITERARY REVIEW*

'Edric's method in this novel is one of stealthy revelation, detail by detail . . . The prose, in contrast to the historical events, is almost colourless, written in pointed, often short, sentences, keeping a steady, beating momentum, a constant heartbeat signalling writing alert with engaging, persistent life. Thereby, the agony, the despair and the madness of war, with its troubled aftermath, emerge with a fierceness and starkness . . . Yet the novel's quiet, persuasive power, its recreation of time and place and a mood of hiatus, continue their work. A fine achievement, not swiftly forgotten'

TOM ADAIR, *SCOTLAND ON SUNDAY*

In Desolate Heaven

Robert Edric was born in 1956 and lives in East Yorkshire. His previous novels include *Winter Garden* (1985 James Tait Black Prize winner), *A New Ice Age* (1986 runner-up for the *Guardian* Fiction Prize), *A Lunar Eclipse* (1989), *The Earth Made of Glass* (1994) and *Elysium* (1995). His short stories have appeared in *Pen New Fiction*, *London Magazine* and *Winter's Tales*.

IN DESOLATE HEAVEN

Robert Edric

TRANSWORLD PUBLISHERS LTD
61–63 Uxbridge Road, London W5 5SA

TRANSWORLD PUBLISHERS (AUSTRALIA) PTY LTD
15–25 Helles Avenue, Moorebank, NSW 2170

TRANSWORLD PUBLISHERS (NZ) LTD
3 William Pickering Drive, Albany, Auckland

Published by Anchor – a division of Transworld Publishers Ltd

First published in 1997 by Gerald Duckworth & Co. Ltd

This paperback edition published in Great Britain by Anchor, 1998

A catalogue record for this book is available from the British Library.

ISBN 1862 30012 7

Typeset in 11/14pt Adobe Caslon by Kestrel Data, Exeter.

Printed in Great Britain by Mackays of Chatham Plc, Chatham, Kent.

We have fallen in the dreams the ever-living
Breathe on the tarnished mirror of the world,
And then smooth out with ivory hands and sigh.

W. B. Yeats

For Friends

Switzerland, 1919

PART I

Each morning she watched the procession of nurses and invalids as they made their short, slow journey to gather at the lakeshore. They came from the town's hospitals and convalescent homes, the converging tributaries of a single flow, the nurses mostly young women, the invalids mostly young men. And despite the seeming chaos of this convergence and gathering, it was clear to her, watching from her hotel window, that these various parties congregated there by some prior arrangement; that despite the apparent confusion and the numbers involved, some governing reason of organization and order existed.

Those in wheelchairs were always taken across the lake road first, with wooden ramps laid at the kerbs to lower and raise the chairs.

The carriage drivers and few motorists held up by the

procession did not complain at the delay. Others, the interrupted morning walkers, the late season tourists, kept a respectable distance and watched from among the flower beds and beneath the plane trees. Some, those who came upon the procession unawares, and who inadvertently came too close to it, stood and watched as though they were watching a passing cortège. It was how she herself had originally felt. She had seen some among these onlookers take off their hats and hold them to their chests, and she imagined the other lost brothers and sons and fathers they, too, might be unexpectedly remembering. She saw what a cold wind this shuffling line of men and nurses blew through those failing days of warmth and light.

On other days she had seen women among the onlookers turn away from the procession. Young women and old women, turn their heads and shield their eyes with gloved hands, as though even a glimpse of these young men was too much for them. She wondered what it was they resented most about the intrusion of the invalids. Some even let down veils and watched with their hands clasped in protective prayer.

Usually the procession moved to the lakeshore in silence, but occasionally a cry of pain or a shouted word could be heard, and when that happened a further cold draught passed through those who stood and watched; it was often more the echo of a cry than the cry itself, but the effect was the same.

She watched all this now from her small balcony. On either side of her stood the other guests who had come out to share in the spectacle. She overheard their remarks; she spoke some French and German and did her best to understand what was being said. But she listened most intently for any sound from the adjacent room, in which Mary, her sister-in-law, slept. By leaning forward she could see that the curtains to the room remained drawn. She hoped, too, that the young widow was unaware of what was happening on the street below, but again she did not deceive herself.

She had woken several times during the night to hear the sound of pacing, of objects – books, photographs, glasses – being picked up and put back down. And she had heard, too, the sound of uncontrollable and convulsive sobbing, muffled, it seemed to her, though she could not tell if this was simply a consequence of the wall through which the noise came, or if her sister-in-law was forcing her face into a pillow in an effort to contain her uncontainable grief.

When Elizabeth had woken and heard this, her first instinct had been to unlock the door which separated them and go through to offer comfort, but she knew that the woman was beyond comforting and that she would have resented being forced to exhibit or share her grief in this way.

On several occasions, home in England, the two of them had cried together over their loss, but even then, even in the days and weeks immediately following her brother's death, she had never felt it to be a shared loss, only a common source of grief in which the roots of two separate plants were so suddenly struggling for survival.

She was here now as a companion to the young widow. She herself was twenty-three, and despite her sister-in-law being a year younger, she would never think of the woman as being anything but ten years older than herself, of a different generation almost, distanced by her loss.

She seldom smoked in public, but on this morning, with the procession of invalids half passed beneath her, she lit a cigarette and sat in the outdoor chair. She slid her hand through the scrollwork of the balcony and flicked ash into the air beyond. She heard the voices of the Gottliebs in the room to her right. The German couple and their daughter had already taken an unwelcome interest in her and Mary. She assumed this was because she and her sister-in-law were the same age as the daughter, Gerda, and because they were two unaccompanied women. The girl behaved like a fifteen-year-old. She had three brothers, two of them twins, all three of whom had fought in the war during its closing months; only two, the twins, had survived. Elizabeth learned all this within minutes of meeting the family.

She heard Gerda now, heard the excitement in her voice as she called to her parents to come out and see what was happening below.

'Elizabet, Elizabet.' She pronounced the name with a hard 't'. Her parents spoke English only in rudimentary phrases, precise meaning drowned in their glutinous accents.

Elizabeth acknowledged the girl with a nod, unwilling to encourage her further.

Herr Gottlieb appeared. He was dressed in the same heavy suit, soft hat and the broad leather belt which he wore over his jacket and which exaggerated the globe of his stomach. He bowed to Elizabeth and told his daughter to lower her voice. His wife called to him from their room and he returned indoors.

'You are smoking?' Gerda called.

In response, Elizabeth let out a plume of smoke.

A horn sounded below, and both women turned back to the street. A motorist, more impatient than the others, had driven forward in an attempt to edge through the men in wheelchairs, and now his engine had stalled, blocking their path and causing the chairs to be manoeuvred around him. Resenting this intrusion, some of the invalids were banging their fists or canes against the sides of the car. In response, the driver sounded his horn at them, the same piercing note over and over, as though the men in chairs and the women pushing them were a flock of sheep that had gathered around him and needed to be frightened into continuing. Several of the nurses tried to reason with the man, and one of them tried to pull his hand from the horn, but he was too strong for her and he went on sounding it until a male orderly intervened.

Only then did it occur to Elizabeth why the nurses had been so insistent on stopping the noise, and she watched as a party of the women returned to where a group of men stood beneath the trees. She could not see clearly what was happening because of the foliage, but she could see that each man in this small group was being held and comforted by at least two of the women, sometimes three, holding themselves in a close wall around him. Beyond them, other men stood with their hands pressed to their ears and their eyes tightly closed.

Eventually the stalled car was pushed clear of the crossing place and the chairs were moved on. Only then were the men beneath the trees led out and across to the lake.

After these came the remainder of the walking wounded, some moving as though they had forgotten how to walk and were now learning anew, the details of which – the co-ordination of bone, muscle, flesh, will and energy – they had yet to master.

And following these came the blinded, held and led, reassured, whispered to of what they could not see. Her pilot brother, Mary's husband, had been blinded, and had then lived sightless for six months before finally succumbing to the infection nurtured by his wounds and burns. It was for this reason that she felt an uncertain affinity with these men, and she watched them closely, already able to distinguish between those who had grown accustomed to their sightlessness, and those who had not. She saw, too, those who would never grow accustomed to the dark worlds they now inhabited, and those who were content to be led everywhere – if not by these women, then by others – and those who resented this new and childlike dependency; those men who would forever stab and slash at the air ahead of them with their canes as though the sticks were antennae and they were insects, and as though the persistence and violence of their actions might somehow miraculously cleave the darkness of these new black worlds and flood them with light.

She watched until the first of these men reached the railings above the lake and then she left the balcony and went silently through to her sister-in-law.

She was surprised to find Mary sleeping, her body length-ways across the bed, and with the bulk of her bedclothes piled on the floor. Several books and photographs lay on the mattress beside her, and her night-gown had been pushed down so that she lay naked from the waist up. Elizabeth felt beneath the pillow for the pill box she knew to be hidden there. She counted the pills it contained and returned it. Mary's skin was pale, even in that half-light, and the pattern of her ribs was visible. Her breasts were small and flat. Elizabeth had seen her naked before, but this was not how she had looked then, and it shocked her to see how little substance and vitality remained.

She met Jameson for the first time four days later. She was
sitting in the dining-room watching the waiters and waitresses clear away the breakfast dishes. Two would strip a
table and carry away its detritus in the bundled cloth, two
others would wipe the table and lay a clean cloth, and yet
two more would immediately arrange upon this the crockery
and cutlery ready for the mid-morning customers. They
worked in silence, watched by the maître d', who directed
them by clicking his fingers and pointing. Occasionally, he
stopped one of the girls and inspected whatever she was
carrying. He, too, worked largely in silence. When he discovered something he did not like – an insufficiently polished
spoon, perhaps, or a less than perfectly folded napkin – he
would pick it up between his thumb and forefinger, hold it at
arm's length, consider it distastefully for a moment, and then

let it drop to the floor. The waitress would then have to put down her tray and retrieve whatever had offended the man. The maître d' wore a pair of starched white gloves, against which he measured the perfection of everything he encountered. Few of the guests ever spoke to the man directly, and he in turn seldom communicated with them. He was the helmsman and they were his passengers – his presence need only be reassuringly felt.

Predictably, the Gottliebs sat at a nearby table. Herr Gottlieb in particular watched the man and the waitresses, most of whom were younger than his daughter, and Elizabeth overheard his comments to his wife about how important it was that someone should be correcting the girls and keeping everything running smoothly. Neither Frau Gottlieb nor Gerda responded with anything other than discreet, obedient nods to his remarks.

Earlier, Elizabeth had been accompanied by Mary. She had ordered breakfast for her, but the food remained untouched. All Mary had eaten was a small piece of dry toast, and most of this she had contrived to wipe in crumbs from her lips. She had again been sick during the night, and the barely-disguised smell of this had struck Elizabeth upon entering her room. She had not remarked on it. The sight and the aroma of the cooked food laid before them had nauseated Mary and she had left the table at the first opportunity. She told Elizabeth she would cross the road to the lake, but Elizabeth knew that this was unlikely, and that she would return instead to her room.

Other guests rose and left until fewer than a dozen remained. The later arrivals were directed to tables alongside Elizabeth and the Gottliebs.

When the last of the food had been delivered, the maître d' placed a card on a pedestal announcing that breakfast was no longer being served, and it was as he did this, as he balanced the card and then stepped back to ensure that it was properly positioned, that the door behind him opened and a man entered, smoking a cigar and reading a newspaper which he had folded into the shape and size of a cricket bat. He collided with the maître d', almost toppling the pedestal. He looked over his paper, considered the notice for a moment, said, 'Coffee, please,' and then crossed the dining-room to a table distant from the others.

The maître d' followed him, waving both his gloved hands through the smoke which trailed the newcomer as though he were pushing through undergrowth.

'You cannot sit there,' he said.

'Coffee, please. The table is vacant. This is where I am sitting.' The man spoke without looking up, engrossed in whatever he was reading. He seldom took the cigar from his mouth. He was clearly English, but spoke with an accent Elizabeth could not identify.

'You will please oblige me by sitting with the other guests,' the maître d' said, his anger now barely controlled.

'Your countryman,' Herr Gottlieb said aloud to Elizabeth. 'Hardly the finest ambassador for your country. I wonder he doesn't take off his boots to make himself feel more at home.' He spoke in German and laughed at his remarks. His daughter began to translate what he said, but he stopped her.

'And you will oblige me by doing as I ask and fetching me a jug of coffee,' the Englishman said to the maître d'. His voice was low, calm; he took no pleasure in the discomfort he caused the man.

'You are not a guest here.'

'Nor do I need to be.'

The maître d' turned and walked away.

'His name is Jameson,' Gerda said to Elizabeth. 'He comes here often. Always the same.'

'And is the maître d' always so unhelpful?' Elizabeth said.

Her answer came from Jameson himself: 'The word is "offensive". "Rude", perhaps. Please, don't let me disturb you.' He looked around the room at the few others, most of whom were now watching him. 'My apologies,' he said directly to Elizabeth. He continued looking at her, making some further silent assessment of her.

Around her, Elizabeth heard his words translated in whispers. Fewer waitresses now moved among the diners. The girl who cleared Elizabeth's table did so without taking her eyes from where Jameson sat.

'Do you know him?' Elizabeth asked her in French.

'Everyone knows him,' the girl said. There was a protective, almost affectionate edge to her voice. She scraped Mary's uneaten food from one plate to another. 'Your companion is ill?' she said. It was a remark rather than an inquiry.

'She's been unwell,' Elizabeth said, but the girl was no longer listening.

Across the room, Jameson refolded his paper and stubbed out his cigar. He watched the door. It opened a moment later and a waiter entered carrying a tray of coffee. In readiness for this, Jameson pushed aside the cutlery already set out before him.

The boy put down the tray and began taking things from it.

'Leave it,' Jameson said. He dipped into his breast pocket and handed the boy a note.

'We are instructed to set out the coffee and milk and—'

'And I'm asking you to leave it,' Jameson said. 'I doubt the world will spin from its axis or this blessed palace of delights crumble and collapse for want of an improperly laid out coffee service.'

'I don't understand,' the boy said.

'I know.' Jameson wiped a hand across his face. He seemed suddenly tired of whatever small drama he had instigated. 'Tell your captain of the tables in there—' he motioned to the kitchen '—that I insisted you leave everything. He won't punish you. He expects it of me. I merely live up to his expectations.'

'But—'

'Please, just go.'

The boy backed away from the table, his hands still going through the motions of setting out the crockery, as though the impulse were too strong, and as though this in some way compensated for his failure.

Jameson poured his coffee. He drank a mouthful and put down the cup.

'No poison,' he announced to those still watching him, at which those who understood him turned away.

He sat in the bay of one of the windows, the panes of which rose from the floor to the high ceiling at the front of the hotel. The morning light fell in on him in a block of yellow. He leaned back in his seat, closed his eyes and turned into this.

Only then did it occur to Elizabeth, still watching him, but without making her interest obvious, that he looked like a man who was finally relaxing after a long night of work. As a young girl she had seen her father, a country doctor, return home at dawn and sit in his study in the same way. She envied men this reassurance and reward and tranquillity of physical exertion; it was something she had never felt.

Jameson sat like this, turning into the rising light, now and then with his hand over his eyes, for several minutes before turning his back to the window and refilling his cup. He caught her eye.

'Cold-blooded,' he said to her. 'A cold-blooded Englishman sitting on a rock like a lizard dependent on the heat of the sun to get him moving.' He shook his head. 'Ignore me.'

Without considering what she was doing, Elizabeth rose, picked up her own empty cup and went across to him.

'She's going to join him,' she heard Gerda say behind her.

'They deserve each other,' her father said.

Jameson rose at her approach and pulled out a chair for her.

She knew without asking that she had been right in her guess and that he had been awake all night.

'My name is Jameson,' he said, holding out his hand to her.

'Elizabeth Mortlake.' She sat opposite him.

'Who is staying here with her sick sister-in-law,' he said unexpectedly.

'It's hardly a secret,' she said.

'No. And this place is considerably smaller than it believes itself to be.'

'Why does everyone call her sick?' Elizabeth said.

He considered this. 'Perhaps because everyone here is sick in one way or another. Shut up, Jameson. Flippancy. Forgive me again.'

She nodded her assent.

'She's a widow, then,' he said. 'She, but not you. You, unfortunately, have lost only a brother, and so in the eyes of the world you are deemed less worthy or deserving of sympathy.' He fell silent and she watched him.

'You forgot to say "Forgive me",' she said. 'Have you had a busy night?'

The remark did not surprise him. 'Reasonably,' he said. He spoke as though he believed she was already familiar with what he did.

'Are *you* sick?' she asked him.

'You only have to look at me.'

'You seem tired, that's all.'

He smiled. 'Thank you for that.' He looked around them at the watching faces. Few now felt obliged to turn away. 'I feel I ought to warn you that you have, by virtue of your small kindness, become the second most unpopular person in the hotel.' He raised his cup in a toast to the onlookers.

'Don't call it kindness,' she said. 'I'm sick of what passes for kindness these days.'

'Me too,' he said.

'Where are you from?'

'London,' he said. 'You?'

'Oxford. I couldn't place your accent.'

'My mother was Irish. Cork. Most of the rest of it I had drummed out of me.'

'At school?'

'Various. And Cambridge.'

'And what were you?'

'Captain. Artillery. And your brother?'

'RFC. He was a flyer. He saw his first aeroplane when he was a small boy.'

'I used to build kites,' he said. 'I never asked his name.'

'Michael,' she said. 'Michael.' She filled her mouth with hot, bitter coffee. And so they collided and then moved apart in their shared silence.

'What will you do today?' he said eventually.

'Find Mary.'

'There really is nothing here,' he said.

'I know. Perhaps that's the point of being here.'

'The small calm eye at the centre of the dying storm? Don't fool yourself. I can recommend a good doctor if your sister-in-law needs or wishes to see one. Be warned, the place is full of quacks, feeling wallets before pulses.' He took out a pen, tore a piece from his paper and wrote down a number.

'Thank you.'

'And now I must go,' he said. 'You'd be wise to stay a while longer. God knows what—' He was interrupted by the arrival of Frau Gottlieb, who crossed the room to stand stiffly beside him.

'Gerda wondered if you wished to accompany us on a visit to the distillery this morning, Elizabeth.' She kept her face turned away from Jameson as she spoke.

'What a good idea,' Jameson said. 'We could all go.'

'The offer was made to Elizabeth, and of course her sister-in-law,' Frau Gottlieb said. 'Elizabeth?' She was anxious for Elizabeth to speak.

'Mary is unwell,' Elizabeth said.

'Of course.' Frau Gottlieb returned to her husband and daughter. Gerda half raised her hand to Elizabeth, as though this somehow enhanced her mother's offer. Herr Gottlieb sat tapping a ringed finger against the side of his cup.

'She came to rescue you from me,' Jameson whispered.

'I've offended her,' Elizabeth said.

'So? They'll be back later to ask you what we talked about.'

'Nothing,' Elizabeth said.

'Exactly.' He rose and held out his hand to her, then withdrew it at the slightest touch. 'Like I said, cold-blooded.'

He crossed the room, nodding to everyone who remained, and the instant the dining-room door swung shut behind him, the kitchen door opened and the maître d' came directly to where Elizabeth still sat, intent on clearing the table himself and securing his own small victory.

3

She spent the following days exploring the town. It was not a large place – she read in her Baedeker that it contained fewer than twenty thousand people – due largely, she supposed, to its physical situation. The lake ran east to west and all the major buildings, mostly hotels, faced south over it. Mountains spread in every direction around them – high, steep pastures rising to barren arêtes, screes, and sharp, snow-capped peaks. The mountains to the south rose precipitously from the water. There were no buildings on that side of the lake, no farms, no roads, no cultivated fields, only what appeared to be an abandoned quarry, and it was difficult to believe, even at the height of summer, now two months past, that the north-facing slopes received any lasting sunlight. In winter, she was told, the rivers and falls which ran out of these mountains were frozen for months at a time.

She was told, too, of the living glacier which filled the head of the valley, which advanced and then retreated each year, and which blocked the narrowing space to the east like the high sheer wall of a dam.

She had suggested a visit to the glacier upon their arrival. Booklets and leaflets had been displayed in their rooms, and she had examined them all, intent on filling their days. She quickly realized how unlikely this was to happen.

Two days after Elizabeth's meeting with Jameson, Mary was sick again, and Elizabeth sat with her in the bathroom until her retching was over. There was little to show for all the painful exertion.

'We'll stay in the hotel,' Elizabeth said, disappointed that they would not now visit the old centre of the town as she had hoped.

'No. Whatever you want to do.' Mary spoke through the towel she held to her mouth.

It had occurred to Elizabeth that Mary was deliberately making herself sick, but she did not fully understand her motives for doing this, and so she vaguely imagined it instead to be some kind of self-inflicted punishment for her inability to absorb whatever confusion, uncertainty or grief she was still suffering.

Mary pushed her long hair from her face. Her brow and cheeks were slick with sweat. 'I know what you're thinking,' she said. 'And if I do starve myself to death then I will have made at least one positive gesture with my life this past year.'

Elizabeth did not take the remark seriously. She held her sister-in-law's hand.

'It isn't what I'm doing,' Mary said, eventually.

'I know.'

'I just never believed anything could be this bad, this painful. You are taught to believe that everything improves with the passing of time. It doesn't. It gets worse. Everything loses its purpose. There's no focus. To anything. Nothing matters. Everything becomes worthless, tawdry. Things, people . . .'

'And is that how you feel?'

Mary nodded. 'I feel as though I've been falling. It sounds so glib and easy to say it. I felt when Michael died – when he was killed – that I'd been broken in half. I should be mending by now, but I'm not. It just goes on. On and on and getting worse each day. Everything has become a diversion, a side-show. I walk, I talk, I look, I hear, but none of it matters to me, none of it makes any sense to me.'

'Do you try and understand it?'

'It's beyond understanding. I always considered myself an independent, intelligent woman, but this, it all just—' She began retching again.

Elizabeth released her hand and waited beside her, gently stroking her back as Mary spat the last of the liquid into the bath.

'I need some air,' Mary said when it was over, rinsing her mouth and examining her teeth in the mirror. 'It must disappoint and offend you to hear me talking like this, to turn you into nothing more than my prop or keeper.'

'You know it doesn't. We could go and sit by the lake.'

Mary laughed coldly at the suggestion. 'With all the other lost souls?'

'Why not?'

They left the hotel an hour later. It was almost midday. The bright sunlight and clear skies of the previous week had been replaced by a layer of thin cloud, through which the sun was only intermittently and vaguely visible.

They crossed to the promenade above the lake and walked to an empty bench. It was a windless day and there were no waves, only ripples and washes where the water touched the boulders and the curving wall at its edge. In contrast to the wild far shore, this side of the lake had been tamed and contained along most of its length. The water lay twelve or fifteen feet beneath them, hidden by the overhanging lip of the promenade. A double row of railings ran along the entire length of the walk, broken at intervals by granite steps leading down to the water. It was here that jetties had been built, and where the boatmen and fishermen sat, tempting the tourists to outings on the lake, mending nets, unloading their small catches.

Elizabeth and Mary sat above a group of these men and watched and listened to them. There were a dozen of them, of all ages. The younger ones whistled and called out to passing women. The passing women laughed to themselves and pretended either not to hear or to be offended.

Mary said, 'I heard all about your meeting with the infamous Captain Jameson. The waitress told me. The way she spoke, I wouldn't be surprised if there wasn't something between the two of them.'

'Oh?'

'No-one else in the hotel seems to think particularly well of him. She wouldn't say why.'

'So?'

The harshness of this surprised Mary. 'I wasn't being critical,' she said.

'What else did she say?'

'Not much. Just that I was fortunate not to have been there. Have you seen him since?'

'No.'

On each of the three mornings since her meeting with Jameson, Elizabeth had expected him to return. No-one else had remarked on his absence.

'Why did she say that, do you think?' she asked Mary.

'No reason. You know what these girls are like.'

'Do I?'

Elizabeth turned and looked behind them. The road facing the water was lined with hotels. At the centre of these stood the most imposing buildings, those most recently painted, those with grander entrances and awnings. On either side, the buildings, though still impressive in their size and uniformity, were less grand. Their own hotel was in this group. To the east, the sweep of this frontage stopped abruptly at a casino, beyond which an outcrop of rock running down from the higher pastures into the lake formed a natural boundary to the town. To the west lay the old part, the façades of white and pale blue and cream giving way to the browns and reds of natural stone and tile. Smoke rose from countless chimneys and gathered over the buildings.

There were no leaflets describing this old part, and when Elizabeth had asked the desk clerk for a map of the streets and small squares, he had looked at her puzzled and asked her why she wanted one. He told her that there was little for tourists to see there. But she had insisted, and the next day the hotel manager himself had presented her with a simple hand-drawn diagram of the principal streets and points of interest. He, too, told her that there was little to be seen in the old town and that her time would be better spent elsewhere. His map, she saw, contained only monuments, churches, museums and the few other public buildings.

'This is all so . . . so unreal,' Mary said, waving her arm. 'Look at those mountains, look at the lake, at the hotels, none of it's real. Even those forests, look at them, each tree identical; none of it real. It's an illustration from a book of fairy stories.' She seemed pleased by this realization and grinned to herself as she looked around them and pointed these things out.

Elizabeth could not bring herself to disagree with her and so she remained silent.

There was some truth in what Mary said – just as there was a fixed order in the routines and events of the place, so there was an order and an artificiality in its appearance – and one which became increasingly apparent the more it was sought out. But the peaks and trees were seen at a distance, the small fields were all the same size and colour and shape for a reason, and the lake was still because it was a windless day, and it faded into the hazy distance because the light was not strong enough for them to follow it.

'Even those gulls,' Mary said. She pointed to the birds beyond the jetties, each one a perfectly white and abstract shape. They were diving for fish, hovering in a cloud and then individually closing their wings to plummet and dive, barely disturbing the surface of the water as they disappeared. When they resurfaced, even at that distance, Elizabeth could see the small silver fish flashing in their beaks before being swallowed.

They sat without speaking for several minutes, and when Elizabeth next looked at her sister-in-law there were tears running down her cheeks. Mary trembled and caught her breath, but made no other sound.

'We'll go in,' Elizabeth said.

'No. I don't want to move. Leave me. Don't ask. Don't try to comfort me.'

They sat like this for several minutes longer. Passers-by paused to look at the crying woman, but no-one approached her or spoke to her. Elizabeth warned them away with gestures and reassuring nods, and people were content to make their own imperfect guesses at what they were seeing.

The only person who showed any genuine concern was another young woman, who stood with her back to the water and watched them with a hand held to her mouth. She wore a dark coat, with a black scarf drawn over her head, covering half her face. Elizabeth looked at her and shook her head, fearing what might happen if she came any closer. Beside her, Mary had grown calmer and was sitting now with her head bowed, breathing deeply. Elizabeth doubted if she had even seen this other woman, and she wanted to motion for the stranger to move away, for the contagion of her sister-in-law's distress to be contained.

But the woman took a step towards them, and as she did so Mary looked up at her and saw her for the first time. The woman stopped. The two of them looked at each other for a moment and then this other woman turned and walked away.

'Was she watching me?' Mary asked Elizabeth.

Elizabeth nodded. 'Perhaps she wanted to console you.'

'No, that's the last thing she wanted. She just wanted to know.'

The remark puzzled Elizabeth. 'To know what?'

'That she wasn't alone. She wouldn't have come any closer, she wouldn't have said anything.'

Elizabeth looked in the direction the woman had gone, but was unable to see her among the others there. 'I see,' she said.

Out on the lake two of the larger steamers approached each other, their double black and white plumes braiding behind them until the pattern was lost to scribble in the still air. From where she sat, it looked to Elizabeth as though the two vessels were on a collision course, but at the moment their bows should have riven into each other the two vessels passed a hundred yards apart.

Distracted by the steamers, she did not notice Mary rise

from beside her and walk to where the woman had been standing.

'You see how interchangeable we all are,' she called back.

Elizabeth went to join her. One of the fishermen below called up to her, but she did not understand him.

Mary stared back in the direction of their hotel. It was not yet one in the afternoon, but already there were lights along its front in some of the lower windows.

'I never told you this,' Mary said, her gaze fixed, 'but a few months ago I took out Michael's service revolver, made sure it was loaded, and then spent an entire day walking round with it either in my pocket or my bag. I visited the doctor, the bank, various shops, I saw friends and went through the motions of talking with them, and all the time I knew that I had this loaded pistol so close to my hand. Afterwards, I put it away again. All day I was intoxicated with the knowledge of what I might do.' She spoke absently. 'All day. And no-one ever knew. I set myself apart from them all, just imagining what I might be capable of; I kept myself apart from everything. It really was that simple, that straightforward.'

Elizabeth was uncertain if she was talking about being capable of shooting herself or someone else.

37

4

She next saw Jameson the following morning. He was standing beneath the tree, occasionally scanning the road on either side of him, giving the impression that he was waiting for someone.

She was alone. She paused for a moment in the hotel entrance and then went out. He saw her immediately. She expected him to raise his hand to her, to beckon her, but he did nothing other than watch as she descended the steps and crossed the road to join him. They shook hands.

'Are you waiting for someone?'

'I'm early,' he said.

Anyone else, any of the men with whom she had socialized in Oxford, might have made a small game of this denial and then admission, their remarks salted with intrigue where none existed. But then he disappointed her by continuing to search along the street. He rolled up his newspaper and pushed it into his pocket.

'You read German,' she said.

'Not very well. You?'

'I once thought I might learn. Not now.'

'I see.' He seemed suddenly uncomfortable in her presence. 'How is your sister-in-law?' he said.

'I'm not certain. I wish I knew. I wish there was some way of differentiating between her physical suffering and whatever else it is that torments her.'

'I know what you mean. Will she return home?'

'Why should she? Our plan was – is – to stay for six or seven weeks and return to England at the end of November. At least then she'll have Christmas to look forward to.'

'Her first without her husband,' he said.

'Don't. There isn't anything I haven't considered.'

'And the first without your brother. I know.' He blew into his hands. 'Cigarette?' He took out his case.

She took one and he lit it for her.

'What will you do if she does decide to return home early? Will you stay on alone?'

'I don't know. You seem very convinced that she'll leave.'

He shrugged. 'Are your parents alive?' he asked.

'No. My mother died when I was a girl, my father three years ago. Two years before Michael, a year before his son even learned to fly. A blessing, really.'

'And Michael was your only brother.'

She nodded. 'There was only a year between us. People always mistook us for twins.' She smiled at this sudden memory, and then said, 'Why do they dislike you so much?'

'Who?' He understood her perfectly. 'Surely not all of them. Mostly it's just the manager and that supercilious head waiter.'

'The maître d'.'

'I wouldn't glorify him with the name. But he's a powerful man. They hire and sack on a daily basis at the height of the season.'

'Is it because you're English?'

'I doubt it. Why should that matter now?'

'In addition to which, you deliberately antagonize him.'

'I know.'

'But you could take your breakfast anywhere; there must be a dozen cafés and bars within walking distance.'

'There are.' He looked again along the lake road. 'England in late November, what a miserable prospect.'

'So do *you* never intend returning home?'

'I haven't given it much thought. I'll stay here for as long as I need to be here, and then I'll find somewhere else. Have you ever been to North Africa?'

She shook her head. She had only once been out of England before, to Calais.

'It's over there, over the water and over the mountains.' He pointed without turning, as though he were talking of some mythical land. 'It's desert. Unimaginably vast and hot. I'd live like an Arab.'

'I believe you,' she said. 'And where would you go after that? China? The Amazon?'

'Perhaps. It wouldn't matter.' He looked at his watch and said, 'Damn,' but with no real feeling.

'What's wrong?'

'He isn't coming. He said he might or might not.'

'I hate unreliable people,' she said. She was suddenly and inexplicably anxious that he was about to leave. Her day ahead was empty.

'He isn't unreliable,' he said. 'He said he might not be able to come.'

'What will you do now?' She felt herself tense against his answer. But he said nothing. Instead, he looked over her shoulder in the direction of the hotel. She turned. Crossing the road towards them came a short procession of the blind. It surprised her to see them. It was long past the usual time for the invalids.

'They're late,' she said.

'Something must have happened.'

Among the blind, in addition to the usual nurses and orderlies, she saw that there was an even greater number of nuns and their young novices. Each woman held the arm of a man. Some of the sightless came with their eyes still bandaged, some with most of their faces hidden; others wore dark glasses or caps with their brims pulled low. A few among them had lost their eyes completely; others crossed with fixed stares.

'Ought we to move?' she said, seeing that the first of the nuns and the men were coming directly towards them.

'No. Stay where you are. They won't harm you.'

'That wasn't what I meant.'

'Margaret,' he called out.

The first nun to approach them shielded her eyes to look at him. She held the arm of a boy, no more than eighteen, and brought him towards them, whispering to him as they came. The boy grinned at what she said. When they were closer she lifted his hand so that Jameson could shake it.

'Give him one of the young, attractive nurses,' he said to the woman. He leaned forward to kiss her on both cheeks.

'Whatever he says, believe one sentence in ten,' the woman said to Elizabeth. She held out her hand. 'And no, before you ask, it is not something of which our Mother Superior approves, kissing men like Jameson in public.' She spoke English well, with a strong accent.

'This is Andrew,' Jameson said, holding out the boy's hand for Elizabeth to take.

The boy said, 'Miss.'

'Call her Elizabeth,' Jameson said to him. He lit another cigarette and put it in Andrew's mouth. 'She's twenty-three, brown hair, brown eyes, too pale, too thin. Her brother was in the RFC and he was killed.'

Elizabeth was unprepared for this directness.

'I'm sorry,' Andrew said.

Jameson looked at her, waiting.

But she could think of nothing to say, and so instead she lifted the boy's hand to her face and let him feel her cheeks and her chin.

Jameson gave the remainder of his cigarette to the old nun.

'Why are you so late?' he asked her.

She glanced at Elizabeth before speaking. 'There was some disturbance or other in the night. I don't know what. We arrived at the usual time, but no-one was ready for us.' She turned back to Elizabeth. 'Our convent is adjacent to the Military Hospital,' she said. 'Most of our sisters and girls give their time there. We find uses for ourselves.'

'God forbid,' Jameson said. 'Useful nuns.'

The remainder of the blind and the women leading them arrived around them. Everyone, it seemed, already knew Jameson. The women greeted him quietly and the men and boys shouted his name, turning their heads from side to side to better gauge where he stood. He did not introduce Elizabeth to any of these others and she felt invisible, guessed at, left solely to the assessment of the women.

Several more of the older nuns came forward to either kiss Jameson or shake his hand. Some of the novices curtsied to him; they acknowledged Elizabeth with curt nods.

Jameson left her and went through the crowd to one of the nurses. He patted arms and shoulders and spoke to everyone he passed. He spoke with the nurse, and in response she turned and pointed back across the road in the direction of the hotel. There, standing at the kerb, was a man accompanied by both a nurse and a nun. Jameson waved to him, but the man gave no indication of having seen him.

After this, Jameson returned to Elizabeth.

'Is that who you were waiting for?' she said.

'Hardly. It's someone I know from the hospital. His name's Hunter.'

'He isn't blind,' she said.

'No.'

At the sound of her voice, the men nearest to her drew even closer. The boy to whom she had been introduced described her to them. They greeted her in chorus. Some of them, having been led safely across the road, left the women and paced alone; others clung more tightly to the girls who held them.

'They only bring out the most stupid and most cheerful,' Jameson said aloud, raising a cheer of agreement from the men. Some edged towards the railings with their arms held in front of them.

They spread all around her, and Elizabeth apologized to each one who brushed past her. They all slowly made their way to overlook the lake. Only later did it occur to her that the men had bumped into her deliberately, playing to their blameless advantage.

'They can feel the breeze coming off the water,' Margaret said to her.

Elizabeth walked with Andrew to the railings. When he was able to hold these, the boy relaxed a little. She thought of what she might say to him.

'I was gassed,' he said to her, but with neither self-pity nor remorse in his voice.

'I'm—'

'You're sorry,' he said. He smiled at her, and she found herself moving a few inches to one side so that he was facing her. She wanted to say something about her brother, but did not. She had long since realized that suffering was not in the slightest relieved by being shared, however indirectly or inconsequentially, only that it was diluted and confused by regret and embarrassment and insincerity, and that in this way it lost its potency. This was now how Mary suffered, wandering in exhausted tangles of evasion and platitude. It was not how she, Elizabeth, wanted to behave and to be thought of.

'You don't have to see the mountains,' the boy said. 'And you don't have to keep talking; I know you're there.'

'How long have you been here?' she asked him.

'Three months. I'll be here until the spring.'

'And then?'

'Back home, I suppose.'

'Do you have any family?'

'Just my mother.'

They were joined by several others, all of whom introduced themselves and held out their hands, and all of whom, she noticed, held her for longer than the gesture required, using their fingertips to caress her palm and then her fingers as they withdrew. She enjoyed this and reciprocated with small pressures of her own.

'They're feeling to see if you have any rings on,' Andrew told her. Some of the men had held out their left rather than right hands.

'No, no rings,' she said.

They came as close as they could to her and sniffed her scent.

Several nuns joined them, including Margaret, and warned the men against making nuisances of themselves. They all denied this.

Elizabeth looked for Jameson. He was not where she had left him.

Margaret saw her looking. 'He's gone to say hello to Hunter,' she said. She indicated the man still waiting on the far side of the road.

'Will he come across?' Elizabeth said.

'Sometimes he does. He and Jameson know each other. They are great friends. Jameson comes often to the hospital. You must get him to bring you. Come to the convent.'

'Is he ill, Hunter?'

'He's a charming, intelligent man, no different from Jameson.'

'He was waiting for someone else,' she said.

'He has many acquaintances in the town.'

It was clear to Elizabeth that the woman did not want to discuss Jameson in his absence.

'Tell him I said he was to invite you to see us,' Margaret said.

One of the novices arrived beside them and waited for them to finish speaking.

'This is Ruth.'

Ruth bowed her head.

'She and Jameson and Hunter have also become firm friends. She thinks I'm an old woman who can barely hear or see, but I see and hear enough to know that they have already led her into evil ways. She gambles with them at cards. She drinks coffee with them, and probably a great deal worse.'

The girl kept her head bowed, but took none of what was said about her seriously. Her affection for the nun was obvious. Elizabeth guessed her to be sixteen or seventeen, but it was difficult to tell with her hair tied back in her scarf.

'Go and look after someone,' Margaret said to her, and the girl went immediately. 'She just came to get a look at you,' Margaret said conspiratorially. 'She spotted you with Jameson the instant we emerged on to the front.'

'Does she—?'

'She's of an age. We are each given responsibility for one of the novices, and she is my charge. She is French, like me, from the Nord. She came here a year ago.'

Elizabeth sensed a great deal more in what the woman left unsaid. 'Will Jameson want to spend some time with Hunter?' she said.

'I doubt it. There's plenty of opportunity for that at the hospital. The town isn't always the best place.' And again she became evasive. Someone called to her and she left Elizabeth to join the others.

The men were now spread along the promenade, the women and girls among them. Ruth, Elizabeth saw, walked with her hand on the arm of one of the younger men. They turned frequently and crossed back and forth over the same length of street. Watching them, it occurred to Elizabeth that the boy was not totally blind, that he possessed a fluidity and an assurance that few of the others displayed. It also occurred to her that if she hadn't been introduced to Ruth, then it would be easy to believe, looking at her from that distance, that she was a girl of little more than eleven or twelve.

'You met Ruth, then.' Jameson was beside her.

'She's over there.'

Jameson searched her out. He saw who she was with and shook his head.

'What is it?'

'Nothing. I have to go.'

'Sister Margaret said you'd take me to the hospital.'

'Why would you want to go? It isn't Bedlam. You're not going to feel any better in yourself for seeing them all up there.'

She was surprised by the hostility of this response, but remained silent.

'Of course I'll take you,' he said eventually, realizing she would not be dissuaded. 'You can sit and talk to them, walk with them, read their letters, write their letters.'

'See,' she said. 'I'll become as useful as a nun.'

'I'll call for you.'

'Is Hunter sick?' she said quickly, clumsily.

'Why do you ask?'

'I—'

'You ask because you're another one of those people who cannot bring themselves to ask any more directly. Hunter suffers from what is commonly and conveniently known as neurasthenia. Surely you've heard of it. You probably have as much idea as the rest of them about what it means, but you must at least have heard of it.'

She looked across to where Hunter had waited with the two women, but neither he nor they were any longer to be seen.

'He went back,' Jameson said. 'Today he couldn't bring himself to cross the road. Yesterday he crossed it, tomorrow he may cross it, but today it was beyond him. Anything else you want to know?'

She shook her head.

He turned, and without a word of farewell to her or any of

the others, he walked quickly away from her. She watched him go, and saw for the first time that he had a slight limp, so slight that she could not even say for certain which of his legs was injured.

5

She set off to visit the convent alone two days later. The hotel clerk gave her instructions. He told her it was in the direction of the glacier and that there was a regular bus service from the town to the hospital, and then on to the lodges beyond, from where visits to the glacier usually began.

'Why are you going there?' he asked her.

'I was invited.'

'There's nothing to see. They won't let you into the hospital, if that's what you were hoping.'

Elizabeth ignored the remark.

'The bus passes in front of the hotel.' He looked up at the clock behind him. 'Another hour.'

'I intend walking,' she told him.

'It's five kilometres.'

'So?'

'Mostly uphill.'

Elizabeth had not realized this. 'It should still only take me two hours.'

'At least three,' he said.

Earlier, she had tried to persuade Mary to accompany her. They had all day to make the round trip. They would see part of the surrounding countryside. They would be away from the claustrophobic confines of the hotel and its routines. They could always take the bus back into town if the outward journey proved too much for them. But Mary refused. She had spent another largely sleepless night and had already accepted the Gottliebs' offer to accompany them on one of their own meticulously-planned excursions.

'Where to?' Elizabeth said.

Mary wasn't certain. She listed several places Herr Gottlieb had previously mentioned. 'They've hired a taxi,' she said.

'They only want you to keep their dullard of a daughter company, so she can practise her English on you.'

'So? Perhaps being in the company of someone duller than myself for a day may be what I need.'

Elizabeth had grown accustomed to these constant rebuttals and evasions.

Mary sat on her bed, still in her nightclothes. The brief argument exhausted her. Elizabeth did not pursue it.

She left the hotel half an hour later.

Initially, the road followed the lakeshore. She passed the broad curve of other hotels and then the casino. Men and women sat on the wide steps leading up to the building. The men wore evening suits, and the women looked out of place in their gowns. Someone had arranged a row of empty champagne bottles along the top of the steps.

For a kilometre further the road was flanked by small

meadows in which cattle grazed. The promenade ended at the casino, and for the first time she walked along the natural lakeshore, out of sight of the town. Pieces of wood and other flotsam lay strewn among the boulders and exposed roots at the water's edge.

Beyond the meadows, the encircling forest came down to the road. Sawn and fallen trunks lay amid the undergrowth. It became much cooler walking beneath the trees. She tried to see through them, but their canopy shut out most of the light. She saw signs nailed crookedly to trunks warning visitors not to enter. In places, the road was covered in shallow drifts of needles, which released their scent as she walked on them.

Then the road began to rise ahead of her and she paused every few minutes to regain her breath. It turned again and became more level. She passed a lifesize crucified Christ, unpainted and rotting at the edge of the trees. There was an inscription on the cross, but this, too, was lost to rot.

She walked on. In places, the forest thinned and she felt tempted to enter it. The bus to the glacier lodge passed her and everyone on it looked out at her. Wayside markers told her that the glacier lay twelve kilometres ahead. Bridges spanned the fast-flowing streams draining from the mountainside into the lake. She rested at each of these and watched the rushing water beneath her.

After more than two and a half hours she finally reached the hospital. It was surrounded by a high wall, above which only the central roof with its tall, ornate chimney stacks was visible. Recent, crude paving had been laid beside the road.

As she approached, a man sitting on a bench by the entrance signalled to her, and she went to him. He was a soldier. His tunic was open and hanging outside his belt.

'Wait,' he said, then, hesitantly, *'Attends. Bleiben sie hier.'*

'I'm English,' she told him.

He came to her with his rifle slung over his arm and carrying a clipboard.

'What do you want,' he said. 'Did you get off the bus? What's your name?'

She told him and he inspected the clipboard.

'I'm visiting the convent,' she said.

'You want me to put you on the list?'

'List?'

'Of visitors. You come and go all the time, but you have to be on the list.'

She wondered if he had misunderstood her.

'I can put you on it if you like. There are rules and regulations, of course, but they don't count for too much, not now.'

'Put me down,' she said, seeing that this was the least confusing way of proceeding.

'Trouble is, I can't let you in today. I can only put you down provisionally for further visits. Corporal Cox confirms all the new names first thing each morning. That's tomorrow now. Was it someone special you wanted to see? More than my life's worth to let you in without Cox knowing about it first.'

'Is Jameson on the list?' she said.

'Jameson? You know Jameson? Of course he's on the list.'

He searched the sheet again to show her, but Jameson's name was not on it. 'Christ, I never knew that,' he said. 'He's here all the time. Everyone knows Jameson. You a friend of his?'

'An acquaintance,' she said.

'Then it's an even bigger pity that I can't let you in.'

'Why? Is he in there?'

'Not today. Come up with him next time – that way we can forget about the list.'

Behind him, the high gate opened and an ambulance emerged.

'Step back,' he said. He walked with her to the far side of the road. The ambulance stood for a moment, filling the air with its smoke. Then it turned in the direction of the town. Two men followed it out. Seeing her and the guard, they came over to them.

'She knows Jameson,' the guard said.

Both new arrivals looked her up and down. They, too, wore their tunics in the same dishevelled manner. One of them, a squat, crop-headed man, wore corporal's stripes.

'I'm Cox,' he said, as though he believed the name might already mean something to her.

She introduced herself.

'And you're a so-called friend of *Mister* Jameson, are you? Well, *Mister* Jameson isn't here, and you can't come in. Not without my say-so. Which you don't have.'

'I explained all that to her,' the man with the rifle and clipboard said.

'You did, did you?' Cox turned to the guard. 'Then why is she still here?' He prodded the man in the chest. 'Why don't you show her where the bus stops and takes them all back to their fancy hotels?'

She did not understand Cox's hostility towards her, but she sensed enough not to provoke him any further. The two others stood in awe of him.

The corporal turned back to her. 'Like it or not, I daresay there's not much I can do to stop you from coming back and getting in. Not if you're a friend of Jameson's.' He half turned from her and spat heavily. Then he and the man who had accompanied him went back inside, pulling the gate shut behind them.

'Does he hate everyone, or just Jameson?' she asked the guard when the two of them were again alone.

'Not really. Just the way he is. He's like a lot of us here – we shouldn't be here, we should be home. He was never in France or Belgium or anywhere like that. He was only drafted ten months ago and they sent him straight here. We're nursemaids, that's all, not soldiers. We've got them all here. Blind, legless, armless, faceless, crazy. You'll see for yourself when you get in. Ignore Cox. He jumps up and down a lot, but it's the medical staff who run the place. See this rifle? Won't fire. Pin corroded and I can't get it out. I haven't seen a bullet since Zonnebeke.'

' "The Storm of Zonnebeke",' she said. 'Were you there?'

He seemed embarrassed that she had remembered or even heard of the place. 'Briefly. Afterwards, mostly. Never saw anything much, never really did anything. Clearing up, mostly. Thank Christ. Look, I've put you on the list for tomorrow onwards.' He showed her her misspelt name.

'Can I look inside?' she said.

He led her to the gate.

'First off it was a castle,' he said. 'Some nobility or other. Then it was a hotel for the visitors, and then it was taken over two or three years ago and turned into this.' He pointed out where other buildings had been more recently built around the original structure. Broad and well-kept lawns ran between these. Men walked in every direction; a cricket match was in progress.

'There's the asylum to the back, just before the trees begin,' he said.

'Asylum?'

'That's what we call it. Not for the insane, just somewhere

more private for some of the more serious injuries. Even once you're in the hospital, I doubt they'll let you in there. Ask Jameson. He knows all about it, he knows Armstrong and Sinclair well enough.'

'Who are they?'

'Armstrong's the big chief and Sinclair's the face man. He builds faces for those that – you know . . .' He ran a hand over his own face in explanation.

'Yes, of course,' she said, then, 'Thank you,' hoping to put him at ease.

It was as they stood at the gate, waiting only to part, that they were approached by a group of women leaving their work in the nearby fields. They congregated on the far side of the road, sitting on the low bank there. Nuns in their habits approached them from the opposite direction carrying baskets.

The soldier propped his rifle by his chair and crossed to join them, leaving Elizabeth standing alone.

There was a shallow drain running along the bank and some of the women washed their hands and faces in this. Those with the baskets distributed bottles and bundles of food. Some of the novices among them took off their scarves and shook out their hair, and it was then that Elizabeth saw Ruth. She sat apart from the others. Her hair was deep auburn, almost red. She brushed it vigorously and then pulled it back from her face and tied it in a ribbon. The girl looked across at her. She scooped water from the drain and washed her face, skimming the water from her eyes and mouth with her thumb.

Elizabeth went over to her.

'We met two days ago,' she said.

'You were at the lakeshore,' Ruth said in French.

'I was with Jameson when you and Sister Margaret brought

the blind boys across.' Elizabeth also spoke in French. Her fluency clearly surprised the girl and she could not disguise this.

'Have you been to the hospital?' Ruth said.

'They wouldn't let me in. I really came to see the convent.' She hoped the girl might offer to act as her guide.

'It's there,' Ruth said. She pointed to an archway further along the road. 'If you went, they'd find someone to show you round.'

'Perhaps you—'

'I'm working. We have to clear the fields.'

'Jameson speaks very highly of the sisters.'

'They're nuns. Everyone speaks highly of nuns. Nuns, missionaries, even priests sometimes.'

Elizabeth smiled at the joke. 'And you,' she said. 'It's obvious he thinks very highly of you.'

Ruth turned away from her.

'Or perhaps that's because you, too, are about to become a nun.'

'Who told you that?'

'No-one. I assumed—'

'I won't become a nun,' she said. She lowered her voice, glancing at the others nearby. She opened her own bundle of food. 'Have some,' she said, breaking a piece of bread in half. Elizabeth took it.

'How long has Jameson been here?'

'About a year.'

'Have you known him all that time?'

Ruth nodded.

'It's none of my business,' Elizabeth said. 'I'm sorry. Do you live inside the convent itself?' She knew it was a stupid question before she'd finished asking it.

'Where else is there? I share a room with five others. Some

of *them* are going to become nuns.' She indicated the girls among the women, most of whom were now watching them. There was envy in Ruth's voice.

'How old are they?'

'Seventeen. Same as me. I'll have to get back soon. Go to the convent. Ask for Margaret. Tell her you saw me. I'll show you something first.' She rose and waited for Elizabeth to follow her. She led her to another cross set into the side of the road midway between the hospital and the convent. It was much smaller than the other she had seen, and on it was carved a date, a year old, and the name of a man.

'Surely it's not a grave,' Elizabeth said.

'No, it's more than that,' Ruth said. 'This is where he was killed. Margaret had this made for him.'

'How did it happen?'

'He was from the hospital, one of those men who look to have nothing wrong with him, no wounds or anything like that. A lorry had come with some timber and cement – the nuns were building some new porches – you'll see them – and he and some others had been sent to help unload the lorry. Someone threw a bag of cement down for him to catch, but he either wasn't watching or didn't raise his arms in time and it caught him on the face and chest and knocked him backwards. He didn't even try to stop himself from falling, didn't even cry out. I saw it.'

'And it killed him?'

'There was a rock in the bank. His head went straight back on to it. They said he was dead before they lifted the sack off his face. The men sent me and the others away. Margaret was there. She knelt beside him and gave him the last rites. She washed his face. Someone told her not to bother, that it was too late, but she went on doing it. She says it's never too late. She believes in heaven; most of them do.'

'*All* of them, surely?'

Ruth refused to answer.

'Do you believe in it?'

'There was no blood on his face, nothing to see, but Margaret kept his head back down in the grass. It was summer and the grass was high. I saw her sleeve afterwards where it was caked with his blood.' There was a childish eagerness in her voice, despite the facts of the story.

'It's a sad tale,' Elizabeth said.

'I suppose so. Some said it was a blessing. I saw the way he stood waiting for that sack to be thrown.'

They stood over the small monument for a moment, and then Ruth walked back to the others.

6

She looked out for the nuns over the following days, but neither they nor their charges appeared in the town. When she asked the hotel manager if there was any reason for their absence, he said she might as well ask him why it was raining, or why visitors chose one hotel and not another. He was examining a ledger and slapped it shut as he spoke.

'Does it affect your trade?' she asked him.

'Of course it does,' he said.

She prompted him to explain and he told her that only a month before her arrival, he and many other hoteliers and restaurateurs along the lakefront had petitioned the Town Council in an attempt to force the invalids and convalescents to be taken elsewhere, to sites further from the lake and the centre of the town. An offer had even been made by the hoteliers and restaurateurs to provide benches and wooden shelters at these more isolated places.

'But most people don't appear to mind,' she said.

'So what? What will happen to the place if these – these people continue to come here? Do you know how many hospitals and clinics already exist here?'

'No.'

Neither did he. 'At least two dozen. No – more – nearer forty,' he said.

'Then perhaps you ought to capitalize on the fact,' she suggested.

'Do you think the owners of this hotel haven't already considered that? I receive endless letters from them suggesting I advertise for the custom of those here to convalesce, and for those who come to visit them.' His voice rose again in exasperation. 'They want me to turn *my* hotel into a hospital waiting-room. *I'm* the one who knows what's happening here, *I'm* the one they're content to leave in charge while they're away somewhere else living like princes on the profits I make for them.'

'I see,' she said, waiting for him to calm down. He tugged the hem of his jacket and pressed a finger to the knot of his tie.

'About the nuns,' he said eventually. 'It is a difficult time of year for them. I imagine they are working against the weather to get their crops in. In the past, before the hospital, it was no problem, but now they have so much else to attend to.'

They were approached by a waitress – the same girl who had cleared the table on the morning she had met Jameson, the one who knew him. She stood beside the manager for a moment and then whispered something to him. He turned.

'You have a visitor,' he said to Elizabeth.

Jameson waited for her in the hotel doorway.

'I can tell him you do not wish to see him,' the manager said.

She considered accepting his offer; she knew it would please and surprise him, and surprise and amuse Jameson.

'There's no need,' she said. 'We have an appointment.'

The manager whispered behind his hand to the waitress. The girl shook her head. 'Then please do not let me detain you any longer. There is a great deal that I, too, must attend to.' He bowed slightly and left her. The girl remained where she stood.

'You could have brought the message directly to me,' Elizabeth told her.

'Mister high and mighty wouldn't have liked that.'

'Especially where Jameson is concerned?'

'Especially.' The girl left her, waving to Jameson as she went.

Elizabeth went to the doorway. Jameson invited her to accompany him to a nearby café. He carried a briefcase, and beneath his arm he held a folder tied with ribbons.

'We could stay here,' she suggested.

Jameson glanced into the dining-room, at the dozen or so other guests taking coffee there, and shook his head. 'I think not. Anyway, I have to deliver these. It's enough that I show my face every now and again to give them all something to talk about.'

'You have a very high opinion of yourself,' she said. She drew on her gloves.

He turned away from her at this remark and she knew that she had offended him.

They left the hotel and walked towards the town centre. She offered to carry his folder. At first he declined, but she insisted and he put it beneath her arm. She slid her hand over the arm he now had free, and he immediately folded this across his chest.

'Do you mind?' she said.

'No,' he said. 'It's just that it's been some time since I held a woman's hand.'

'You aren't now,' she pointed out to him. It was the first time she had seen any sign of uncertainty in him. 'We could hold hands if you'd prefer,' she said.

He made no attempt to do so.

They arrived at a café and went inside. The waiter recognized Jameson and indicated to him that he knew what he wanted. He brought a tray of coffee, and then returned with a second, smaller tray containing a bottle of clear liqueur and two thistle-shaped glasses. He poured this drink, filling the glasses to their rims.

'They distil it locally,' Jameson told her. 'Frau Gottlieb's distillery visit. From cherries.' He poured their coffee. Then he indicated both the briefcase and the folder to the waiter and the man picked them up and carried them away.

'What's he doing?' Elizabeth said, surprised by the casual nature of the transaction.

'I'm afraid that on this occasion I'm only the messenger boy. They belong to my associate. One of his customers will collect them later. He was unable to leave the studio today, and so, to deflate my high opinion of myself, I allowed myself to be used as his errand boy.'

'And you decided to combine your business with the pleasure of seeing me.'

'And holding your hand, yes.'

'What does your "associate" do?' she said, intrigued by his choice of word.

'My associate is a photographer. I thought you might have known at least that much by now.'

'Why should I? Are you a photographer too?'

'I thought perhaps someone at the hotel might have told you. No, I'm not a photographer.' He picked up one of the small glasses, raised it carefully to his lips and drained it in a single swallow, following it immediately with a mouthful of coffee. He waited for her to do the same.

She had expected the liqueur to be sweet, but it was not. It was raw and made her eyes water.

'The trick is to swallow it without really tasting it,' he said. He smiled at her discomfort.

She tried to talk, but had no voice.

'Drink some coffee.' He refilled their glasses.

When her voice eventually returned, her throat warmed by the coffee, she asked him if his association with the photographer was in some way responsible for the way he was treated at the hotel.

'Of course,' he said. He drained a second glass of the liqueur. 'Why don't you ask me what it is that I do? You'll be disappointed.'

'Shall I tell you what I thought originally?' she said. 'At first, I thought you were something to do with the War Office, someone involved with Army Intelligence.'

He laughed. 'Army Intelligence. What a magnificent contradiction in terms. You mean you thought I was a spy. Do you really think I'd be capable of it?'

'Why not? You appear to enjoy the air of mystery which—'

'You're wrong,' he said abruptly, and again she saw that she had in some way misjudged him.

To release this sudden tension between them she picked up her second glass of liqueur. 'Without tasting it,' she said, and she threw the drink into her mouth, tipping back her head. The effect was the same as before – she coughed, her eyes watered.

'You'll get the hang of it before you leave,' he told her.

'I doubt it,' she said.

He raised his hand to order more coffee.

When she had again composed herself, he said, 'I deal in rare and precious books and manuscripts. I'm a bookseller.'

Her first instinct was to say that she did not believe him.

'The briefcase I handed over contained Blomfield's own proof of his unbound Euripides, his Aeschylus working copy, and most of the letters sent to him by Norton.'

As intended, the names, other than those of the authors, meant nothing to her.

'And were there photographs in the folder?'

'How perceptive.'

'Do you have a shop, here?'

'No. I have rooms above the studio which serve as my office. I deal privately. I have a network of customers. They tell me what they want and, by and large, I know where to start looking.'

'Why here?'

'Why not? Most of my business depends only on the postal system. I employ people on commission in London, Paris, Berlin, Madrid. I even have my contacts in your own home town, even there.'

'And does all this provide you with a good living?'

'I don't need it to provide for me. I have a private income, family money. I no longer have the two brothers with whom it might once have been shared. I do it because it satisfies my need to do it. It was what I did before the war.'

This last remark surprised her. 'You always seem to me like a man constantly severing his ties with the past,' she said.

'Perhaps.'

'Is there a great demand?'

'For the particular books I deal in, yes.'

The waiter returned with a fresh pot of coffee. Jameson took out his cigarette case. 'This belonged to my elder brother,' he said. 'And this lighter to my younger brother.'

'I'm sorry.'

'Why should you be sorry? You never knew them. You are sorry for my brothers – or for me – in the same useless way I am sorry for your own and for you. Please, don't be insulted, I'm not criticizing.'

'I know.'

Neither of them spoke for several minutes.

'In the hotel . . .' she said, uncertain of what she wanted to say.

'In the hotel what?'

'I don't know. You seemed restless.'

'Did I?'

'Constantly on edge, bracing yourself against something you believed was going to happen, something you even had to provoke into happening so that you could at least be in control of the situation. For instance, when the Gottliebs—'

'Ah, yes, fine upstanding Herr Gottlieb.'

'Meaning?'

'Meaning perhaps I have good cause to feel restless in his company.'

'It's more than that,' she said. 'He resents you.'

'I know. And as you've already surmised, he's not alone in feeling that way. Who knows, perhaps I was the man who ordered a field piece to be fired into the void of their lines one fine day, and somewhere over a hill, in a trench, in a dugout, his son was just then sitting down to cook himself breakfast.'

'That's a ridiculous connection to make.'

'Is it? It makes as much sense as a thousand other expla-nations.'

She refused to concede the point.

'Tell me,' he said. 'What do you think Herr Gottlieb does?'

'Does?'

'His profession.'

'He owns a factory, several factories, making machines, tools.' This, too, she had learned in that first hour.

'He makes – made – weapons. Gottlieb Munitions. How do you imagine he squares that with the loss of his son?'

'I imagine—'

'You imagine someone had to do it. You're right, someone did, and in this instance it just happened to be fine, upstanding Herr Gottlieb, who also managed to make himself a vast fortune in the process.'

She refused to continue the argument, uncertain of the true source of his anger, but convinced that the Gottliebs were only a small part of it.

'And what about now, here?' he said.

'Now?'

'Do I still seem restless to you?'

She considered this. 'No, you seem at ease,' she said.

He nodded slowly in agreement. There was a further short silence between them.

'Where is the studio?' she said eventually.

'In the old town.'

'Can I visit it?'

'You wouldn't want to go there.'

'I might want my photograph taken.'

'Then ask the hotel manager. I'm sure he'll know of a dozen other photographers, all considerably more respectable than—'

'Than your associate.'

'His name's Emil. It's no secret.'

'Tell me about him.'

He considered this for a moment and then told her.

Only later, when they had parted and she was back at the hotel, eating a cold and silent dinner with Mary, did she realize that by speaking of Emil, he had been able to avoid all further mention of himself and his own work.

She drained a third glass of the liqueur.

'I met Emil at the hospital,' he told her. 'He works there occasionally.'

'As a photographer?'

'Why not? The men there want photographs to send home to their families, to reassure them. You'd be surprised how full an empty sleeve can be made to look, and you can always photograph a legless man in a wheelchair from the waist up and with a grin on his face.'

She let the remark pass.

'He sometimes does more technical work for Sinclair when he needs it. Emil photographs the injured faces and then helps Sinclair keep a record of their repair.'

'Is it a large part of his business?'

'Not really. And other parts of it are certainly more lucrative.'

'Do you visit the hospital together?'

'Occasionally.'

'I went to the convent,' she said, conscious of his growing unease at her questioning.

'And saw Ruth. I know.'

'Have you seen her?'

'Yesterday. I went with Emil. I didn't go into the hospital. I waited in the cab outside. Ruth saw me and came over.'

'She thinks you—'

'I know exactly what she thinks of me,' he said. 'And if you

67

want to believe she's jealous of you, then you'd be right in assuming that too.'

'It's none of my business,' she said.

'You're wrong. Everything belongs to everybody in this place. Only not knowing something sets you apart.'

Like everything I'm not being told about you, she thought, but said nothing.

'Ruth showed me the marker for the man who'd been killed unloading cement,' she said.

'Is that what she told you, that he was unloading cement?'

'Isn't that what happened? She said she saw it.'

'I don't know. I only heard the story afterwards. It happened before I came here.'

'And you've heard a different version?'

'Does it matter? I know a man died there. Margaret told me that much. Does it really matter to know the details?'

'I think it does,' she said.

'Then I envy you.'

He poured the last of the liqueur from the small bottle, dividing it between their glasses. She wanted to refuse the drink, but took it. She was starting to feel intoxicated. She half rose, more to test her legs than to leave, but Jameson grabbed her arm and held her in her seat.

'Wait just a moment,' he said. He looked closely at a man who had just then entered the café. This man went to the counter and spoke to the waiter who had served them. Elizabeth tried to follow what was happening, but found this difficult. The waiter gave the man the folder she had carried, and the man gave the waiter an envelope. Following this, he left the café.

'He took the photographs,' she said absently to Jameson.

Jameson waited for a signal from the waiter before

answering her. 'Yes, he took the photographs. He was Emil's customer.'

'Shouldn't you have said something to him?'

Jameson shook his head, smiling. 'He wouldn't have wanted that.' He rose, waiting for her to follow him.

7

She didn't see him the next day, nor the one following. Instead, she spent her time with Mary. They went together into the town, taking one of the horse-drawn carriages which plied for trade along the lake road. They visited the few sites of supposed interest, the larger churches, the spa building, the dull museums and the small opera house.

Mary held Elizabeth's arm as they walked. She had been sleeping better during the previous few nights and claimed to have regained some of her strength. But she still ate very little, and when Elizabeth suggested Jameson's doctor to her, Mary refused to even speak until Elizabeth promised her she would receive no treatment or medication against her will.

They went into the spa building and watched the bathers from the public gallery.

A broad staircase led to a mezzanine, and they sat there

among the few other onlookers. The men and women below all wore blue and white towels fastened round their chests or waists, and most of the women had their hair wrapped in flannel turbans. They sat around a succession of shallow, steaming pools, and their whispered voices and the noise of their splashing echoed in the domed ceiling above them. Sunlight shone down in columns from patterned skylights.

Around the edge of the larger pool, the only one in which anyone actually swam, stood a line of leather-padded tables, alongside which sat the masseurs waiting for their customers. The rhythm of kneading and slapping echoed loudest of all, providing a regular beat to the cacophony of other sounds.

'We could have a steam bath,' Elizabeth suggested. 'A sauna.' These were the first she had seen.

Mary responded by drawing her coat shut and holding it tight at her chest. 'You go,' she said. 'I'll stay up here and watch.'

'It wouldn't harm you,' Elizabeth said, knowing her argument was already lost.

'The heat would make me feel faint.'

The bones of Mary's forearm showed in outline through her flesh. She trembled in silent panic at the thought of having to expose herself.

'I didn't think,' Elizabeth said.

Mary started crying, and her gasps for breath echoed in the space above them like the beating wings of birds. And listening to this, Elizabeth understood then, as fully as she was ever able to understand it afterwards, the precise nature of the tragedy of which her sister-in-law was the only true victim. There was no contagion, no casting of cold shadows. She pressed Mary's head hard into her shoulder and absorbed her trembling.

Mary allowed herself to be cosseted and calmed like this for several minutes before finally pulling herself free.

Elizabeth turned her attention to the bathers below. 'The Gottliebs come here,' she said.

'Only because the stupid woman thinks she has a good figure, and because her stupid husband thinks it's something to admire.'

'I thought you got on with them,' Elizabeth said, encouraged by the remark. 'You've spent enough time with them recently.'

'I spend time with them because I despise them, all three of them, and because I have to pay them no real attention. They use me, but they get nothing from me in return. Nothing they say to me antagonizes or upsets me. If they all died tomorrow I wouldn't think anything of it.'

Elizabeth wondered how much of this Mary genuinely believed, and how much of it was merely what she wanted to believe.

'Is it because they're German, do you think?'

'Because the Germans killed Michael? It may be, but I doubt it. It would make as much sense for me to hate all men with blue eyes if I knew a man with blue eyes had killed him.'

'No-one likes the Gottliebs,' Elizabeth said. 'Perhaps there are people who exist for that purpose alone – to make everyone else feel better about themselves.'

'I wish they understood that. Perhaps I should tell them.'

'You couldn't be that cruel.'

'Not now, perhaps.' Mary rose and edged along the seats to the marble staircase.

8

The same guard sat at the hospital gate. He recognized her immediately and rose as she and Jameson approached him. He held out his hand, first to Jameson, then to her. He asked Jameson what was happening in the town, and Jameson quizzed him on what, if anything, was happening at the hospital.

'They've taken a lot of them out over the past few days,' the man said.

'Out where?'

'No – out, away. Gone. Home, most of them, I should think. Word is they're starting to run the place down. They'll close it eventually, want us out.' He spoke with some enthusiasm for the plan.

'Are they ready to leave?' Elizabeth asked him. She saw that Jameson was concerned at the prospect.

'Who's gone?' Jameson said before the man could answer her with another of his guesses.

'Mostly leg injuries so far. They can learn to walk anywhere. Best place for them to be, home. Sooner the better.'

'What about Sinclair?'

The man glanced at Elizabeth before answering. 'No talk of that yet. How do you go back out into the world looking like that?'

'And Hunter?'

'Hunter's still here. Saw him earlier. Does he know you're coming?'

Jameson took a bottle of wine from the satchel he carried and gave it to the man, who slid it into the knapsack at his feet. Beyond him, through the gate, Elizabeth saw the same mix of patients, nuns and orderlies walking on the drives and lawns. It was a warmer, brighter day than when she had come a week previously, and the sun was reflected in the glass along the fronts of the buildings.

'Is Cox around?' Jameson asked.

'Somewhere. He's always somewhere. He's been put in charge of organizing the transport to take them out. In his element, he is. They want most of it doing at nights.'

'Where to? The town station?'

'Mostly. Some they take straight through to Altdorf and Berne. Ask me, they'll turn the place back into a hotel for the tourists. Sinclair's already complaining about the number of visitors we're getting.'

'People like me,' Elizabeth said.

'I didn't mean – Mostly they just stand around out here. It's something to see, I suppose. Cox wants me to move them on. What does he expect me to do, point my rifle at them?' He nodded in the direction of the useless weapon.

'You could let them pose with it for photographs,' Jameson suggested.

'I do,' the man said, a hand over his mouth to mask the confession.

Jameson and Elizabeth left him and went into the hospital. Some of the patients they encountered exchanged greetings with Jameson; others passed them by and looked straight through them.

He pointed out the various buildings to her. She asked where Sinclair did his work, and he indicated a copse of firs in the distance. A high wall ran alongside the trees; nothing of the buildings beyond was visible. 'Everything's kept apart,' he said, then added, 'I imagine they'll wait until a particularly dark and moonless night before they evacuate Sinclair and his men.'

Beyond the copse was a strip of open land, and beyond this the steeper slopes and wooded foothills.

'Will they manage to rebuild their lives back at home, do you think?'

'Some of them. Given the chance.'

'And the others?'

'They can't even imagine what they will have to face.'

She moved closer to him. 'How did you get your limp?' she said.

'Glencorse Wood,' he said without pausing, indicating to her that he did not want to explain any further.

'It's barely noticeable,' she said, immediately regretting the platitude.

'I'm surprised you saw it,' he said. 'It's only really evident when I walk for any length of time on hard ground. Apparently, what you see now is what I'm stuck with for the rest of my life. It'll get worse, eventually, but at least I have to grow old for that to happen.' He raised his hand to a man standing on the path ahead of them. The man watched him closely, and then as Jameson drew near, he pulled his legs together, straightened his arm and saluted. Jameson returned the gesture. 'Keep walking,' he whispered to her as they passed the man.

'Sir!' the man shouted.

Elizabeth turned and looked at him.

'You'll get used to it,' Jameson said.

They arrived at the path skirting the hospital.

'There used to be a moat here,' he said, indicating the driveway ahead of them.

They passed the barred windows of the ground floor. She caught glimpses of the interiors, of the lines of beds and the men in them.

'Hunter will be at the rear,' Jameson said. 'They all make some small, private space of their own.'

'How do you know him?'

'We served together. I believe the phrase is "fellow officers".'

As before when she had asked him, he was reluctant to discuss the man.

'So do you come to see him out of some sense of obligation?'

'It isn't something I think about.'

'And what about when he returns home, will you go with him?'

'I doubt he'll go. He'll probably just set himself adrift.'

'Like you,' she said. 'Africa, China . . .'

'Mock me,' he said. He turned from her briefly to talk to two nurses sitting on a bench against the hospital wall.

When he returned to her, he resumed their conversation. 'Except in Hunter's case there are complications.'

'His illness, you mean?'

'Illness?' It was clear that this was not what he had meant.

He stopped talking. Ahead of them, another patient stood a short distance from the wall throwing a ball against it. Or this was what she thought he was doing, but when they came close to him she saw that he was merely going through the motions of throwing the ball and catching it, and that he never actually released his grip on it. He counted aloud to himself each time the gesture was completed.

They turned a corner. The grounds to the rear of the hospital were less extensive than those at its front. A conservatory ran the full length of the building, the doors of which opened on to a paved area, from where steps led down to yet another lawn. Wicker tables and chairs stood inside and out, most of them occupied. There were fewer men here than at the front; the space felt more enclosed and private.

Jameson paused and searched ahead of them.

Elizabeth felt suddenly exposed. Men looked up from whatever they were doing and watched them. Several rose from their chairs on the driveway and walked away ahead of them.

'Can you see him?' she asked.

'I know where he'll be. Inside. You won't see him from here. He'll see us.'

'Will he know I'm with you?'

'I doubt it. But don't worry, you're not as terrifying as you sometimes like to pretend.' He paused. 'Just don't be alarmed by anything anyone does or says to you. And try not to show any pity. Most of the more severely injured will still be indoors. You might see them, but I doubt it.'

She looked around to see if there were any other visitors among the nurses and the men, but saw none.

A nun came to them, and she recognized Margaret.

'Did you know about the departures?' Margaret asked

Jameson after the three of them had exchanged greetings.

'I share your concern,' he said, 'but I don't know what anyone can do. I'll find out what I can. I brought your magazine.' He took a magazine from his satchel.

'It's two months old,' she said.

'And it's meant to be read by women a third your age.'

'What do they know?' She rolled the magazine and slid it into one of her deep pockets. She looked around her. 'Ruth's here, somewhere.'

'She'll know I've arrived.'

'Naturally. Will you come to the convent afterwards?'

'Not today. Soon.'

'Bring Elizabeth. Show her what decrepit creatures we all are. So many small planets going round and round each other.' She held up her hand to him. 'Here, save your worthless soul.' He took her hand and lightly kissed it.

'Is that it? Am I saved?'

'Only until nightfall.'

Elizabeth envied the old woman her familiarity, this near-intimacy with Jameson.

'Look at me,' Margaret said to her. 'I have nothing better to do? There aren't a hundred more important tasks waiting to be done?' She turned to Jameson and saw that he was looking at the conservatory. 'He's fine,' she said. 'Stop worrying.'

Jameson nodded, unconvinced.

'It was good to see you,' Margaret said to Elizabeth. 'Come again. They must get sick and tired of the sight of me and all the other ancient brides of Christ forever wandering among them like unwelcome angels.' She left them. 'I know, I know,' she called back to Jameson without turning. 'Half of all the angels were cast out of heaven and into hell. I'm going, I'm going.'

9

They entered the conservatory. Men sat along its entire length. Most wore part of what remained of their uniforms, but some were dressed only in pyjamas and dressing gowns. Few showed any outward sign of their injuries. Orderlies pushed men in wheelchairs noisily over the tiled floor.

It was immediately warmer beneath the glass. Doors led from the rear of the conservatory into the darker spaces of the corridors and wards beyond.

'Can you see him?' she asked him.

He was reluctant to point Hunter out to her amid all these others. 'Just follow me.'

He took her to the far end of the long room, to where a man sat alone at a table, writing. Others stopped what they were doing to watch her pass; conversations faded and then resumed in their wake.

Hunter stopped writing and looked up at their approach. He screwed the cap on his pen, slid the paper into a card folder, and rose to greet them.

He was the same age as Jameson – she had guessed early to mid-thirties – and several inches taller. He wore a tweed jacket and a dark shirt, open at the collar. Jameson introduced her to him and he shook her hand, holding it until she pulled it free.

There were two other chairs at the table and Hunter drew these closer. With her back to the rest of the men, and facing only Hunter and the glass wall behind him, Elizabeth felt cut off from these others, and she saw why Hunter had made this small space his own.

She waited for Jameson to speak.

'Why no processions?' he said.

'Armstrong has had another complaint from the Town Council. We're lepers, still bad for trade.'

'An official complaint?'

'Everything they do they try to make sound official. You know what a high opinion they have of themselves.'

She had expected to see some indication of Hunter's illness, some nervousness or reticence, perhaps even some slight uncontrollable tremor; but she saw nothing. Hunter appeared calm and assured of himself; he behaved as though he were sitting in the hotel lobby rather than the hospital where he had already been for almost a year.

He caught her watching him.

'I'm afraid there's nothing to see,' he said, but without making the words a rebuke. 'Apparently it's all in my mind. I realize how confusing and inconvenient that is for some of them, but there's not a great deal I can do about it. Whatever he's told you about me—' he nodded to Jameson, who sat looking out over the lawn '—ignore it. He pretends, for my sake alone, to understand it all, but in truth he knows as little as the rest of them. I tell him he ought to go, to leave, but he refuses to listen. He pretends to care about what happens to me, and I in turn pretend to take some interest in the dreary life he himself leads out there.'

Jameson refused to be drawn. He sat with his eyes closed against the sunlight caught in the panes above them. She saw the strength of the bond between the two men; she saw how vital they were to each other.

'I'll wait until they certify him sane and release him, and then I'll disappear,' Jameson said, his eyes still closed.

The word 'sane' caught her by surprise.

'Don't worry,' Hunter said. 'I'm as hopeless a cause as most of them here. Admittedly, that might not be saying much, under the circumstances, but I'm content to stay until—'

'Until the place gets turned into another watering hole for the wandering rich,' Jameson said.

'That's what's being said.' Hunter turned to Elizabeth. 'You see how he worries for me.'

In the ward, someone called for a nurse, then shouted again and again until he was screaming. Of the three of them, only Elizabeth turned to look. She couldn't see who was calling; she heard only running footsteps and then silence.

'It happens all the time,' Hunter said. 'It means nothing to anyone.'

'Except the screaming man,' Elizabeth said.

'I doubt it. One minute they scream, the next they blithely deny ever having opened their mouths.'

'Do you know who it is?'

'A scream from in there—' he indicated the adjoining ward '—signifies nothing. A man waking from a nightmare, a man wetting himself because of a moment's loss of control.'

'And a scream from elsewhere?'

'You quickly learn which ones not to listen to,' he said. 'Some of us are on permanent display here; others they aren't so keen to put in the window.' He was distracted by a line of blind men walking close to the glass, each man with a finger hooked into the belt of the man in front of him. At first Elizabeth believed the man at the head of this line to be sighted, but then saw by the way he barely lifted his own feet that he, too, was blind. A nun followed a few paces behind the shuffling procession.

Jameson took several newspapers and books from his bag and put them on the table.

Elizabeth studied the titles. The papers were English and French, the books mostly in Latin.

'Hunter considers himself something of a scholar,' Jameson said. 'If this glorious war hadn't come along to show him the error of his ways, he might be grazing in the fields of academe by now.'

'Ignore him: it's not true,' Hunter said. He picked up the books. 'This is the wrong Heywood; I need Shepherd's.' He laid it back down and Jameson put it immediately back in his bag.

She saw how adeptly they kept themselves at the surface of things.

'You taught Latin?' she said to Hunter.

'No, never,' he said. 'It's just a passion of mine. Something I might have done. Something I now have the time to indulge.' There was neither longing nor regret in his voice. 'Useless momentum. What else is there for me to do? Did Jameson tell you that he applied to the authorities – *the authorities* – to allow me to live in the town? He even offered to accept responsibility for me.'

She looked to Jameson, who looked away from her.

'*Him*, responsible for *me*. They turned him down, of course. Thank God.'

'Do they allow it?'

'Sometimes. Especially if the families arrive with the money to pay for private nursing. Have you seen where he lives?'

Elizabeth shook her head.

'This place is a palace compared to that.'

An orderly approached them with a jug of water. The men he passed held up glasses to be filled.

'Do you want some water?' Hunter asked her.

She said she did. He took a glass from the table and held it out to be filled. The orderly appeared not to notice him.

'It's for the young lady,' Hunter called out.

The orderly came to him and filled the glass, deliberately slopping water over the rim onto Hunter's hand and sleeve. 'Thank you, so kind,' Hunter said to him. He made no attempt to dry his hand. 'You have to excuse them,' he said loudly to her. The orderly flicked his hand at him and walked away.

'One of Cox's cronies,' he said to Jameson. He turned back to Elizabeth. 'Corporal Cox, proud in his ignorance of all matters medical, doesn't believe I should be here. He thinks I'm depriving someone more worthy than myself of a bed and treatment.'

'I see,' she said.

'He was wounded on four separate occasions,' Jameson said. 'There are still sixty splinters the size of a thumbnail in his back.'

'Completely unimpressive,' Hunter said.

'You ought to make a formal complaint about the man,' Jameson said.

'And what good would that do?' Turning to Elizabeth, Hunter said, 'Jameson here still believes that all those old rules and regulations, those balances and checks are still in operation. He professes not to, but he does. Something is right, something is wrong, there is a natural order to things, some common understanding of justice, fairness, all that.'

She waited for Jameson to protest, but saw that his silent acquiescence was all a part of the game of which they were the only two players, and of which she herself would forever remain a spectator.

They left the hospital an hour later. There had been no further interruptions.

On their way back across the lawn they met Ruth. She held the arm of a blind boy, the same one she had been with on the lakefront. She led him towards them, talking to him as they came. She stopped a few paces from them and let go of the boy. She told him to wait where he was and then came to them alone.

She spoke first to Jameson, asking him how long he'd been there, how Hunter was. Then she greeted Elizabeth.

'That's Mitchell,' she said.

The boy stood with his gaze fixed on them.

'Is he totally blind?' Elizabeth said.

'He suffers from what they call "hysterical blindness",' Ruth said. 'Don't ask me.'

'He no longer believes he can see,' Jameson said, his voice low. 'No actual physical damage to his eyes, but whatever part of his brain it is that controls his vision has convinced him that he is sightless. If he does see anything, then apparently it makes no impression on him.'

'There are one or two others like him,' Ruth said.

'It's just the way he's standing and looking at us . . .' Elizabeth said.

'I know,' Jameson said.

'You don't sound convinced.'

'I'm not.'

'But why would he want to fake something like that? I could understand it if there was still fighting for him to be sent back to, but not now. Is it because he'll receive some kind of pension if he's blind?'

'Would you spend the rest of your life pretending to be blind for whatever pittance they hand out?'

Elizabeth watched the boy turn his face in a full circle. 'What do you think?' she asked Ruth.

'I don't care,' she said. 'I just do what they tell me to do.'

It was clear to Elizabeth that the girl resented her presence, resented her being with Jameson.

'I'll go on ahead,' she said. 'I want to see the convent before we leave.'

Jameson understood and nodded.

Leaving them, she heard Ruth's conversation become more animated.

She paused for a few minutes to talk again with the guard, and then she walked to the convent entrance. She did not enter; instead, she stood in the shadow of the wall and looked inside.

The building was constructed in a square, with a central courtyard and with colonnaded walkways along each of its walls; its roofs were terracotta-tiled, and the rendering of its walls was pocked to reveal the bricks and plasterwork beneath. The courtyard was paved with small round cobbles, pavé; shuttered windows were set deep in its walls. There was a trough of clear water close to where she stood, and she could hear the splash of running water – a tap or a fountain – somewhere inside.

Two nuns emerged from a doorway, saw her, but passed

her without speaking. A single bell began to toll. Other nuns came and went from the courtyard entrances. She imagined they were being summoned to their devotions.

She returned to the hospital.

Jameson and Ruth stood where she had left them on the lawn, with the blind boy still apart from them and facing them. Ruth now held Jameson's arm and did most of the talking.

As Elizabeth watched, she saw the blind boy turn and walk stiffly away from them, swinging his arms as though he were marching. Ruth called out for him to stop, but the boy marched directly towards a parked ambulance, showing no sign of having seen it, and making no attempt to avoid walking into it. Ruth called again, and then released her hold on Jameson and ran to stop the boy. She did this by running ahead of him, turning to face him and then shouting at him as he came close to her and threatened to knock her over. He stopped immediately, and stood with his hands on his waist, panting. Then he started laughing.

Elizabeth called to Jameson, who signalled for her to stay where she was. He came to her, never once turning to see what was taking place between Ruth and the boy.

When she asked him what had happened, he said, simply, 'Not now.'

10

The following day, she went with Mary out onto the lake. Most of the other hotel guests had already made the trip. The Gottliebs had recommended the excursion to Mary, who in turn repeated everything they told her to Elizabeth, causing Elizabeth to again feel as though she had been neglecting her sister-in-law.

The small steamer left from the jetty below the hotel. The larger vessels, those which ran from one end of the lake to the other, were moored further east, in an excavated dock with its own booking offices and refreshment rooms.

A week earlier, Elizabeth had watched the unloading of one of these boats, surprised to see that, following its cargo of roughly-hewn timber, it had then discharged a load of ice, cut into yard-square blocks and wrapped in straw. One of the fishermen explained to her that this was fresh ice cut from the glacier and that the better hotels paid a high premium for it. Some had ice-houses built into their cellars where the ice was stored. He told her that now was the time the ice-cutters visited the glacier, now its summer streams were not flowing so vigorously, and before the new winter snow camouflaged its surface and made it unpredictable. The man offered to take her to watch the cutters at work – he named a price – but she declined.

The boat she and Mary took sat lower in the water than most. It contained seats for forty passengers, though there were fewer than half that number waiting to depart as they went down the steps to the water. Smoke rose from a single stack. The boatman wiped the exposed parts of the engine with a rag, his hands and forearms already black. He directed them to their seats. A woman Elizabeth recognized from the hotel warned them against sitting where the man showed them, pointing instead to empty seats further forward. She said the smoke from the moving vessel would blow down onto their faces and clothes. Elizabeth felt the shallow vessel rock beneath them as others came on board.

A few moments later the Gottliebs arrived in a cab from the town. Herr Gottlieb called down for the boatman to wait. They were accompanied by an Italian family, also from the hotel. The four children came aboard first, ignored the directions of the boatman and ran to the prow.

'Did you know they were coming?' Elizabeth asked Mary. It was the first time she had seen the Gottliebs, other than across the hotel dining-room, since Jameson's revelation. She was still not completely convinced of what he had told her.

Mary seemed distracted. She sat wrapped in her coat and scarf, gazing over the calm surface of the lake. 'What?' she said.

Elizabeth indicated the Gottliebs, who had by then come down to the boat and seen them.

Gerda waved and called and came to them.

'I don't know,' Mary said. 'They said something about coming. They take the trip all the time.'

'I wish you'd told me,' Elizabeth said.

Mary turned away.

The Italian and his wife took the seats across the aisle from them. The Gottliebs arranged themselves close behind. Herr Gottlieb was angry that better seats had not been reserved for himself and his wife and daughter.

'I meant for you to take one of the larger boats,' he said to Mary. He smiled at her, but the smile did nothing to disguise his anger.

Elizabeth wondered if Mary had forgotten or confused some arrangement she had made with the Germans.

Mary turned to face him, but said nothing.

'With these smaller ones you are exposed to the elements. What good is that—' he indicated the canvas canopy above them '—when the wind and the rain start?'

'Perhaps it won't rain,' Elizabeth suggested.

'Of course it will rain.'

'He knows all about weather,' Frau Gottlieb said.

'You only have to look at the surface of the water to know it will rain. Believe me, I know about these things.'

Elizabeth looked up at the sky instead, most of which was clear and bright; only towards the head of the valley was it darker with gathering cloud. Herr Gottlieb followed her gaze.

'That is where the bad weather will come from,' he said. 'Off the ice.' He beckoned the boatman to him and quizzed the man on their route and the duration of the trip.

At the prow of the boat, two of the Italian children started fighting. This lasted several minutes before their father called for them to stop. They paid him no attention. The other passengers shook their heads at the noise made by the children. The two boys grabbed the boat rail and rocked the vessel. Their father called to them again.

'They need to be punished,' Herr Gottlieb said to the man. 'If you wish me to—' He stopped abruptly as the Italian rose and went to his children. The man pulled the smaller boy from the rail and pushed him into an empty seat. Then he grabbed the other by his collar and pulled him back to where he sat with his wife and other children. He shouted at the child and then struck him hard on the side of his head. The boy started to cry and his father struck him again.

'Pay him no attention,' Herr Gottlieb said. 'They cry for no reason these days. What does he have to cry over?'

While all this was happening, Elizabeth watched the children's mother. She made no attempt to discipline the boys or to restrain her husband. She sat in silence with her hands clasped. She made a gesture towards the crying child, but gave no indication of wanting to hold or console him. From somewhere further back in the boat, someone shouted 'Bravo.' Only the father turned to see who had called out.

Herr Gottlieb indicated to the boatman that it was time for them to leave. The man cast off the ropes which held them to the jetty and then pushed the steamer slowly away using an oar. He started up the engine. Smoke rose more thickly in a faltering plume and then drifted to one side in an unravelling ribbon. The small stern paddle started to turn with a more regular rhythm and they moved out onto the broad surface of the lake.

It surprised Elizabeth to realize how swiftly they were beyond all hearing of the shore. The water lay still and smooth, broken only by the pattern of their own motion through it. They passed amid the ever-present gulls, hundreds of birds riding on the surface, none of them rising at their approach.

'Do you know where we're going?' she asked Mary. It hardly mattered to her where they went during the two hours of the trip; she merely wanted Mary to speak to her.

Ever since calling for her earlier that morning, Elizabeth could not rid herself of the impression that there was something Mary was putting off telling her. She tried to decide what this might be, and guessed it was to do with her decision to return home earlier than they had originally planned. Elizabeth had already decided that if this was what Mary wanted, then she, Elizabeth, would not return with her.

'We go directly to the far side,' Herr Gottlieb said. He came across and sat behind them, pushing his head between them. 'Over there, directly towards the mountains, the abandoned quarry.'

Elizabeth looked. That side of the lake lay in impenetrable shadow, the sunlight shaped in a silhouette of peaks.

'Wait until we get there,' Herr Gottlieb said. 'Wait until we leave the sun behind. Tell me then if you shouldn't have done as I suggested and taken one of the larger vessels.'

His wife called him back to her, and he went.

Out on the open water, with no other small craft around them, they moved more swiftly, and for the first time Elizabeth was able to look along the full curved length of the lake, ten miles in each direction, and she saw how totally enclosed it appeared, with no sign of either the road or the railway which ran to the west and the world beyond through tunnels and gorges in the rising land.

Their movement from the sunlit surface of the lake into

the cool and half-light of the shade was as abrupt as Herr Gottlieb had predicted.

Elizabeth looked back to the town and saw how far they had steamed from it. Moving cars heliographed their presence to her. Beside her, Mary began to shiver. The boatman opened a basket and announced that there were blankets. Elizabeth took two of these, wrapped Mary in one, and draped the other loosely over her own shoulders. She overheard Herr Gottlieb warning his wife and daughter against using the blankets. The Italian mother swaddled each of her children against the cold and they sat cocooned with only their small round faces showing.

She heard the sound of falling water and looked ahead to where a waterfall fell from a high lip of overhanging rock into the lake below. Her eyes became accustomed to the gloom. There was a low mist on the water along this shore. In places the rock wall was sheer, almost concave; elsewhere the forest came down precipitous slopes to the water's edge. Trees lay where they had lost their footing and fallen, their trunks, branches and roots in a half-submerged and moss-covered tangle. The boatman pointed out where other streams and cascades came down off the peaks into the water. He pointed out the abandoned quarry to them as they passed it by. He cut the engine and the paddle slowed and stopped. Its echoing slap quickly faded and they drifted in silence. No-one spoke. Then, without warning, the boatman took out a hand-bell from the basket and shook it vigorously. The noise it made was deafening so close to the overhang, and people put their hands over their ears and Frau Gottlieb called out for him to stop. Her husband told her not to complain, that it was an interesting and memorable experiment. The boatman stopped ringing, but the fading echo of the bell could be heard for long afterwards.

They continued to drift towards the wall of the shore. They passed black rocks in the shadows, some of which rose higher than the steamer; others barely broke the surface and lapped in the water like the bobbing heads of inquisitive seals. It grew even cooler. They drifted to where a slender spout of water fell from a cliff and was blown to spray before reaching the lake.

The boatman altered their course by pushing with his oar against the rocks. Herr Gottlieb put his hand over the side into the water and announced that it was freezing. Anyone falling into the lake, he said, would very quickly die. Elizabeth felt Mary edge away from her and closer to the rail.

They turned into a bay of deeper water. Ahead of them hung the leading edge of a small glacier, a tributary of the much larger ice-floe to the east. The sun shone along the rim of this and meltwater dripped sporadically. Elizabeth saw that the ice also extended beneath them, that a fallen slab of this glacier lay under the lake. She guessed their draught to be no more than four feet, and she waited, bracing herself against the scrape of their keel along this submerged shelf.

The boatman explained to them how the face of the ice frequently broke and fell into the lake, and that this could be heard from the town, especially when it took place during the night and the wind was in the right direction. Elizabeth looked at the ice above them. She had heard the stories of falling ice, but had so far neither seen nor heard this, and she wondered if the boatman had hoped to encourage this spectacle by the ringing of his bell.

Beyond the glacier they drew closer still to the shore, and Elizabeth was surprised to see there the ruin of a large house, set back from what remained of a simple stone pier, now nothing more than a strip of submerged rubble from which a few posts still rose.

'How long has it been empty?' she asked the boatman.

The man didn't know. He had lived all his life, thirty years, in the town, and it had been empty and abandoned all that time.

'It can only ever have been a folly,' Herr Gottlieb said. 'Who would want to live in the cold and dark and damp for nine months of the year and with only uncertain light and sun for the remaining three?'

Elizabeth ignored him. The building, though derelict, appeared substantially intact. A toppled trunk lay propped against one end of the structure.

They passed it slowly. She tried to imagine who might have lived there in such uncomfortable isolation. Even a boat with an engine would have taken twenty minutes to cross the lake to the town, and there were no roads or paths on that side of the water.

A minute later they rounded another small headland and were out of sight of the house. The boatman restarted his engine and turned them back over the deeper water.

Before they began their return journey to the town, he took them close to the skeletal wreck of another, larger vessel. He told them that these were the remains of a steamer that had been blown off course and onto the rocks during a storm twenty years earlier. Sixty-one people had lost their lives in the wreck; a hundred others had been rescued by the fishermen of the town. As he spoke, Elizabeth saw him take out a large tin from the basket and stand this beside him on the step by which they would all soon disembark. He continued with the story, exaggerating the bravery of the boatmen, his father and uncles among them. The tin was to collect his gratuities.

He steered them closer to the iron spars of the lost vessel, warning them against trying to reach out and touch these.

Anyone coming into contact with the wreck would suffer misfortune, he said.

As he spoke, Elizabeth saw Mary withdraw one of her arms from her blanket, reach out and touch the nearest of the spars. But before she could comment on this, something else caught her eye: they were again manoeuvring among half-submerged boulders, and she saw that the exposed surface of the largest of these had been covered with vividly white crosses, almost luminous in the poor light. Everyone else turned to look, and some started to count until the boatman announced that there were sixty-one of these, and that it was a tradition in the town for the boulder to be repainted and blessed anew each year in the spring. He picked up his tin and rattled the few small coins it already held. Elizabeth saw that some of the crosses were half the size of the others, and she wondered if these were for the children lost in the wreck. She turned to look at the Italians, and saw all of them sitting with the knuckles of their thumbs held between their lips. She understood how unexpectedly and forcibly such connections were made. The father withdrew his hand from his mouth, and his wife and children followed him. He then took a coin from his pocket, kissed it and threw it into the water, where it flickered briefly before sinking.

11

'There's something you ought to know about Hunter,' Jameson said when they next met.

They were sitting beneath the awning of one of the cafés overlooking the town square. It was a cool day and they were the only customers outside. It was Elizabeth's choice; they sat in their coats. A waiter came frequently to the window and looked out at them. She wore the gloves which had been a gift from her brother, bought from the same outfitters who had provided him with his flying helmet and gauntlets. She still had the embossed box in which he had given them to her. She showed Jameson where the stitching was coming loose on several fingers.

'This place used to be famous for its gloves, I believe,' he said. 'Gloves and fine leather-ware. The old town is full of the places. Hard to say which ones are still in operation, though; a lot of dark little shops and back rooms.'

'What about Hunter? Something about you and him?'

'Me and him? Not really.'

They sat side by side, facing the square.

'What do you mean, about me and him?' he said.

'I only meant that you seem to have taken on some kind of responsibility for him. His remarks the other day . . .'

'Oh, that. No, not really.' There was little conviction in the denial.

'Then tell me,' she said. She felt the steam from her cup rise into her face.

'He may be court-martialled,' he said.

'For what?'

'I'm not entirely certain of the specific charges they've brought against him. They tried once before.'

'What happened?'

'His appointed defender argued that he was too ill, too unstable—' he raised a finger, as though about to tap his forehead, but then thought better of the gesture and lowered his hand '—to face the charge. That's why he's here.'

'To make him well? To wait until he's well enough to be tried again? But the war's been over almost a year now. They surely can't—'

'I doubt if that has the slightest bearing on the matter. The Army remains the Army. Where would it be without its routines and regulations?'

'How does Hunter feel about it?'

'Detached. He certainly doesn't feel angry or even aggrieved. I wish he did.'

'When will it happen?'

He shrugged. 'I suppose when they deem him sufficiently recovered from whatever it is they imagine him to be suffering from to face his accusers. No point in confronting an insane man with the rock of sanity and duty upon which to break him.'

'But he isn't insane. Anyone can see that.'

'As you say. I believe it's all a matter of definition. We await an announcement.'

'We?'

'They'll take him home to try him. When that happens . . .'

'What? You'll go with him?'

'And offer him the services of a family lawyer, if they allow it.'

'Won't they just let it drop? What purpose will it serve for them to try and punish him now?'

'Loose ends. They all need to be tied up.'

'Do you know what happened? Were you there? Is that why you're here?'

'I'm afraid not. Nothing so simple.' He paused. 'Yes, I know what happened. And the only reason I'm telling you this is because I think someone else ought to know, and because you'd probably have heard it all sooner or later in some twisted-up version from somebody like Cox.'

'Who, presumably, doesn't know.'

'Not the whole story. Court-martial someone and they're either a coward or a deserter. Christ knows, there were enough of those.'

'Cowards and deserters?'

'No – trials. Mostly lower ranks. Mostly *pour encourager les autres*. A lot of sick and frightened men, boys, tried and punished and executed.' He stopped abruptly.

She put down her cup. 'Are you saying Hunter could be executed?'

She received his answer in silence. They stopped speaking for several minutes. She watched the people passing them by. There were fewer tourists now, fewer guests at the hotels. In her own hotel, a quarter of the tables had been removed from the dining-room. Each day, late in the afternoon, the cabs and carriages queued along the road to the station piled high with luggage, the waiting-rooms and platforms filled with departing visitors.

'He was married,' Jameson said eventually. 'His wife petitioned for a divorce and was granted one. There was little point in him contesting it.'

'Because of his trial?'

'No. It started before then, but you can imagine how a fat patriotic old judge sitting in the Home Counties might look on a thing like that.'

'Did he have any children?'

'Has. He has two daughters. One of them called Elizabeth. Both young, four, five, something like that. The first time I saw him here, he took out their photographs from one of his books and tore them into small pieces.'

'Why?'

'Because he couldn't bear to look at them, simple as that. He was denied the right to even visit them until the outcome of his trial was announced. I imagine that someone somewhere decided it would be too distressing for the children to have a father who—'

'You don't have to,' she said. She put her hand on his.

'No. Perhaps they've already been told he died wreathed in glory somewhere.'

'Won't his wife do anything for him?'

'Why should she? Imagine the shame she must be suffering. The proper marriage was over long ago.'

'Did you ever know her?'

'I met her, once. In London, on leave. Just after he'd been wounded and hospitalized for the second time. She came to visit him. I was in the same small hospital in Elstree. I think even then she'd started the proceedings against him. I remember how disappointed he was that she hadn't brought his daughters to see him. She told him it was no place for children. He'd expected to be allowed home for a few weeks before returning to France, but that never happened.'

They were interrupted by the arrival of the waiter. He stood in his shirt-sleeves blowing into his hands and gently stamping his feet. 'There are plenty of tables inside,' he said.

Jameson looked through the window. 'So there are,' he said. He waited for the boy to leave them before going on.

'He's a civil engineer. He designs bridges, buildings, roads, whatever it is that civil engineers do.'

'My brother wanted to be an architect,' she said. The words almost dried in the sudden and unexpected memory.

He stopped speaking and looked at her. 'Is it still that painful for you?'

'When I was a girl I used to say that I'd be his secretary or his assistant. We made plans to go into business together.'

'It must have been comforting, sustaining, to grow up together thinking it might happen.'

'It was.' She tugged at the open fingers of her gloves.

The waiter returned, this time speaking to neither of them.

'Do you remember the massive mines they exploded at Messines?' Jameson asked her.

'I remember something about them. Wasn't it the start of an offensive?'

'They wanted it to be the start and the end. The biggest explosion the world had ever seen. Whole hills levelled in a minute, thousands of men killed, buried or shocked into numb disbelief. Hunter was transferred to help with the preparations, with mining the tunnels from our lines under theirs. Hundreds of Durham miners did the digging.

Durham Light Infantry. It took them the best part of six months. I saw them once while they were working. The strangest thing of all is that they were digging through blue clay for part of the way, not coal, and they came out at the end of each shift blue and marbled with sweat, looking more like statues than men. Hunter got on well with them, and they with him. Up until then he'd spent most of his time building support roads across plains of mud and bridges across canals.'

'Did the mines work?'

'Up to a point. The real problem was that it was such a large operation the Germans couldn't help but know what was going on. They had their own miners working towards our lines at the same time. Sometimes we'd try and find out where they were tunnelling and set off smaller charges in the hope of stopping them.'

'Of burying them alive? That's awful.'

'Of course it was. But the point was, if you could hear them tunnelling, then you could be reasonably certain that they weren't about to let off anything of their own. When they stopped digging, that was the time to worry. When there was no more digging, all they then had to do was take down the ammonal and gun cotton, wire it up and stand well back. When that seemed likely we'd just withdraw from our own front line, wait for the big bang and then get back forward as soon as possible afterwards. In truth, the mines looked impressive, but they did little real damage. That was why the explosions had to get bigger and bigger for them to have any real impact. They demoralized more than they destroyed. The mines at Messines were going to be the last word in that kind of thing. No-one was ever going to better them.'

'And what was Hunter's part in it all?'

'He understood the geology and the lie of the land. He

worked out the best route to take. He worked well with those men, and they had a lot of respect for him. He went into their diggings with them. He told me afterwards that those tunnels were as perfectly built and supported as any he'd seen. They knew what they were digging them for, but they still took that pride in their work. According to Hunter, there was no other way they could do it. They worked naked, most of them. It worried them that they had to devise ways of stopping their German counterparts from coming too close. One day, Hunter said, everyone in the tunnel he was inspecting fell silent, and a man led him to where three or four of them sat with their ears pressed to the wall. He did the same and heard the voices of the German miners not a foot away from him. All down the tunnel men blew out their lamps. He said most of them were grinning, suppressing laughter. Someone told him that earlier they'd signalled to each other, making sure that they and the Germans kept to different paths, but when someone back at Command heard about this they'd warned of charges of collaboration being brought. After that there'd been a messy incident where a German tunneller had broken through one of our walls and then been beaten to death with picks. It happened in the dark and the fight started and finished without anyone really understanding why, or how to prevent it. Everyone felt bad about it. Apparently, the German tunneller was as small and as naked as our own diggers. They cleaned up his corpse and left it to be collected. They told Hunter that judging by the dead man's physique, he too had been a miner before the war.'

'What happened?' she said.

'The court-martial, you mean?'

A sudden gust of wind brought dead leaves down all around them, some onto their table, where he absently gathered them up.

'What happened was that Hunter was called to a meeting to decide when and how best to explode the mines, and how to do it without giving too much advance warning to the Germans.'

She noticed he never used any of the other names which had long since become common currency. She noticed it the same way she noticed his insistence on calling himself and others by their surnames alone, thereby maintaining a formality and a measure of detachment. She had noticed something similar elsewhere – how men were kept boys by their diminutives – the Johnnies, Billies and Tommies – and how the Jonathans, Williams and Thomases were a different breed entirely.

He went on. 'At this meeting someone had a marvellous idea how to catch the German unawares, how to avoid signalling to them that the digging had finished and that the explosives were in place and ready to be detonated.'

'Which was?'

'Why not start packing the excavated chambers with the explosives while the digging was still in progress – perfectly safe, no detonators, no fuses – and then, when everything was ready and there was enough stuff down there to blow a hundred-foot hill to Kingdom Come and the word came from upon high to do it – why not do it while there were still men digging down there and making all their usual disarming noise.'

'Surely not?'

'Why not? It was all for the common good. No-one would actually *feel* anything, no-one would actually *know*, no-one would *suffer*, it would all be very sudden, no-one would be merely injured and left wounded, not at the heart of an explosion like that.' He paused and caught his breath.

'And presumably Hunter objected,' she said.

'Of course he objected. Who, apart from a sadistic idiot, wouldn't object?'

'Then I take it he was alone.'

'Essentially, yes. Some others voiced their concerns about the deliberate taking of life, but the "Greater Good" and all that.'

'And so they were persuaded to agree?'

'It's the way most of those big campaign decisions were made. You were usually only ever consulted to see how enthusiastically you were prepared to go along with them.'

'So what did he do?'

'What could he do? He insisted on going on record with his objections and they told him that because the meeting was a secret one no record of it was being kept. He was told they would abide by a majority decision. He was also told that he was not to repeat a word of what had been said to anyone outside the meeting.'

'And he did?'

'Not immediately. They were still a fortnight away from detonating the mines.'

'So he lived with the knowledge of what was going to happen all that time?'

'He spoke, privately, to anyone he believed might have had some influence. He even spoke to the Durham men's padre.'

'Surely *he* would have been able to do something?'

'He wasn't a Durham man; he'd been recently attached to them after their own padre was killed.'

'Was there no-one?'

'Apparently not. There was a great deal at stake. What was that one small sacrifice against the supposedly impressive gains all set to be made?'

'But how would they decide – *who* would decide – which men to send down the tunnels on the morning they knew they were going to detonate the explosions? It's unthinkable.'

'Not in that world. They even found a way to convince the miners themselves that even though the explosives appeared to be ready for detonation, this was just temporary wiring and dud fuses to help them get it right for the big day.'

'Did Hunter know when the explosions were going to happen?'

'He believed he did. And then he was convinced that because no-one could be sure of his own silence they would fire them off before he'd had a chance to do anything about it. They wanted to transfer him to another sector. After all, the digging was finished.'

'Why didn't they?'

'I don't know. Perhaps because not letting him see the job through would have raised suspicions. And because a week had passed and no-one had sided with him, I imagine they thought he'd seen sense himself.'

'Couldn't he have secretly warned the miners?'

'There was never a time when there weren't at least sixty or seventy men in the tunnels. Three shifts, all overlapping, with men on their way to and from the ends of the tunnels. The diggings were never empty. Nor could they fire the explosions at a moment's notice. They needed time to build up a charge, and anyone forewarned would be looking out for that happening.'

'So what did he do?'

'He took the only course he believed was open to him. He waited ten or twelve days and then went into the main shaft himself, having first told his mess orderly to inform High Command of what he was doing. The choice was theirs. He'd also left several copies of an account of his reasons for doing what he did. He made it clear to everyone in the know, and to the few men prepared to listen to him, that whoever now took responsibility for the explosions did so in full knowledge of what he was doing.'

'Would it make such a difference to them, killing an officer alongside all those enlisted men?'

'Apparently it would, and he knew that. Officer and Gentleman, several times wounded, decorated, cited for bravery . . .'

'What happened?'

'What do you imagine happened? There was a panic. They sent other officers in to reason with him. I imagine they tried to persuade the diggers that he didn't know what he was saying or doing, that he'd been too long at the front. The trouble was, those men believed him. They'd known him too long. Their only reassurance then was knowing – or so they believed – that the explosives wouldn't be fired while the negotiators themselves were still in the tunnel. Hunter told the diggers to insist on the top brass coming down to talk to them. Those men stayed with him. Someone on the surface even had the clever idea of insisting that the sounds of digging be kept up all the time they were talking. Imagine that.'

'Did he succeed?'

'Not really. A compromise was reached. Normally a full twelve or twenty-four hours would pass between the end of the digging and the explosives being detonated. On this occasion they would evacuate the tunnels and then fire the detonators immediately. There would be some risk involved, but once the men were out of the deeper tunnels and the line of the blast, they would be reasonably safe.'

'And Hunter?'

'He insisted on coming out last, with the negotiators. I think by then some of the others were beginning to see the sense in what he was saying.'

'And did they all get out?'

Jameson shook his head. 'Someone, whether by accident or design, pressed the plunger fifteen minutes early. Seventeen of the miners and two of the negotiators were killed. By some miracle, Hunter survived. He was buried, along with a dozen others, for two days, but they eventually got everyone who was still alive out.'

'You think they set the mines off early deliberately?'

'It would certainly have solved a lot of problems, but the written records suggest a genuine error.'

'How convenient.'

'I try to believe it for his sake, if not my own.'

'How could they be so inhumane? They were punishing him.'

'Perhaps. But they achieved that more in the deaths of those other miners than through his own injuries. One of his legs and both his arms were broken, most of his ribs. His skull was fractured. He was concussed, unconscious for a week.'

'And when he came round they said he'd lost his reason?'

'And that he was directly responsible for the deaths of those others. They had everything they needed.'

Neither of them spoke after that. She knew without being told not to repeat any of what she had heard.

The strings of lights beneath the trees were switched on, emphasizing the falling dusk.

'They'll find him guilty, won't they?' she said eventually.

Jameson rose, took out his wallet and pushed a note under his saucer. He left her without saying anything else.

Alone, she considered what he'd told her, and she felt numbed by it – not only by the events and people he had described, but also by the act of disclosure itself, which seemed to her no less brutal or unavoidable than those events. It was something she would have insisted on knowing, but even that wanting had made the revelation no less of a shock to her.

She waited at the table half an hour longer before making her way back to the hotel. On the steps she passed those guests who were leaving, and who stood anxiously watching as their luggage was carried down to the road and waiting cabs.

12

At the centre of the courtyard stood a dovecote, built of pale, powdery brick, and with freshly-painted perches. A dozen or so of the birds clustered together on the conical roof. Several of these rose at her approach, fluttered above it for a moment and then resettled. Small white heads appeared in the dark holes of the miniature doorways. Grain lay scattered around the base of the structure, but here there were only sparrows running back and forth between the sunlight and the shade.

She came through the archway and saw that three others led out of the courtyard into other, smaller yards beyond. Through one of these, the one which faced in the direction of the hospital, she could hear the chanting of girls' voices as they repeated a lesson by rote to the rhythm of a conductor.

She had asked at the entrance if she was allowed to wander alone into the buildings, and had been assured that she could go anywhere except those doors marked private. But now, entering this peaceful space with its murmuring birds and its warm echo of voices, she felt as though she were an intruder, and that her presence would soon be noticed and acted upon.

Beside her stood the small fountain she had heard on her first visit. It was a simple, font-like basin with a lead spout emerging from the wall above it. The basin was dry, its worn inner bowl caked with dust and a mat of dried stems.

Ahead of her, the chanting ended and she heard instead the instructions of a single voice. She was about to leave when a nearby door opened and two nuns came out. They saw her and approached her. They were both young women; one carried a fork and the other a hoe, and both wore heavy gauntlets. As they came closer she saw the dirt on their faces, their foreheads and cheeks striped by clear lines of sweat. The sparrows scattered at their approach.

'Are you looking for someone?' one asked her. Both women nodded vigorously in expectation of her answer.

Elizabeth's first instinct was to mention Margaret, but instead she said, 'I was just looking around.'

The two women propped their tools against the fountain, took off their gauntlets and dropped these into its bowl. The one drew back her cowl and rubbed both her hands through her short blonde hair, before drawing the material forward and securing it again. Elizabeth saw that they were both her own age, perhaps a year or two younger.

'We've been working in the fields,' the one with blonde hair said. Elizabeth guessed her to be German or Austrian.

'The Lord's blessed harvest,' the other added, wiping her face with a cloth. The two women hesitated, glanced at each other and then laughed at a shared joke.

'And in twenty minutes we must attend to our devotions.'

'May I?' the first said, and reached out to feel the material of Elizabeth's coat.

'Cashmere,' Elizabeth said.

'Yes. I had one the same,' the woman said, a sigh of long-subdued regret in her voice.

'I was hoping to see Sister Margaret,' Elizabeth said. 'I know her from the town. I've spoken with her several times.' She now felt the need not so much to explain her presence, but simply to share something with them. She remained uncertain of her reason for having returned alone to the convent, knowing only that it had something to do with what she had learned of Hunter, and what she now understood of the bond between him and Jameson. It also had something to do with what both men saw in the place, and what it meant to them amid the uncertainty and turmoil of their own two unsettled lives.

'Someone could fetch her for you,' the blonde nun said. Nothing of her hair was now visible, her anonymity secure.

They sat with her, sharing news of their work and of her time in the town, until a bell rang and they both rose. They took up their tools, said their farewells and went through one of the smaller archways. Elizabeth heard them greet someone, and a moment later Margaret appeared.

'I heard you were here. Someone saw you arrive. My apologies. I would have come to join you sooner. No doubt you feel as though you're intruding on us. Nothing could be further from the truth. We need these contacts.' She lowered her voice. 'To be perfectly frank with you, some of us here crave them.' She led Elizabeth closer to the preening birds.

'Is that why you work at the hospital?' Elizabeth said.

'Partly. And partly because it gives us some purpose. There are some of us trained as nurses, some as cooks. And we can all be company for the men. You can imagine how different life here was before the hospital was created.'

'And how different it will be when the place is finally emptied and turned back into a hotel?'

Margaret considered the prospect. 'When that day comes, yes.'

Ahead of them, the chanting voices resumed.

'Lessons,' Margaret said. 'Come and meet some of our students.'

Elizabeth followed her into a smaller yard, where she saw a group of novices being instructed by an older woman tapping words along a blackboard. The voices faltered at her appearance, but then resumed their rhythm at a gesture from Margaret.

'Some of them will join us when the time comes,' Margaret whispered. 'But not all. Some are here because there is no-where else for them to go just at present, no-one to care for them, or because they are uncertain in themselves what they want. They use the convent as a breathing space. Some of the other sisters consider this a waste of our resources and would like to demand some greater commitment from them, but there are enough of us here who understand the true nature of the times in which we live to allow these girls to find their own way.' She looked fondly at the pupils as she spoke. Ruth was not among them.

'Are they mostly from the town?' Elizabeth asked her.

'Some are local. Others find their way to us from other convents. Some come because we can care for them, and some simply because to be here is to be away from the eyes of the world.'

'Care for them? In what way?'

But Margaret did not answer her. She went to stand in front of the girls. She apologized to the teacher for her intrusion. She beckoned Elizabeth forward and introduced her. The girls answered her in chorus. They were all, Elizabeth guessed, between fourteen and seventeen, some dressed in the simple smocks and aprons of the other novices, some in their own clothes; some already wore their hair covered, while others kept it loose. One girl, she saw, had an almost shaved head, crudely cut, with small tufts of hair sprouting longer than the rest, as though she had cut it herself in some small private act of devotion.

'Elizabeth comes from England, from Oxford,' Margaret said.

Several of the girls looked at her intently, as though this added to their understanding of her.

It was then that Elizabeth saw that one of the girls sitting on the back row of chairs appeared to be pregnant, and noticing this in the one girl, she saw that the girl sitting beside her also looked to be in the same condition. These were the only two. Both girls wore their own clothes and had their hair uncovered, and one was clearly in a more advanced state than the other.

Elizabeth looked away from them, uncertain of what precisely she had seen, of what to say. No attempt had been made to disguise the girls' condition.

'Follow me,' Margaret told her. She said goodbye to the girls and again they answered her in a single voice.

'Is that what you meant when you said you cared for them?' Elizabeth asked her as they came out onto the open land at the rear of the convent.

'It's something the nuns here have always done,' Margaret said. She avoided Elizabeth's eyes as she spoke. 'I myself am a trained midwife. You seem surprised. Are you shocked?'

Elizabeth was not certain what she felt.

'Do you deliver them here?'

Margaret indicated a building set apart from the main body of the convent, only partially visible to them through an old orchard. They walked towards the trees.

'Do they stay with you afterwards?'

'The mothers, sometimes.'

'And the babies?'

'Sometimes the mothers and babies are found new homes together.'

'And sometimes they are separated?'

'In many cases it is the only course available. You saw how young some of the girls were.'

They entered the first of the trees.

'You must use your imagination,' Margaret said. 'But, please, try not to judge them, and certainly try not to judge them harshly; there are enough people elsewhere only too willing to do that. They come here, we do what has to be done for them – hopefully always for the best – and when we have done all we can do, they leave.'

'Except the ones who remain to become nuns.'

Margaret smiled. 'I'm afraid not. The girls who come to us with the intention of one day joining us in the order must of course come to us in a state of grace. A clumsy phrase, I know, but these absolutes remain.'

Elizabeth regretted her mistake. 'And so the pregnant girls – even those who might want to join you – are denied?'

'I'm afraid so, yes. There are those among us who might occasionally wish it were otherwise, but it is something so far beyond us.'

They walked further into the trees. Elizabeth saw that there had once been a design to the orchard, but that now that order had been lost through time and neglect. Trees stood unpruned; many had fallen, others lay propped but living, grown into strange shapes. Dead branches covered the ground at their feet.

'I'm afraid we're going to lose it for ever,' Margaret said, looking around her. 'Apples, pears and cherries. Most of the trees have outgrown their own strength. There were once gardeners, horticulturists, men who understood what needed to be done, but we lost the last of them three or four years ago. There is still a small harvest to be had, but this grows less each year. The fruit is smaller than it ever was, and the cherries have barely any flesh on them. You must watch where you walk.'

'It's a great pity,' Elizabeth said.

'I know. Dr Armstrong has offered us the use of able-bodied men from the hospital to help remove all the dead wood. There is even a man from Kent who has offered to acquire new trees for us and to train some of the sisters in their care.'

'Will you accept?'

'Possibly. I don't know. It is not for me to say.'

They arrived at the high wall which separated the convent from the hospital. Beyond it, men's voices could be heard. Someone was singing, someone else playing a harmonica.

'I sometimes come and stand down here alone – sometimes with Ruth – just to hear them,' Margaret said. 'I try to imagine them all at peace with themselves, and all safe. Throughout the war, I always regarded this failing and over-grown place as a true haven.'

'I imagine the whole convent must have been that to many.'

'Of course. But this was my own, private place. Let me show you something else.'

Margaret walked ahead of her, past the last of the trees and away from the high wall. She led Elizabeth to yet another archway, whose door hung loosely on its hinges, but which opened only when both of them pushed on it. Ivy trailed from the arch to the ground. The once-blue paint of the door had mostly peeled away and the wood beneath was bleached grey.

Margaret led the way.

Beyond lay a small graveyard.

'No longer in use,' Margaret said. The plot ahead of them was even more neglected and overgrown than the orchard. A few stones still rose above the grass and weeds. 'There has been no burial here for twelve years. We have a new grave-yard alongside the road.'

'But why neglect this one?'

'It is not neglected in our hearts.'

Elizabeth went forward alone. She saw other, smaller stones hidden by the tall grass. 'Are those the graves of children?'

'Babies, mostly,' Margaret said. 'And some of the unfortu-nate young mothers. There were some girls who only found their way to us after they had tried other means. Some of them were beyond our help from the start, but we did every-thing we could for them, even if it was only to provide them with a Christian burial. Things have improved greatly over recent years. We now have a properly-equipped delivery room. Most of the burials these days follow the deaths of the older sisters.' She paused and looked around her. 'A pity. I always intended that I should be buried here, among all these desperate girls and their quiet children. I imagined I would one day meet them all again up in heaven, and that they would all remember me.'

Elizabeth looked up at this.

Margaret caught the look on her face. 'Do I embarrass you with my talk of heaven?'

'Not at all.' Elizabeth remembered what Ruth had said.

'Yes I do. You imagined I must have grown at least a little sceptical, a little hardened by all that I've seen next door.'

'It's not that.'

'Then what? You can speak here, of all places.'

'It's just that I've never heard anyone speak with such *flat* conviction of something so . . . so . . .'

'Of heaven. I see. Then let me tell you – sometimes I know with absolute conviction that there must be a heaven, and at other times I cannot convince myself of even its tiniest detail. Swedenborg was once a great favourite of mine. Does the name mean anything to you?'

'Were they not his angels dancing on the head of a pin?'

Margaret laughed at this. Then she said a brief prayer over the small space and led Elizabeth back to the archway, pulling the clumsy door into place behind her. 'Soon it will fall from its hinges and everyone will be able to gaze in at what lies there.'

Passing back through the lost orchard, Elizabeth saw Ruth waiting ahead of them, and only then did it occur to her that she too might have had this other reason for coming to the convent.

'There's Ruth,' she said to Margaret, who had not yet seen the girl.

Margaret considered the distant figure for a moment. 'Perhaps she imagined Jameson was with you,' she said.

Ruth watched them approach, and it seemed to Elizabeth as though she was practising the smile with which she would greet them.

'I suppose the town is full of talk of the first snow,' Margaret said loudly as they came close to where Ruth waited.

'The first snow? I don't know. I haven't heard anything.'

'It's already on the peaks at the head of the valley, and those further to the south.' Margaret shielded her eyes against the sun and looked in that direction. There was nothing to see.

'Does it usually come at this time of year?'

'Normally later.'

'What does it signify?'

'A hard winter. A long one. Impassable roads and lost power. Don't worry – you'll be long gone by then.'

They emerged from the trees and Ruth finally came forward to greet them. Her hair was uncovered and freshly brushed. Margaret spoke to her in rapid French. The girl slid her hand through the old woman's arm.

'I am wanted elsewhere,' Margaret said. 'Ruth will walk with you back to the road.'

The girl was about to object to the offer made on her behalf.

'Ruth?' Margaret said.

Ruth nodded.

Margaret left them, entering a doorway at the rear of the convent.

'She was showing me your orchard,' Elizabeth said.

'And the graveyard, I imagine. Is that why you think I came here?'

'It's none of my business,' Elizabeth said, speaking as abruptly to the girl as she had spoken to her, making no allowance for her age.

'Well, it wasn't. I came because there was nowhere else for me to go when my parents were killed. My aunt was a nun at another convent.' There was neither embarrassment nor anger in her voice.

'Then you arrived in a state of grace,' Elizabeth said.

Ruth laughed. 'Some of them are so pathetic,' she said. 'No more than cows led one way and then the other.'

This sudden change surprised Elizabeth. She knew the girl would never have spoken like this in front of Margaret.

After that, perhaps because this outburst had not had the desired effect, they continued in silence to the convent gates.

Ruth waited in the shadow of the entrance with her until the bus finally arrived, coming out onto the empty road only as it pulled away and left her standing behind and waving. Elizabeth waved back. Something about the girl's outburst had reassured her. Then, remembering Margaret's talk of snow, she looked beyond the swiftly receding figure, still waving, and saw the falling sun reflected amid the scatter of distant peaks above the glacier.

13

She was surprised, several mornings later, to see the return of the invalids with their nurses and the nuns. She watched them from her window. She saw Margaret walking with Hunter, and a short distance ahead of them, Ruth leading Mitchell. She stopped him at the steps leading down to the lower walkway, and Elizabeth saw Mitchell signal to her that he wanted to go down. She watched more closely as the boy reached out to locate the rail, swinging his hand from side to side until Ruth finally guided him to it.

Elizabeth put down the book she had been reading and went outside.

In the hotel entrance she passed the manager and the maître d', both standing out of sight of the men and women below, watching and discussing them. They stopped speaking at her approach, and the manager bowed to her.

'I would delay your departure,' he said to her, indicating the crowded pavement.

'Why?'

The maître d' whispered to him.

'Ah, yes,' the manager said. 'Then of course you must go out.'

She refused to be drawn by these cryptic remarks, assuming they were in some way connected with her friendship with Jameson and all that this implied.

At the bottom of the steps she looked again for Margaret and Hunter, finally spotting them on one of the benches overlooking the lake. She saw several others she recognized from the hospital.

She crossed the road to the lake. Ruth and Mitchell sat beneath her. Ruth put small stones into the boy's hand and he threw them into the water. After each throw she spoke to him, redirecting his aim, or his trajectory, or perhaps telling him of some invisible target.

Hunter was the first to see her. He rose and indicated the space on the bench where he sat with Margaret.

'I don't want to intrude,' Elizabeth said.

'Then you ought to,' Margaret told her. 'Captain Hunter believes I am capable of understanding his wayward philosophical discussions. I agree with him when I see he is convinced of what he says, and every ten minutes I disagree with something merely for the sake of argument.'

Hunter dismissed the remark. 'This woman,' he said to Elizabeth, briefly clasping Margaret's shoulders, 'is an acknowledged expert on the labours and writings of Jean de la Ceppède. She is a published author.'

Margaret pushed him away. 'Twenty years ago. Two small volumes. Very academic, very dry, read by no-one.'

'Read by me,' Hunter said. He brushed the bench with his palm. 'Sit down.'

Elizabeth sat between them. She saw that they had positioned themselves to catch the morning sun, which had by then risen above the peaks, and was streaming in misty lines across the water towards them, its growing warmth exaggerated in the chill air.

'I didn't expect to see so many of you,' Elizabeth said.

'There have been some problems with the transport,' Hunter said. 'That's all.'

'I'm afraid that at present pleasure trips to the lake come very low down the list of someone's priorities,' Margaret said.

'She means Cox,' Hunter said. 'And yet this is where most of them are cured.' He waved his hand to include the men and the walkways and the lake beyond.

'What were you discussing?' Elizabeth asked him.

'I was trying to convince God's bride here that there was little to choose or distinguish between the suffering of the survivor – the suffering of one who has seen or heard and endured – and the suffering of those who died of their injuries.'

'Ah, yes,' said Margaret, 'but he then goes on to confuse the issue by wanting to include the suffering – if he will allow it to be called that – of those who lost people close to them. It's a tormented equation.'

Hunter laughed. 'I thought only souls were ever truly tormented.'

'You see how quickly he evades and skirts the issue,' Margaret said to Elizabeth. 'It's as much as I can do to hold him up and hold him together with my prayers.'

'People like me, you mean?' Elizabeth said to Hunter. 'My brother, Mary's husband.'

'Jameson told me,' Hunter said. 'I'm sorry for her loss, of

course I am, and your own, but I won't apologize for having raised the subject.'

'And nor will he respect your feelings on the matter, however close or painful it may still be to you,' Margaret said to her, both protecting her and warning her.

'She is at perfect liberty to leave,' Hunter said, and then put his hand on her arm and said, 'But don't.'

'I won't leave,' Elizabeth said.

'I know. Otherwise why are you here? Why are any of us here? Switzerland. What an excuse for a nation. And they know it. An impenetrable basin of a country. Impenetrable mountains, impenetrable hearts, impenetrable minds. Empty of everything, just holding itself in sanctimonious readiness for times like these. A cold planet in an overheated universe.' He turned to Margaret. 'Even you must admit that much at least, that this, here, now, is where the world stops.'

'Which is precisely why you, why all these others, need it so much,' Margaret said softly.

'Do you think places like this are the best places to begin anew?' Elizabeth said to Hunter.

'What a strange idea. Who can ever begin anew? All those savaged and discarded by the world they knew? All those who had everything they ever possessed taken away from them? I think not.'

'He takes pleasure in leading people into mazes,' Margaret said to Elizabeth. 'He refuses to see how convoluted his arguments become, flabby with sentiment and rhetoric.'

'He's letting off steam,' Hunter said. 'That's all.'

Someone called Margaret's name and she turned to see a woman waving to her. 'I'm wanted,' she said. 'I can only apologize for leaving you alone with him. Call me back when it all gets too much for you.' She turned to Hunter. 'And you—'

Hunter raised his hands to her.

Margaret left them.

'You think very highly of her,' Elizabeth said.

'I'll miss her.'

'Oh?'

'Whenever it is they decide I'm well enough to return home. I suppose Jameson told you about why I'm here. Please, there's no need to spare my feelings. My so-called predicament holds no fear for me. The sooner the better, as far as I'm concerned. Except Armstrong and Sinclair and all the others at the hospital insist on protecting me and hiding me in their reports and assessments. I imagine they hope, like some of these others, that the world will one day resume turning at its normal speed and I will be happily overlooked, forgotten and abandoned. Perhaps I'll become one of those men starting anew.'

'You could leave,' she said, the thought only then occurring to her. She watched the men on the jetties below.

'Leave? Run away, you mean? Escape?'

'It surely wouldn't be that difficult. Have you never considered it?'

'For the first three months I was here I considered nothing but.'

'And?'

'What would it achieve? Jameson is convinced they want to stand me in front of a firing squad. They won't. Those days are over. I doubt they'll even hang me.'

'Don't.'

'I'm sorry. No, they won't do that, either. The worst I can hope for is to be committed to some institution or other until I'm old and harmless.'

'But surely they'll see what you are, what you—'

'I still did what they said I did. I still have to answer for that. Men were still killed. If they say I must be punished, then I must be punished.'

'But the right publicity – the facts of the matter becoming known – will ensure you fair treatment. People won't stand for it, not after everything else that's happened.'

'People? What people? I no longer exist in the public domain. Besides which, I was once only too happy to live by their rules and regulations, so I must now abide by them again. Like Jameson, I still believe in those checks and balances.'

She could not accept this perverse logic, but said nothing.

'Shall we walk?' he said, indicating the steps.

They went down to the water and turned away from those already gathered down there.

'Did Jameson also tell you about my wife and daughters?'

'Yes.'

'I regret the loss of them more than I regret anything else.'

'Including, possibly, your own life?'

'Of course.' He took several paces ahead of her, speaking to her over his shoulder. 'I used to harbour a notion of pleading with her to return to me – largely, I imagine, so that I might see the girls. I doubt if I ever truly loved *her*, but the thought of seeing *them* again once fed me with hope.'

'But not now?'

'No, not now. I see now that it is unattainable, and we should never strive for the unattainable.'

'Nonsense. Surely, striving for the unattainable is what drives men forward.'

'The complete domination of most of Europe was thought attainable not so long ago.'

They walked beyond the stone jetties and came to the first of the flimsier wooden walkways. Hunter turned onto this and waited for her to follow him.

'I *am* sorry for your brother,' he said. 'In the way that I'm sorry for all of them. I know what it's like to have men – men I've never met or spoken to – wish me dead.'

'Did you wish yourself dead?'

'At the time. I can see how many problems it would have solved. Tell me, do you still have all the letters and notes of condolence sent by your brother's colleagues?'

'Mary has them, his wife.'

'Do you imagine she ever rereads them?'

'I don't know.'

'She does. I promise you. Every day. Those letters are where her husband last lived. She knows nothing – *nothing* – of that part of his life, and it drives her to despair, this not knowing. How much do you imagine he told her about it all?'

'They were very close.'

'Then he told her even less. The more he loved her, the more he would feel the need to keep her apart from it all.' He paused. 'In fact, I imagine he told *you* more than he ever let on to her.'

Elizabeth acknowledged the truth in this. There were a great many things Michael had told her and then made her promise never to tell Mary.

They continued along the jetty. The water grew darker beneath them. They passed the last of the small tethered boats. There was a wind, and waves rode the surface of the lake, rocking the shallow vessels. The water in their flat bottoms slapped from side to side.

'Are you all right?' he said to her, finally waiting until she was alongside him.

'In what way?'

'The jetty.'

There was another sixty or seventy feet of walkway ahead

of them. She looked back to the shore and saw how far they had already come out along the flimsy structure.

'Beyond those posts—' Hunter pointed '—it's a floating pontoon. Tell me if you want to turn back.'

'Why? Because I'm a woman?'

'What does that have to do with it? We can all drown. I was just thinking of your shoes, the hem of your dress. The further out you go, the rougher the water becomes; it rises over the boards occasionally.'

She walked past him. She felt the swell beneath her, water splashing between the wooden slats.

She waited for him at the junction of the fixed and the floating jetty. Ahead of her the walkway rose and fell a foot along the edge of each wave.

'We can't go any further,' he said. 'It wouldn't be safe.'

She nodded in agreement. She saw how a man who had survived four years of war might now carefully prepare himself to cross a busy road.

'Look down here,' he said.

She went back to him and looked down into the water. Fish congregated around the wooden supports, copper and silver in the dark water, and nibbled at the weed which coated the wood.

'Did Jameson tell you anything else?' he said after they had watched the fish for several minutes.

'Is there anything else to tell?'

'About himself, I mean.'

'I know he lives somewhere in the old town and that he shares a building, a studio, with a photographer.'

'Emil.'

'You know him?'

'Not well.'

'And I know that the manager and staff of the hotel where

I'm staying are suspicious of Jameson, that they hold him in low regard. Which, incidentally, he enjoys.'

'Which he likes to give the impression of enjoying. You know, of course, that he is here because he believes himself capable of catching me should I fall.'

'I know that you give him some purpose.'

Hunter considered this. 'There are worthier causes.'

'You won't convince *him* of that.'

'No. I wish you'd known him before all this, before he let everything in himself die.'

The remark surprised her. 'What do you mean?'

'What I said. Whatever faith he might once have possessed – I don't necessarily mean religious faith – he lost it, let it go, all of it. You might even say he deliberately destroyed it in order to survive. What do you know about his work?'

'Only that he deals in valuable books and manuscripts.'

'Have you never visited him? At the studio, I mean.'

'I don't even know where it is. Do you have the address?'

'Ask him,' he said. He walked back along the jetty to the shore. 'They'll be wanting us all back soon. Not a single bus or ambulance will be allowed to return until we're all correct and accounted for.'

They walked above the calmer water.

Nearer the land, Hunter paused. 'Did he tell you that when they first brought me here they kept me sedated and strapped to my bed like an animal for a week?'

'No.'

'Only when Armstrong was appointed did they release me. He ordered it. They would have been happy to have kept me like that for a lot longer. There are still men up there today who are tied to their beds each night.'

'Even after all this time?'

'I'm afraid time has no bearing on their suffering; time

merely allows them to go on enduring whatever it is they endure.'

In the distance ahead of them she saw the others starting to draw together, men and women coming slowly up from the water and along the walkways to a central point.

'Does anyone ever try to run away?' she said.

'Where to? How far do you think they'd get?' He pointed ahead of them. 'There's Margaret.'

The distant figure waved to them.

'She'll be keeping an eye on me. I might have dived into the water and swum off to freedom. Ask Jameson to show you the studio. It'll tell you a lot about him.'

Climbing the steps back to the street, Margaret once more beside him, Ruth and Mitchell walking ahead, Hunter told Elizabeth to walk away from them, not to go back to the waiting ambulances and buses with them.

'Is there a reason?' she asked him.

'Only what remains of my pride,' he said.

'It can sometimes get confusing, distressing,' Margaret said. 'There are always those who want to stay longer.'

Elizabeth understood what she was being told. She watched Ruth help Mitchell through the gathering crowd. Margaret led Hunter to one side. He seemed unsettled, less confident of himself now that he was back among so many others.

Elizabeth kissed him on the cheek and left without speaking.

14 _____

Herr Gottlieb entered the dining-room alone and came through the few other diners to where she sat, also alone. She was not aware of him until he appeared beside her.

'May I . . . ?' He tapped a folded newspaper on the chair beside her, and then drew it out without waiting for her answer.

'Of course.'

He raised his hand to attract one of the waiters.

'I am alone,' he said. 'My wife and daughter are too tired to eat. They do too much. They do not possess my constitution.'

'Of course not.'

'Have you seen the paper?' he said. 'Go on, pick it up. It's all over the front page.'

She unfolded it where it lay. It was the local paper, concerned only with the affairs of the town. The top half of the page was filled with the face of a man, the accompanying headline announcing that he was due to arrive there later that same afternoon. She read no further.

'I prefer the international editions,' she said.

He ignored her. 'Coming here. Today. To this very hotel. Apparently, it was his custom before the war to visit here every year with his entire family and staff. He, too, has a wife and a single daughter. They are arriving later.' He clearly expected something to come of this simple connection.

'Who is he?' Elizabeth said.

'Who is he? You ask who is he? He is a great statesman, a Hapsburg, a relation of Wilhelm himself. A man instrumental in suing for peace, in negotiating for settlements.'

'The war,' she said, making it clear to him that she did not wish to discuss the subject.

He finally acknowledged her disdain. 'Yes, the war.' He took back his paper. 'What you do not seem to grasp, Miss Mortlake, is that without great men like these—' he tapped the photograph '—we would be nowhere. He is widely spoken of as being about to form a new government.'

'When that is allowed, presumably.'

' "Allowed"? How allowed?'

She dusted her fingers. 'Crumbs,' she said. She swept them into a mound on the cloth.

'Whatever you may think, he is a great man,' he said. 'And I shall do my utmost to meet him and introduce myself. He comes here because he is a private man, again a man like myself.'

'Private enough to have his picture on the front page,' she said.

'What, of this rag? Precisely. Who else will know? He will arrive by floatplane. Imagine that. There is talk of establishing a regular service. Even during the war, when things were not so good, he was always admired and trusted. He himself planned some of our more—' He stopped abruptly. 'As you say – the war. And now all that is past.'

A waiter arrived and took his order.

'You'll see,' he said. 'A crowd will gather to watch him arrive and to applaud him.'

'Then it's to be hoped that Frau Gottlieb and Gerda are sufficiently recovered to share in the occasion.'

'Yes, I hope so too. In fact, I will make certain of it.'

'I'm sure you will. Tell me, why does he come here? To this hotel, I mean, and not one of the more elegant or fashionable ones?'

'How should I know? It is all a matter of taste, of judgement. Perhaps he prefers to avoid some places because of the publicity that might ensue.'

'Of course,' she said. 'Let me see.' She took back the paper and read the rest of the short piece announcing the man's arrival. His achievements, positions and awards were listed in separate paragraphs. He was seventy-two and had first visited the town when it was little more than a village, fifty years earlier. He came here because of the peace and stability it had always represented to him. She almost laughed. The remainder of the article was little more than an advertisement for the place.

'He comes for the peace and the stability,' she read to Herr Gottlieb.

'A wise choice, then.'

She wanted to ask him what right he believed the man had to that peace and stability when he had done so much elsewhere to destroy the peace and stability of so many others. But she said nothing. The man endorsed the town and the town sought his blessing.

She left Herr Gottlieb as his food arrived.

'I'll see you later,' he said. 'At his arrival.'

'Perhaps.'

'You'll be there,' he said. 'Jameson too.'

By mid-afternoon a small crowd had formed along the lake road in front of the hotel. The seats beneath the trees were filled. Townspeople and tourists alike sat around the stone walls of the empty flower beds. A covered launch waited at the water's edge, crewed by a dozen men in uniform. Street vendors moved among the crowd selling food and drink.

Elizabeth watched all this from her room, dismayed to see how right Herr Gottlieb had been. She saw people she recognized, English, Americans, Germans, Italians. Banners flapped along the front of the hotel; others were strung amid the lights beneath the trees. The town band arrived and cleared a space for itself above the launch. Popular and patriotic tunes were played to entertain the crowd.

Earlier, Mary had been with her briefly. Elizabeth told her what was happening, but Mary refused to accompany her outside, even to stand with her and watch the proceedings from the window.

It was as the band fell silent after half an hour's playing that Elizabeth saw Jameson. He stood with a group of men and women, none of whom she recognized, but all of whom seemed familiar with each other. She watched him for several minutes, knowing that he would soon turn and look up to where she stood.

When that finally happened, she waved to him and he motioned for her to go down to him.

She went first to Mary and told her what she was doing; again Mary refused to accompany her.

Skirting the crowd, she made her way to where Jameson had been standing. He was no longer there, and it was difficult to find him in the shifting mass. She stood beside the resting bandsmen. One of them offered her his stool and then held her hand as she stood on it to look over the heads of the people around her. She eventually saw him closer to the steps leading down to the lake.

Nearer the water, the crowd grew thicker, and it was difficult for her to get through. She regretted not having signalled for Jameson to join her in her room and for them to have watched the proceedings from there.

She finally reached him. Several of his companions turned and looked at her, but he made no attempt to introduce her.

'Surprising how many people will turn out to applaud a warmonger,' he said. He was forced to raise his voice, and several of those standing beside him turned to see who had spoken before turning their attention back to the water. A sharp heel caught Elizabeth's shin.

'Can't we go somewhere less crowded?' she said.

'Why? It's important to be at the centre of these things. History will insist on its witnesses, even if most of them are only ever innocent or ignorant bystanders.'

'I thought you'd had enough of being at the centre of things.'

'Precisely.'

'So why are you here? Are you going to stand and jeer?'

'Nothing so childish. I just want to see the man. I just want to remind myself of what that kind of man looks like.'

'You won't achieve anything by it.'

'I'll be scratching an itch. I bumped into Gottlieb earlier. He looked as though he was going to burst.'

He was interrupted by the noise of a distant engine. The crowd fell silent. One man pointed and then another hundred pointed in reflex.

The plane came from the west and passed low over the

surface of the lake, sweeping from one end of the town to the other, its silver fuselage and floats catching the sun, impressive against the darkness of the opposite slopes and the water.

'This is the man who shuns publicity,' Jameson said.

'I read it.'

The plane returned, lower this time, and closer to the shore. People applauded and cheered. Someone called out that they could see the man inside and the applause grew louder.

The aircraft banked for a second time, and then came towards them more slowly, its pilot now certain of a surface calm enough to make his landing.

A further cheer rose at the first splash of spray as the floats touched the water. The aircraft rose and fell several times and then slowed and stopped. Its engine note grew dimmer. It stood for several minutes and then turned to the shore. Beneath them, the launch drew noisily away from its moorings.

The plane finally came to a halt fifty yards from the shore and waited for the launch to reach it. A man stepped out onto one of the floats. The crowd cheered again.

'Save your breath,' Jameson said to the silent Elizabeth. 'That's the pilot.'

The man carried a coil of rope. He fastened a weight to this and tested the depth of the water. Then he took out an anchor and threw it away from the plane into the lake. He drew in the slack and tied the rope to a ring beneath the engine.

Only at the arrival of the launch did the statesman himself appear. He stood briefly to acknowledge the waiting crowd, lifted an arm to the applause, and then stepped into the launch and was lost to sight beneath its canopy. The applause along the shore continued in anticipation of his arrival. But the launch, instead of retracing its course back to the jetty, turned and headed away from the town. There were cries of surprise and disappointment. Only then did Jameson raise his own hands and start clapping.

'What is it?' Elizabeth asked him.

'Who knows? Perhaps he was no longer convinced of his reception.'

One of the men with whom Jameson had been standing whispered something to him and they both laughed.

The launch moved quickly along the lake and the applause died with the sound of its engine.

'Wait a moment,' Jameson told her. Around her, the disappointed onlookers began to disperse. He spoke briefly to someone else and then returned to her. He led her out of the disintegrating crowd. 'Apparently, the plane's going to be moored here throughout the duration of his stay. He may be called away on urgent *diplomatic* business. These men always are. Or if they aren't, then they like to live with the thought that it might happen at any moment. And they like the people around them to know it too. It creates the tensions within which they are better able to define themselves.' He looked along the lake. 'Four years of all that filth and he still behaves as though he were responsible for none of it.'

'Is that what disgusts you the most about him? The fact that he can convince himself that his own hands are clean, while yours remain dirty?' She regretted the remark immediately. He considered her for a moment. She wanted him to deny what she had suggested, or perhaps to turn and walk away from her, to return to the company of his companions. Instead, he looked out at the moored plane. The pilot still stood on one of its floats.

'Perhaps I could bribe him to take us up for a flight,' he said. 'Have you ever flown?'

'Never.'

'We could get above the peaks and see something of the world beyond.'

This she found less appealing. She did not wish to discover that beyond these peaks lay another valley, another lake, another small, enclosed and self-regarding town like this one, oblivious of the world beyond its own close horizon; and beyond that valley another, then another and another until the whole world was transformed.

'What do you think?' He held her arm and steered her beneath the trees.

'I doubt it will happen. What if he is called away? According to Gottlieb, he's a genuine Hapsburg.'

'So what? Look at them – the Hapsburgs, the Hohenzollerns – all dead wood. Look at the Romanovs, look what happened to them. Cut out like rotten flesh.'

'Don't.'

'Don't what?'

She pulled free of him and found an empty bench.

The band resumed playing the same songs they had rehearsed to greet their visitor.

He sat beside her.

'You shouldn't have come,' she said.

'I know. I'm no different from the rest of them. What is it that makes us think so highly of these people?'

'Yourself excepted.'

'It can't just be me. What is it that makes us follow them when we know nothing about them, when the evidence of their incompetence and disregard for life is all around us?'

She couldn't answer him. 'He's staying at the hotel,' she said.

'I know. Perhaps he'll invite you to dine with him.'

'I'd accept,' she said.

'I know that too.'

The playing bandsmen still attracted a small audience, but their music now served only to add the twin notes of disappointment and regret to the occasion, as though they were playing in an empty ballroom.

The people Jameson had been standing with gathered to say their farewells. The women kissed him. He made arrangements to meet some of them later that evening. Elizabeth wondered if she, too, might be included, or if, as previously, she was again to be kept apart from this other life of his. She said nothing, merely acknowledging the nods and smiles of these acquaintances.

'Were you being honest?' she said when they were again alone.

'About what?'

'About not telling me how dirty you still felt.'

He looked at his hands. ' "Dirty" seems barely adequate. There must be thousands like me.'

'Millions. Do you think it will pass?'

'I don't know. Perhaps there's something I should be doing, I just don't know.'

She knew not to pursue the matter.

They sat together for an hour longer, until he asked her about Mary and she knew she would have to return to her sister-in-law.

15

Almost a week passed before she saw him again.

She spent her time with Mary. For four days neither of them left the hotel. It rained, not heavily, but Mary used this as the latest of her excuses to stay in her room. For three days she would not even accompany Elizabeth down to the dining-room, insisting instead on food being sent up to her, and then on eating it alone.

On several occasions, Elizabeth tried to raise the subject of Michael, hoping it might now help for Mary to talk about him, about her feelings, but Mary refused to even consider discussing her dead husband. It was during those four days that Elizabeth realized how unbridgeable the distance between them had finally become; and the more she considered this, the more she found herself resenting the fact that her own feelings for Michael were somehow becoming contaminated by these cold silences into which Mary constantly retreated. She even began to consider if there was any way forward for her without detaching herself completely from her sister-in-law, thereby allowing the two of them to move apart even more rapidly.

Jameson eventually telephoned her one morning with the news that he had business at the hospital and that he wanted her to go with him. She agreed immediately.

He arrived an hour later, carrying a card folder similar to the one he had delivered to the café. He told her they were going to see Sinclair.

Arriving at the hospital, they were directed to a room at the rear of the main building while an orderly was sent to fetch Sinclair.

Jameson stood at the window and Elizabeth sat in the seat behind him.

'An hour,' she said, after they had waited that long for the orderly to return. 'Perhaps he isn't here.'

'Someone would have come and told us.' He remained unconcerned by the delay.

'Perhaps he forgot.'

Jameson shook his head.

'Perhaps someone gave the orderly something else to do,' she suggested.

'I know him,' Jameson said, and she knew by the tone of his voice to stop questioning him.

There were men working in the hospital grounds, digging the dark soil even darker. Others raked the gravel of the path and picked out the grass that had seeded there.

'This obsession with order,' she said, rising to stand beside him.

'Perhaps it serves some greater purpose,' he said.

She watched the gardeners and saw that only a few of

them were actually working; most simply stood and watched, occasionally pointing out something they had seen which required the attention of these others.

'Do *you* understand it?' she asked him.

'Of course.'

His folder contained photographs of the burned and mended faces of men in Sinclair's care. Earlier, at the hotel, she had asked him if she might see, and he had refused her. He showed her how tightly taped the folder was, but said that he would not have shown her anyway. The photographs were confidential. There was an address plate on the folder and she made a note of the street on which the photographer's studio was located; there was no number.

Boarding the bus to the hospital, Jameson would not even allow her to hold the folder while he sought for their fare. She saw with some surprise the thick wad of notes in his wallet, and when she asked him why he carried so much money on him, he dismissed the question by saying that she had no idea of how little each of the notes was actually worth. She knew he was lying to her.

'He's coming,' he said unexpectedly.

The orderly came back across the grass. Beside him walked a man at least a foot shorter. As he came he pulled on a jacket and straightened his tie.

'You'll make him nervous,' Jameson said, smiling. 'Last week he was offered a job in Washington. He could become an incredibly wealthy man.'

'Wealthier than you?' She tapped his pocket.

'Probably.'

'Will he go to America?'

'I don't know. Perhaps, eventually. They want him in London and Paris. Armstrong reckons he's five years ahead of the game.'

'It must be a costly process,' she said, indicating the folder.

'I imagine it is. That's why he'll be forced to leave.' He raised his hand to the man now approaching them.

Sinclair smoked a cigar, which he threw down and ground out before coming in to them. He spoke to the orderly, directing him towards a man who lay on the damp grass, and who moved his arms and legs as though he were swimming.

Sinclair came into the room speaking loudly, as though in conversation with someone immediately behind him. He stopped abruptly at seeing Elizabeth.

He was dark-skinned. His hair was black. He had not shaved. He again checked his tie and brushed his hand on his sleeve before holding it out to her. Thick dark hairs grew along the backs of his wrists and fingers.

'And you must be . . .' he said, paused, closed his eyes for an instant, and then recited her full name, the name of her sister-in-law and the name and room number of her hotel. He held her hand long after he had finished speaking. Then he lifted it to his face, making her think he was going to kiss it, but instead he pressed her palm to his nose and sniffed deeply.

'Unused flesh,' he said. 'One day I'm going to cut it from the corpses of children and keep it alive. I'll build faces from it instead of the third-rate substitutes I'm forced to use now.' He released his grip on her. She felt him studying her own face as he spoke to her. 'You have no idea how rare and valuable a commodity good skin is.'

Jameson came forward. 'Perhaps if you ask nicely she might find an inch or two to spare for you.'

'Do you take it?' Elizabeth asked him, fascinated and repulsed in equal measure by the idea.

'To little avail,' Sinclair said. He turned to Jameson. 'Are these the photographs?'

Jameson handed them over. Sinclair took out a small knife and slit the tape which bound them.

'Don't you think . . .' Jameson began, indicating Elizabeth.

Sinclair stopped. He looked first at Jameson and then at Elizabeth.

'Do you know what these are pictures of?' he asked her.

'Faces.'

'They *were* faces.' He clicked the small knife shut. 'I'm sorry, I wasn't thinking.'

'Show me,' Elizabeth said.

'Don't,' Jameson said immediately.

'Why not?' she said. 'You haven't taken it on yourself to protect me from anything else so far.'

'No, he's right,' Sinclair said. 'You *would* be shocked by what you'd see. You wouldn't be human if you weren't. I sometimes think I ought to show these pictures to everyone who had some hand in it all, however distant, however indirectly involved they were.'

'Then let me see.'

'No – it wouldn't be fair on the men,' Sinclair said. 'Most of them are still here. It would have to be their decision. I imagine – I *know* – most of them would be terrified of the thought that someone like you was looking at them. They may only be photographs, but they're still men, boys.'

'By "someone like me" you mean a woman?'

'How old are you?'

'Twenty-three.'

'Then you're older than ninety per cent of them. Here.' He handed the folder to her. The tape was sufficiently slit for her to be able to take the pictures from it. 'It's up to you.' He turned to Jameson. 'Have you seen them?'

Jameson shook his head. 'I once saw a man without a head, and without any mark on him, sitting among daisies beneath

143

a tree at Langemarck. Someone had tipped his helmet down over what remained of his neck. His rifle and pack were beside him. He looked as though he'd just sat down for a minute to rest and had fallen asleep.' He spoke almost fondly of the memory, certainly with no distaste. 'I wasn't going to wake him, but the man I was with insisted on rapping on his helmet with his cane.'

'How awful,' Elizabeth said.

'You could say that,' Jameson said coldly.

'Ignore him,' Sinclair said to her. 'You're right, it is awful. It's just that we've grown immune to—'

'We live in an age of evasions and platitudes,' Jameson said loudly.

'Somebody fetch him a soapbox,' Sinclair said. He took Elizabeth's arm and led her to the door which opened onto the garden.

They went outside. Jameson followed behind a few minutes later. She handed the folder back to Sinclair, who tucked it beneath his jacket.

'One day I'd like you to come and meet some of my patients. Not now.' He turned towards the wall separating his clinic from the hospital. 'I sometimes wonder if keeping them hidden away for so long doesn't do them as much harm as good.'

'What do you believe?'

'I'm not sure. I'm more concerned with the bone and flesh and blood of it all while there's still time to do anything about it. I'm sure some of them would be grateful for the chance to meet—'

'Someone like me.'

He smiled at her. She slid her hand beneath his arm, conscious both of Jameson walking behind them, and of Sinclair's height.

'I hate tall women,' he said.

She guessed him to be only an inch or two shorter than herself.

'I'll wear flat shoes when I next come,' she said. She was grateful for this easy understanding between them.

They approached the digging and raking men, most of whom stopped as they drew close. She saw that some of them wore artificial limbs. One man wore a flat cap with a strap connecting it to a rigid leather pouch which covered his chin. Sinclair spoke to him, and only then did Elizabeth realize that the pouch was the man's chin. His words came distorted through teeth which barely opened, but Sinclair understood most of what he said.

'The trick,' Sinclair told her, 'is to pretend to hear everything, and to make good guesses where you don't. You seldom need to hear every word of what someone's telling you to make sense of what they're saying.'

'Like you and Jameson?' she said. 'Like him and Hunter?'

Jameson had fallen further behind them and was out of earshot.

'He's been into the clinic a few times,' Sinclair said. 'Him and Hunter. We had a bit of an emergency one night and they came to help out.'

'What sort of emergency?'

'Nothing, really. I make a point of keeping out all reflective surfaces. I even had all the window panes painted over. One of the nuns brought in an empty cooking pot she'd polished. She thought she was returning it to where it belonged. One of the new arrivals saw his reflection in it, that's all.'

'What happened?'

'What I would expect to happen. He couldn't contain his anguish, his repulsion, whatever. He tried to harm himself. Jameson and Hunter were walking outside. I needed to get the man into the hospital as quickly as possible. I couldn't sedate him. Jameson and Hunter picked him up and ran with him. Can you imagine – we put a blanket over his head. We covered him up and ran with him to Armstrong dripping blood all the way. Everybody here has a knife of some sort or other, most men do, and he'd used it to try and slit his wrists.'

'Did he survive?'

'Yes, though I doubt he considered himself fortunate. I couldn't keep him here after that. They sent him home. Glasgow, I believe.'

'What about his face?'

Sinclair shrugged. 'I've got forty men here. How many do you imagine there are who would like to come and join them?'

She looked back to Jameson, who was now talking to a group of men forking cut grass into a wheelbarrow.

'I see,' she said.

They came close to the entrance of the clinic, and Sinclair guided her away from it.

'Are we keeping you from your work?' she asked him.

'I was up all night. Men who require operations on their skulls and jaws have to be transferred to the operating theatres in the main building. Night is the best time to do it. You'd be surprised how many there are, even here, staff *and* patients, who still object to being exposed to what I'm doing. I'm convinced some of them still wish I'd go away and do it all somewhere else.'

'Paris? Washington?'

'Perhaps. Anywhere where we wouldn't be seen.'

They walked around the building until they came in sight of the conservatory. Jameson followed them, coming closer.

'You're married,' she said to Sinclair.

Sinclair held up his hand and rubbed the ring with his

thumb. 'Charlotte,' he said. 'Do you like the name, do you know anyone else called by it?'

She thought for a moment and shook her head.

'Not married, only ever engaged. She was a nurse, killed on the *Marquette*, off Salonika, leaving Gallipoli.'

The remark caught her by surprise. She had been expecting to be told more of the woman, of their plans for their happy and successful future together.

'Almost three years ago now. She'd only been out there a month. I still miss her, still think of her every day. Emil enlarged and framed a photograph for me.'

'Is it in your office, your room?'

'Hidden away. Her body was never recovered.' He looked at the men around him. 'You begin to wonder if there isn't a single corner or refuge anywhere in the entire world into which that bitter wind didn't blow or isn't yet about to probe.' He paused. 'My apologies. I compose poetry. I know how inadequate it all is, but I still insist on doing it.'

'I'd like to read it,' she said.

He considered her for a moment. 'I believe you,' he said. 'Except I never write it down, that would be too much.' He tapped his forehead.

Jameson finally caught up with them.

'I was telling Elizabeth about my poetry,' Sinclair said.

Jameson appeared not to hear him; he was distracted.

'Is something wrong?' Elizabeth asked him. She looked behind him, but the men to whom he had earlier been speaking were no longer in sight.

'Ruth's been injured,' he said.

'I saw her yesterday,' Sinclair said. 'She was all right then. Are you sure?'

'It happened last night. Someone saw her this morning' – he, too, turned and looked to where the men had been standing — 'and said her face was cut and bruised. She was stripping beds in one of the open wards.' His agitation grew.

'Calm down,' Sinclair told him. 'It can't have been anything serious if she was at work in the hospital this morning.'

'We could easily go and find out,' Elizabeth said.

'No, don't — I mean, I'll see her soon enough.'

'You'd think they were lovers,' Sinclair said to Elizabeth.

She said nothing in reply. Jameson stood with his back to her. She guessed then, watching him, seeing him compose himself before turning, that he knew, or believed he knew, how the girl's injuries — if they existed — had been caused.

'Sinclair gambles, did he tell you that?' Jameson said eventually, turning back to face them.

Sinclair put his arm round Elizabeth's shoulders. 'I'm a reckless character,' he said. 'But at least I gamble according to a plan. Unlike Jameson here.'

'You also gamble?' she said.

'At the casino.'

'You never told me.'

'We'll take you along with us the next time we go,' Sinclair said.

She could see that the idea of her accompanying them did not appeal to Jameson, but again he said nothing. Despite his attempt to appear otherwise, he was still distracted by the rumour concerning Ruth, and she knew that if he had been there alone he would have gone to discover if there were any truth in it.

'Go to the convent,' she said to him. 'Sinclair can keep me company until you find out.'

But again Jameson refused.

'And I'm due back,' Sinclair said. He held up the folder.

'Emil will keep the plates in his safe in case you need any more prints,' Jameson said.

'Thank him for me.'

Sinclair left them and returned to his clinic.

'You can see how hard he works,' Jameson said.

'He told me about his fiancée.'

'I'd known him three months before he told me.'

They walked the length of the lawn in front of the conservatory.

'Do you want to go and look for Hunter?' she said.

'Not today.'

'I just thought . . . It seems a pity to come all—'

'Not today. He had a bad night. I spoke to one of the orderlies.'

She felt angry at this rebuff. 'What does that mean, he's had a bad night? Has he not slept? What?'

He stopped walking and looked at her as though she did not understand the smallest part of anything around her.

'Then tell me,' she said.

He shook his head. 'Use your imagination,' he said.

She held out her hand to him and he took it, holding it until they encountered the next group of men on the lawn, when he let it go.

'We ought to leave,' he told her.

Walking out onto the road, something occurred to her. 'Sinclair said there were nuns in the clinic,' she said.

'So?'

'Isn't that distressing for the men, to have women among them?'

He smiled. 'That's the whole point – they're nuns, not women. Besides, they know which of them to send.'

'So none of the young girls ever go there?'

'Never.'

'If it was a genuine offer of Sinclair's, I'd like to go back one day,' she said.

He neither encouraged nor tried to dissuade her.

Waiting for the bus, their conversation turned to the possible closure of the hospital, and then to the end of the tourist season and the nature of the town during winter, but even though he answered all her questions, she saw that he remained distracted, that his thoughts were still with the injured girl.

16

The following day she was woken before dawn by the sound of something being dropped or thrown in the next room. She lay in the half-light, listening, unwilling to be drawn into the cold of waking. She wondered if she had woken from some noise in a forgotten dream. Then she heard Mary, half coughing, half retching. Something else was thrown or knocked to the ground. She switched on her bedside lamp. It was not yet five. Lights from the road below were reflected on the ceiling of her room, shimmering where they swayed in the wind, creating an impression similar to that of sunlit water reflected on the hull of a ship. Then Mary called her name. Elizabeth pulled on her dressing-gown and unlocked the connecting door.

Mary lay panting on the floor, and beside her lay the jug and bowl she had pulled from her cabinet. Water from the jug soaked her hair, her night-gown and the rug on which she lay; it ran in streams over the boards beneath the bed. She lay in an awkward position, her legs caught up in the bedclothes, and propped against the bed. She clawed the rug ahead of her, trying to pull herself free. Her wet hair was plastered to her face, and her night-gown was stuck to her chest. She seemed not to notice that Elizabeth had come into the room, and continued to clutch at the rug, coughing and choking at her exertions. She was trying to pull herself free of her bedclothes, which twisted themselves more tightly around her as she struggled. Elizabeth watched her for a moment, still convinced that Mary had no idea of her presence. Then she went to help her. She knelt on the wet rug and pulled the hair from Mary's face. Mary put a hand on her shoulder. 'Help me,' she said, the words barely out before she resumed her choking. There was vomit on the rug, and Elizabeth could smell it on Mary's breath. She saw it, too, splashed on her night-dress. Elizabeth tried to calm her, holding her head and stroking her cheek for a moment, before turning her attention to the twisted sheets. She pulled Mary's night-dress free, exposing her legs and her groin. She loosened the sheets and Mary was finally able to pull herself free of them. She knelt on all fours. Bile ran in a string from her mouth onto the backs of her hands. Elizabeth screwed up the sheets and used them to mop up the spreading water.

After several minutes, Mary grew more composed and sat back against the bed. She brushed at the wet mess down the front of her night-gown, turning her face from side to side as though to avoid its smell. Then she pulled the night-gown over her head and threw it across the room.

Elizabeth looked at her thin naked body for a moment before pulling the eiderdown from the bed and draping it over her shoulders. She tried to pull her from the puddle of damp in which she sat, but Mary made no attempt to help her. Tears ran down her face.

'It isn't all water,' Mary said eventually. She pointed between her legs. The eiderdown was too heavy for her shoulders and she let it fall behind her, sitting in its arch as though it were a bishop's cloak.

'I'm sending for a doctor,' Elizabeth said. She expected Mary to object, but she said nothing.

'Help me get dry first,' Mary said. 'I need to wash myself.'

Elizabeth knelt and put her arm around her. Mary winced at her touch. Lifting her from the ground, Elizabeth felt the plates of her shoulder blades move beneath her hands; the line of Mary's spine was visible from her skull to its base.

She eventually sat her on a dry part of the bed and wrapped the eiderdown back around her, this time ensuring that Mary bore none of its weight. She propped a pillow behind her. She took the towels from Mary's bathroom and rubbed her face, her arms and legs. Mary picked off the strands of her hair which came away in the rubbing. She screwed a corner of the towel into a knot and stuck it in her mouth.

Elizabeth dialled the single number to connect her to the hotel reception. There was no answer. She put down the receiver, waited a few seconds and dialled again. She imagined the night porter making his way across the room to answer the ringing. But there was still no answer.

'I'm going down to find someone,' she said.

'Wait,' Mary told her.

'What happened?'

'I woke with a start. I wanted a drink, that's all. I reached out and caught my arm in the bedclothes. I knocked the bowl over. And the jug. Then I overbalanced.' She spoke in a monotone, drawing breath after every few words.

'You can't have eaten for days,' Elizabeth said.

Mary looked surprised, as though this remark had no bearing on what had just happened to her. 'I have no appetite.'

'It's more than that,' Elizabeth said.

Mary combed her hair back from her face with her fingers. Elizabeth dialled again.

'There will be no-one there,' Mary said.

But this time the phone was answered immediately. It was the hotel manager. Elizabeth explained the situation and said she wanted a doctor to be sent for.

'I'll come up myself,' the manager said.

'I need a doctor.'

The receiver went dead.

He arrived several minutes later, making no attempt to disguise his annoyance at having been woken and summoned.

Elizabeth let him into the room. He ignored the woman on the bed and instead he looked around at the soaked and scattered sheets, the wet rug. He breathed deeply and then screwed up his face at the smell which filled the room.

'What has she done?' he said. He picked up the jug and bowl and inspected them.

'She's ill. She needs a doctor. I have a number.' She searched her bag for the piece of paper Jameson had given her.

'For what?'

'For a doctor.'

'No need. There is a hotel doctor. In the morning I will call him and he will come then.'

'We're not waiting,' Elizabeth told him. She remembered she had put the number in a drawer in her bureau and went through to get it.

When she returned the manager was sitting on the end of the unmade bed, his feet propped on the mound of bedclothes. Mary sat where she had left her. The eiderdown had fallen away to reveal her chest. The manager looked quickly away from her at Elizabeth's return.

'I couldn't . . .' he said. He rose from the bed and went to the window, opened the curtains an inch and looked out. 'Raining,' he said. 'No-one will come at this hour.' He pulled a watch from his pocket. 'Quarter past five. Not at this hour. Please . . .'

Elizabeth dialled the number. For a full minute no-one answered.

The manager shrugged in sympathy.

Then Elizabeth realized she needed the number which would take her beyond the hotel switchboard.

'What is it?' she asked him.

He told her. 'I thought you'd dialled it,' he said.

Beside her on the bed, Mary began to shake. Elizabeth pulled the eiderdown tighter over her shoulders and pressed its bulky slack between her legs.

This time the phone was answered immediately, and only then did Elizabeth realize that she did not know the doctor's name. It was not on the piece of paper, and if she had been told it, she had forgotten.

'Hello, doctor?'

The man said, '*Ja.*'

She asked if he spoke English.

'We all speak English,' the manager said behind her. 'Why else do we exist?'

Elizabeth explained where she was and what had happened. The man on the phone said hardly anything, and it was only when she told him that Jameson had given her the number that he paid any real attention to what she was saying. He repeated the few details as though he were writing them down. She felt reassured. She asked him to come to the hotel as quickly as possible. She waited for his answer, and as she waited the line went dead.

'Well, is he coming?' the manager asked her. Everything he now said was again given an edge by the knowledge that Jameson was involved. 'Perhaps I ought to call our own doctor. Just in case. He is certain to be here sooner.'

Elizabeth kept her hand on the phone.

'What's wrong with her?' he said. 'Look at her. She woke from a nightmare, that's all. She was like this when she came here. You pay for her food, but every day she refuses to eat it. Whole meals sent back to the kitchen uneaten.'

On the bed, Mary made a sudden, involuntary noise. She started to retch again and Elizabeth placed the bowl in her lap. A knot of saliva swung from Mary's mouth.

The manager turned back to the window in disgust. The sound of horses' hooves rose from below, but the animals passed without stopping.

'Gamblers,' he said.

'I think she should be taken to a hospital,' Elizabeth said. 'Mary?'

Mary nodded once in agreement. Her hair, still wet, had again fallen over her face. Elizabeth pulled it away from her mouth. The smell in the room grew stronger. 'Open a window,' she said.

'A hospital?' the manager said. 'But your rooms—'

'The rooms are paid for. *I* won't be leaving.'

'It is not hotel policy to offer refunds as a consequence of circumstances beyond our control.' He grew confident at having injected this formal declaration.

'I'm not asking for one,' Elizabeth told him.

'Of course, it will be impossible to relet the room so late in the season.' He buttoned up his waistcoat.

'Besides which,' Elizabeth said, 'half the rooms are empty anyway.'

'That is not the issue.'

She refused to enter into this pointless argument while Mary sat ill and confused beside her.

'Go down to the lobby, wait for the doctor, send him up,' she said.

'There will be no-one to gather up the soiled sheets and replace them with clean ones,' he said. 'At least not until morning. And then not until after breakfast is served. The hotel cannot stop because of one sick woman.'

'I'm taking her through into my room,' Elizabeth said. 'You can send the doctor there.'

'Your room? But . . .' He could think of no further valid protest and so he left.

'Can you walk?' Elizabeth asked Mary.

Mary nodded. She took several paces and stopped. Again she winced with pain and held her chest.

'What is it?'

'My ribs.'

Elizabeth looked, but there was nothing to see.

'When I fell . . .' Mary said. She resumed walking.

In Elizabeth's room, Mary sat on the bed and allowed Elizabeth to lift her legs for her and then to settle her onto the pillows. The bed was still warm. Elizabeth helped her into a clean night-gown.

'Will he be long, do you think?' Mary asked her. It was the first sign of concern she had shown.

'Not long,' Elizabeth told her, still not even certain if the man was actually coming. She wished she had a number to contact Jameson. The reflected light from the street below still wavered over her ceiling. She poked the cooling embers of her fire and threw on more of the small chips of coal.

There was little flame, only a slowly rising heat. She pressed her palms to the tiles surrounding the fire and carried the warmth back to Mary's face.

Mary lay in a half-sleep. She murmured to herself. There was a smear of blood at the side of her mouth where either her lips had cracked or she had earlier bitten herself while being sick.

The doctor arrived half an hour later. It was still dark. Mary had fallen asleep and Elizabeth had turned off the lamp. She stood at the window, watching, unseen by anyone below. Two men approached from the town, paused before reaching the hotel, and parted, one turning back, the other coming on. As this man drew closer, she saw that he carried a bag. He looked up at each of the hotels as he came. Beyond the road, neither the lake nor the mountains were visible, only the reflection of the few lights on the wet paving.

She left the window, switched on the lamp and waited.

She opened the door the instant the man knocked.

'You called me,' he said, avoiding all formalities, and went directly to Mary. She remained asleep. He drew back the single sheet and blanket Elizabeth had folded over her. He studied her. He pulled away the sheet to expose her feet. He took off one of his gloves and examined her ankles and her knees. Then he felt her wrists and elbows. He did all this with his left hand; his right arm hung by his side.

'Has she vomited recently?'

'Just bile. She retches, but little comes up.'

'Often?'

'I don't know.'

'Tell me,' he said. He stepped back from the bed. He slid his coat over his right arm and caught it as it fell, throwing it over a chair.

'Can I do anything?' she said.

'I have only one hand. You can open my case and take out my stethoscope.'

She knew from his voice that he was not the man to whom she had spoken on the telephone.

'I asked you how often she was sick. Every day, most days?'

'Most days.'

'Or perhaps every day, but she is secretive about it?'

Elizabeth nodded.

'You do see what she's doing?' he said matter-of-factly. 'You do see that she's starving herself to death, and that as far as she's concerned, the sooner this happens the better.'

'She's only twenty-two,' Elizabeth said. She could not bring herself to admit to the truth in what he said. It was the first time she had heard it put so bluntly.

'And what difference does that make? Hasn't she ever tried to tell you that this was what she was doing?'

Elizabeth handed him the stethoscope.

'Open her night-dress for me. My hand is cold. I can do all this while she's asleep.'

Elizabeth unfastened the buttons to Mary's waist and gently peeled the two halves apart.

The doctor looked at Mary, leaning over her to inspect her more closely. He saw something and pressed a finger to one of her ribs. Mary jumped in her sleep, but did not wake.

'I think she's bruised or cracked it,' he said. 'It'll mend. It might take some time with her in this condition, but it will heal if she lets it. Where did she fall?'

'From her bed.'

'This one?'

'Next door.'

'Where she was also sick?'

Elizabeth nodded. She looked at his rigid glove as he spoke.

'I can take it off if you'd prefer,' he said. 'The hand is a perfectly good and completely useless match.' He gripped the tip of one finger in his teeth and pulled the glove off. The hand beneath was smooth and tan-coloured, the thumb and each finger slightly curved, as though he were holding an invisible ball. 'Shake,' he said, and he held it out to her. Elizabeth took it.

'Why didn't you call me sooner?' he asked her. He went back to the bed and listened to other parts of Mary's chest and stomach. 'You can cover her up,' he said. 'Jameson told me a fortnight ago what was happening. He wanted me to come then, but knew he had to wait for you to make the decision.'

'Was that him with you outside?'

'No, that was no-one.'

'How do you know Jameson?' she asked him.

By then the fire had grown warmer and she offered him a seat beside it. He took the lamp from the bedside table.

'We served together,' he said.

'That doesn't account for why you should end up here.'

'Coincidence. By virtue of my injuries, I am no longer able to practise in England. Here, a one-handed doctor can scrape a living.'

'Is that what you do?' She saw that the arm and the lapel of his jacket had both been patched.

'Just about.'

'There's some brandy,' she said. She took the decanter from the bureau and poured them both a drink.

He drank his in a single swallow and held out his glass to be refilled.

'What time will it be light?' she said.

'About two hours yet.' He glanced across at the bed. 'She'll have to go into a clinic. I can recommend one. I'll stay here until it can be arranged. You might have to get the manager to call the hotel doctor. They'll listen to him more readily than to me.'

They sat in silence for several minutes, listening to Mary's tortured breathing. Elizabeth built up the fire. She brushed coal dust from her dressing gown.

'I'll get dressed,' she said.

'It might be wise.'

She saw him balance the brandy glass in the bowl of his artificial hand and raise it to his mouth.

'Would you rather put your glove back on?'

'No. I don't mind.'

The glass rattled in his rigid palm and he lifted it clear. She went into Mary's room to get dressed.

She returned to find him back at the bedside, looking down at the sleeping woman.

'Is it serious?' she asked him.

'Who was it?'

'Her husband.'

'Sorry, yes, I already knew that. Jameson told me. Your brother. Yes, I think it is serious.' He drew her away from the bed back to the fire. 'We are instructed by the powers-that-be that we may no longer cite grief as a contributory factor in the cause of death when filling out a death certificate. But I ask you – can you think of any more valid or potent cause?'

'What will they do at the clinic?'

'I'm not certain. A lot will depend on what she allows to be done to her. My advice would be for her to recover her strength sufficiently for her to return home. This isn't the place for what's happening to her. She might think it is – you too – but it isn't, believe me.'

They were interrupted by the return of the manager, who entered without knocking, and who then stood looking at them sitting by the fire with their drinks.

'I took the liberty of informing our own doctor,' he said. He looked at Mary, waiting until he was certain she was breathing. 'Is it serious?' He spoke to Elizabeth rather than the doctor.

'She can die here or she can die in the clinic,' the doctor said.

Elizabeth made no response to the callous and deliberately provocative remark.

'Surely not,' the manager said.

'Can you leave us with her?' Elizabeth said.

The man went.

Outside, it began to rain more heavily, blowing against the window in squalls. She drew back the curtains. Dull light flecked with yellow came into the room.

The doctor fell asleep where he sat. She picked up his glove and put it in his lap.

17

The small clinic lay to the west of the town, built on a broad knoll overlooking the lake and surrounded by forest. She signed the forms which admitted Mary and then sent a telegram to her bank in Oxford requesting the transfer of further funds to her tourist account at the bank in the town. On the hotel doctor's advice, she had taken all the money she possessed and used this to secure the room and treatment for Mary.

Jameson's doctor had accompanied her only as far as the outskirts of the town, where he had insisted on being let out of the cab. The hotel doctor had gone on with her and Mary, impressing upon her his influence in getting Mary admitted at such short notice. He behaved no differently to the hotel manager, and listening to him it occurred to Elizabeth that some private financial arrangement existed between the two men. He spoke about his bill when he was alone with her. He asked her where the other doctor had come from; he referred to the man as a charlatan.

At the clinic, they undressed Mary and washed her. Nuns worked alongside the nurses here too, but they were formal and distant and said little, only speaking when spoken to.

Mary slept in the cab and woke briefly only upon being carried to a wheelchair. She was confused, and called out for Elizabeth. Elizabeth reassured her that she was still with her. She held Mary's hand, but once inside the building, Mary pushed her away, saying she wanted to be admitted alone and for Elizabeth to have no part in what was now happening to her. She became near hysterical in her demands. A nurse laid a heavy blanket in her lap, more to restrain her where she sat than to cover or warm her. Mary had no real strength to fight back and so she stopped shouting and struggling. Watching her, surprised by this sudden outburst, Elizabeth wondered how much of what Mary now did, she did to protect her, Elizabeth, and how much of it was genuine, fear-induced confusion. They were not questions she could ask of anyone. She stood back and watched. A doctor held his palm against Mary's chest, pulled up her sleeve and deftly pushed a syringe into her upper arm. Mary fell silent almost immediately, her eyes closed.

The room to which they took her overlooked the rear of the clinic. There were no grounds, and immediately beyond the high wire fence of the clinic boundary was a cutting through which the railway ran. The cables of telegraph poles could be seen rising above this. The forest began immediately beyond, and only at the top of the small barred window was any sky visible. The light in the room remained on throughout the day. The window shook with the passage of the trains, and soot and steam rose in mixed columns from the gorge.

Elizabeth asked if there wasn't a room available at the front of the building, one where Mary might convalesce overlooking the lake, perhaps even a room from which the town itself was visible. The doctor told her it was of no consequence where her sister-in-law lay; her treatment meant that she would seldom be awake. Surely Elizabeth understood that much? Surely she had been told? He also pointed out to her that Mary was there for treatment and not merely to convalesce, that she was seriously ill.

She was asked to leave for a short time while tests were made. She wanted to refuse, but saw that Mary now had no awareness or understanding of what was happening to her.

She wandered along the corridor, pausing to look through the viewing panels of other doors. There were no open wards, no room containing anything other than its single patient, bed, screen and various pieces of medical equipment. She spoke to no-one. No-one stopped her and asked her what she was doing.

She went outside. The sun had risen and had gone directly from its cradle of rock into a bank of low cloud. She had missed it, and she knew from her experience of the place that it would not reappear later in the day. For the first time, she considered seriously the prospect and practicalities of returning home with Mary. She wondered what other provision needed to be made for the sick woman. In that sense, their visit to the town had failed completely.

She returned indoors. Apart from its new occupant, Mary's room was empty. Mary lay asleep. A moist cloth had been draped over her forehead, obscuring her eyes. Elizabeth raised this an inch. A metal bowl sat on the bedside table.

She considered drawing out Mary's hand from beneath the sheets and holding it, but the bedclothes had been tucked tightly around the sleeping woman, allowing her no movement.

She sat in the chair with her head against the wall, and after a few minutes she, too, fell asleep.

She woke to the sound of the door opening. Jameson had arrived.

'I woke you,' he said.

Beside her, Mary still slept.

'Come in. He told you where we were.'

'Have the doctors told you anything?'

'Not really. They seem to believe that whatever's happening to her is more serious than *I* think it is.'

He came into the room and stood beside her.

'What time is it?' she asked him.

'Almost midday.'

She was surprised by this. She had slept for three hours.

'Have they said anything about feeding her?'

'No. What do you mean? You mean feeding her by force?' She saw by his evasive glance away that her guess had been right. She remembered the women and the apparatus she had seen in some of the other rooms.

'She was brought here because they understand the types of treatment required. They'll let you stay with her.'

'There isn't much point. She'll sleep all day and all night.'

'And after that?'

'The doctor said he'd talk to me about it.'

'Whatever happens, let me know.'

'So you can find out from your friend if what they're doing is the right thing to do?' She shook her head. 'Thank him for me.'

'No – so *you'd* know,' he said.

'Of course. And what good has me "knowing" done her so far?'

He went to the barred window. 'I came an hour ago. I didn't want to wake you. I wanted to ask you a favour.'

'Oh?'

'I'm going to the convent. I wanted you to come with me.'

'To see Ruth?'

'To find out what, if anything, has happened to her.' He stood with his back to her as he spoke.

'You already know what's happened to her,' she said. 'You think the boy who might or might not be blind hit her. Don't look so surprised: you knew that's what I'd guess.'

'It's only a possibility,' he said, but with no conviction.

'But *you're* convinced of it. He's jealous of you, of her, of her feelings for you. He's dependent on her, he's her own age, give or take, and he probably feels he has the greater claim on her.'

'Because she feels sorry for him?' He turned to her. 'I doubt she's ever felt genuinely sorry for anyone in her entire life. It was part of what first appealed to me about her, understanding that.'

'Do you know her that well?'

'I think so. They have guest rooms at the convent. When Hunter first came here he was in a far worse physical state than he is now, believe me. I used to stay up there, spend my days with him. Mostly like this, sitting beside his bed and watching him sleep. It wasn't much, but it was enough for me to feel that I was doing the right thing.'

'And Ruth?'

'Margaret used to come and wash Hunter. Ruth was with her. It was Margaret who persuaded me to take one of their guest rooms. She saw to it that I was fed, that my clothes were washed. Everywhere she went, Ruth went. The girl kept me company. I practised my French on her, and she her English on me. She spoke it well enough before I met her. Margaret still keeps an eye on Hunter for me when I'm not there. I have to stand back from him occasionally.'

'I understand that.'

'It's probably against all the rules and regulations, but she always lets me know how he's being treated, whether or not his medication is changed. You've seen Cox. Cox has the power to make life comfortable or uncomfortable for the patients. He doesn't know the first thing about why Hunter's there, and like I said, what little he guesses at only makes things worse. I need Margaret to act as a counterbalance to him. You see how close Hunter is to setting himself adrift.' He looked at Mary as he spoke.

'Does Margaret know this?'

'That she's being used? Yes. I sometimes find books for her, small presents. She's not allowed to buy anything herself. She isn't even allowed to ask me for them, but she lets me know and I do my best.'

Beside them, Mary groaned in her sleep. She moved her arms beneath the sheets, but made no effort to pull them free. She grew still after a few seconds. Elizabeth lifted the cloth from her head, refolded and replaced it. Mary's mouth was open, and she noticed for the first time the discoloration of her teeth.

'What will they do if she refuses to eat?' she said.

'I imagine it's something they prefer you *not* to think about.'

Waiting until Mary was breathing soundly again, she told him she was ready to leave.

In the corridor she saw the doctor who had treated Mary and she told him that she would return. Her sister-in-law was to be given whatever she asked for. There was money.

Jameson went on ahead of her.

'Money?' the doctor said. 'Money buys the room, the bed. It buys my attention and expertise, it buys the nurses. But, please, do not harbour the belief that your money has anything to do with your sister-in-law's cure. That lies within her and her alone. Money? No.' He left her.

She could not understand why he had behaved so abruptly towards her.

Jameson waited for her at the clinic entrance. She repeated what the man had told her.

'He's right,' he said. 'They may be a cold and calculating breed, but there are some things that ought not to be obscured. Will you come to the convent?'

She looked down at her coat and shoes. 'Yes,' she said, adding that first she needed to change her clothes.

The clinic was quickly out of sight once they reached the lake road. Smoke from the chimneys of a dozen other hidden buildings rose through the trees all around it.

18

Ruth sat where Elizabeth had seen the class of girls. Scattered chairs showed where an earlier outdoor lesson had been held. Beside Ruth lay a pile of books. She was reading as Jameson and Elizabeth passed through the arch into the courtyard. In one corner a woman with a brush swept the cobbles. The bristles were stiff and the brush bounced along the ground ahead of her. Leaves from the orchard had blown into the space. At their approach, the sweeper stopped and watched them. Her progress through the leaves was unnoticeable; there were no clear spaces, no mounds to show where she had been.

Ruth, too, looked up at their arrival.

Jameson raised a hand to the woman with the brush, and she stood it against the wall and left through the arch. Only then did it occur to Elizabeth that Jameson's meeting with Ruth – which he had earlier spoken of as though his seeing her were not entirely certain – had been arranged via Margaret, and that the sweeper was there to ensure Ruth was waiting for them, waiting herself only to leave at their arrival. She felt deceived, manipulated, by this realization, and she began to consider what part she herself now played in the arrangement. She soon understood, however, that little other than her presence was required, and accepting this, she expected Margaret also to appear and participate.

Jameson entered first, Elizabeth several paces behind him. She saw the surprise and pleasure on Ruth's face turn to disappointment. She saw, too, how quickly she composed herself as they came closer to her.

The bruise on Ruth's face followed the line of her cheekbone, purple but already fading to yellow. Beneath her eye was an inch-long cut, uncovered; that, too, was already healing.

Jameson sat beside her. Elizabeth watched as Ruth leaned briefly against him, her arm touching his, before drawing away to let him look at her. Elizabeth took one of the chairs a short distance away, facing them.

'I like your shoes,' Ruth said to her.

Elizabeth kicked them off. 'Try them on.'

Ruth remained seated. 'They'll be too big. I'll look like a small child dressing up.'

Elizabeth retrieved her shoes. She acknowledged Jameson's glance.

'Tell me what happened,' he said to Ruth.

'Did Margaret tell you? Did she tell you to come and see me?'

'No and no. You don't think I wouldn't have come, do you? Does it still hurt?'

Ruth ran a finger beneath the line of the bruise. 'Not

really. It did when it first happened, but not now.'

'Was it Mitchell?'

'It was an accident.' She spoke slowly, hesitantly.

'How did it happen?'

'I told you, it was an accident. He had a stick. I was telling him to guess where things were. He was swinging it round. I got too close, that's all.'

Jameson made it clear to her that he knew she was lying, but that he was not going to force the issue. 'And would you tell me if he'd done it deliberately?'

Ruth looked at Elizabeth. 'Probably not. Why? Why do you think he'd do it deliberately? He's blind.'

'He could still lash out at you. I imagine he's pretty strong.'

'Perhaps, but he's like a baby,' Ruth said. 'He's twenty-one. He lives with his parents. Can you imagine, he doesn't even know where he was when he was wounded and blinded. He has a rough idea, but to listen to him talk it could have been anywhere.' She paused for a moment. 'He does everything I tell him to do.'

'I don't doubt it. You're very attractive.'

'Is that supposed to be a joke? He's blind. I'm attractive to a blind man?'

'That wasn't what I meant.'

Elizabeth understood what he had done; Ruth understood an instant later. She laughed at him.

'You still think he can see, don't you? Does she think it as well?' She pointed without turning.

'It isn't just me,' Jameson said. 'I know it makes no sense for him to keep up the pretence. I imagine there are millions of men who wish they hadn't seen what they've seen over these past years. But, of all people, *you* must know whether he's telling the truth or not.'

'Why must I? Next you'll be saying that he's only pretending to be blind so that he can stay here and so that he'll get to be with me. That's what you came here to tell me, isn't it? I don't care this much—' she snapped her fingers '—for him. He's never tried to lay a hand on me.'

'He's cut and bruised your face,' Elizabeth said.

Ruth stared at her for a moment. Then she whispered something to Jameson, which Elizabeth could not overhear, and at which Jameson shook his head, not in answer, but in the sad understanding of something.

The three of them sat without speaking for several minutes.

'What was your lesson?' Jameson said, eventually. He picked up one of her books and opened it. 'An anonymous poet,' he called to Elizabeth. 'Listen. "What is one person's grief but a single flake in a snowstorm?" '

'They make us recite them until we know them by heart. Some I like, most are worthless, meaningless.' She sat with her elbows on her knees, her face resting in her palms. When she straightened, she smiled at Elizabeth. 'Did he drag you all this way just to listen to what I had to say about this?' She pressed a finger into her bruise, causing its colour to rise. 'I don't mean to be rude, but you must have guessed by now how weak and stupid he sometimes is. He pretends to understand everything, but somewhere, right in the middle of everything, there's something missing.' She spoke with affection, and Jameson nodded in agreement with her.

'I sometimes think there's a great deal missing,' Elizabeth said.

'I've told him to get it back, but he makes no effort,' Ruth said. 'Poor old Jameson.' She put her arm across his back, as though he were the child and she the consoling adult. 'Have you guessed how old he is yet?' she said to Elizabeth.

The question surprised Elizabeth, and she wondered if Ruth was trying to prove another point, if knowledge and intimacy had become confused in her own feelings for the man. She entered into the game.

'I thought early thirties,' she said, dropping several years from her true estimate.

'He's twenty-eight,' Ruth said.

Jameson looked from one to the other. 'Did you really think I was that old?' he said to Elizabeth.

'Thirty-two, perhaps. I'm not very good at . . .'

'Lying? If it's any consolation, I guessed you to be three or four years older than you are.'

'Women mature faster,' Ruth said. She withdrew her arm and took back her book. 'There's a boy in the hospital, in one of the basement rooms, whose hair turned white overnight. He's supposed to have seen something that made it happen. Thing is, it struck him dumb too, so he can't even tell anyone what it was he saw.'

There were a thousand such tales, most with their grains of lost and painful truth.

'You ought not to talk about them,' Jameson said, seriously.

'That's what Margaret says. But why not? Everyone else does.'

'That's still no reason.'

'You talk about Mitchell to people.' She took pleasure in this simple defeat of him, and again as though to console him she slid her hand back into his.

Elizabeth left her seat and walked round the small court-yard. She looked through the arch to the trees beyond. Women worked beneath them. At the centre of the yard, Ruth and Jameson continued their conversation. She saw that he had underestimated the girl's understanding of the situation. It was also obvious to her that Ruth herself was not convinced that Mitchell's striking her had been wholly accidental, and it occurred to Elizabeth, watching the girl with Jameson, that there was also something to be gained by dwelling within this uncertainty. Knowing Jameson's real age forced her to look at him and the girl together in a new light. She tried to imagine how she might feel in the girl's place. She wondered, too, what signals, what deliberate or inadvertent encouragements Jameson had given her. She knew that his friendship with Ruth fulfilled some need in him, but she did not yet understand the precise nature of that need. She saw it, too, in his relationship with Hunter, with Sinclair, and with all the others, mostly men, with whom he surrounded himself, both at the hospital and in the town.

A bell rang in one of the nearby buildings. Ruth rose immediately and picked up her books.

'I'll tell Sister Margaret that our meeting was satisfactory, shall I?' she said mockingly. 'It'll save you having to find her and make your own report.'

Elizabeth laughed at this.

'We run circles round him,' Ruth said to her behind her hand.

'What did she say?' Jameson said.

Elizabeth refused to tell him. Ruth came to her and held out her hand. It was a genuine gesture – the first Elizabeth had received from the girl – and she took it.

'You could have tried my shoes on,' she said. 'They aren't that much larger than your own.'

'I know,' Ruth said. 'But it was just something to say. I don't particularly like them.' She looked down at her own clumsy second-hand shoes that might have been worn by a hundred others before her. 'I prefer these. The nuns have them specially made for us by a Parisian shoemaker.'

The bell sounded again, followed this time by the sound of running feet in one of the corridors.

Ruth reached up and kissed Jameson on his cheek before leaving to join the others.

The nun who had been brushing the leaves reappeared. She studied the ground around her, shook her head, retrieved her broom and left.

'He did it deliberately,' Elizabeth said, meaning Mitchell. 'He was proving a point.'

'Which was what?'

'You know exactly what it was: that he could do it, and that she'd make excuses for him.'

'So do you think he'll do it again?'

Elizabeth shrugged.

'Excuses to me, you mean.'

She walked out of the courtyard ahead of him.

They parted an hour later in the main square of the town, and Elizabeth returned alone to the clinic.

Mary was still asleep when she arrived. There was no longer a cloth on her head, and the bowl which had been beside her had been removed. A stain on the sheet close to Mary's chin showed where something had been wiped away. She sat with her, feeling her outline beneath the sheets. She had no idea what she might now do for her except be with her. She tried to turn off the light in the room, but the bright bulb did not respond to the switch. Outside, it had grown dark, and she could see only her own reflection in the small window. She felt suddenly hungry, and realized that she herself had not eaten since the previous day.

PART 2

19

She went first to a café where Jameson had taken her. She sat in a window seat and ordered a drink while she decided what to do. She had with her a map of the town, and she ran her finger along the length of the street she was looking for. It was a long street, one of several running parallel from the main square to the ourskirts. A warren of passages and alleyways connected these streets, and she guessed that an address along one of the main thoroughfares might equally apply to a building situated somewhere between them. It had also occurred to her, so evasive had Jameson been about inviting her to visit the studio, that the address on Sinclair's folder might have been an old one, or have belonged to a different business entirely.

She watched the walkers and the shoppers passing by in the hope she might see him. There were troughs at the centre of the square and the carts and horse-drawn cabs pulled up at these.

She left the café and approached one of the drivers.

He pointed out to her where the street she sought left the square. Because she had nothing more specific, she asked him if he knew of a photographer's studio somewhere along it.

He told her there were several, many, that they came and went, prospered and failed.

'Emil,' she told him.

That, too, was of little use to him.

'The studio was recommended to me,' she said.

'There are perfectly good ones here in the centre of town.' He indicated a brightly-lit shop in the corner of the square, and then another where the lake road entered in a broad curve. But she had already visited these, knowing before she had entered that neither was the place she was looking for.

'It's a long street,' he told her. He looked at her map as though he had never before seen the town laid out like this. 'It's misleading,' he said.

'Oh?'

'This makes it look too simple, too straightforward. These small passages and courts running from the main drives, there are far more than are shown here, most without names, local ones at best. Few of them are numbered. There are buildings which exist, here and elsewhere, which are not marked.' He turned the map to one side. 'It's useless,' he said.

'I could hire you to help me look,' she said, hoping this might encourage his interest.

'In there? I couldn't get into most of those places.'

'Then along the street.' She expected him to be pleased at this suggestion. 'I could hire you by the hour.' She took out her purse.

'What will you do?' he said, still unconvinced, weighing profit and futility.

'Stop at the first studio we come to and ask.'

'And you expect to be told? About places in there, about those places?'

The strangeness of the remark did not immediately strike her; she was preoccupied with the map.

'I insist,' she said.

The man shrugged, turned back to his drinking animal, patted its side and then drew it away from the trough. The horse snorted. Water dripped from the hairs of its mouth. The driver opened the door for her and pulled down the folding step. She sat facing his back, waiting for him to manoeuvre them out of the crush of other carriages and animals and turn them in the direction she wanted.

They crossed the square. The horse's hooves sounded like hammers on the cobbles.

They turned out of the square.

A hundred yards along the street she called for the driver to stop. She pointed out a shop to him.

'That isn't the one you want,' he said.

'Do you know who owns it?'

'I know.'

'Then if it's not the one I'm looking for, he may know where I can find it. Stop. I'm going to enquire.'

'Please yourself.' He reached back and opened the door for her.

She stepped down into a mulch of drifted leaves. They already felt like soil beneath her feet. Water ran in thin streams along the side of the kerb.

There was a single light in the shop window. She looked in and saw a man in a white apron standing at his counter reading a magazine.

He put this down and folded it shut as she entered. He gave the impression of having expected someone else.

She told him the name of the man she was looking for.

'He's not on this street, whoever he is,' he said. 'I've been here ten years, longer, I'd know. You could look for a month, you'd never find him. Is he new? Some of them in there don't last, come and go, think it's an easy trade to take up. If you—'

'He may be new,' Elizabeth said firmly, silencing him. 'A man called Jameson lodges with him, a book dealer.'

The man's expression changed, and for a moment she imagined he was going to tell her where to find the studio. But instead he grinned, and said, 'A book dealer and a photographer under the same roof. That's convenient.'

"You find that strange?'

'I don't find that strange at all, madam. Amusing, perhaps, that you yourself – a lady like you – should set such store by it, but not strange, no. I could show you twenty such establishments. I can point to two of them from that very window.' He pointed behind her. 'What I *do* find strange is that a young woman like yourself should come here looking for something she knows nothing about, for a man whose name she does not know, at an address which may or may not even exist, *that* I find strange.'

'Give me one address,' she said. 'Another book dealer is sure to know of Jameson. Perhaps he can direct me.'

'Why should he? You wouldn't ask in a bakery for the address of another baker. And even if you did, why should he tell you?'

A thought occurred to her. 'Because I might be willing to pay for the information.'

'Pay?'

'Possibly.'

He considered this. 'I can give you the name and address of someone.'

'Who?'

'Someone who may know. But just because he is a dealer in books does not guarantee he will know, and even if he does—'

'He may not tell me. You made yourself clear the first time.' She was losing patience with him. She wondered how much to offer him for the information.

'You understand very little,' he said. He wrote down the name, folded the piece of paper in half and handed it to her. He named his price. It was less than she had anticipated. 'You'll be leaving soon,' he told her. 'I wish you luck.' He put her money into his magazine and walked with her back to the door. She heard him draw the bolts behind her. The lamp above the counter was extinguished.

It had seemed bright, sitting in the square, but here the tall buildings and the narrowness of the street shut out most of the sun. The shop behind her sank into darkness. She saw only the man's white apron as he passed through into a back room.

She returned to the waiting cab.

'See,' she said, holding up the piece of paper.

'Give it to me.' The driver took it, read it and handed it back. 'Get in.'

'He didn't explain how to get there.'

'I know where it is. We can only drive so far.'

The horse drew them at a walk for fifteen minutes. The street was longer than she had anticipated, far longer than suggested by her map.

They stopped. The driver climbed down and helped her out.

'In there.' He pointed to a side street.

'Will you come with me?'

'If you like.' He tethered the horse to a thin tree.

They entered the darkness of the alleyway. Somewhere ahead of them children played unseen. They passed unlit doorways. A woman came out of one of these, watched them for a moment as though expecting to be approached, and then went back in.

'Is it far?' Elizabeth asked him. She began to believe she had made a mistake, convinced that Jameson lived closer to the centre of the town. They were by then half an hour's walk from the hotel; he had always given her the impression that he lived much closer.

'In here,' the driver said eventually. He led her into an unpaved court.

'How do you know?'

'There.' He indicated the shop. 'It's not the man you're looking for, but if anyone knows, he will. Give me the paper.'

She handed it to him and he tore it into small pieces and scattered them.

'Will you come in with me?'

'I'll wait here.'

The man in this second shop watched her without rising from his seat. The wall behind him was hung from floor to ceiling with framed faces, groups, couples, landscapes.

'Are you buying?' he asked her. His eyes never left her. 'I don't know you. Perhaps there's something special I can do for you. You only have to say. Something special. I assure you, we are quite alone.'

She looked around, pausing at the bookcase by the door.

'If it's books you're after? Do you know the titles? It doesn't matter, of course.'

'Jameson,' she said, unable to frame her request any less directly.

'Ah, Jameson.' He knew the name. 'I am not he,' he said.
'I know.'
'Then you know Jameson?'
'I'm trying to find him,' she said.
'One moment.' He rose from his seat, went to the glass cabinet which filled one wall of the small shop and pulled down a heavy gold and maroon drape, which covered it. She had paid no attention to the contents of the cabinet. 'You've come too far,' he said, 'I assume you've come from the centre of the town.'
'From the Hotel Lepontine.'
'The Hotel Lepontine. You *are* keen to find him.' He looked into the yard and saw the cab driver there, the glow of his pipe. 'Is he with you?'
'My driver. He's waiting.' She imagined he was about to become as evasive as the first man, that he, too, expected to be paid.
'If you just tell me the address, I'll leave,' she told him.
'So soon?' he said, adding, 'I do know the address, of course.'
'Then you'll know the photographer's name.'
He told her.
She grew relaxed. A connection had been made. She wanted to give the impression of being confident of getting what she wanted.
'Who told you to come here?' he asked her.
'Oh, just a man.'
'I see. The world is full of men sticking their noses into other people's business.'
'May I see the cabinet?' she said.
He hesitated. 'You may look where you like. Feel free.' He returned to his chair and watched her.
She lifted the gold and maroon cloth.

At first she saw nothing but other framed photographs, books open at their illustrations, small etchings and ivory carvings. Then she looked more closely at this collection and saw the bodies, the men and women, the acts and actions on display.

'Are you shocked?' he asked her, smiling.

She went on looking, determined not to reveal her confusion to him. 'Is this how you make your living?'

He laughed. 'How dare you suggest such a thing. I'm a respectable photographer and bookseller. You only have to look around you.' She looked up at the groups and the faces on the wall.

'You didn't know,' he said. 'I knew the instant you opened your mouth.'

She looked more closely at individual objects in the cabinet.

'If there's anything you wish to inspect more closely . . .' he said.

She could not bring herself to ask him if this was how Jameson's associate made his living.

'*Should* I be shocked?' she said, but her voice was dry.

'Be whatever you like.' His smile dropped and then rose again.

They were both distracted by the noise of footsteps in the room above them. He rose from his chair, pulled aside a curtain and called up the stairs for silence. A man's voice answered him. She knew from the noise that there was more than one person above them.

'I'll give you Emil's address,' he said.

'But I'm not to tell him where I got it?'

'Tell him what you like. Why should I care?'

She lowered the cloth back over the cabinet.

There were more footsteps above them. She heard a woman's laughter.

He looked up, waiting for silence. 'You don't even know how you got here,' he said, and for the first time there was something close to malice in his voice. 'And without that simpleton out there to guide you back, you'd spend an hour trying to find your way back to the centre.' This near-threat satisfied something in him, and he gave her the address.

'The pictures,' she said. 'Are they all local girls?'

'Mostly. Why? Do you think this kind of thing only goes on here? I don't know where you live in England, but wherever it is, believe me, this goes on there too.'

She resisted the urge to deny this.

'Tell me, are you truly shocked?' he said. 'I mean shocked inside, made off-balance, sick even, by what you've seen? Or are you merely surprised and offended? Surprised, perhaps, because you find Jameson is involved in all of this?'

'Jameson deals—' She stopped herself.

'He deals in what?'

She could think of nothing to say which would not further reveal how little she knew of him.

'People come here from all over,' he said. 'Some to buy. Some – some merely to indulge themselves.'

She wanted to leave. She fumbled with the clasp of her bag and took out her purse.

'It would insult me,' he said, holding up his palm to her. He closed his eyes, waiting for her to leave.

20

She returned to the clinic the next morning. The hotel manager intercepted her on the stairs on her way down and asked if she intended taking Mary's clothes and possessions into her own room. She told him that Mary's room was paid for and that the clothes and possessions would be staying where they were until Mary returned.

'Until she returns?' He stopped on the stairs above her. It was not something she had considered. 'You mean you intend to bring a sick woman, a woman as sick as your sister-in-law, back here?'

'When they've done all they can for her at the clinic, yes. Why not?' She saw how ambiguous this sounded. 'When she's cured.'

' "Cured"? No-one is ever cured in this place. Not properly cured. Year after year they come back to be "cured". Cure, sickness, cure, sickness. In some of them it is a need, a desire for sickness, a genuine longing.'

She refused to answer him.

He followed her into the lobby.

'No breakfast?' he asked her. He behaved now in his usual solicitous manner. The other guests turned to watch them. She saw the waitress she had seen with Jameson. The girl stood at the reception desk, a shabby coat beneath her arm, either just coming on duty or just leaving. She was talking to the young clerk, who leaned over the desk to hold his face close to hers. They interrupted their conversation to watch Elizabeth and the manager. The clerk said something and the girl laughed. The manager called to them. He told the girl to leave and the clerk to attend to his duties. They drew apart. The girl left, crossing the lobby towards the entrance with a deliberate swagger. Elizabeth wondered if this was meant for her or the manager.

'When they are finished here they should leave by the rear, not the main entrance,' he said to her, as though this explained his own sudden anger at seeing the girl.

Now that there were fewer guests in the hotel, so there were fewer staff; where there had once been a dozen waiters and waitresses serving meals, now there were only six. A whole upper floor had been emptied and cleared, sheeted and closed off. She had learned from the Gottliebs that another hotel, further out, closer to the casino, had already closed down completely for the winter, its remaining guests having been transferred elsewhere. It had surprised her to hear the word 'winter' used so early in the season, and long before its first true indicators — the distant, quickly-lost high snow excepted — were apparent, but she knew that the word had its more precise, commercial implications regarding the town and its trade.

'Why not sack her?' she said to the manager. He held the door for guests leaving the dining-room.

'It is not that simple.'

'You get rid of others easily enough.'

'Please, it is not policy to discuss such things with the hotel guests.' He threw up this flimsy but impenetrable wall to shield his evasions.

Outside, the girl had stopped at the top of the steps and was looking back in at them. It occurred to Elizabeth that she was waiting for her.

'I'll need a cab,' she said.

'There will be plenty down on the street.' He was pleased at this opportunity to leave her. He bowed slightly and went into the dining-room, where she saw him approach the maître d' and then start pointing at the empty tables around them, already planning the next stage of the hotel's withdrawal into the sleep of its own eventual closure.

She went outside. The waitress descended the steps ahead of her. At the bottom the girl pulled on a hat as nondescript as her coat. She carried a bag. She leaned against a stone portal and waited for Elizabeth to come down to her.

'I heard about your sister-in-law,' she said as Elizabeth reached her. 'It's a good clinic.'

'Aren't all clinics supposed to be good?' Elizabeth maintained her guard, surprised that the girl had made this approach.

'Not here. A new one opens up every month in the summer. Some open in the spring and close in the autumn. You'd be surprised how many supposedly sick people recover their strength sufficiently to leave and spend their winters in the south of France, at home in America, wherever. We call this month, October, the Lazarus month. Are you going there now?'

'Yes.'

'I'll share your cab as far as the town. I can't pay for it. I normally walk.'

'Have you been working all night?'

'In the kitchen.'

'Doing what?'

'Whatever they tell me to do.'

'Will he fire you soon?' Elizabeth asked her.

'Probably.'

'He doesn't have a very high opinion of you.'

The girl laughed. 'Is that what it is? Did *he* tell you that?'

'It's just the way he behaves and talks.'

'The only person he has a high opinion of is himself.'

A cab drew up alongside them and the girl put out her hand for it. It was she who gave instructions to the driver. The man clearly knew her, waiting for Elizabeth's nod of confirmation before opening the door.

'You work for Jameson's friend,' Elizabeth said when they were headed towards the town. She had asked Jameson about the waitress several days earlier, before her search for the studio, but, as usual when he spoke of his business or life in the town, half-truths had shaded everything.

'His friend?'

'The photographer, Emil.'

'Jameson didn't tell you that.'

'He told me you cleaned for him, that occasionally you stayed there.'

The girl considered this. She relaxed. 'I clean—' she placed a special emphasis on the word '—for several of them. It's a good trade in this town, photography.'

'But not at this time of year, surely?'

'Why not? They make postcards, there are still sittings.

Summer is the busiest time, but most of them have ways and means of surviving through the winter. We all have.'

It was a game they were playing; Elizabeth understood that.

They entered the busier streets. The cab stood in traffic.

'It might be quicker for you to get out and walk,' Elizabeth suggested.

'It might.' The girl gave no indication of leaving. 'Will you employ someone to sit with your sister-in-law, to look after her?'

'A companion?' The thought had not occurred to her. 'I doubt it. Why should I? There are nurses, there's me.'

'I only wondered,' the girl said.

'Do you think I should? Is that what normally happens?'

'Sometimes. It depends. Sometimes. I'm Monique, by the way. I'll get out here.' She waited for the cab to slow at an intersection, opened the door and stepped out. The driver gesticulated at her. She gestured back and slammed the door. 'Ignore him,' she said to Elizabeth. She waited until the cab drew away before turning and disappearing into one of the nearby alleyways.

Mary was awake when she arrived. She was sitting up, supported by pillows. A tray of uneaten food lay on the cabinet beside her. Elizabeth watched her through the door: Mary's eyes were closed; she held a hand to her mouth and methodically wiped a finger back and forth across her lips. She slid her hand beneath the sheets the instant Elizabeth opened the door.

Elizabeth tried to sound cheerful. She remarked on how much better Mary was looking. She commented on the dismal view from the room and related what little else she had learned about the clinic.

But Mary was distracted.

'Do you feel unwell?' Elizabeth said. 'Should I call for someone?'

Mary closed her eyes and spoke. 'They say they'll leave it here until I eat it. I've told them I still have no appetite, that the smell alone sickens me, but they insist on leaving it.'

Elizabeth examined the plate. It contained cold mashed vegetables and two small slices of cold meat. A thin liquid filled the spaces between these few pieces.

'They know what they're doing,' she said.

'How can they? They don't understand what I'm suffering, so how can they pretend to know how to cure me? They think that if I can just get my appetite back, then I'll be saved.'

'It wouldn't hurt,' Elizabeth said, wanting the remark to sound neutral, not wanting to repeat the word 'saved'.

'If that's what you think, then you're as blind as the rest of them.'

Elizabeth forgave her this remark.

Mary opened her eyes and studied her.

Elizabeth expected her to ask questions concerning the medication she was being given, how long she would stay in the clinic, what other arrangements had been made on her behalf. But she asked none of these things.

'I'll get you another room,' Elizabeth said. 'One at the front, overlooking the lake.'

'No, don't,' Mary said. Again she closed her eyes, as though by this simple and obvious gesture she might deny responsibility for what she said.

'But there's nothing here for you to look out at,' Elizabeth said.

'You and your precious lake. I don't *want* anything to look out at. That's what I want to look at – nothing. What does it matter what I look out at? *You* look at the lake, let me just look at the walls. Do you really think some attractive scenery – because that's all it is, a backcloth – is going to tempt me to get well enough to go out and walk among it again? It's scenery, no-one here cares about it; to them it's just an expensive picture hanging on the wall of their dull little houses, dull big houses.' This outburst exhausted her. She raised her hand back to her lips and repeated the motion Elizabeth had watched through the door. She looked as though she were searching for some morsel of food, something she needed to be rid of for fear of unexpectedly tasting it later.

'Here.' Elizabeth handed her a handkerchief.

'What's that for?'

Elizabeth took it back.

'Tell them I'll eat when I'm hungry again. Tell them that this has nothing whatsoever to do with eating or not eating. Tell them it's here . . .' She lowered her hand to her chest, reluctant rather than embarrassed to say more.

They were interrupted by the arrival of the doctor Elizabeth had spoken to upon Mary's admission. He saw the plate of uneaten food, said, 'No matter; you will eat,' and picked up Mary's arm by the wrist. He measured her pulse and then pulled her forward to listen to her back and sides with his stethoscope. Mary remained silent through all this, and kept her eyes closed.

More denial, Elizabeth thought.

'I hope you are talking some sense into her,' he said to Elizabeth, but then left before she could answer him.

'How did I get here?' Mary asked when they were again alone.

Elizabeth was uncertain what she meant by this. 'Jameson—'

'I knew he'd have something to do with it all, the blessed Jameson.'

'Don't. I sent for the doctor he recommended.'

'I don't remember anything.'

'You passed out. He thought you'd cracked a rib.'

'I have. Look.' Mary pulled up her night-dress to reveal the broad bandage which flattened her breasts even further; there was no shape beneath the material.

'Is it painful?'

'What else? How did I get here?'

Elizabeth told her.

'Was this room Jameson's idea too? I imagine that he, of all people, understands the false promises of your beautiful lake and forests and mountains. If no-one else understands it, Jameson will.'

'Now you're being ridiculous,' Elizabeth said. Again, she barely understood what Mary was saying to her.

'Ask him. Ask him why *he* stays here. Ask him why he closets himself away in the town and spends so much time up at the hospital. He's a wealthy man, he could just as easily stay in a hotel — a hotel much better than ours — and pamper himself as we pamper ourselves. Ask him why he doesn't. Ask him why —'

'Stop,' Elizabeth shouted. 'I know all that. It's none of my business.'

Neither of them spoke for several minutes. A train passed noisily through the gorge. The telegraph wires shook above it.

'I'm sorry,' Mary said eventually, exhausted, letting her head fall back against her pillows. 'You can blame all this on the sedatives they give me. We're going to need a lot of excuses soon, aren't we?'

'Do they intend giving you more?'

'I imagine so.'

Elizabeth pulled her chair closer to the bed. It was impossible to avoid the smell of the cold food. She took the tray and put it on the floor beside the door.

'They told me I could ask you to bring food in for me,' Mary said. 'If there was anything I particularly wanted, anything that might stim-u-late my appetite.'

'And is there?'

Mary smiled and shook her head. She closed her eyes again.

An hour later, when Elizabeth left, Mary was asleep. Her lips were dry, and the edges of her mouth red from her constant rubbing.

21

She next saw Jameson three days later. He came into the hotel while she sat in the lobby reading a newspaper. It was his first visit there in over a week. She made a point of putting down the paper and watching him as he came towards her. Something in the way he did this – his slight hesitancy at seeing her so soon after his arrival, the way he raised the package he was carrying to his chest, the way he watched her – told her he knew.

He sat beside her and put the package between them.

Across the lobby, the clerk went through the motions of seeing off a family of departing guests. The closer they came to the final point of departure, the more obsequious he became in the hope of a gratuity. He carried their bags and stood with his hands on the shoulders of their children. He wished everyone a safe journey home.

It was a cold day, and a wind chilled by the lake blew into the lobby each time the door was opened.

'You don't need to say anything,' she said to him.

'I'm on my way to see Hunter, to take him these.'

'Did you think I'd come with you?'

'That wasn't why I came. How's Mary?'

'She ate something yesterday.'

'Did she tell you that, or the doctor?'

'She isn't any worse.'

'I never lied to you,' he said. He coughed to clear his throat. 'I kept certain things from you, that's all, but I never lied to you.'

'Please, don't apologize; it's none of my business.'

'It wasn't an apology. And it *is* your business. Everyone else who knows what I do, what I am, will make the assumption that you know too.'

'And they'll judge me because of it?'

'Possibly.'

'The way they all judge you?'

'I doubt you could sink quite so low in their estimation.'

She smiled at that. 'You did lie to me,' she said. 'Your rare books and manuscripts.'

'It wasn't a lie. They are still part of my trade. And they are rare, and some of them, many of them, are beautiful and impressive works. That is not only my opinion. It's unfamiliar to you, that's all.'

She nodded her acknowledgement of this.

'I'd like to try and explain something to you,' he said. 'But not now, and certainly not here.'

'There's really no need.'

'I know. But I believe there's a need for me to try. I know what you must think of me. I'm not going to make excuses for myself. I'm not ashamed of anything I do. I'm not doing anything against my will. There is a reason, a purpose behind all this.' He remained calm as he spoke. She saw how long he had rehearsed what he wanted to say to her.

'All right,' she said.

The clerk followed the last of the departing guests out of the lobby. They sat in silence. The boy returned a minute later counting the notes in his hand. He grew angry at the realization of how little he had been given for all his efforts.

'How is Hunter?' she asked him.

'He's heard from the man appointed to represent him. They want to set a new trial in motion. They're pushing the hospital for an assessment; they want a date for his release.'

'Will it happen?'

'These people make things happen. There's nothing he can do about it.' He was unable to hide his concern from her.

'Will you go with him if it's allowed?'

'I don't know. I just want to see him, find out for certain what's happening. It all seemed so far away until now.'

'In addition to which, you'd almost succeeded in convincing yourself that whoever or whatever was reaching out to get him would either forget about him or be unable to find him hidden away here.'

'I suppose so. Something like that.'

She had wanted to be angry with him.

'It was stupid of me to go looking,' she said.

'You would have done it sooner or later. Jameson, Man of Mystery.' He tapped the package. 'Once, back home, I remember weeping, actually weeping, with joy, pleasure, excitement, whatever, at receiving a manuscript I'd been looking for for five years. It just arrived out of the blue one day after all those years of searching. I paid twice what I'd anticipated, but it was worth it. Back then, it was what I lived for.'

'And now? Is that why you deal in . . . why you . . .'

'Deal in pornography? It would be far too simple and misleading for me to say yes, but it's partly the reason.'

'Is that what you call it, how you refer to it?'

'I try not to be too dishonest about it. No more than I'm needed to be.'

The clerk leaned across the desk, watching them.

'I'm going to see Mary,' she said. She rose.

'When can I see you?' He half reached out to stop her going.

She suggested that evening. She did not intend spending more than an hour or two at the clinic, less if Mary was sedated and sleeping.

'I'll come on my way back from seeing Hunter,' he said.

'Give him my regards.'

'He told me he'd like to see you again. He said you reminded him of his wife when he first knew her, when he—' He stopped.

'When he loved her?'

He rose beside her, and for a moment she thought he was going to hold her, perhaps even kiss her. But instead he reached down and picked up his package.

She pulled on her gloves. 'I'd better go,' she said. She saw how quickly they had both retreated from their vague and uncertain intimacy back to the common ground of propriety. She held out her hand to him and he took it. She called 'Goodbye,' to the inquisitive clerk, who turned away and pretended to occupy himself with the hotel register.

'Does your knowing change whatever feelings you may have for me?' Jameson said.

She considered the question. 'Why should it?'

'You can no better lie than I can,' he said.

'If that's what you want to believe.' She left him and he watched her go. The clerk, too, watched her again, making no attempt now to disguise his interest.

22

She was prevented by a nurse from going directly to see Mary.

'Is something wrong?'

'The doctor wishes to see you before you talk to your sister-in-law.'

'What is it?'

'Please, the doctor will explain. Your sister-in-law is fine.'

'Fetch him.'

'He'll be here shortly. Someone has gone to find him. I saw you arrive. Please, you can wait here.' The nurse indicated a line of chairs.

The doctor arrived several minutes later.

'What's wrong?'

'Your sister-in-law continues to refuse to eat. I would like your permission to start feeding her by force.'

'Of course she's eating.'

'I assure you, what she eats would not keep a snail alive. She vomits. Please do not make excuses for her. I know what's happening; you know it too. You are doing her no favours by entering into this fantasy with her.'

'What fantasy? What are you talking about?'

'Your sister-in-law wishes to return to a time and a place before all this happened to her.' He sighed, exasperated.

'That's absurd. I've never heard anything more ridiculous.' But even as she spoke she felt the weight of truth in what he said, felt her own resolve fail.

He waited for her anger to subside. 'Her problem,' he said, 'has more to do with her mind than her body. You know that. She expected her suffering and her grief to grow less, to diminish, to be replaced by something else. Instead it continues, on and on and on, the light grows darker, the weight heavier. She starts to search for new ways to escape from it, to make things change, to make herself change. And because whatever she tries either does not work or lasts only a short time, so she becomes increasingly desperate in her search for salvation. That is why she came here.'

'Are you suggesting that what she's doing, what she's suffering, she is doing deliberately?'

'You know she is. Does it make it easier for you to accept to hear me say it? We have patients here who have mutilated themselves. What your sister-in-law is doing is no different.'

'What good will feeding her by force do?'

'Very little. Keep her alive. But unless it is accompanied by some attempt to understand the causes of her actions . . .'

'Her husband was killed.'

He sighed again. 'We know that. But this is something far more complicated. You yourself must have endured something of what she now endures.'

She held her face in her hands.

He sat beside her. 'In a way, you are her anchor,' he said.

'You said you wanted my permission. Do you need it?'

'We can proceed without it if necessary.'

'Would you do that?'

'The time will soon arrive when she will endanger her own life.'

'But she only came here eight days ago. How can . . .'

'How can a woman who, to all outward appearances, has merely lost her appetite – and quite understandably so – turn from that into someone so close to death in so short a time?'

Elizabeth nodded, grateful now for his blunt and direct manner.

There was nothing more to say. He rose and left her, taking off his jacket as he went.

Elizabeth waited a few minutes and then went to see Mary.

'You're late,' Mary said harshly as she entered.

'I had to wait.'

'Why?'

'I don't know. People were busy.'

'I see. People were busy and so I'm left waiting.' She slapped her hand on the bed. 'Have you done anything about getting me another room yet?'

'You said you wanted to stay here.'

'I didn't. Why would anyone want to stay in here? When did I say it?'

'I must have misheard you,' Elizabeth said. She was alarmed by this change in Mary, and by this new and sudden distance between them.

'You're probably like the rest of them – you only hear what you want to hear,' Mary said.

'Have you been able to eat anything?'

'I eat everything they give me. Look around you – no plates

of uneaten food.' Mary still fretted at her mouth with her fingers as she spoke.

It occurred to Elizabeth to tell her what she had been told, but even as the thought entered her mind, she knew she could never be that cruel.

'Why don't you sit down,' Mary said. Her voice was softer.

Elizabeth sat beside her.

'What does Jameson think about all this?'

'I haven't seen him.'

Mary looked at her in a way which suggested her own lies were equally transparent.

'So what do they intend doing to me?' she said after a minute of silent reconciliation between them.

'To help you get well.'

'Is that all? What a surprise. Why can't they want what I want?'

'And that is?' Elizabeth said, fearful of the answer.

Mary turned away from her. The line of her jaw had grown more distinct. There was now a small hollow at the centre of each of her cheeks, as though an invisible finger were pressed into them. She started to cry. Elizabeth wiped her face. 'What I want is unthinkable,' Mary said. She made no attempt to take out the hairs which fell into her mouth as she spoke.

Elizabeth waited.

'They wanted to take off my rings,' Mary said, holding up the bands for Elizabeth to see.

'You were right not to let them.'

'Not that *they* understood that.' She looked around her. 'You needn't bother about changing the room. All this would happen wherever I was.' She finally pulled the hairs from her mouth. 'I lied about eating and you lied about Jameson,' she said. 'What is it?'

'Nothing, really.'

'Have you and he . . . ?'

'No.'

'He came here the day before yesterday, just after you'd gone. I saw him looking in at the door. I pretended to be asleep so he wouldn't feel obliged to go through some charade with me. I thought at first he might have been here in the hope of seeing you, but it was something else. He knew you weren't here. He just stood and watched, came and went.'

'He's concerned about you,' Elizabeth said, uselessly.

Mary pulled up the sheets to cover her face.

23

They turned off the road above the lake – a sharp bend which forced the carriage driver to back his horse between the trees.

'Why are we turning?' she asked him.

Jameson sat with his head out of the window directing the driver.

'I thought we were going to the hospital.' She held onto her seat as the carriage rocked.

They moved from the smooth surface of the public road on to a logging track, deeply rutted, embedded with stones and with a ridge of grass along its centre.

'Somewhere else,' Jameson said.

'Where? There is nowhere. I assumed we were going to see Hunter.'

'You might need to brace yourself; I'm afraid the track gets no better.' He reached under his own seat and pulled out a wooden case. This was the first Elizabeth had known of it.

'What is it?'

He lifted the lid to reveal rolls of bandages, packages and dark bottles.

'Medicines?'

'Basic stuff. It was all I could find.' He pulled a canvas satchel from the case and began to load it with the rolled bandages. When the satchel was full he felt its weight and passed it to Elizabeth. Then he began stuffing his pockets and a second bag with the packages and bottles.

The driver called in to them, a dialect Elizabeth did not understand.

'He's telling us to hold on. We have to negotiate a rock step ahead.' As he finished speaking the carriage slewed and tipped them both sideways in their seats. They rose and rocked again. 'Hold my arm,' he said. He braced himself against the roof. Elizabeth took his arm. The carriage tipped forward. The empty case slid across the floor; Elizabeth's purse fell from her lap. She heard the driver coaxing his horse forward; she heard the clatter and slide of the animal's hooves on the bare rock.

They finally came level.

'Is that it?'

He nodded. 'Another mile or so of this and then we have to walk.'

'Walk?'

'Perhaps half a mile, a little less.' He looked down at her feet. 'You'll manage.'

The track ahead of them began to rise again. It looked disused: grass covered it from side to side, and the trees which bordered it came closer, their lower boughs pleached into an arch above them.

They drove more slowly now. There were other obstacles

to negotiate. Behind them, nothing of the road or the lake was visible, and for the first time, Elizabeth realized, even the broader view of the distant peaks was lost to them.

Eventually they stopped, and the driver called in to them again.

'This is where we walk,' Jameson said. He helped her out and then adjusted the satchel of bandages for her until it rested comfortably against her side.

He spoke to the driver, who answered in the same unintelligible accent.

'We can save time by cutting through here.' He indicated a slope beside the track. It was a steep path, but she saw by the way it was trodden into steps that it was in regular use.

She was exhausted after only ten minutes' walking, and she called for him to stop. They sat on a boulder at the crest of the rise.

'It's all downhill from here,' he assured her. He breathed deeply and told her to do the same. She smelled woodsmoke.

They went on. The path widened and he walked beside her, helping her where the footing came loose. Around them, the pines gave way to chestnuts and other, smaller trees growing in coppiced clumps.

The smell of smoke grew stronger. She heard voices ahead of them, the voices of men and the calls of children. She heard the crackle of burning wood.

'Wait,' Jameson told her. He cupped his hands and called out. The sound echoed around them. The voices fell silent. He called again, less loudly this time, adding his name to whatever it was he yelled. She watched the path ahead of them. A man appeared carrying a long-handled axe; another came out of the trees beside him.

Jameson raised his arm. The men recognized him immediately and came towards them. Jameson laid down his load and the men embraced him. After this they stood and looked at Elizabeth.

Jameson introduced her.

She held out her hand to them.

Both men raised their own hands, but then hesitated.

'What's wrong?' she said.

'Your gloves.'

She looked at the two hands still held out towards her.

'They won't want to soil them for you,' he said.

Elizabeth considered taking them off, but instead she pushed her hand into that of the man standing closest to her and shook it. His companion followed.

A group of old women appeared and came forward.

'Who are they?' Elizabeth said, as the women gathered around her.

'Gypsies.'

Children and younger women appeared. The children ran forward, but the women held back. It was difficult to guess their ages. Most wore thick clothing and their heads were scarved. They had the same dark skin and hair as the men.

Several of these younger women gathered together. Jameson raised his hand to them. They all waved back, but none of them came any closer to greet him.

'Are they shy of you?' Elizabeth asked him. 'Are they not allowed to approach?'

He shook his head at the suggestion.

A single woman came forward, taking off her scarf as she approached. She was little more than a girl, Elizabeth guessed, Ruth's age. She wiped the dirt from her face and kissed Jameson on both cheeks. He took several packets of cigarettes from his pocket and handed them out to the men.

The old women began urging both her and Jameson along the path.

They arrived at an encampment, a circle of caravans and other crude shelters. The ground was trodden clear, but dry. Half a dozen fires burned at the centre of the space; ponies stood tethered in a line, and a large number of dogs lay sleeping around the camp. Most of these woke and started barking at their approach.

The crowd around them grew even larger. The small children were drawn to Elizabeth. The young women, she noticed, continued to keep their distance, with the exception of the one who had kissed Jameson, and who now walked beside him, her arm through his. She walked with him like this until approached by one of the older women, who berated her until she pulled herself free and walked away.

A space was cleared beside one of the fires, and the bags of medicines and bandages were laid on the ground. Jameson indicated for the old woman who supervised this to empty them.

'Who are they for?' Elizabeth asked him.

She was answered by another of the women, who took her by the arm and led her to one of the canvas shelters.

Inside lay a line of men on simple wooden pallets. The man nearest the entrance had his whole head bandaged. He called out at her approach and the woman introduced her. She wished she had some of Jameson's cigarettes to dispense. It was dark inside the shelter, the air fetid.

There were a dozen injured men, and beside each one sat a watching woman.

One man raised the bandaged stump of his missing arm to her.

The old woman who had taken her there led her further inside. She spoke to Elizabeth as though she believed she could understand her, and Elizabeth tried to explain to her until eventually their conversation held together in a few common words and gestures. The other women rose to greet her. She handed out bottles and bandages, and they treated these like the precious things they were. The dressings on most of the men were old and soiled. A pot simmered on a small stove, and the bandages were unwound and put into this, to be used again.

A young man with half his leg missing hopped towards Elizabeth and kissed her. She held him while he regained his balance after the embrace.

On pallets pushed together in the darkest part of the shelter, four men lay without moving. They were covered with blankets, making their injuries less obvious and difficult to guess at. A woman knelt on the ground beside each one. It was clear to Elizabeth that these men were the sickest and that all were now close to death. She could only wonder at the nature of their suffering so long after sustaining their injuries.

As she stood over them, uncertain and uncomfortable, there was a commotion behind her as Jameson and some of the others came in. It shocked her to see men so obviously healthy and vigorous apparently so unconcerned by the suffering of those alongside them.

Jameson came to her and spoke to the old woman.

'What are you saying?' Elizabeth asked him.

'I'm telling her how sorry I am that her son is shortly to die and that he has suffered for so long.' He indicated the closest of the silent men, a young man whose skeletal chest and shoulders lay exposed. Another woman wiped his brow and lips, eliciting only the slightest of responses. The old woman looked down at him and uttered a silent prayer.

'How did it happen? I mean here, so far from anywhere?'

'The war was here too. Close enough for them to be

involved. They acted as guides and scouts for the Italian and Austrian mountain troops.'

'They fought with the enemy?'

He ignored the remark. 'I doubt if any of them actually fought.'

'But their injuries . . .'

'Do you truly believe that because the mountains *look* so solid and clean and perfect, nothing of that stinking mess out there ever reached into them?'

She nodded, confused.

'Don't worry, you're not alone. Her son was wounded at Caporetto. The miracle of it is that any of them have survived for so long.'

'Can't they be admitted to the hospital?'

He shook his head, unable or unwilling to answer her in front of all these watching women.

Beside her, one of them lifted a blanket and the smell which rose from beneath it made her wince.

'Come outside,' Jameson said. It was not what she wanted, but he took her arm and led her out.

Another of the younger women approached them with a tray of enamel mugs. She, too, flirted with Jameson.

'Do you know her?'

'I know most of them.'

'How? I mean – Emil?'

He shook his head. 'Later.'

She sipped the drink she had been given and grimaced at the taste.

Jameson drank his. 'It's disgusting,' he said.

'But we have to drink it?'

They went to sit in a circle of men.

'They're talking about you,' he told her.

The men around her all laughed.

'Don't tell me what they're saying,' she told him.

A small child – she could not tell if it was a boy or a girl – came and stood in front of her.

'It must be a hard life for them,' she said.

'It is. They're outcasts.'

'They live like—'

'They live like animals. I admire them for it.'

'I was going to say they live like they must have lived for centuries.'

'Easy enough to do, I suppose, until that first unseen barrage comes whistling over the horizon.'

She was about to say something to the small, staring child, when the girl who had stood with Jameson on the path returned to sit beside him. She carried a baby now, nursing it as she came. She held out the child for him to see. It looked pale against her dark breast. She wiped a hand over the milk which still flowed.

Elizabeth looked away.

Jameson took the child. 'This is Maria,' he said. 'The child is Tomas. Her husband died recently. He was one of the wounded. Maria cared for him.' He handed the baby back. 'Did you imagine that the child was mine, that that was why she'd brought him to me?'

She was too slow in her denial. 'Of course not.'

'Yes, you did,' he said, but with no anger in his voice. 'And before you ask again, yes, Maria has worked for Emil; several of them have.' He spoke to the girl and she buttoned up her blouse. Elizabeth saw that something in their brief exchange had disappointed her, and she wondered if Maria had expected to return to the town with them, if that was why she believed Jameson had come; she saw how appealing that place must appear to her and the other young women.

'Our driver is Maria's brother,' Jameson said softly. 'His

wife was unfaithful during one of his long absences and he has vowed never to return. She was punished in childbirth six months later. No-one would welcome him if he did try to come back to them.'

A man threw logs on to the fire.

'We ought to be leaving,' Jameson said eventually, looking up at the darkening sky.

'Does anyone else know they're here?' she asked him.

'I imagine so. Margaret comes occasionally. She walks from the convent. They have no consecrated ground here; the convent obliges.'

They left shortly after, followed up the slope by twenty others. The children were braver now and clamoured to hold Elizabeth's hand.

At the top of the path all these others stopped and drew back as though at some invisible divide. None of the younger women, Elizabeth noticed, accompanied them out of the camp.

Here, she realized on their journey back down through the trees, was another of Jameson's checks and balances, another of his small and vital acts of atonement.

The carriage waited where they had left it, the driver asleep where he sat.

24

The visiting diplomat did not, after all, come to the hotel he had supposedly visited all those previous summers. He went instead to the newest and grandest hotel in the town, a hotel built back from the road to the west, a hotel with its own spa and bathing pool, with its exclusive and wealthy clientele, and with plans to construct a small-gauge railway up the slope of the mountain beneath which it stood.

Elizabeth occasionally saw the man on her excursions into town, surrounded wherever he went by his family and entourage.

On one occasion she saw him returning from a trip out on the lake in a boat similar to the one she and Mary had taken. There was an argument at the jetty and she overheard one of the diplomat's aides express anger at being charged by the boatman. The Great Man himself stood apart from the scene, turned away from the arguing men as though they didn't exist.

It was Herr Gottlieb's opinion that the new hotel had lured this influential guest away by offering him his accommodation and meals free of charge, and his disappointment at not now meeting the man as a fellow guest was tempered by the knowledge that he had been swayed in his decision to go elsewhere by something as base as expense.

She saw the Gottliebs once, all three of them, standing at the window of the restaurant in which the diplomat was eating. She stayed on the far side of the busy street from them, avoiding them, and as she walked away from them she instead encountered Cox, who emerged from a shop directly ahead of her.

Alone, away from the hospital, he seemed less sure of himself. He saw her and stopped.

'I heard about your sister-in-law,' he said. He avoided looking at her.

'She's in good hands.' She wanted to avoid this small talk and ask him immediately and directly what it was about Jameson and Hunter he despised so much, and why he felt the constant need to challenge them. But she knew that he would not answer her, that he would in all likelihood walk away from her and then remark on her 'interference' to Jameson.

'They treat him like royalty,' he said, indicating the restaurant. 'I saw him arrive. Anywhere else they'd line the streets to spit at him.'

'Is that what you'd do?'

'Bloody right it is.'

She knew this language was meant to provoke her. 'There are some here who seem to worship the ground he walks on,' she said.

'Them, you mean.' He pointed to the Gottliebs, who were only then drawing away from the window. 'His own sort.'

'You think we should still be fighting them?' she said.

'I think the job should have been properly finished, that's all. There's plenty of us still think that.'

'People like Mitchell?'

He grew more cautious at mention of the boy's name. 'He doesn't think anything about anything. That much must be obvious, even to you.'

'He thinks something of the girl,' she said.

He laughed at this. 'Her? You're wrong. I've put him right on that score. He knows what she is. Perhaps it's you who doesn't know the half of it.'

'Was that why he hit her?' she said.

'What? She's just as likely to have done that to herself and then tried to blame him. Perhaps it's you who wants to get things straight before you go accusing people.'

'Perhaps he was provoked,' she said. 'Perhaps he was put up to it.'

But before he could respond to this, they were interrupted by a call from Herr Gottlieb, who now stood at the centre of the street, waiting for his wife and daughter to join him.

'Like I said,' Cox said, his caution now curdled to hostility, 'you want to watch who you're accusing.'

Herr Gottlieb called again.

'You and him friends, are you?' Cox said.

She watched as Frau Gottlieb and Gerda came through the traffic. She hoped Cox might leave at their approach, but he waited beside her.

'Fräulein Mortlake,' Herr Gottlieb said, finally reaching her. He nodded to Cox, waiting for the introduction which did not come. 'We were just considering whether or not to eat in that particular restaurant. I believe it has a good reputation.'

Cox laughed at this.

'You know something about the place?' Herr Gottlieb said to him.

'Me? I can't afford to eat in restaurants.'

They were joined by Frau Gottlieb and Gerda.

Elizabeth resented this intrusion.

Cox grimaced at hearing the two women speak.

'Cox works at the hospital,' Elizabeth said.

'Corporal Cox,' Cox said.

'My son, too, was a corporal,' Herr Gottlieb said, but this revelation – another of those futile connections – did nothing to appease Cox, serving instead only to feed his contempt for the three Germans.

'I've got to go,' he said.

Herr Gottlieb half raised his hand to him, as though the two of them might now shake, but Cox made no effort to reciprocate. He pushed past Frau Gottlieb and Gerda, both of whom said 'Goodbye' to him as he went.

'You saw us, didn't you?' Herr Gottlieb said to Elizabeth. He indicated the restaurant. 'The doors have been locked. A private luncheon. Twenty empty tables.' As before when talking of the diplomat, he could not disguise his disillusion.

'They were having such dishes delivered to them,' Gerda said enthusiastically. 'We saw everything.'

'Until they lowered the blinds on us,' Herr Gottlieb added coldly.

Frau Gottlieb put a hand on her daughter's arm to temper her excitement.

'Have you eaten?' Herr Gottlieb asked Elizabeth.

She lied and told him she was expected at the clinic.

'Of course,' he said. 'Then you will excuse us.' He left her, motioning for his wife and daughter to follow him.

Elizabeth waited where she stood until they were out of sight. Across the street a man hung a sign in the restaurant window announcing that the place was closed and would not reopen until later that same evening.

25

Three days later, the doctor treating Mary called the hotel and left a message asking for Elizabeth to go to the clinic immediately. She was out when the message came, and four hours passed before she returned and the manager emerged from his office to inform her.

On her arrival at the clinic she imagined someone would be waiting for her, that her sense of urgency would be shared, lessened, but she was met only by the nurse who unlocked the door to let her in, and who was unaware of why she had been summoned. She was told to wait while the doctor was sought.

He came soon after, rolling down the sleeves of his jacket. His necktie was pulled away from his collar.

'I called you five hours ago,' he said, brusquely.

'I was out.'

'Then I'm afraid you may have had a wasted journey. Your sister-in-law is sedated.'

'What happened?' The crisis – whatever it had been – had clearly passed, and she knew that by her presence she was now only prolonging it unnecessarily.

'I should have called back,' he said. He paused, but did not stop walking. She walked alongside him. She wanted to tell him to stop, to stand still and explain to her what had happened; more than ever before she needed the details, confirmation of what she already knew.

Eventually he stopped. He brushed at a stain on his shirt. 'An emergency elsewhere,' he said. His tone had changed, and she wondered if this was his apology. They stood at the bottom of a staircase, its window looking out over the railway.

'Tell me,' she said.

He took a deep breath. 'Your sister-in-law is a very stupid young woman.'

'What has she done?'

'A nurse was in her room, delivering fresh water, when she was called away. She believed your sister-in-law to be sleeping. She went, leaving her tray of empty jugs and some medicines on the table by the door. When she returned a few minutes later, it was to discover your sister-in-law in bed surrounded by a dozen empty bottles. She had not been asleep and had deliberately tricked this nurse – herself no more than a stupid girl – into believing she was.'

'What was in the bottles, what medicines? Tell me.'

'Little of consequence, fortunately. Appetite stimulants, nothing dangerous, some laxative and emetic drugs; nothing that will do her any lasting harm.'

She sensed now that he was beginning to protect himself, and she considered whether or not to exploit this weakness and demand to be told more.

'Are you certain she's all right?'

'Absolutely, absolutely. In fact, the emetics she swallowed . . .'

'She was sick?'

'Fortunately for her. Most of the pills she took – stole – were regurgitated intact. As you know, she is in a very weakened condition and any introduction of such potent medicines into her stomach . . .'

She didn't want to hear any more. 'Can I see her?'

'Of course.' His relief was obvious. 'It's very distressing, naturally, but I'm afraid the Institution really cannot accept any responsibility for what has happened, for your sister-in-law's deception and deliberate criminal act.'

It was the first time she had heard the place called an institution.

He walked with her to Mary's door.

'I'll go in alone,' she told him.

'Of course. But one thing . . .'

'What?'

'You must understand – I hope it was made clear to you when your sister-in-law was brought here – you must understand that her actions today make it very difficult – impossible, I might say – for me to go on treating her. Her will to recover . . . Her co-operation . . .'

'You think she tried to kill herself,' Elizabeth said flatly.

'What else?'

'She isn't herself,' she shouted. 'Her mind . . . You said yourself that her unwillingness, her inability to eat was a symptom of something much deeper.'

'And I still believe that. But what has happened today casts the whole affair in a different light. Before, I didn't know that she had it within her to attempt something so stupid, but now . . .' He shrugged, and she saw how far he, too, had distanced himself in those five hours of waiting.

'She isn't thinking straight, that's all. Her mind is unbalanced. She isn't a stupid woman.'

'Stupid enough to attempt what she attempted.'

'Perhaps she knew what she was swallowing.'

'She still deceived the nurse, she still stole, she still tried to deliberately cause harm to herself.'

'You can't seriously believe that she fully understood what she was doing? She's been sedated; most of the time she's barely awake.' She knew that her argument was losing both its momentum and its edge, and that his mind was already made up to stop treating Mary and to make room for a more compliant patient.

'It is all very unfortunate,' he said, confirming her guess.

'Where can she go?'

'There are other institutions, sanatoria.'

'Will you recommend one? Will you write a letter of recommendation for me? You must know someone, a colleague . . .'

Again, he became evasive. 'I'm afraid your sister-in-law's condition . . . My advice to you would be to take her home. Who knows, familiar, friendly surroundings and people might make all the difference to how she—'

'You think she's losing her mind, don't you?' she said.

He smiled at the clumsy phrase. 'Of course not, no.'

She saw that her argument was lost, and she saw too how reassured he felt by this same understanding.

'Perhaps you might like to seek the opinion of someone else,' he said. 'Perhaps the doctor who accompanied her on her arrival. Perhaps even the doctor who treated her in the hotel. I forget his name.' He raised a clenched fist. 'Not one of the more reputable practitioners, but I understand you have some not inconsiderable faith in him.' He smiled.

Unlike you, you mean, Elizabeth thought, knowing that nothing would now bring him back to her.

'Go in and see her,' he said. 'Go and talk to her.'

'You're washing your hands of her.'

'She is quite welcome to stay until she is recovered following today's small misadventure.'

'I could lodge a complaint,' Elizabeth said, the threat betrayed by her lack of conviction.

'Complaint? With whom?' He seemed genuinely surprised at the remark. 'If it is any consolation, the nurse who was so irresponsible in her duties – as I say, more of a girl, really, an orderly rather than anyone appropriately qualified – was dismissed instantly.'

'How convenient.'

'I can see you are upset,' he said. He turned sharply and walked away from her.

She went in and sat beside Mary, who was asleep. The room still contained some faint, sour odour of its recent drama. Two enamel basins sat on the floor beneath the bed.

After several minutes, Mary opened her eyes and looked up at her.

'I know,' Elizabeth told her. She took her hand. 'You don't have to explain.'

Mary's dull gaze moved from Elizabeth to the wall beside her, and from there to the ceiling above.

You lost your balance, that's all, thought Elizabeth. You fell.

She knew how many of her own attachments had grown weak and unreliable over the previous months.

'Does he want me to leave?' Mary said, her voice dry.

Elizabeth poured a glass of water and held it to her lips. Mary sipped at this, but most of it ran down her chin.

Elizabeth straightened her sheets. She saw new bruises on

Mary's shoulders, at the top of her chest, and lower down, against her ribs. She made no effort to disguise the fact that she had seen these; Mary was beyond caring.

'I'll find you somewhere else,' Elizabeth said.

'No.'

'Somewhere for you to convalesce.'

'I want to go home.'

'Somewhere where they know what you need.' She was fooling neither of them.

'Home,' Mary repeated. Her eyes moved more rapidly around the room. She smiled, as though already imagining herself elsewhere.

'You'll need to recover some strength first. It was a stupid thing to do.'

'No, it wasn't,' Mary said. 'But I know that's what you've got to tell me.' She began to cough, then choke, recovering only slowly. Elizabeth waited in silence until the spasm subsided. 'It's the role I've forced you into playing,' Mary said.

'I know,' Elizabeth said. It was the first time she had acknowledged so directly and destructively the pact into which the two of them had entered all those months ago, yoked in their shared and unspeakable grief, bound together and yet kept apart by that grief: it was why Elizabeth was there; it was the rock in which her responsibilities and concerns also struggled to root themselves; it was why she understood so perfectly Jameson's concern for Hunter.

'I'll make the arrangements,' she said. 'We can travel by train from here to—'

'Alone,' Mary said.

'What?'

'I want to go alone. Hire a nurse to accompany me.'

'That's ridiculous; of course I'll come back with you.'

Mary shook her head. 'If you come back with me now you'll never be rid of it. Stay here. Wait.'

'Wait for what?' But even as she asked she knew that she would allow herself to be convinced, and knew too that Mary's reasoning formed only the smallest part of that conviction.

'Please,' Mary said.

Elizabeth nodded her agreement, and as though her final effort had been made and something precious achieved, Mary fell immediately back to sleep.

26

She saw Jameson the following day and told him what had happened. He told her his friend, the doctor, would accompany Mary home and then return alone. He said that he himself had long-overdue matters to settle, old business, and that these could be attended to by the man at the same time. Only afterwards did she realize that this was his way of preventing her from arguing against the arrangement. All this was decided in the bar of a hotel close to the casino, where Jameson had gone to visit a client.

'Will you take me to the casino?' she asked him, watching a party of Americans gathering to depart for the place.

'You're not a gambler,' he told her. But she persisted.

They went that same night. She wore what she considered to be the most fashionable of her dresses, but saw upon her arrival how poor her judgement had been. She wore jewellery

– earrings, a full necklace, several bracelets – but then removed all these at the first opportunity.

Jameson changed a wad of notes for coloured chips. He gave her half of these and took her to one of the roulette tables. She followed his lead. She won on two small, unadventurous bets and grew less cautious. She lifted drinks off a tray and gave him one. The woman beside her stood with the straps of her shoes hooked over her thumb; she saw others walking barefoot on the thick carpet. She became more daring in her wagers.

Jameson, she saw, was not a true gambler, either. He had no system, no plan for limiting his losses. He was content to place his chips on the same number spin after spin. She alone, or so it seemed to her then, saw the futility of this, but nothing she said could persuade him to change. He had one big win – thirty times his stake – but even this appeared not to excite him, or even to encourage him to move to another number. He behaved like a man who possessed an unspendable fortune, and who, because his life was dulled and blunted by this wealth, was more interested in the science and nature of loss and disappointment than that of gain or achievement; where there was nothing to lose, so there was no risk.

At the end of the night all her own chips had gone.

'How much was there?' she asked him, expecting to be told she had gambled and lost fifty or sixty pounds.

Jameson shrugged. 'A hundred and fifty, two hundred.'

He had tripled his own share. Her surprise and concern at what she had lost disappointed him and she saw this.

He cashed in his own winnings without counting the money he was given. He handed the woman at the grille a note, and then gave another to the cloakroom attendant. It was a large amount – what Elizabeth considered to be a day's wage for both women – but neither showed surprise at the gift, only the appropriate discreet gratitude.

Outside, a black space existed between the lights of the casino and those of the nearest hotels.

'Is there no pleasure at all involved in it for you?' she asked him.

'Not really. Not like you mean. The same pleasure another man might get, say, by pointing a pistol into the darkness of the town and pulling the trigger.'

It struck her as a strange remark, a strange comparison to make, but she said nothing.

'Risk and chance are grossly overrated,' he said. 'Mostly by people whose lives contain neither.'

'Lives like mine, you mean?'

'Don't worry – you're in the majority.'

'And the select minority consists largely of men like yourself?'

'I never think about it.' If he had heard the veiled criticism, then he showed no sign of it.

They walked in silence for several minutes. Then he said, 'I can make all the arrangements for Mary.'

'There's more than enough money in the bank,' she said.

'I'll pay Osborne what you lost tonight.'

It seemed an exorbitant sum to her, but she stopped herself from remarking on this. It was the first time she had heard the doctor referred to by his name.

'Does it surprise you that I'm not going back with her?' she asked him.

'Not really. I can see that to most it would be the logical solution, but that in itself isn't a good enough reason for doing it.'

'People might think me callous, that I have responsibilities.' She wanted to be convinced.

'And some people might see the truth of the matter.'

'Which is what?' She stopped walking and pulled his arm so that he faced her. 'Which is what?'

'That the time has come for you to sever yourself from her, and to do it now, while the opportunity still exists.'

'Meaning what?'

'You know precisely what I mean. I'm not being cruel, only realistic. You asked me to tell you because you knew what I was going to say. The time has come for you to decide for yourself what kind of life it is you're entering into.'

The remark silenced her. Their breath rose in plumes in the night air.

'She isn't a weight around my neck,' she said.

He didn't answer, and she, in turn, could not bring herself to ask him if he would accept the same irrational argument when the time came for him to sever himself from Hunter.

'I want to go back there,' she said, indicating the casino illuminations now far behind them.

He looked at his watch and told her it was four in the morning.

27 _____

She woke to see a dense fog covering the valley floor. She could see neither the lake nor the road which skirted it, and it seemed to her as though a dam had burst higher up in the valley and this sea of cloud had rushed down on them in the night. Beneath her, the bare tops of the trees emerged from the fog like reeds from shallows. From her vantage point she could see the height at which this cloud grew thin; the distant peaks were visible to her like some far-off rugged shore, a watery sun already rising and brightening above them. She saw, too, where some movement in the depths of the fog disturbed its surface. She imagined the boats, the traffic and the people moving through it as though they were walking on the bed of an ocean. Something higher up caught her eyes, and she watched as a sunlit flock of gulls passed slowly above.

The changed view mesmerized her, and she studied it, realizing how little she remembered of what the fog obscured. She guessed where the lake began, where the road ran, where the flower beds and other buildings stood. The fog curled against the glass of her window. She saw where chimney smoke rose briefly above this cloud, cooled and then fell back into it and thickened it.

She left the window and put coal on the embers of her fire. Sparks blew out at her, dying wherever they touched.

She dressed and went down to the dining-room.

She was late and there were few other diners.

Four days had passed since she had gone to the casino with Jameson, and today she intended visiting him and Emil in the studio they shared. He had given her instructions on how to find the place.

But first she would visit Mary. Arrangements were already being made for her departure, and the knowledge that she was soon to return home seemed to Elizabeth to have encouraged her. She could still not bring herself to eat all the liquid food she was now being fed, but she did at least make some effort. The doctor was no longer so insistent in his treatment of her: she would live until her departure, and hopefully be strong enough and sufficiently recovered to withstand the rigours of the journey home; these were now the limits to his concern.

The Italian family sat at the far side of the dining-room. The husband called for Elizabeth to join them, explaining that this was their final day in the town, that they were returning to Milan later that afternoon. This was the last she would see of them, and for that reason alone she accepted the man's invitation. The children were subdued. The husband made a space for her beside him, watching closely as she slid into the chair. He took her hand and kissed it. His wife busied herself with the youngest of the children while he did this.

'We looked out for you,' he said. 'We wanted to ask you to join us for dinner last night. Perhaps you and your friend, Mr Jameson. It would have been an honour.'

His wife said something sharp to him. Elizabeth did not understand the words, only the message they conveyed. Her husband flicked his hand at her. It was a gesture close to a slap.

He knows about Jameson, Elizabeth thought. He knew about Jameson, and he knew, or imagined he knew, about her relationship with him. Perhaps he had even bought whatever it was Jameson and Emil manufactured and sold. The more she listened to him, the more she felt him watching her, so the more convinced she became that this was the source of her new attraction for the man.

His wife said something and the children picked up their glasses of milk and drank from them. When she spoke to her husband, he ignored her.

The maître d' arrived and asked Elizabeth what she wanted. She ordered her meal without looking up at him.

They all know, she thought, every one of them.

The waitress Monique cleared a nearby table, and the two of them exchanged a glance.

She asked the Italian how he and his family would travel home and he told her in every detail. He told her how much he regretted having to leave, but that he owned a business, several businesses, employing hundreds of people, all of them depending on his return. He told her all this in English, further excluding his wife from the exchange.

'I'll tell Jameson you were asking after him,' Elizabeth said.

'Is there anything else you want me to tell him, to ask him?' She raised her eyebrows to the man.

He hesitated at this. His wife wiped the face of the smallest child.

'You might give him my card,' he said. He took one from his wallet. 'You see that it contains the address of my office.'

'Not your home address?'

'No, not that.'

The longer they continued, the more she enjoyed his discomfort.

'Anything else?'

'Just that I would appreciate very much hearing from him. We businessmen must form strong alliances if we are to survive in this new world.' Now he was talking merely to disguise meaning, to camouflage it with dead words.

'Of course you must,' she said. She slipped the card casually into her bag.

'You won't lose it, will you?' he said. 'You will remember to give it to him. He may wish to contact me.'

'Of course,' she said. She dropped the bag to the floor beside her. He watched as it landed and then slowly fell over.

Her food arrived, and as it was put on the table, the Italian rose and announced that it was time for them to leave. He was now angry – whether because he felt insulted by her, or threatened, she could not tell. His wife complained that the children had not finished eating. He shouted at her, threw down his napkin onto his own empty plate and left them.

His wife watched him go. His anger did not concern her.

'Jameson,' the woman said. 'Mr Jameson.'

'You understand?' Elizabeth asked her.

'Of course I understand. Only *he* thinks I am stupid. How can a wife not know and understand such things?' She turned back to her children, hurrying them through the remainder of their meal.

28

The fog persisted. The street lamps remained lit through the day, as did the coloured lights beneath the trees, but neither did much to penetrate the darkness, serving instead only to heighten it and to shape a ceiling above the heads of the people beneath.

She followed the line of the railings, coming upon men and women looking out over the invisible lake, more impressed, it seemed to her, by what they could not now see than by what had been visible to them before the fog. Not even the edge of the water was to be seen, only the sound of it slapping against the stone steps, and the creak of the moored boats. She saw the chains and cables running from the quays into nothing. None of the larger ferries were sailing, and their stationary illuminated outlines rose up through the fog further from the shore.

She went from the lake into the town square. Jameson had assured her that the studio was only a ten-minute walk from there.

She entered the side street he had named. It was cobbled and stepped and she rose quickly. The fog was thinner here, kept out by the narrowness of the alley and by the buildings on either side.

She counted the passageways leading off to her right. She stopped at the tenth of these and searched for the sign Jameson had told her was hanging there. She could not see it. She went on, but there was no sign at the entrance to the next alley, either. Retracing her steps, she found what she was looking for further down the hill. She had either miscounted, or had passed a passage so narrow that she had mistaken it for a doorway.

The one she entered now was little more than twice her own width. Windowless walls rose on each side of her, and she was quickly beyond all hearing of the street behind. The studio was again on the right, a minute's walk along the passage. She had asked Jameson for a more specific address and he had told her there was none. There were no other photographers nearby; she would not mistake it.

She passed several shops. Women and children congregated in the doorways; some of these whispered as she passed; she heard their voices long before she arrived where they stood. One of the shops was a butcher's, and in its window lay the whole steaming carcass of a recently-killed pig. Three men scraped at the flesh with curved blades; another stood beside them sharpening knives.

The alley widened slightly, a gutter ran down its centre. She began to think that again she had come too far when she saw ahead of her an illuminated window filled with framed photographs. A gas lamp burned above the door.

She paused, preparing herself. Ahead of her, beyond the studio, the passage grew narrow again and ended at an archway and a closed gate.

She looked at the pictures in the window. They were all landscapes, family groups and portraits, identical to the ones she had already seen. The name of the business and its original proprietor, long-dead or vanished, she imagined, was spelled across the upper window in flaking paint. The flame above her wavered.

She had expected Jameson to answer her knock, but instead the door was opened by a man who seemed surprised that she had not gone straight in.

He led her into the shop and she saw that this, too, was little different from the ones she had already visited.

The man lifted the counter and went behind it. He waited for her to speak.

'I came to see Jameson,' she said.

'You're Elizabeth,' he said immediately. He came back out to her and shook her hand. 'He's upstairs. With a customer.'

'Who will no doubt not wish to be disturbed,' she said.

'Have a seat,' he said.

He sat beside her and offered her a cigarette, scrutinized her as she lit it.

'Are you Emil?' she asked him.

'Emil Simenon. I should say "At your service", but I doubt that's the case.'

He was younger than Jameson – or possibly not, considering how she had miscalculated Jameson's age – French, and outgoing. He possessed none of Jameson's reserve. She supposed he might be called flamboyant.

'He's told me all about you, of course,' he said. 'He is planning a visit to the glacier with you. You really ought to see it before it's too late. I was there earlier, taking pictures of intrepid explorers. Intrepid enough, that is, to walk fifty yards from their coach and then insist that I make them appear to be in the middle of a wilderness in the photograph. They were back in their hotel congratulating themselves on their adventure by midday.'

'And you were back here?' Jameson had frequently mentioned a visit to the ice field, but had arranged nothing more definite.

'Of course. Developing the plates and making sure they got what they wanted.'

'Is this all your stock?' She looked around her for the hidden cabinet or case.

'You mean do I keep my more illicit, my more sought-after wares in here? Of course not.' There was neither surprise nor reproach in his voice. 'There's another room.' He indicated a curtained doorway. 'A sense of decorum, you understand.' The accent with which he spoke English made it seem as though he were making fun of her, but she knew by the way he behaved towards her that this was not the case.

'Listen,' he told her, cocking his head to the ceiling. 'If you listen hard enough you can hear them turning the dead pages of some long-lost scribbler or other. The man up there is a serious collector, very wealthy.'

'Is it a lucrative trade?'

'That depends on what one is prepared to do. Like my own, it is a trade that must constantly change, that must remain responsive to the demands of its market. Am I phrasing all this delicately enough for you? I don't want to insult you by being evasive.'

She wondered how much Jameson had told him.

'I'm not keeping you from your work?' she said.

'It can wait. I'd rather sit and talk to you. The women

who—' He stopped abruptly. 'I'm sorry, I shouldn't have put it so crudely.'

'I do understand,' she said.

'I believe you.'

'I know some of the waitresses at the hotel,' she said.

'Where they are treated like slaves and paid a pittance. At least here the pay is good. They are not what most people believe them to be.' He stopped at the sound of scraping chairs and footsteps above them. 'He won't be long. He knows you're coming. He said you would arrive early and then wait outside until the exact time.'

'Can I see?' she said, indicating the curtained door.

'I would rather you waited for Jameson, but we can pretend you are a customer if you like.'

'Do other women come here, customers, alone?'

'Of course.'

'Many?'

'No, not many. I would say only one in twenty of our customers is female. Do you know how many brothels there are in this town? Most of our custom from women is for prints for their walls. Feel free.' He indicated the doorway.

'I'll wait,' she said, more for his sake than her own. She enjoyed his openness, the way he treated her. She knew Jameson would have told him very little, almost nothing.

'Postcards,' he said. 'Most of our trade involves the manufacture of postcards.'

She stopped herself from asking him if he meant views of the lake, the town, the mountains.

They both fell silent at the sound of footsteps coming down the stairs. Jameson entered the shop, followed by an old man. Jameson helped the man with his coat and saw him out into the passageway.

'Did he get what he wanted?' Emil asked when he returned.

'Possibly, possibly not. He's happy with what I gave him. I'll go on looking for the rest.' Jameson looked at Elizabeth as he spoke. 'Have you been here long?' he asked her.

'Not very.'

'I was keeping her amused with tales of the sordid little lives we lead here,' Emil said. 'Tales of the terrible and degrading depths to which we have sunk.'

'She knows that already,' Jameson said. 'Shall we go upstairs?'

'She wanted to see the studio,' Emil said, rising.

The shop was warm, filled with the smoke of their cigarettes and the smell of burning gas. There was the smell, too, of perfume, and of the chemicals used in developing prints.

'Why not?' Jameson said. He held the curtain aside and opened the door to reveal a short corridor, at the end of which was a second door.

Emil led the way. He unlocked this second door and went in.

The room beyond was in darkness. He lit a wax taper and then used this to ignite the mantles on each wall. The light from these rose slowly, revealing the room to her in rising glows and falling shadows, theatrically, calculated, just as a stage might be lit in dramatic sequence.

A rack of costumes stood along one wall; there were several sofas and a variety of tables; she saw the underside of a folding bed fastened to another wall. Drapes and rolls of cloth, emerald, sunflower yellow and scarlet, were spread at her feet. A small palm tree made of card stood in one corner. Against another wall hung a painted backdrop: the lake, the mountains, the balustrade of an overlooking balcony. More panoramas hung behind this; a dozen others were rolled and propped in a corner. There was a fireplace, before which was spread the skin of a polar bear. She saw other skins – leopard, zebra, tiger – bundled and tied on a dresser beside the fireplace.

'Anything you want,' Emil said, 'we can reproduce. The Orient, the African jungle, the endless desert. Slave girls, handmaidens, Amazons.' He picked up a spear from where it lay on the floor. A plumed helmet stood on one of the couches. The smell of perfume was stronger here than in the shop. A gramophone stood beside the door. There were no windows that she could see; if they existed they were hidden by the backdrops and tapestries. A large, ornate mirror, pocked with age, hung above the fireplace.

In one corner the carpet was rolled back and a tripod and camera stood on the bare boards. Boxes of equipment stood around it.

The room was larger than it first appeared. She moved around it, inspecting its contents.

'I wish I'd come sooner,' she said to Jameson.

'This is Emil's domain. I live and work upstairs.'

'Are there any of your photographs in here?' she asked Emil.

He indicated the couch upon which the plumed helmet sat. 'Do you want to see?' He looked at Jameson, clearly expecting him to answer for her.

Jameson said nothing.

Elizabeth shook her head. 'I just wondered,' she said. She continued moving around. She looked at herself in the mirror, almost stumbling over the snarling head at her feet.

Along the corridor, the shop door rattled open and shut and Emil left immediately, closing the studio door behind him.

'Is it what you expected?' Jameson asked her when they were alone.

'I don't know. I suppose so.'

'He was working in here last night, late, until one, two. Monique was here.' He looked slowly around him. 'We'll go upstairs,' he said. He reached up and extinguished the first of the lights.

The room was darkened in stages, just as it had been illuminated in stages, until it was as black and as devoid of shape and content as when the door had first been opened.

They went back along the short corridor. Jameson paused to listen at the door leading into the shop before opening it and leading her through.

Emil was in conversation with a young woman, little more than a girl, poorly dressed and sitting where Elizabeth had sat. Jameson apologized for interrupting them and took Elizabeth through to the staircase. The girl was unconcerned by their presence. She greeted Jameson and simply watched Elizabeth, waiting for her to leave before resuming her conversation with Emil. She held the front of her coat together at her chest. She wore soft shoes. Her legs were bare and there was dirt on her shins.

Elizabeth passed through the room without speaking.

29

The first of the winter storms arrived. Like the fog, it came in the night, sweeping down the valley from the east, fanning its sleet and snow to the west and south. The strong wind along the lake was uneven, gusting and falling, driving the snow across the water; the surrounding forests swayed like fields of blown wheat.

It was dark when Elizabeth woke. Sleet pattered against her window. Shutters rattled in their frames all along the hotel front. It was not yet three. Her curtains billowed and sagged in the draught. There had been a fall of soot in her fireplace, and she smelled this the instant she woke, believing it to be smoke.

She went to the window. The snow spun in circles around the street lights below. The illuminated sign which normally shone through the night above the hotel entrance had been switched off. The few trees she could make out shook against each other, and for the first time she saw fountains and waves of spume curl high above the edge of the promenade.

She heard running footsteps in the corridor outside; someone shouted. Putting on her dressing-gown, she opened her door. One of the hotel porters ran past her carrying two empty pails. She asked him what was wrong, but the man was in too great a hurry to stop and answer her.

She followed him to the top of the stairs.

The manager stood below her. He wore a smoking jacket. There was a woman with him. He called out orders to the porter and to the few others already gathered there. A sheet of water flowed under the hotel door. Everything the manager shouted, the woman beside him repeated, adding her own urgent note to the proceedings. She was taller than him, and with her hair elaborately styled and fastened up at the back of her head.

As she watched from above, guessing what had happened, Elizabeth saw the manager push the woman behind the hotel desk and then into his office. A fire burned in the room, lamps were lit. The woman protested at being ordered away, but the manager continued pushing her. He followed her into the office, pulling the door shut behind them.

Others appeared, mostly kitchen staff. Two men rolled up the carpets in the entrance, revealing the full extent to which the water had spread over the tiles beneath. Several other guests arrived to stand beside Elizabeth and watch. They asked her what was happening, but she merely pointed in explanation.

Something heavy blew against the hotel door, smashing one of its coloured panes. The tip of a severed branch appeared and was then sucked away. Snow began to blow in.

The manager reappeared alone several minutes later. He took a mop and joined the line of men clearing the water. Someone stuffed a rolled sheet or curtain along the bottom of the door. Snow continued to blow in through the broken glass.

After several minutes of this frantic activity, the emergency was over. The water coming in was stemmed, and most of what had already collected was cleared up. The men and women below relaxed.

For the first time, the manager saw that they were being watched. He came halfway up the stairs to where Elizabeth and the other guests stood.

'Nothing serious,' he said. 'A little water. The outer door was left open, a broken branch, the wind, that's all.' He behaved as though he himself were responsible for the damage, practising his explanation in advance of having to report to the hotel owners.

Most of those standing beside Elizabeth returned to their rooms.

Someone nailed a panel of wood over the broken pane. Several others went to the window to look out into the snow-filled darkness before returning to their beds or their work. Men from the kitchen congregated in the lobby and drank the coffee which a waiter took out to them. The sense of relief now that the night's small drama was over translated itself into raised voices and laughter.

Elizabeth returned to her room.

The shutters still banged along the front of the hotel. Snow had started to collect on her own window; it blew across her small balcony. The lamp beside her bed wavered and flared in the new draughts.

She returned to her bed, but knew she would not sleep. She tried to read, but was preoccupied with thoughts of

Mary, who was leaving the clinic and the town and returning home that same day. She hoped the storm had done nothing to interrupt the passage of the trains. She knew that Mary would be awake, listening to the same wind, the same few thoughts in her mind.

30

The storm brought down a tree across the road to the clinic, and a section of this had to be sawn through and removed to allow the traffic to pass. Men chopped at the branches and trunk on either side of the road. Propped on its stouter limbs, the fallen tree rested ten feet above the ground, shaking and sagging each time some part of it was removed. Horses waited to drag away the cut timber. The few pedestrians along the road were led under the trunk by the foresters.

Directly above the lake, part of the road had collapsed beneath the weight of the fallen tree, exposing the crushed rock of its foundations. Elizabeth saw how quickly this had been scoured by the wind and water, creating a half-crater which overhung the shore, and in which snow had collected. A makeshift barrier had been built around the hole. She asked the cab driver if there was any other way around the obstacle, knowing this was unlikely. He threw up his hands in answer. Even reversing and returning to the town was beyond him. He turned off his engine and waited. Elizabeth considered leaving and completing her journey on foot, but it was still another mile, and the road was snow-covered in some places, and flooded in others where dirty meltwater streamed down from above.

Further back, she had seen where other fallen branches had already been cleared from the road and left in high tangles along the lakeshore.

Eventually, after a delay of an hour, they were able to move. The driver reached the clinic, but refused to enter and negotiate the paths over which the meltwater flowed in shallow rivers. He pulled off the road and waited for her.

The storm had died by dawn, but there were still flurries of snow in the cold wind. She was not properly dressed against this, and her face grew numb as she walked from the road to the clinic entrance. The ground beneath her was waterlogged. Men laid planks beneath the wheels of an ambulance.

She went first to see the doctor.

'She has been waiting for you since daybreak,' he said. His every remark seemed a rebuke to her. She had absolved him of all responsibility for what was happening to Mary, and everything he now said made this clear to her.

'I was delayed. The storm,' she said. It was pointless to explain any further – as pointless as fighting or resisting the man.

'She was dressed and waiting at five. Five in the morning. Ridiculous. She sat at the window watching the storm. She was concerned.'

'That the track would be blocked?'

'I don't know. She was concerned about everything.' He

turned his attention back to the sheet of paper he had been reading upon her arrival.

'I'll go to her,' Elizabeth said.

'First the forms.'

'What forms?'

'The forms for her release. Everything must be made official, the exchange of responsibilities properly acknowledged.'

She almost laughed at hearing him say this; before, there had been some room for negotiation; now there was none, only a single road ahead.

'You must mean the forms whereby you wash your hands of her.' She regretted the remark immediately. In the past he would have countered with some platitude. 'Give them to me,' she said.

He spread the sheets and she signed them without reading them.

'And if she falls ill along her journey home?' she said.

He sighed and gathered up the papers. 'It would be better if the person – I won't say doctor – to whom her health is now to be entrusted were also present to sign. That way there would be no misunderstanding. I assume the man has shown you his qualifications, I assume you have seen them.' He knew this was unlikely.

'He knows what's wrong. He knows as much as you do,' she said.

'Still . . . ' He shook his head. He put the papers in a file and fastened a ribbon around it. 'Should you or anyone else require to see your sister-in-law's notes during her treatment here at any time in the future . . .' He tapped a finger on the sealed file.

'Surely all your notes will do is show anyone who might be interested how miserably you've failed her.' Only then did it occur to her that he was talking about a coroner, a surgeon performing an autopsy perhaps. The thought stopped her.

'And where is her companion?' he asked. He dropped the file into a metal cabinet and locked the door.

'He's meeting us at the station. He said he'd call if there was any problem with the train. He and Jameson have arranged everything.'

'There has been no call,' he said.

'Good.'

'Or perhaps the telephone lines have come down; it has happened before. Frequently. They pass through the trees, you see.'

She wondered if he was being deliberately provocative, but knew that he was as anxious for Mary to leave as Mary now was to go.

'I'm sure there are no problems,' she said. She also knew how tightly the schedule of Mary's return to England had been organized, how one delay would lead unavoidably to a sequence of others.

She had spoken to both Jameson and Osborne before coming to the clinic. Jameson had offered to accompany her there, but she knew that this was not what Mary would have wanted. She regretted that Mary had not had a good night's rest; she would need whatever strength she still possessed for the journey.

Osborne would do all he could to help her sleep on each of the trains on which they travelled. Arrangements had already been made in London, and further away still, in Oxford. And listening as Osborne told her about these arrangements, Elizabeth had realized for the first time how distant those familiar places had become to her, how great an effort would now be required of her to return to them.

'Down comes a tree and down come the cables with it.' He made his arm into a falling tree.

'When did she last eat?'

'Eat? She never eats. She is fed; it is not eating. Fed, she is fed.'

'All right, when was she last fed?'

'I would have to consult my notes.'

'Just tell me.'

'Yesterday evening. Before the storm. Seven o'clock.'

It was then midday. The train left at three.

'I need some transport down to the road,' she said.

'Impossible. You were to make all the arrangements your-self.'

'And if she walks to the road and collapses on the way?' She watched as he calculated more precisely the limits of his responsibility.

'Go to her,' he said. 'I'll arrange something. You must appreciate – the storm . . .'

She rose and left him.

Entering Mary's room, she was surprised to see Mary sipping tea from a china cup, the saucer balanced in her free hand. She already wore her coat with its fur collar, her gloves and her hat.

'I knew you'd be late,' Mary said immediately. She put down the cup and saucer, as though holding them had been something done solely in preparation for Elizabeth's arrival. 'I'm all packed.' She indicated her bags. Elizabeth had sent her trunk directly from the hotel to the station.

Elizabeth began to explain the arrangements.

'I want to go now,' Mary said. 'I'd rather wait on the train in the station than here.'

Elizabeth picked up the bags. There was almost nothing in them. The books and magazines she had delivered to Mary over the previous two weeks lay scattered around the room, most of them, she guessed, unread.

Mary saw her looking. 'The girls who come in will gather them up,' she said. 'They take everything else.' She fastened a scarf beneath her collar.

They walked to the clinic entrance. A car was waiting. The doctor stood talking to its driver. He saw Elizabeth and Mary and stepped aside, holding open the door for them.

'See how well she looks,' he said loudly to Elizabeth.

Elizabeth said nothing in reply.

Beside her, Mary sat gasping at the slight exertion.

The doctor closed the door. '*Bon voyage*,' he called out.

'Are you all right?' Elizabeth said to Mary.

Mary nodded once.

Elizabeth imagined the doctor watching them all the way down to the lake road. The driver remained silent throughout the short journey.

At the road, Elizabeth told Mary to stay where she was. She crossed to where the cab waited and offered the driver money to carry Mary to her seat. The request surprised him, but he agreed. Mary made no effort to resist. She sat with her collar pulled close to her face, only her eyes and nose visible. And seeing her like that, swaddled, hidden, it was not difficult for Elizabeth to believe that her sister-in-law was at last, and against all expectation, recovering, that her cure had started, that she had never been so seriously ill in the first instance, and that everyone, Mary included, had over-reacted and then panicked because of the uncertainty of what was happening and because there had been no other course open to them.

Mary said little on the journey into town, commenting occasionally on the lake or on the snow which still clung to the canopy of the trees. More often than not she simply pointed instead of speaking, leaving Elizabeth to fill the silence.

They were delayed again at the fallen tree, but only briefly this time. A section of the trunk had been removed, allowing the cars and carriages to pass through. The web of roots with their thin cake of soil rose twenty feet into the air. Elizabeth pointed all this out to Mary, but Mary, her few nods of acknowledgement aside, now kept her eyes on the road ahead, anxious for her first sight of the town.

Jameson and Osborne were waiting for them at the station. Mary put on a show for them. Osborne had with him a wheelchair. Mary protested at the use of this, but allowed herself to be helped into it. Elizabeth tucked blankets over her legs, drawing back as Mary flinched at some sudden pain. Elizabeth did nothing to alert the others to this.

'I want to say goodbye here, now,' Mary said unexpectedly.

Jameson and Osborne moved away.

Elizabeth knelt beside her and kissed her.

'Don't make me talk,' Mary whispered. 'Tell Osborne I'm tired, sedated.'

'Write to me,' Elizabeth told her. 'A telegram when you get home. Tell Osborne to send one.'

Mary nodded.

'I'll let you know of my own return.'

She felt Mary push her away.

She rose and returned to Jameson. There was nothing she needed to say to Osborne. He gave her his hand and told her not to worry. She wondered if he and Jameson had made secret arrangements whereby Mary would be taken from the train at any of its stops if she became too sick to continue. But it was beyond her to ask. Like the doctor at the clinic, she had long since absolved herself of the privileges conferred by responsibility: the baton had been handed on.

Osborne pushed Mary to the waiting train. A guard helped lift her on board.

'Come away now,' Jameson told Elizabeth, and she let him lead her out of the station. He had never before held her so tightly.

Outside, it had grown dark. Cars and carriages came and went. The last of the departing tourists congregated in the booking halls and waiting-rooms, their luggage piled around them. They looked to her like a small surprised army in retreat. It had grown much colder since the storm. Water had been trodden over the polished floors and lay in pools. The voices of children echoed in the high room.

Jameson went with her back to the hotel. It started to snow again before they left the centre of the town. She watched the flakes melt into the lake.

Later, in the night, she woke with a start from a forgotten dream. She lay in the darkness and silence remembering what had happened, and only then, having remembered every detail of the day, did she finally cry for the lost, sick woman that Mary had become, drawn off now into her own uncertain orbit through the infinite darkness of her suffering.

She spent the next three days alone, in the hotel, taking her meals in her room, remaining there even when the chambermaids came in to clean and to change her bedding. She spoke to no-one; no-one spoke to her. And then on the fourth day, Jameson called suggesting a visit to the glacier before the ice and the weather grew too unpredictable. The idea appealed to her, following her confinement, and she agreed to go. He told her what to wear and when he would call for her.

As before, she waited for him in the hotel lobby. She saw the manager there and told him where she was going. The sound of her own voice seemed strange to her.

The manager considered this for a moment. 'Impossible,' he said.

She imagined at first that he was referring to how she was dressed.

'There are no guides,' he said. 'You have hired someone privately?'

'I'm going with Jameson.' She rose from where she sat.

'Jameson?' He shook his head.

'What do you mean, there are no guides?'

'Look around you. Too few tourists. All the organized visits ended a month ago. There are still men who will take you up on to the ice, who know the few safe routes across the glacier, but now you must hire them privately.' He rubbed his thumb and fingers together to suggest the expense of this.

'That's what he's done,' she said.

'Do you know the man's name? Some are very unreliable. You should have told me you were going. I could have recommended someone.'

It was clear to her that he didn't believe her, but she was less affected by his animosity towards Jameson now that she understood its true cause.

'I'm sure Captain Jameson knows what he's doing,' she said. 'I doubt he'd be taking me, otherwise.'

'Of course. Perhaps Captain Jameson himself has become such an expert.'

A horn sounded in the street below; Jameson waved to her from a cab.

'He won't come in?' the manager said. 'He visits us less and less often.'

'I imagine there's a very good reason for that, don't you?'

Once in the cab, she told Jameson everything the man had said and implied.

'I know what I'm doing,' he told her.

'Have you been recently?'

'No, not recently.'

'He said it changed from year to year.'

'So?' He rapped on the glass and called for the driver to stop.

'The more he told me, the more I wanted to go,' she said.

Jameson rapped again and they went on.

The journey lasted an hour. They passed the hospital and the convent. The guard at the hospital gates waved to them. Beyond the convent they passed three nuns leading a horse dragging logs from a track amid the trees. She recognized none of the women.

She had not been so far in this direction before. The road grew steeper, rising and falling in mounds which grew progressively higher.

The cab stopped at a gate across the road and the driver climbed out to open it.

The road beyond was less well maintained, rutted, and lined with water-filled holes.

Eventually, the trees thinned and they emerged onto a broad stony plateau.

'There,' Jameson said. He pointed to the wall of ice ahead of them. She leaned out of the cab to look.

The glacier filled the narrow valley, its edges folded against the exposed rock on both sides. The vegetation ahead of it had all but disappeared, replaced by a wrack of dark rock, of screes and scattered trunks.

The cab pulled off the road and stopped.

Jameson arranged with the driver for them to be picked up later. The man handed out the rucksack and sticks from the space beside him.

It was colder on that higher land close to the ice. Jameson sat beside the road and changed his shoes for a pair of boots. He gave her a pair. She watched the departing cab until she could no longer see it. The boots felt stiff, too large for her feet. She looked again at the ice. Water ran from it, just as she had seen it run from the ice at the far side of the lake, and it occurred to her only then that the town in its cradle of valley was surrounded on all sides by this living ice, kept only in temporary abeyance by the summer warmth and the moat of the lake.

'What would happen if the temperature fell over succeeding years?' she asked him.

'You mean before the place was crushed out of existence?'

'Until it became a problem.'

'It isn't going to happen. Apparently, there's less ice now than there ever was. They only have to keep the railway and the road to the west open. Don't worry about the place.'

'Does the river freeze?'

'Over some of its length. Up here. Not where it enters the lake. The lake itself freezes in its bays and shallows, especially in the shade of the far side. Ice sometimes floats across to the town.'

She walked ahead of him to the glacier. 'How do we get up there?' The closer she came to the sheer wall, the less convinced she became of their ability to mount it.

Jameson walked at an angle to her. 'We climb beside it. There are gulleys. We follow one of these until a way out on to the surface of the ice presents itself. Don't worry. The guides have been using them all summer. They're well enough marked.' He stopped at a post driven into the rock. She felt reassured by this. He told her what food and drink he had in the rucksack. The driver would return for them long before darkness fell.

They walked for half an hour, rising gradually. They passed beyond the limits of the ice. A second post marked the entrance to a gulley. Jameson led the way. They walked up loose scree. He pointed out to her where the ground was firm, which boulders were secure, which were loose, and which showed signs of recent movement and were to be avoided. She stumbled several times as the path slid away beneath her. In places it was necessary to climb rock steps. He helped her up these. She paused frequently to catch her breath, and when she dislodged the stones beneath her she stopped to watch them rattle down the slope below.

'Will we go down the same way?' she asked him.

He studied the path and said, 'Probably not.'

In places, she lost sight of the ice, but wherever they now went she could feel it. Water drained down the path they climbed, forcing them to detour briefly on to steeper, un-trodden slopes.

The gulley became a chasm, and they entered its dripping walls. Again, she could not see how to continue, but Jameson led her upwards. He pointed out the smaller posts driven into the rock faces.

Coming out of the chasm, they emerged onto a flat expanse and she saw that they were at last level with the surface of the ice. It was a dramatic revelation. The sun shining down on the glacier blinded her. Jameson gave her some tinted glasses. She estimated that it had taken them almost an hour to climb three or four hundred feet.

She walked towards the level plain of ice, pausing where it came abruptly to the rock at her feet. She continued out onto it, surprised to find she could walk on it. She had expected it to be wet and slippery, but a powder of soil and small stones gave her a good grip; most of the meltwater drained swiftly away. Jameson wandered alongside her on a parallel course. She estimated the glacier to be half a mile across. The black, scoured rock of the upper valley rose abruptly on the far side.

As she walked, she imagined she could feel the gentle movement of the ice beneath her feet.

'It's possible,' Jameson told her. He warned her against going too close to the leading face of the glacier, where the most fissures occurred, and where the ice was most active. He warned her too against leaping over even small cracks, telling her to avoid them by walking carefully around them.

She followed him away from the edge towards the mass of snow-covered peaks from which the glacier was fed. In places the surface was ridged, crumpled by some deep disturbance.

'Over there,' he called to her, waiting for her to join him. He pointed to where a mass of rock broke the surface of the ice, rising above it by seventy or eighty feet. Fragments of stone lay at its base. 'We can climb onto it and eat there.'

She looked back in the direction they had come, but could see nothing of the forest, pastures, lake or the town beneath. The ice stretched in a dazzling plain, destroying perspective and all idea of distance, appearing to run on into the mountains in the west, which she knew to be at least twenty miles away.

They reached the outcrop and climbed onto it. She saw where ledges and seats had been hammered out of the loose rock. The litter of other meals, empty bottles, bones, peel and pieces of food lay scattered there.

'Look,' he said as she arrived at a broad ledge beside him, fifteen feet above the surface of the ice. She shielded her eyes. In the distance, following the line of the valley side were six small figures, moving in a manner which suggested to her that they were roped together.

'Listen,' he told her. He cupped a hand to his ear. 'Sound carries across the ice. You can hear them talking.' She copied him and heard the unintelligible voices of the distant walkers. She heard too the crackle of a rockslide and saw where a length of frozen scree had just then come loose and was sliding down onto the ice. She watched as individual boulders and stones spread quickly outwards over the lubricated surface, some travelling several hundred yards before coming to rest.

'Have you been here before?' she asked him.

'I came here with Hunter four months ago.'

'They let you bring him?'

'They didn't know. I told Armstrong and Sinclair. I thought it might do him some good, let him clear his head.'

They ate the food he had brought. There were bottles of water and a flask of wine.

'I heard a strange thing yesterday,' he said.

She shaped the half-empty rucksack into a cushion and leaned back on it, closing her eyes and turning her face into the strong sun.

'Oh?'

'A customer in the shop.'

She waited for him to go on.

'He used the expression "between the wars". Have you ever heard anything more terrible in its implications? Do you think he was right to think like that? Is that how we will all come to think, how we will *have* to think?'

'I suppose it depends on whether or not you accept that aggression and the release of that aggression is a natural part of what we are,' she said.

'Of what men are, you mean.'

'I suppose so.'

He said nothing for several minutes after that.

She watched the distant figures fade from view in the glare. Large birds circled high above them.

'I used to believe that what I did – my bookselling – was all I wanted. It used to sustain me, excite me; it fed all my appetites. When I took over the running of the business I had hopes of bringing it properly to the Continent. I wanted it to be much more than it was. My own passion was for the seventeenth century – pamphlets, diaries, Books of Scripture, personal instruction and religious duty, most of them gathered in from private collections.'

'There must be a considerable number of private collections being sold off now,' she said.

'There are. The war saw to that. Thousands of collections. Everything you could possibly want. And all at good prices. Death duties – what a phrase.'

'Is that why it no longer appeals to you? Is that why you became . . .' She waited for him to answer.

'You can say it,' he said, but then went on before she could speak. 'My father died an old man only a month after war was declared. My brothers were both killed. My mother died twelve years ago. Last year I sold all our stock. I sold it all before those thousands of private collections flooded the market. I cut away all my anchors, you see. At least, all the ones that had not been cut away for me. I knew what belonged to that world, just as I know what belongs to this one.'

Sometimes, both then and afterwards, it seemed to her as though he were talking to two different people, one an intimate, the other merely a business acquaintance, or perhaps someone taking notes of what he said, keeping a record for some third party to examine later. But what she did not then understand, and what she never fully understood afterwards, was the precise nature of her own role in these proceedings, the true extent to which she herself was becoming a part of this strategy of loss, withdrawal and self-destruction.

'Did you know about the dealers in this place before you came here?'

He nodded. 'I used to think I was performing a kind of penance.'

'For what sins?'

'For unimaginable sins.'

'You surely can't still believe that.'

'Can't I? Tell me, did you nurse your brother yourself?'

The question surprised her. 'Towards the end, the very last days.'

'Was he at peace with himself?'

'No,' she said honestly.

'If he'd recovered, survived, do you think he would have coped with being blind?'

'No. He used to paint. He wanted once to be an artist. He knew he would become an architect, but he drew and painted endlessly.'

'And I was once a great dancer,' he said, in a voice which suggested he was rewarding her intimate revelation with one of his own.

'I can imagine you were,' she said.

'Can you?' He was genuinely surprised.

'I think so.'

'And can you imagine me once married?'

She could think of nothing to say to this.

'It lasted a month,' he said. 'One month.'

It seemed to her now that his first revelation had been a dam holding back these others, and she wondered what else might come pouring out.

'Four years ago,' he said. 'It was what is commonly referred to as an "unsuitable match". A very unsuitable match.'

'Did you love her?'

'In the beginning, perhaps. But never afterwards. It made it easy for her to go. We both regretted it by then. Some things, it seems, are built solely to collapse. We agreed on a settlement. She told me she could see nothing whatsoever of any value in my books and manuscripts. She said looking at me was no different from looking at my father. A month. I knew her for several years before that. She said it at a time when I still needed to believe that I was fulfilled and sustained by my work, before it came to disgust me as much as I had apparently come to disgust her.'

'And so you hated her for it?'

'No, not for that. I never truly hated her.' He took a swig from the flask and passed it to her.

The sun glared over the ice below, sudden flashes and shadows marking breaks in the surface. She heard both the silence and the splash of falling water.

'What then?' she said.

'I don't know. Her remark, her departure – they formed the boundary over which I had been reluctant – terrified – to cross. At the time I didn't know what to do, whether to cling to the past and sink back into it with all its comforts and securities, or whether it was best to cut it all loose and struggle up to the surface of this new world.' He picked up a handful of stones and threw them down onto the ice.

'Will you ever marry again?'

'No. I believe there is a price to pay for everything we do, for good or ill, a price, and that there is also a price to be paid – a far higher price – for everything that we have allowed to happen to us, for what we have allowed ourselves to become.'

'And how do you believe we pay that price?'

'Oh, it's quite simple – we pay it by the lives we lead. Simple as that.' He turned his attention back to the ice, throwing the stones at some imaginary target.

She felt a sudden great sympathy for him. He stood up beside her and scattered the last of the stones at his feet. He looked to her as though he were about to draw his arms together and dive off the ledge into the ice below.

He saw her watching him. 'Is there anything *you* cling to?' he said.

'What do you mean?'

'Anything at all, any person, any place, anything, an idea even, anything that you cling to above everything else. One single thing that you could not bear to lose, not even bear to have challenged or changed in any way? Just one thing or person or place to which you might be attached, from which you might draw sustenance, for the rest of your life, and for every day of that life?'

He was talking about her brother.

She could not bring herself to say it. 'There must be countless things,' she said. 'And places, and people.'

'The loss of whom or which would leave you bereft, as though part of yourself had been lost along with them?' He saw that he had pushed her too far. 'Don't answer,' he said. 'Of course those things and people exist for you.'

'Perhaps . . .' She hesitated, uncertain of what she wanted to say, of how she wanted to console him. 'Perhaps there are times, like now, when everything needs to be made anew. Perhaps one day . . .'

'What? I shall be resurrected? I have none of those precious things, none of those people.'

She wanted to say 'Hunter, Ruth, Emil, Margaret, me.' 'You have other attachments,' she said.

'Not really. Everything I touch I soil in some way. I'm not apologizing for myself. I don't feel any self-pity.'

'Which is why you feel none for anyone else.'

'Hunter, the other sick and wounded, your sister-in-law, your own lost brother, you mean?'

'Anyone.'

He laughed at this. 'So do you think I should hold myself in readiness for that miraculous day when this feeling, this humanity returns to me? Do you imagine that a life of feeling is any more or less valid than a life devoid of it? You surely can't be another of those idiots who believe that suffering ennobles the soul.' He signalled for her not to answer him. 'You can hear all this from countless others,' he said.

'I know, but if it helps you to say it . . .'

'Not really.'

'You can still tell me.' She could only wonder at the depth, at the darkness of what he had tried to tell her.

'We ought to set off back down,' he said.

They retraced their route over the surface of the ice. The sun had begun its descent into the west and she saw where the outline of sharper peaks waited to impale it.

32

Hunter met them on the lawn and walked with them back to the conservatory. He listened to everything Elizabeth told him about Mary. A telegram had arrived from Oxford the previous day. Mary and Osborne had arrived safely. It said no more. She did not even know if the journey had been prolonged, or if there had been some delay in sending the telegram; she could only guess.

Jameson interrupted them. 'Have you heard anything?' he said to Hunter.

'Not really. Only that the Board of Inquiry is still pressing Armstrong for a decision.'

'Do they suspect him of delaying?'

'What do you think?'

They arrived at the conservatory to find it full of men. The adjoining wards were being cleaned, and their occupants had been driven out. Those who could find no place beneath the glass congregated on the paved area above the lawn. There were few walkers, no men playing cricket or kicking balls. Beds and cabinets were being wheeled around inside the building and the noise of this came to them amplified.

It was clear to Elizabeth that Hunter again felt uncomfortable amid such a crowd. He suggested going back outside, and they followed the path around the side of the hospital.

'There's Armstrong,' Jameson said, indicating a man on one of the seats beneath a line of barred windows. Several patients stood at the nearest of these windows and looked passively out.

Jameson introduced Elizabeth to Armstrong. He rose and shook her hand. They sat beside him.

'He's told me about the pressure being put on you,' Jameson said.

'Him? What does he know? His mind's unbalanced. You can tell just by looking at him that he's unfit to stand trial.'

Hunter sat apart from them as Armstrong said all this, keeping himself beyond the pretence.

Watching the three men, Elizabeth wondered how swiftly everything might now happen if Hunter were deemed fit to be prosecuted. She saw how easily and fully he himself would acquiesce in what might happen to him; she knew he would make no excuses for himself, that he would abide without complaint or appeal in whatever was decided for him.

'Are they still moving men away?' Jameson asked Armstrong.

'Some. They're talking now about a new influenza epidemic. One to match last winter's.'

'Not here, surely?'

'Why not? Who knows? I doubt it. It may just be panic.

There have been several outbreaks in various French hospitals. They think this time it may come back further east and south.'

'*Who* thinks?'

Armstrong shrugged. 'There's an expert for everything. Don't ask me what good evacuating men from one place to another will do.'

'Except it will scatter them,' Jameson said. 'They'll all have to go somewhere. They'll all be back out in the open, exposed to some bureaucratic whim or other.'

'You're not telling him anything new,' Hunter said, his breath forming in the cold air.

'Go inside,' Armstrong said.

'Too crowded,' Jameson said.

'Go to your room,' Armstrong said to Hunter. 'You have my permission.'

Hunter considered this for a moment and then rose. He waited until Jameson and Elizabeth were several yards from where Armstrong remained sitting, and then he returned alone to the man and the two of them spoke in low voices. Elizabeth sensed Jameson's frustration at being excluded. She saw that just as Jameson felt the need to protect Hunter from what might now happen to him, so Hunter himself understood the need to keep some vital distance between himself and Jameson whenever these outside forces were eventually brought to bear on him. She saw too how destructive this bond between the two men might suddenly become, and she knew that when Hunter was sent for or collected then he would keep the news of his departure from Jameson until it was too late for him to intervene. She guessed that Jameson understood this too, and that this understanding between the two men remained unspoken, each of them making his own preparations.

They went through the main entrance and up a broad staircase. They were in the original building. Hunter pointed out to Elizabeth the architectural features. He spoke to her as though she understood the terms he used.

'Just go along with everything he says,' Jameson told her.

'I'm interested,' Elizabeth said. She took Hunter's arm, feeling him tense and then relax.

They were stopped at the top of the staircase by Cox.

'And where might we be going?' he said, holding out his arm as a barrier.

Hunter stopped. He raised his own arm slightly so that Elizabeth might pull back her hand, but instead she held him more firmly.

'Dr Armstrong said we might go to my room,' Hunter said. He avoided looking at Cox.

'Dr Armstrong said we might go to my room,' Cox mimicked.

'Just let us get past, Cox,' Jameson said. 'I'm sure you've got some menial task or other you could be getting on with, something more commensurate with your abilities.' He came forward until Cox's arm was across his chest. 'Put your arm down, Cox, be a good man. Don't make yourself look any more stupid or petty than you already are.'

'We're working up here,' Cox said. 'No patients back in until we're finished. You know the rules.'

'Good, then it should be nice and peaceful for us, shouldn't it.' Jameson walked past him.

Elizabeth went forward, taking Hunter with her.

'I'll come and see you later, Hunter,' Cox shouted after them. Everyone else along the corridor turned to look.

'Why not come and see me, instead,' Jameson called back.

Unhappy at having become the centre of attention, Cox turned and went down the stairs.

Elizabeth put her hand over Hunter's.

'Why does he insist?' she asked him.

'You'd have to ask him that.'

'You must resent the way he treats you.'

'Why must I?'

'He thinks Cox is a valuable reminder of what others, people elsewhere, people just as ignorant, might come to think of him,' Jameson said.

'But not if they knew the truth, surely?' Elizabeth said.

'It has no bearing,' Hunter said. 'Please, I'd rather we didn't spend our time going over old ground.'

'Me, too,' Elizabeth said.

'She agrees with me, Jameson. Two against one. Shut up.'

Jameson waited at a door ahead of them.

'Go in,' Hunter told him. 'It won't be locked.'

Jameson opened the door and waited for Elizabeth to enter first.

It was a large room, with two high windows overlooking the roof of the conservatory and the garden beyond. There was no carpet, only a bed, a table, several chairs and a bookcase filled with books.

'Make yourself at home,' Hunter said. 'I'd ring for room service, but . . .'

Against the far wall was a sink and a mounted mirror. Hunter collected two cups and a glass and rinsed these out. He filled them with water and proposed a toast: 'To Cox and all those others like him.'

'Did you read the Petronius?' Jameson asked, inspecting the bookcase.

'I tried. It's an abysmal copy. Annotated. What's the point

of an annotated copy? Who wants to be distracted by what someone else might or might not think?'

'Petronius?' Elizabeth said.

'A Roman satirist at the court of Nero,' Jameson said.

'Who slit his wrists in a bath made of sea shells,' Hunter added.

'If you live to be a hundred,' Jameson said to Elizabeth, 'you will never meet anyone as ungrateful as Hunter.' He went from the bookcase to the window and looked out.

'He slit his wrists to avoid being put to death by Nero,' Hunter said. 'It was from Petronius that I discovered that Nero had a pair of eye-glasses made from ground emeralds, and that, apparently, he regarded the world through these for days on end.'

'Much like your own rose-tinted ones,' Jameson said, then signalled his apology.

'I'm surprised you've got a room to yourself,' Elizabeth said, releasing this sudden tension between the two men.

'Privilege of rank,' Hunter told her. There was room for a further ten beds. 'Armstrong insisted. There used to be a dozen of us along this corridor, but most of them have gone now. The rooms on either side are empty. They occasionally bring in someone who's kept here for a few days before being moved on, but there are fewer and fewer of those. All you see now are the men like me, the never-ending ripples, the echoes that refuse to fall silent.'

'Ignore him,' Jameson said.

Hunter laughed and drained his cup. 'Ruth was here yesterday,' he said, knowing how effectively the remark would divert Jameson.

'Was she alone?'

'With the boy Mitchell. It seems he's taken it into his head to wander round those parts of the hospital out of bounds to him.'

'To what end?'

'Who knows? Perhaps he just wanted to make a point, all men being born equal and all that. Cox was with them. Not with them, exactly, but following on behind. Some of the others objected to the boy wanting to go into their rooms, but Cox made sure he got in.'

'How did Ruth feel about it?'

'There wasn't much she could do. I just waited by the window while she let him wander round. He wanted her to describe things to him. She did everything he asked. She seemed afraid of him. Not afraid, apprehensive.'

'And?'

'That was the strange thing. She told him lie after lie. She described wallpaper, paintings, a chandelier. She told him there were high shelves he couldn't reach filled with drink and all manner of luxuries.'

'What did Cox think of it all?'

'I'm not sure. That was strange too. I thought at first he was going to tell the boy what she was doing, but he let her go on with it.'

'What do you think she was doing?'

Hunter shrugged. 'Catch him out? Prove something to herself? Revenge? You'd have to ask her. She was caught between them. Cox never took his eyes off her. They're neither of them particularly noble characters. I imagine she was just doing what she could to keep them away from her. Whatever, it worked. Cox thought it amusing, and the boy got to hear what he wanted to hear. You know what a good actress she is.'

'He means liar,' Jameson said.

'Do *you* believe he's blind?' Elizabeth asked Hunter.

'No, I don't,' Hunter said bluntly. 'True, he walks into things, into furniture, doors, walls, but he never really injures himself. Beside, the blind don't actually do that very often. He may not see most of what he supposedly looks at, but some protective instinct, based on his sight, still exists which protects him from genuinely harming himself. I don't honestly know how you'd ever put a thing like that to the test. He might stumble into a wall and knock his arm or leg, but would he walk on to a knife, for instance, that someone held out in front of him?'

'We could try it,' Jameson said. 'Did Ruth say anything to you?'

'About what?'

'Anything. About her injuries.'

'They're hardly that. A small cut and a bruise, not much left of either.'

'No, of course.'

Elizabeth saw that Jameson regretted having asked.

'I saw her just before you arrived, with Margaret,' Hunter said. 'They were stripping the empty beds. Armstrong thinks there might be call for an isolation ward if there is another epidemic.'

'Where?'

'He wasn't certain. One of the newer buildings. Perhaps Sinclair's.'

'They can't move him out of there,' Jameson said.

'I think another epidemic would overrule most other considerations.'

There was a knock at the door and Margaret entered. She carried a stack of clean, folded linen. 'Cox told me you were here,' she said. She dropped the linen on the bed and pulled back her head dress. 'We're all working hard in advance of the plague, but I doubt it will take any account of our efforts if it really is on its way. Do you have a cigarette for a worn-out old nun?'

Jameson lit one and gave it to her.

'Still no news?' she said to Hunter.

Hunter shook his head, unwilling to speak.

Jameson, Elizabeth noticed, kept his eye on the door, expecting Ruth to enter.

Margaret, too, saw this. 'She's downstairs. In the conservatory. Cox kindly informed her I could manage this alone and that she was to stay where she was. He really is a wretched man. She knows you're here.' She turned her attention to the bookcase beside the bed. 'Anything new?' She traced her finger along the spines. Sweat ran from her brow and her cheeks and she wiped it on her sleeve. 'Such ignorance,' she said, meaning Cox. 'I sometimes wonder if this war will ever end.' She took out a book and flicked her fingers through its pages in a manner which suggested she was familiar with its contents.

'Take it,' Hunter told her. 'Jameson won't mind. There can't have been a pound profit in it for him.'

'A guinea,' Jameson said. 'Take whatever you want.'

Margaret let this pass. She sat beside Hunter and took his hand. 'If there's anything we, the sisters, can do for you . . .' she said. 'I know how useless that sounds, but Mother Superior said she would be pleased to put in a good word for you. I don't imagine it will impress the authorities involved, but if there's anything else . . .'

'Thank her for me. Your prayers are as good as anything.'

'We *do* pray for him,' Margaret said to Elizabeth. 'We pray for mankind as a whole and Hunter here in particular. No-one thanks us, of course, but we do it out of a sort of instinct, the way a farmer might pull out individual weeds while walking through a vast field of his corn.'

They were distracted by a commotion below. A group of men ran from the conservatory out onto the lawn. Several orderlies ran after them. Two of the men carried a third who had no legs. The orderlies called for them to go back indoors. The running men ignored them. Others, nurses and nuns, gathered to watch. Ruth stood by the open door. Then one of the men carrying the cripple stumbled and fell, pulling the other down with him. They dropped the man they held. He landed to one side of them and cried out in pain. Orderlies and nurses ran to him. The group of able-bodied patients stopped running and walked back to where the man lay crying on the lawn. Someone pushed a wheelchair out to him, leaving lines in the damp grass.

'I'd better go,' Margaret said, retrieving the linen. 'I'll tell Ruth you were asking after her, shall I?'

'Please,' Jameson said. It was clear that he wanted to say more. He looked back down to where the girl had been standing, but she was no longer there.

He and Elizabeth left an hour later.

They encountered Cox again in the hospital entrance. Ruth and Mitchell stood beside him.

'Johnny boy here wanted to say hello,' Cox called to Jameson. 'We've been waiting. What can you and Hunter find to do for so long?'

The boy laughed at this and Cox encouraged him.

Ruth released her hold on Mitchell and he immediately grabbed her arm. Jameson was about to say something.

'Don't,' Elizabeth whispered. She saw that it was not what Ruth wanted. 'Let's just leave. They're both trying to antagonize you. Don't give either of them the satisfaction. It isn't what she wants.'

Ruth pulled free again, but made no further effort to move away from her charge.

Elizabeth led Jameson towards the door.

'Come back soon,' Cox called after them.

The sound of his laughter, and that of the boy, followed them outside.

33

She entered the dining-room and went directly to where the Gottliebs sat, surprising them by her approach. Jameson sat in the far corner of the room. He half rose at her arrival and then sat back down. Herr Gottlieb pulled a chair from another table for her. The family were leaving in a week's time. Herr Gottlieb insisted they exchange addresses and told his daughter to give Elizabeth one of his cards. Gerda did this. Herr Gottlieb then suggested to his daughter that it might be more appropriate if she crossed out his name and business address and substituted her own name and their home address instead. The girl did this too, behaving as though she were being bestowed a great favour in being allowed to deface the precious card. Waiting for her to finish writing, Elizabeth glanced at Jameson, indicating to him that she would soon join him. Monique served him and then sat beside him in conversation. She laid a hand across his shoulders and kissed him before leaving him.

'You must visit us next spring,' Frau Gottlieb said to Elizabeth, drawing her back to them. 'Bring Mary. She will no doubt be fully recovered by then.'

'Or come alone,' Herr Gottlieb said, frowning at his wife.

'Father,' Gerda said.

'What have I said? All I meant was that poor Mary may not wish to travel so far again after this unfortunate experience. And, perhaps, too, Elizabeth would not wish to take on such a – such a responsibility again. I am only being realistic.'

'Yes,' Elizabeth told him. 'I'd like to visit you.' She knew she would see none of them ever again; they understood this too.

'There are good times coming,' Frau Gottlieb said.

'Of course there are, and we must all share in them.' Her husband spoke as the benevolent victor addressing the forgiven vanquished.

'If you will excuse me,' Elizabeth said, indicating Jameson.

The Gottliebs had what they wanted; they were not disappointed by her departure.

'Perhaps if you are free later . . .' Frau Gottlieb said, unexpectedly. 'I mean now that you no longer have Mary to accompany you.'

'Free for what?'

'I thought perhaps you and Gerda might spend some time together.'

Gerda nodded vigorously at the suggestion.

'But you're leaving,' Elizabeth said. 'You'll be busy.'

'Not for another week.'

'Perhaps,' Elizabeth said. Where once she had pitied the overgrown girl for the way she allowed herself to be dominated, she now pitied her for all her weaknesses, as solid and as natural to her as her limbs.

She went to Jameson. A briefcase and package lay beside his chair.

'I'm going to see Sinclair,' he said. 'I thought you might come. I spoke to him last night. I have some more pictures to deliver. He said we could go into the clinic. They've finally taken some of his patients away; others are about to leave. He's worried that they're going too early. He wants full records to accompany them.'

It was five days since they had visited Hunter.

'Where are they going? Home?'

'Some. Some to Paris.' He indicated the Gottliebs, who were in the process of leaving. 'Are the rats ready to leave the sinking ship?'

'A week.'

He raised his hand to the Germans. Only Gerda returned the gesture.

'And before they go they'll confirm their booking for next year, and then next year they'll confirm for the year after,' he said.

'So?'

He didn't answer her. 'Will you come to see Sinclair?' He checked his watch.

Monique returned and poured coffee for them both.

'Will you come tonight?' Jameson said to her.

'When I finish here. Tell him ten o'clock.'

'Emil has a new client,' Jameson said to Elizabeth. 'A new and very wealthy client.' Monique slapped him on his shoulder. 'Photographs to be taken to his own, very precise specifications.'

Monique left them.

'Doesn't she . . .' Elizabeth began, watching her go.

'Doesn't she what?'

'Nothing,' she said.

There was no-one at the hospital gate. A line of lorries and converted ambulances stood along the drive, most with their engines running. Cox directed a line of men carrying luggage and boxes of files. He saw them arrive, but said nothing to them.

In the hallway were three men on stretchers. They appeared unconcerned, and lay propped on their elbows, smoking. They put their thumbs up to Jameson and told him they were going home. He wished them luck and they cheered themselves.

Jameson used the small switchboard to call Sinclair and tell him they had arrived. He spoke for several minutes, but Elizabeth could hear little of what he said above the noise of the room. Men she hardly recognized came to talk to her, all of them excited by the prospect of their departure.

Jameson came back to her.

'He says we can go straight over. He won't come out because of all this. His patients who were leaving went in the night. There are a dozen or so left, but with no prospect of departure. He's angry.'

'Why?'

'Because I've got photographs of the men who've already gone. Now he's going to have to find out where they are and send them on.'

'That shouldn't be too difficult, surely?'

He shrugged. 'This is still the Army. Connections that exist elsewhere don't necessarily exist here. Everyone travels hopefully.'

'He couldn't have gone on caring for them for ever. They would have had to go sometime.'

'Will you tell him that? He told me to warn you that only the more severe cases remain.'

'Warn me against what?'

'Their appearance. Imagining isn't seeing.'

'You don't want me to over-react. I won't.'

He led her through the hospital and out into the grounds beyond. He seemed relieved to be outside.

'What is it?' she asked him.

'I don't know. Being in there – it felt like a rout. I've seen it.'

'Most of them seemed happy enough with what was happening.'

'They were the ones who were going home. The rest will be locked away, kept apart from it all until everything calms down again.'

'I see.'

The gate leading into Sinclair's compound was open.

Inside stood a man with a cloth wrapped around the lower half of his face, giving him the appearance of an Arab. He turned away at their approach, but then recognized Jameson and came over to them.

Jameson introduced Elizabeth. The man spoke to her, but his words were mumbled, and muffled by the cloth.

'There's no need for it,' Jameson said, indicating the cloth.

The man nodded, but made no effort to uncover his mouth. His nose, eyes, cheeks and forehead above the cloth were uninjured and lightly tanned, giving no indication of what remained hidden. He told them where Sinclair was.

She followed Jameson into the yard. Several others stood

together by the wall. He led her to a door away from them.

Sinclair was in his office. Files lay piled on his desk and on the floor around it.

'Why couldn't they wait?' he said angrily. 'Two hours' notice. Two. Twelve and I could have stayed up all night getting things ready for them.' The appearance of Elizabeth did nothing to lessen his anger. 'They care as little for the poor bastards now as they did when they told them to climb up out of the trenches and start collecting bullets.' He looked at the package Jameson held. 'Is it everything?'

Jameson nodded.

Sinclair took the package and opened it. He cleared a space on his desk and spread the pictures across it. 'Good, good,' he said. 'Want to see?' He turned the pictures for Jameson and Elizabeth to look at. In some, the faces looked like those of damaged mannequins, clean and incomplete; in others, it was difficult to see the damage. Beside them on the desk lay several of the masks Sinclair was building for the men still with him.

'Sinclair got Osborne his hand,' Jameson said.

'And I'm still waiting for a better one for him.' Sinclair gathered up the pictures.

'There are these others,' Jameson said, taking a second, smaller package from his briefcase.

'Ah, yes.' Sinclair took them and immediately put them in a drawer.

'How many are going?' Jameson asked him.

'As many as they can get in the transport. Apparently, it's happening everywhere. I imagine they want them out of here before either the influenza arrives or the winter passes close up.'

'Do they still genuinely believe it's on its way?'

'Ours is not to reason why,' Sinclair said.

'Jameson tells me you're going to become a very famous and a very wealthy man,' Elizabeth said.

'It's true. Jameson, on the other hand, will eventually be reduced to skulking in the shadows, hissing at tourists and shaking a begging bowl.'

'More or less what I do already,' Jameson said. 'I brought you this.' He took a book from the briefcase and gave it to Sinclair.

Sinclair held the book to his face and sniffed it. It was a small, slim volume, bound in yellow leather.

'You owe me twenty guineas,' Jameson said.

Sinclair laughed. 'Send me your bill.'

They were interrupted by a knock at the door.

Sinclair waited a moment before calling, 'Come in.'

The man who entered wore an unpainted mask covering two-thirds of his face, only his right eye and temple remaining exposed. He hesitated, seeing Sinclair was not alone.

'Please,' Sinclair said to him.

The man closed the door behind him.

'You know Jameson,' Sinclair said.

The man held out a gloved hand.

Jameson introduced Elizabeth.

He held out his other hand to her.

She started to apologize for her unexpected presence, concentrating on the man's one good eye, which flicked from her hair to her mouth and back again.

The mask was held in place by thin straps, cupped at the chin, and with a slot through which the man was able to speak.

'Pleased to meet you,' he said, his speech unimpaired. He still had both his ears, and the metal of the mask was cut to fit around these and to cover the injuries to his neck.

'We're going to paint him soon,' Sinclair said.

'Don't worry about staring,' the man said to Elizabeth.

'I didn't mean to.'

'You can't help it. It's something I'm used to.'

'Not for much longer,' Sinclair said.

'If you say so.' He took out a cigarette and smoked it through the slit. When he exhaled, smoke appeared round the edge of the mask and through the hole of his lost eye, causing him to cough and to shake his head to clear it. Sinclair gave him a short rubber tube through which to blow out the smoke.

'Gas gangrene,' the man said to Elizabeth. 'And shrapnel for my hand. Are you a doctor?'

At first Elizabeth did not realize that the question was directed at her.

'No,' she said. She wanted to explain her presence to him, but even as she considered this she knew she had nothing to say to a man who had lost a hand and most of his face which would not sound trite or mockingly inconsequential.

An orderly entered without knocking and handed a package to Sinclair. He spoke to the man in the mask, but not to Jameson or Elizabeth.

Jameson told Sinclair it was time for them to leave. He asked him if he intended visiting the town during the next few days, inviting him to his rooms above the studio. Sinclair said that if he was in town then he would call, giving the impression that it was something he had done frequently in the past.

'Thank Emil for me,' he said.

Elizabeth held out her hand to him, but instead Sinclair took her arm and kissed her on the cheek. His breath and skin smelled of tobacco. The smell remained with her.

When she turned to the man in the mask, he moved away from her.

'What is it?' she asked him.

The man said nothing.

Sinclair still held her arm. 'Kiss him,' he said to her.

'No,' the man said.

'Why not?'

'If that's what you want,' Elizabeth said. She reached out for his good hand and held it firmly in her own. She felt him respond to her. He did not draw away when she moved closer to him. He mumbled something when her face was only inches from his own. 'What?' she said.

He whispered to her. 'Not on the mask.'

She raised herself and kissed his temple, holding her lips against his skin for several seconds. He closed his eye and kept it closed as she drew away.

'Are you smiling?' she asked him.

He nodded. He raised his fingers to where she had kissed him.

'Now he'll probably say "Thank you" and ruin everything,' Sinclair said.

He accompanied Elizabeth and Jameson back to the main body of the hospital. It was midday, but the sky was dark. Blocks of yellow light lay across the grass from the ground-floor windows.

Before entering the building, they were approached by a man who, from only a short distance and in the failing light, appeared to have a moustache and a goatee beard, through which his teeth shone white, and it was only as he came closer that Elizabeth saw that what she had taken for dark hair was in fact a hole, around which the sound flesh of his remaining face had been neatly trimmed, and inside which the man's teeth remained intact. He spoke to Sinclair as though the injury did not exist, and Elizabeth saw that the teeth and pink gums were artificial, clacking together each time the man closed his mouth. She saw where saliva collected in the hollow of his jaw, and after talking for only a few seconds he turned away from her and spat to clear this, keeping his head tipped forward until the last of the mucus dripped free. He left them, having spoken only to Sinclair.

As they re-entered the town, Jameson asked her if she wanted to go directly to the hotel, and without considering what she said, she told him she wanted to return to the studio with him.

34

She woke to the sound of church bells. She lay alone in the bed. There were several peals of bells, and the tolling of each destroyed any overall sense of rhythm or recognizable tune. The bedclothes were bunched around her. She looked along the shelves of books which filled the wall beside the bed. After several minutes, the separate peals one by one unravelled themselves, leaving only a single chime sounding through the narrow streets.

Jameson sat at a table by the window, watching her.

'I knew they'd wake you,' he said.

'What time is it?'

'Ten.' He turned back to the book in front of him. He wrote in a pad and tore strips of paper to slip into the book. The only natural light in the room fell across the desk. She saw the high wall of the building opposite.

Jameson drew back the curtains, but this made little difference.

'How long have you been awake?'

'Since six,' he said.

'Have you been working?'

He held up the pad. 'Cataloguing faults. I have someone coming to inspect it later.'

She sat up, drawing the sheets around her. 'What is it?'

'Latin prayers. For Saint Thomas Aquinas. Sixteenth-century binding, but I believe the actual manuscript dates from the fifteenth. For use before, during and after Mass. Beneventan script.' Like Hunter in the hospital, he spoke as though she might understand him, as though she might even share whatever enthusiasm this understanding fed.

'Is it rare?'

'The prayers were assembled for a nun. I doubt very much they were written by Thomas himself, but they mention him often enough for him to have had some hand in their composition or transcription.' He picked up another book. 'The great E. A. Lowe. I'm boring you.'

'No, tell me.'

Thus they avoided a more obvious, awkward conversation.

'The script's unusual letter form is derived from Roman cursive writing and not Roman capitals, making it hard to read. The recognized authorities on this kind of thing usually agree that Beneventan script died out in the thirteenth century.'

'Not the fifteenth?'

'Making this particular piece somewhat unusual.'

'Is it very valuable?'

'I'm not certain. No provenance. It came to me via an Italian collector who suffered some losses.'

'Can I see it?' She knew now she was talking to conceal what embarrassment she might feel, or be expected to feel; but in truth she felt very little, almost none.

'Your clothes,' he said, indicating the chair over which he had hung them. He handed the manuscript to her and she laid it out on the bed to look at it. 'Margaret would appreciate it,' he said. 'I'd hoped to be able to show it to her before I sold it. It may still be possible.'

They were distracted by noises downstairs.

'Emil,' he said. 'He came back late. He's been working.'

'Is Monique with him?'

'Yes. There were others, but I heard them leave about an hour ago. Monique and Emil, they—'

'I know,' she said. 'Do they know I'm here?'

'I imagine so.' He picked up bottles and glasses from where they stood and lay on the floor around the bed. A small fire burned in the room. She remembered him lighting it the previous evening.

'I'll make a drink,' he said. 'I need to go down to the studio.'

While he was gone, she looked again at the manuscript. Most of the books around her were filled with the same strips of paper. The pages of the volume on the bed were composed of wide margins and illuminated initials. She traced the outline of these and felt the thickness of the ancient ink and paint beneath her fingers.

The door opened. But instead of Jameson returning, Monique came in. 'I've come to get warm,' she said. 'He keeps the studio so cold down there. Something to do with the plates and chemicals.' She wore a man's thick shirt and loose woollen socks which covered her knees. She held a blanket over her shoulders.

'Have you been working?' Elizabeth asked her.

Monique held her hands inches from the coals. 'Hours. Six hours. I'll sleep soon. I'm not back on duty at the hotel until later this afternoon.' Nothing in her manner or voice indicated any surprise at finding Elizabeth in Jameson's bed.

'Is it hard work?' Elizabeth said.

'What, the hotel or this? The hotel's hard work and badly paid. This is just . . . I couldn't live on what I get from the hotel alone.'

'How long have you been doing it – the photography?'

'Two or three years, perhaps longer. There are others at the hotel who do it less regularly. Some of the chambermaids, waitresses, clerks and—'

'Clerks?'

'They're young. It's what Emil's customers want. Did you think it was just poor, stupid young women like me?' She pulled back the blanket to examine the inside of one of her thighs. She licked her thumb and rubbed at a mark there.

'Is the hotel manager one of Emil's customers?'

'I imagine so.'

'Doesn't that bother you?'

'Not really. Whatever Emil sells to him, he'll charge well above the going rate.'

'But he won't let him have pictures of you, surely?'

This, too, surprised Monique. 'Why not? I wouldn't be doing it at all if I felt like that about it. Apart from which, it's probably far too late now.'

'How old are you?'

'Nineteen.'

'I wish we'd spoken earlier,' Elizabeth said.

'At the hotel? As you can imagine, it isn't exactly

encouraged. He wishes you'd leave. You and your sister-in-law have cast a shadow on the place. He prefers the Germans. He wanted them to win the war. They take all his most expensive rooms and buy all the best food and wine. It's not necessarily what they get, but it's what they pay for.' She laughed at this and Elizabeth laughed with her. 'If there's anything else you want to know, about all this, the studio work, feel free to ask.'

Elizabeth wanted to know everything. She had wandered into a strange country, and everything about it was strange. 'I'd feel as though I were intruding,' she said.

'It's up to you. You remember the Italian family?'

'Obnoxious children.'

'He spent a small fortune. Half of Jameson's visits to the hotel before you arrived were in connection with him. Emil thinks he reproduces what he buys and sells it on.'

' "It"?'

'The pictures, postcards.'

'Of course.' Elizabeth tried to imagine how she might have felt had she known the true reason for Jameson's visits to the hotel from the very beginning.

They were joined by Jameson and Emil. Emil carried a tray containing bowls of chocolate, and Jameson a cloth-covered basket of bread. He took butter and a pot of jam from his pocket.

Emil sat in the seat by the window, closed his eyes and pretended to snore.

'He hasn't slept for two nights,' Monique said.

Emil opened his eyes and looked at her affectionately. 'I have to work while I can. In a few weeks' time . . .' He gestured. 'Then I'll rest. Or I'll spend my days taking pretty pictures of the mountains and the lakes. Who knows, I may even cover the cost of my plates for once.' He took a drink and a piece of warm bread. 'Has Monique told you how many times I have asked her to marry me? A thousand.'

'No-one will marry you,' Jameson said.

But Elizabeth saw by the way Monique looked away and avoided speaking that he was wrong.

The previous evening she had asked Jameson to show her his private stock of books, and he had given her the keys to several cabinets in a small closet. She had spent almost an hour in there, while he had laid the fire and then gone out to buy wine. The books were published in all languages; some illustrated by drawings, others by photographs; some were works of erotic fiction, some books of art, some of poetry. Most contained women alone or women together, but some included both men and women in their illustrations. She knew she was being left alone to make her judgement on the collection and to overcome whatever shock or revulsion she might feel. But, as with her discovery of Emil and his work, she felt neither of those things; instead, she felt aroused by what she saw, and if, upon his return, Jameson had asked her what she felt, she would have been unable to lie to him. But he had said nothing, talking instead about the poor quality of the drink he had bought and about an acquaintance he had encountered in the alleyway below. She saw again the extent to which she had been formed in the mould of other people's expectations.

Now, watching him with his rare and precious manuscript amid these close friends, it occurred to her that it was as though this other small room, this other part of his life, did not exist; or, more accurately, that it existed – because he would be the last to deny that – but that it was not allowed to colour the rest of what he was and what he did as it would with some other men – those otherwise empty men who were defined only by their professions, whose substance lay in their work alone.

Emil left the desk and came to sit beside her on the bed. She was naked beneath her wrapping of sheets.

'I'd like to take your photograph,' he said. He pushed loose hairs from her face and ran his hand down her neck and over her shoulder as though he were testing some line or proportion.

'Me?' she said.

'He means a portrait,' Monique said, grinning.

'What else?'

'No,' Elizabeth said.

'Why not?'

'Because I don't like pictures of myself. Back home, it's become an obsession. Everyone has their picture taken, all the time. Every house in the country is filled with pictures.'

'I could take a picture of you that you would treasure for the rest of your life,' Emil said.

'Will it prevent me from growing any older?'

'Of course it will. I guarantee it.'

'You can see how easily I fell for his charms,' Monique said. 'Me and a thousand others.'

'We ought to go out somewhere,' Jameson suggested. He passed around what remained of the bread.

'I'm working later,' Monique said.

'Me too,' Emil added. 'I agreed to take some of my latest work to show the Count. The rent is due.'

'I'll settle the rent,' Jameson said.

'He says that every month,' Emil said to Elizabeth.

She, too, did not want to leave the room. She wanted to spend the day there, in the bed, in front of the fire, perhaps going out only briefly to eat at a café or to walk to the lake and back. She told them none of this.

'Talk to her, Jameson,' Emil said. 'Persuade her.'

They stayed together for several hours longer, until it was time for Monique to return to the hotel.

'I'll walk with you,' Elizabeth said.

'I thought you might stay,' Jameson said, but in a voice devoid of pleading or disappointment.

'I need to go back,' she said. She hoped he would not ask her to explain. She felt like a swimmer in a cold sea who had climbed from the water to briefly sun herself in the warmth, but who must now return to the water and complete her journey.

Jameson and Emil kissed both women at the doorway.

Monique led her through the maze of passages and alleyways, bringing them quickly to the town square. 'I have to call for another of the girls,' she said. She rang the bell of a building in the square. A window opened high above them and a woman looked out. Monique stood back from the doorway so she might be seen. The woman called down to her and withdrew.

Several minutes later, a much younger girl, younger than Monique, came out. Elizabeth recognized her as one of the hotel chambermaids. It was clear she had only just woken. She asked Monique in German what Elizabeth was doing with her. Elizabeth pretended not to understand, but knew by Monique's answer that she, Monique, was aware of the deception.

They left the square in the direction of the lake, turning along the road above the water. It was cold, and both Monique and the girl wore only short thin coats. The girl complained incessantly of the cold. Midway between the town and the hotel, Monique took an envelope from her pocket and gave it to the girl. The girl immediately opened this and counted the money it contained, unable to suppress her delight. She suggested they went into one of the lakeside bars for a drink before reporting for work. She insisted there was time and pulled both Monique and Elizabeth into the first bar they came to.

It was full, mostly of men, fishermen and labourers, who played cards or sat with newspapers. The girl knew most of them. She showed off her money and flirted with the barman.

'Leave her,' Monique whispered to Elizabeth, leading her to a table. She signalled to a waiter to bring them their drinks.

'She seems excited,' Elizabeth said, conscious of the looks of the men at the surrounding tables.

'She doesn't care,' Monique said disparagingly. 'It's why Emil employs her. She has no scruples. She has other . . .' She stopped, watching the girl.

'Other what?'

'You know – other talents, other vices.' She patted her inner arm. She paid the waiter for their drinks. He told her to keep an eye on the girl, that he didn't want any trouble.

'Some of these men are her customers,' Monique said to Elizabeth, her voice low.

Elizabeth watched the girl more closely.

'Imagine that – having to work in the hotel because, pittance that it is, it pays better than most of them do. Can you imagine sleeping with a single man in this room?'

Elizabeth looked at them. Most were overweight and dirty from their labours; most were twenty or thirty years older than the girl, and with shabby clothes and poorly-cut beards.

'That's why they're watching us,' Monique said, her own

cold stare forcing the men to look away from her. 'We're friends of hers, so it stands to reason. It's almost winter so her prices will be going down. I imagine there are some nights when a glass of drink will be enough.'

The girl left her seat at the bar and came over to them. She was pleased by the effect she had on the men.

'Tell the manager I'm sick,' she said to Monique.

'Don't be stupid. They're just waiting to get rid of people. Any excuse.'

'Not me,' the girl said confidently. She winked at the two women and left them again.

'Let's go,' Monique said. She and Elizabeth made their way to the entrance. She called to the girl that they were leaving.

'Good, then go,' she shouted back. 'I'm staying with my friends.'

A chorus of cheers rose around her.

Monique went out first.

'Are you leaving her?' Elizabeth said.

'You heard her. He won't sack her because he's bedding her. Or whatever else it is she does to keep him sweet.'

'Blackmail?'

'Nothing so drastic. He's just taking what he wants. It won't last. He's too powerful and careful. When the time comes, he'll be rid of her as easily as he might wipe something off his shoe.' She looked through the clouded glass to the dim shape of the girl at the bar. Men stood all around her now.

They crossed the road to walk above the lake.

The strings of bulbs flickered into colour and light ahead of them, and what little of the water that had been visible was lost in the sudden darkness beyond their glow.

Monique took Elizabeth's arm as they walked, and only

then did it occur to Elizabeth that she had not once thought about Mary since waking. There was now no limit to the paths ahead of her, no boundary she might not approach and cross, and she felt this change in herself as forcibly as she felt the cold mountain air against her face.

35

'Did Jameson tell you about our "miracle"?' Hunter sat beside Elizabeth.

'It was no such thing,' Margaret said. She crossed herself. She and Ruth stripped Hunter's bed and put on clean sheets.

'What miracle?'

'He called it that, not me,' Jameson said. 'You have to believe in them beforehand to convince yourself you've seen one. Like mermaids.'

'Tell me about it,' Elizabeth said to Hunter.

Ruth came to sit beside them.

Margaret stopped working on the bed.

'It was at Cassel. We were a long way out of the line. I had five days' leave, Jameson was already there. We were staying in a hotel. The Hotel Sauvage.'

'Madame Imbert,' Jameson said fondly.

'A hotel for officers. The lower ranks made do with whatever they could find or were given in the town. It was summer. We spent long warm days and evenings in the garden. Somebody had taken a piano out there. A piano with a candelabra on it under the apricot trees. Surprising what a few days of that life could do for you.'

'Or what it could allow you to forget,' Jameson said.

'Let him go on,' Margaret said.

It was clear to Elizabeth that Margaret had already heard the story, and that what mattered to her now was not its interpretation as a miracle, but the indulgent pleasure the two men got in repeating and sharing it, regardless of Jameson's otherwise dismissive remarks.

'Everyone would be drunk by late afternoon,' Hunter went on. 'Tennis, cricket, croquet, swimming in the river. Elegant young ladies visiting from the town.'

'Elegant?' Margaret said, adding to their enjoyment.

'There was a cellar of drink in that place second to none, even then. There were horses for riding, a taxi service for wherever you wanted to go.'

'I'm surprised you'd want to go anywhere, it sounds such a paradise,' Margaret said.

'It was,' Jameson said.

Both Ruth and Elizabeth looked at him.

Hunter went on. 'We were out in the garden one evening when there was a starburst directly above us. It must have been a misfire from one of our own guns. Theirs were too far off. There was nothing planned, it wasn't nuisance fire, so it must just have been a freak or a dud fired to clear a breech.' He paused for a moment, remembering.

It was a common feature, Elizabeth had noticed, of these men and their recollections: they started out on them like wanderers convinced of the accuracy of the maps they possessed, but who were then deceived by those maps and left lost and uncertain, anxious only to retrace their steps away from the dangerous and unfamiliar terrain back to the known, to common ground, to the present.

'There were flocks of starlings,' Hunter said. 'Thousands of them in the trees. They roosted there. Sometimes they were silent, and sometimes you couldn't hear yourself think above the racket they made. Apparently, they'd gathered there for decades. We tried everything we could think of to get rid of them, but nothing lasted.'

Ruth began to say something, but fell silent at a gesture from Margaret. Hunter appeared not to notice.

'The starburst knocked them out of the trees in their hundreds, thousands. The shock waves. We felt them too, but the blast was too high to do any real damage. Some small pieces of shrapnel, but nothing much. It was all a bit of a joke, really. We knew straight off that there was nothing more to come.' He paused. 'And then the birds just fell from the trees. Some of them scattered, flew off, but the vast majority of them, those caught in the blast, just fell to the ground and lay there. It took us a moment or two to realize what was happening. They fell onto our tables, onto the piano, into our laps, all around us, like a sudden windfall.'

'Were they all dead?' Elizabeth asked him.

'We thought so, at first. Some of them were clearly alive, squawking and flapping around in the grass, but most of them fell without a sound and lay without moving where they landed. It was all over in a few seconds. They were all intact; it's not as though they'd even been damaged by the blast, no stray feathers or blood, just whole fat birds, thousands of birds.'

'What did you do?'

'Nothing. Everyone just left off what they were doing and walked among them. They were so thick in places it was hard to avoid stepping on them. Someone suggested gathering them all up into sacks and either burning them or throwing them into the river. To be honest, we didn't know what to do. Those birds that had flown away returned and started their racket again. I picked one up and looked at it. I don't know why, but I sensed it was alive.'

'Did it revive?'

'Not then. I put it back down.'

'Then what?'

'Nothing. For about an hour we went on doing whatever we'd been doing before the shell. I think someone tried to find out what had happened. And then the birds started to recover.'

'What, all of them?'

'Most. The strangest thing is, they all seemed to come round at exactly the same time. I suppose it makes sense, that there's a reason for it, but it seemed very strange at the time. All those thousands of supposedly dead birds in the long grass and under our tables and feet, suddenly coming back to life, resuming their noise, flapping their wings and all of them rising up out of the ground at practically the same instant. It was like watching a flock of feeding crows rise from a field of corn at a gunshot.' He made the shape of a bird with his hands.

'It sounds like a miracle to me,' Ruth said. She was as mesmerized as Hunter by the tale.

'Me, too,' Elizabeth added. Listening to the story had reminded her of something in her own life.

'The only miracle is that no-one was killed,' Jameson said.

'We were invincible,' Hunter said absently.

'A pity all those poor torn men could not recover and rise up in the same miraculous way,' Margaret said.

Jameson put his arm around her. He told her about the Aquinas prayers. He arranged for her to see them before he sold them. There was genuine excitement in her voice at the prospect of seeing the manuscript.

Ruth watched them, barely able to suppress her envy at Jameson's arm around the old nun.

'I believe in miracles because I know of another,' Elizabeth said unexpectedly. She hoped to distract Ruth, to ease what small uncertain pain she might be feeling. She felt as she had felt before – as though a whole generation and not only six years separated her from the girl.

'Tell us,' Margaret said. She slid free of Jameson's embrace. 'Change places with me,' she said to Ruth. The girl went. 'I don't doubt you,' she said to Elizabeth. 'A world without miracles would be like a world without music. But I was taught to believe in only one – at most two – true miracles.'

'It concerns my brother,' Elizabeth said. Jameson looked up at her but she avoided looking back at him.

She waited a few moments before going on. The room was filled with the muted noise and voices of the men below; somewhere further inside the hospital a gramophone played, and its barely-recognizable song came to them distorted through a dozen walls. There was no-one to be seen out on the lawn. The ground remained wet; there had been further squalls of rain and snow during the nights, and sometimes in the afternoons as darkness fell.

'If it's too painful, keep it to yourself,' Margaret said. She touched Elizabeth's hand.

'No, I want to tell you. I've never mentioned it to anyone before.'

'Not even Mary?' Jameson said.

'Especially not Mary.'

'Tell us,' Hunter said.

She had joined the two men after an hour with Margaret and Ruth at the convent. She had come out to the hospital with Jameson. Something had preoccupied him during the journey and they had travelled largely in silence. He had been pleased at the opportunity to see Hunter alone. Elizabeth had joined Margaret and Ruth in one of their small gardens, removing dead stalks and collecting what few herbs remained to be picked and dried. Margaret and Ruth told her what had happened in the convent over the previous week; Ruth in particular was desperate to talk to someone from outside. Ten days had passed since either of them had accompanied the invalids into town. There was no longer any order or reliable routine in the working of the hospital, and both of them regretted this. Elizabeth told them about Mary, guessing at what she did not know. Ruth tied a small bundle of rosemary and gave it to her. Elizabeth put it in her sleeve, where it rubbed against her wrist and released its scent. There was no longer any sign of the cut or the bruise on Ruth's face.

'Tell us,' Jameson said again.

'Michael told me all this the last time I saw him. I mean before he was injured, when he was home on leave. It was just after Saint Pol. Before Merville. He said he knew then that he was leading a charmed life. But I guessed by the little he did tell me – and Mary – how much more he was keeping from us. I also guessed he was keeping those things from us more for her sake than my own. I wanted him to be able to tell me.'

'It was never encouraged,' Hunter said.

'I know. And I know he had his own reasons for keeping it

to himself. He aged so quickly. I watched him sometimes just standing in the garden and staring up into the sky, shielding his eyes and moving his head as though he were watching something when there was nothing to see. I made all the guesses in the world, but I doubt if I ever came close. That's what separates you from the rest of us – you and Jameson – the knowing, not the suffering. Why do you imagine you keep it all to yourselves? Is it because we could never understand, because we might think you were overdramatizing things, lying even? Or is it because you *can't* tell us, because whatever it is you know, whatever new understanding you have of the things men can do, of the way they can behave towards each other, is it because whatever you know has become some vital part of you, something to be secreted away and clung to for fear that if you lost it or gave it away you'd end up like so many of those others here?' She knew she had said too much, uncertain of why she had prefaced her story in this way. No-one spoke. She felt Margaret's hand on her arm.

'It's all right,' Margaret said. 'We none of us know the answer to that.'

She wanted to apologize to Hunter and Jameson.

'Tell us what he told you,' Hunter said.

She waited until she felt composed.

'He told me he was flying when his engine began to falter. He wasn't being attacked or fired on from the ground; he was over friendly territory. It wasn't uncommon, apparently. According to Michael, his mechanic spent five times longer working on his machine than he actually spent flying it. He said he was as high as he liked to go. Sometimes the air and fuel mixture was affected. He wasn't in the least scared of what was happening. He said there were procedures, techniques. He told me that if the worst came to the worst he could just glide to the ground and find a nice flat field to land in and go for tea with the farmer while someone came out to collect him. You see what I mean about him keeping things from me. Older brother and younger sister. But then something else happened. He said he tried to do whatever it was he was supposed to do, but the machine didn't respond to his controls. He said he started falling and spinning. He was supposed to come down in a gentle curve and somehow get the engine started like that. But he couldn't. He said he just fell, and that he started spinning. He said that even if the controls had been manageable, he wouldn't have been able to do anything under those conditions. He'd seen other machines just break up when that happened, seen them come down like broken kites, all the pieces still held together by their wires.' She took a deep breath. 'He passed out. He didn't even remember it happening, how could he? He didn't know how long it lasted, but when he came round – it couldn't have been more than a few seconds – he was flying on a level course and the machine was responding to his controls. He said he no longer had on his helmet or his gloves, that they must have been sucked off him in the fall. He couldn't believe it. He said he was only a few hundred feet off the ground and that he could see everything below him. He didn't know where he was, he didn't even know which direction he was flying. He could see the men below him. No-one fired at him, so he knew he was still over friendly territory. He landed on a road without so much as a bruise. They sent a tractor out to drag his plane into a barn and a car and driver for him.'

'Why didn't he tell Mary this?' Hunter asked her. 'Why don't *you* tell her?'

'He asked me not to. It wasn't because she wouldn't have

known, or couldn't have guessed about what he did; it was to do with the way he came round.'

'Which was?'

'He said he came round because he could hear me calling his name, and because he could feel me shaking him.' She clasped her hands. 'He swore he could hear me, feel me.'

'You, and not Mary,' Hunter said.

She nodded. 'He was wounded about six weeks later. No, he was wounded six weeks and two days later. What good was I to him then?' She fumbled to light a cigarette. Ruth left the bed and came to her. She lit the cigarette for her and held her hand as Elizabeth put it to her lips. She remained beside her, flanking her with Margaret in an instinctive gesture of comfort and support.

'I've heard others tell similar stories,' Jameson said. 'Wives, sisters, sweethearts. They're not so unbelievable, not when a man wants or needs something so desperately.'

'But why wasn't it *her*?' Elizabeth said. 'Surely, his wife—'

'Those priorities don't exist,' Hunter said. 'Stop punishing yourself.'

'He's right,' Jameson said. 'Perhaps you ought to tell her; perhaps it might help.'

'Not now,' Elizabeth said. 'It's too late now. It would only make things more complicated. And besides—' She stopped abruptly.

'What?' Jameson said.

'She doesn't *want* to tell her,' Margaret said. 'She wants to keep it, to keep that last small part of him for herself.'

Elizabeth acknowledged this, grateful that the confession had not been hers to make.

'And so you should,' Margaret said. 'You need these things as much as anyone, as much as Mary. No-one will judge you. He was all you had.'

Elizabeth started to cry. 'I loved him so much,' she said. Margaret and Ruth moved even closer to her. They built a wall around her. The girl knelt at her feet.

'Cry,' Margaret said, cradling Elizabeth's head in both her hands.

The three women remained held together like this for several minutes longer, until Elizabeth finally raised her face and wiped her eyes. The two men sat and waited. Margaret told her not to try to speak. She touched away the last of the tears draining from her chin. Ruth held one of Elizabeth's hands in both her own, soothing and caressing. Eventually, when both the nun and the girl saw the time was right, they released their hold on her and resumed their positions beside her.

They were still sitting like this, still silent, still watched by Jameson and Hunter, when the door was pushed open and Cox entered. He stopped at what he saw there, and looked at each of them in turn, as though by this means alone he might somehow understand what was happening in the room.

'What do you want?' Jameson asked him eventually.

'The girl.' He pointed at Ruth. 'Mitchell was asking for her.'

'Then tell him he'll have to go without her for once.'

'She was due to take him out an hour ago. You don't tell me what to do.' He whistled and waited for Ruth to look up at him. 'Now,' he said.

'You'd better go,' Margaret whispered to her.

'Thank you, both of you,' Elizabeth said. She held out both her hands for the woman and the girl to briefly hold.

Then Ruth rose and walked slowly to where Cox waited for her.

'I sometimes wonder,' Cox said, looking at Margaret, pausing for effect, and to savour the assertion of his authority, 'I sometimes wonder if you and all the other sisters don't forget what you're here for.'

'Oh, we never forget that, Corporal Cox,' Margaret said. She rose and followed Ruth across the room, collecting the sheets she had stripped from the bed. She stood with her face a few inches from Cox's and looked into his eyes. He turned away from her and left the room.

'You ought to leave the poor little man alone,' Hunter said loudly.

From the corridor, Cox called for Ruth to follow him.

'Wait. I'm coming with you,' Margaret told her.

The two of them left, mouthing their farewells to the men and the woman left behind.

Elizabeth and Jameson stayed another hour before they, too, left and returned to the town.

He sat with his arm around her.

'Will you come back to the studio?'

She considered this and shook her head. He made no effort to persuade her.

The return journey, like the journey out, was made largely in silence.

'Something's happened,' she said to him.

He wiped a hand over his face. 'They've set a date for his court martial. The end of the year. Five weeks.'

'Where?'

'Southampton.'

'Why there?'

'Why not? Because it suits their purpose. Besides, what does it matter to *him* where it happens?'

'How long before they want him to return?'

He shrugged. 'A few weeks, less?'

They parted outside the hotel and she stood and watched as he was driven away from her.

36

A week after he first made his request, Elizabeth finally agreed to have her photograph taken by Emil. She fixed a time with him and then arranged for Jameson to meet her beforehand in the town. She wanted to buy a new pair of gloves – a memento, she told herself – and upon meeting Jameson she asked him to recommend a shop to her.

'Will you be there?' she asked him, meaning the studio, aware of his own lack of enthusiasm for the project, and conscious too that he remained preoccupied with what might now be about to happen to Hunter.

'If you like,' he said.

'I won't do it if you're not there,' she told him.

'I'm not against the idea as such,' he said, but without conviction. 'It's just . . .'

'It's just that you associate the studio with whatever else

goes on there. Surely others must go there for their portraits to be taken?'

'Of course. Tourists. But I doubt if any of them have even the faintest idea.'

Her first instinct was to dispute this, but she said nothing. She saw increasingly that a great deal of what he continually denied to himself was only too obvious to others.

'There's no harm in it,' she said, immediately regretting the trite remark.

He nodded, refusing to be drawn any further into the predictable argument.

He led her across the square and into the narrow streets of the old town.

'You'll find whatever you want here,' he said. He indicated a window in which several hundred pairs of gloves were displayed, most laid flat in tissue envelopes, but with several dozen pairs drawn over plaster hands, splayed and upright, as though waving to attract her attention. The window was brightly lit. A man appeared at the rear of the display, smiled at her and then looked down at his work.

She saw a pair she liked and went in.

The shopkeeper took off his apron. The interior smelled strongly of treated leather and other odours she did not recognize, and she stood for a moment breathing these in.

The glove-maker went first to Jameson and shook his hand. Then he returned to Elizabeth and asked her what she wanted to see. She pointed out the gloves in the window to him.

'A wise choice,' he said, and took a packet from one of the multitude of drawers behind the counter. He laid the gloves on the glass top.

'May I try them on?'

He took her right hand and turned it in his palm. 'These will fit you.'

She pulled on the first of the white kid gloves. She had never bought white before, nor cream, and she heard her mother's voice warning her against it now as she slid her first finger into the supple skin.

'May I . . .' The glove-maker held her wrist, pulling the thin leather tight and then tamping between her fingers. He remarked on the closeness of the fit. 'They may, of course, be a little tight for a day or so. You wouldn't want them otherwise.' He stroked a thumb over the creases in her palm, admiring his craftsmanship. Elizabeth rolled up the sleeve of her coat and the man smoothed the leather along her forearm. Each glove was fastened by a dozen mother-of-pearl studs, which he joined by another deft stroke. 'Hold them up,' he told her. 'Feel them against your cheek.' He returned to his counter and turned a mirror towards her. She put on the second glove, unable to repeat his practised sealing of the studs.

'They suit you,' Jameson said.

'I want two pairs,' she told the glove-maker.

'Two?'

'A pair for my sister-in-law.'

'But, whoever this woman is, her hands may not be the same size or shape as your own,' he said.

'They are,' Elizabeth insisted.

'It would be better if she were to come to me personally to make sure.' He looked to Jameson, alarmed, despite the double sale, at the prospect of letting this second pair go without them first being tried.

'Sell her two pairs,' Jameson said. 'If she can afford them, and that's what she wants.'

The glove-maker acceded to this, but was still not happy.

He took a second packet from the drawer and put it on the counter alongside Elizabeth's old gloves. She alone saw what he was truly losing in being unable to repeat the small ritual of the fitting.

'I'll help you take them off,' he said.

'I want to keep them on. Wrap the second pair.'

'It would be wise not to get them too wet – the snow.'

'Of course.'

'And these?' he said, indicating her old pair.

'Wrap them,' she said. She would never wear them again.

She took out her purse, flexing and closing her fingers for the simple pleasure of feeling them inside the tight and supple skin.

The man told her the price. It was higher than she had anticipated, but she paid with a single note of large currency without remarking on this.

'It seems very expensive,' Jameson said to her.

'It's a fair price,' she said.

The glove-maker took her money. He wrapped the old pair and the second pair, along with the felt-lined pouches in which to keep the new gloves.

'I shall wear them to have my photograph taken,' she said to him, as though this might somehow compensate for his earlier disappointment. The man said nothing in reply. The transaction completed, he opened and held the door for them.

Emil was waiting for them. Monique was with him. They were laughing together as Jameson and Elizabeth entered. A bottle stood on the table beside them.

'Emil made a good sale,' Monique said.

'Oh?'

'Some of her pictures,' Emil said. He spoke to Jameson

rather than Elizabeth. 'Our old friend Baron Varese. More money than sense.'

'He paid well because he likes *me*,' Monique said. She was half drunk.

'He likes you the way *I* portray you,' Emil said. 'I doubt he would be so titillated by you – I almost said "in the flesh".' They both laughed again at this.

Elizabeth wondered if Jameson had known Monique would be present. He threw his coat over a sofa and helped her out of hers.

She held up her new gloves for Emil to see. 'I want you to photograph me wearing them.'

'I'm flattered you agreed,' he said.

'No you're not. I had no choice.'

'I am,' he insisted. 'I am.' He came closer to her and reached out to hold her gloved hand. He stroked her the way the glove-maker had stroked her. 'Of course you must wear them,' he said. 'Held like this . . .' He put her hand on her shoulder and then drew it closer to her throat and down towards her breast.

'When?' Elizabeth asked him.

'No urgency. First we celebrate my sale.' He pulled a handful of notes from his pocket. 'A cash sale, see? Jameson here is happy to rely on promises and credit, but for me there is nothing to beat the smell and the feel of the stuff. You know when you have it and you know when you don't. You know exactly what it can do for you and you know what is impossible when you no longer have it.' He gestured as though he were about to toss the money in the air.

'Speaking of which,' Monique said. She held his wrist and pulled several of the notes from his grip. He let her do this, making a face to Elizabeth and Jameson. Monique counted out what she was owed. 'I ought really to ask for more,' she said.

'Take it all,' Emil said. He laid the notes on the table. 'You might as well. While you can. You'll soon be too old for Varese.' He winked to Elizabeth. 'You'll last a few more years for the general trade, of course, but the time will soon come when I have to keep your face out of things and concentrate on your more, shall we say anonymous assets. A great pity, but—'

'Bastard.' Monique threw the notes she held at him.

At first Elizabeth thought she was genuinely angry at his remarks, but then Monique burst into laughter. She tried to slap Emil's face, but he ducked and avoided the blow. They fell together onto the sofa.

'Rescue me,' Emil called out.

Elizabeth turned to Jameson and saw that he remained unwilling to participate.

'Ignore him,' Emil said to her. 'He doesn't want me to take your picture, so what? Tell him it's none of his business.'

She felt herself caught between them.

'If the picture comes out to my satisfaction,' she said, 'I'll want a copy to leave him as a present.'

' "Leave"?' Jameson said.

'He can put it on his desk like the picture of some doting wife or sweetheart,' Monique said.

'He can blow kisses to it.'

'Just make sure you see the plates,' Monique told her. 'Otherwise, this time next year you could find yourself grinning out from a dozen shop windows.'

'You two are drunk,' Jameson said to Emil and Monique, but good-naturedly, further releasing the tension.

A further hour passed before Emil suggested they should make a start. He took Elizabeth through into the studio and showed her where he wanted her to sit. His camera was already set up, and while he busied himself making the final preparations, Elizabeth inspected the rolled backdrops, any one of which she might now choose to pull down behind her. None of them appealed to her, but she decided finally on a panorama intended to represent the lake and the rising peaks beyond. It seemed the most appropriate to her. She knew how artificial it would all appear on the finished photograph.

Jameson and Monique remained through in the other room while the sitting took place. She heard their voices, the pull of another cork.

'Is it true what you said about Monique?' Elizabeth said.

'What? Regarding the type of picture I take of her? Possibly. To some men it hardly matters. Some appreciate a semblance of innocence, a suggestion of virginity; some pay merely for that which they know is well beyond them in reality; for others I doubt if the face even comes into the reckoning. She has a fine figure for this work. Some deteriorate very quickly, but others hang on to what they have. She isn't stupid. There are places where she could be making considerably more by doing what she does than here. She's very professional, despite appearances. If she has one failing, it is that she refuses to pose for group compositions.'

'Group compositions?' Her voice dried.

Emil stopped what he was doing and looked at her. 'You need me to explain?'

'Of course not.' She looked at the room around her, at the rugs and scattered props and costumes.

'Don't think about it,' he told her. 'You are here for your portrait. Your portrait with gloves. Is that the scene you want behind you? Lady with gloves in the mountains?' He came to her and repositioned her chair. He pulled two plaster urns closer to her, siting them to frame her in the finished picture.

'Like this?' she said, exaggerating her pose.

'Take off your jacket.'

'Of course.' She took it off and threw it to one side.

Emil retrieved it, brushed it with his palm and hung it on the door. He went back to his camera.

'Turn your head from side to side. Look here. Look to the right.' He stepped back from the instrument. 'The backdrop is creased,' he said, coming back to her.

'No, leave it,' she told him.

'If you like.' He studied her, telling her to twist around in the chair. 'Hold your hand to your throat like I showed you.'

She did this, but he was still not satisfied.

'Would you rather Jameson were here with you?' he said.

'Not particularly. No.'

'He won't come unless I call him,' he said. He looked hard at her.

'What do you want me to do?'

'Take off your brooch,' he said.

'My brooch?'

'It holds your collar too far up your neck. I want to photograph your neck. I want to see the whiteness of the gloves against the texture of the skin there.'

She took off the brooch.

'Unfasten a button.'

She did this.

'Fold your collar down, tug it away from the centre.'

She unfastened several more buttons. 'Like this?'

'Hold up your hand.' But still he was not satisfied. 'Pull your shoulders back; make your breasts rise. Lift your chin very slightly.'

She did all this. 'And now your hand.'

She rested her hand above the swell of her breasts, her index finger in the hollow of her throat.

'Do you feel comfortable like that?'

'Perfectly.' She glanced down at herself.

'Unfasten one more button,' he said.

She did this with her free hand. She felt herself through the soft leather. She rose in her seat and drew back her shoulders even further.

'Like this?' she said.

'I believe so.' He covered his head with the camera cloth. 'Don't smile,' he told her.

'Then what?'

'Nothing. No emotion. Imagine you're cold. Imagine you're at the lakeside dressed like this, now, this moment. Don't talk, don't answer me, just imagine.'

It was as she did this that he triggered the flash of chemical light and then slid in the boards of his plate.

She remained posed, reluctant, after so much preparation, to believe that it was all over.

'It's finished,' he said to her. 'You can fasten your blouse, replace your brooch.'

She was just as reluctant to take her hand from her throat. She heard laughter from the other room.

'Do you want your coat?' Emil asked her. He paid her no other attention now – he barely looked at her – busy with whatever it was he had to do with the camera and the exposed plate.

'It surprised me,' she said. She left her seat and went to stand beside him, her blouse still unfastened. She held one gloved hand inside another. 'Are you sure my surprise won't register? Perhaps you ought to take another.'

'Stop worrying,' he said. 'It's a common assumption. By the

time your brain had worked out enough to be surprised, you'd been captured.' He tapped the covered camera.

'I just thought . . .' She began buttoning her blouse.

'What?'

'Nothing. Just to be sure.'

He watched her briefly. The buttons were as small as the studs on her gloves. 'Let me,' he said. He tugged the material away from her skin and fastened the buttons. 'Did it excite you?' he said. 'Sitting like that? Did you feel something?'

She could not speak, and so she nodded.

'Don't be ashamed. Most of my female clients deny it. Some even pretend not to know what I mean, or what else happens in here. With some, I have to enter into the charade of not guessing that this is precisely why they have come to me, and not gone to some other, more reputable photographer. You might say I trade, unadvertised and unspoken, on my reputation. Put your jacket on.'

'Is that why Jameson didn't want me to come?'

'Who knows?'

'You and I know,' she said.

'So what? Some things he pretends not to care about, other things he can never disguise.'

She fixed her brooch and took her jacket from the door.

'Shall we return to civilized society?' he said.

Jameson and Monique applauded their return.

'We have a perfect portrait,' Emil announced. He took Monique's glass from her and drained it.

Elizabeth did not stay long after that. Jameson walked with her back to the hotel. He showed her a way through the town which brought her to the rear of the building. She saw how shabby and undistinguished it looked behind its façade. Steam rose from metal chimneys above the kitchen.

'Ask Emil to show the picture to you before he lets me see it,' she said to him as they parted.

'Why should he do that?'

'Tell him it's what I want.' She was not prepared to indulge his disappointment in her any further.

37

That night she dreamed of Mary, and in her dream her sister-in-law looked as she had looked when she and Michael had first met. But the dream was not of that time because in it Mary carried the revolver she had taken from her dead husband's belongings, and as she wandered along familiar Oxford streets, she called out to the people she encountered, all of whom knew her and stopped to talk to her, and when these people were close enough to her, Mary aimed the pistol at them, told them what she was about to do and then shot them. But despite the deafening noise of the shots, and the holes and bloody wounds appearing in the faces, chests and stomachs of her targets, none of those shot people seemed in the slightest affected by what was happening to them, continuing their conversations and reaching out to embrace Mary as she continued to fire into them at even closer range.

The supply of bullets was limitless, shot after shot, a dozen bullets in a single woman's chest, and that woman laughing and talking and not even brushing the worst of the blood from her coat, or feeling beneath it to gauge the severity of her wounds. Men, women and children, all fired at and hit, all of them wounded and bleeding, and all of them behaving as though nothing was happening, as though Mary had merely seen them and then called out in greeting to them.

But then the dream focused on Mary herself, and on her growing frustration and anger that, despite all her efforts, she was achieving nothing. She jabbed the pistol against her targets' chests, into their faces and mouths, but still she achieved nothing. She cursed and raged at them, striking them with the weapon in addition to shooting it.

And as she shouted and swore, so she turned from the woman she had once been into the woman she had become. She grew thin, her face gaunt; and the louder she raged so the faster this happened to her, until she went beyond what she had become and turned into little more than a clothed skeleton with skin turned yellow and stretched so tight over the bones beneath that it began to tear and bleed.

And when she finally stopped shooting and calmed down sufficiently to see and understand what was happening to her, she let out a long, piercing scream of fear and disgust and then turned the pistol on herself, jabbing it into her own face and neck and chest as she fired. But unlike before, when the ammunition had seemed endless, now there was nothing to be heard except the loud click of the firing pin striking empty chambers; even the stabbing of the barrel into her enervated flesh left no mark.

And it was as Mary did this, as she held the pistol in both her hands and slashed it from side to side across her face, that Elizabeth woke and lay shaking in the darkness, allowing the kaleidoscopic fragments of dream, memory and reality to align themselves into some more understandable pattern. But even as this happened, as dream and reality drew apart, she gained little reassurance that this horror and brutality had taken place in the unreal space of a dream, and saw it instead as the first and outermost tremor of a distant yet equally brutal and inevitable tragedy waiting to unfold.

38

She sat with Jameson overlooking the lake. Margaret stood a short distance away, giving instructions to a group of nuns and orderlies, their charges already scattered along the otherwise empty promenade.

Earlier that morning she had finally decided to leave the town and had told the hotel manager of her intentions. She would stay for a further fortnight. She telephoned the station and secured a seat on the train to Geneva. She made no further reservations.

She told Jameson all this. She expected him to quiz her, but he said nothing. He made no reference to Mary or to Oxford, or to the life to which she might or might not now return. She would leave and she doubted if she would ever see him again.

It was the coldest day yet of the approaching winter; a skim of broken ice drifted amid the boulders below. They had both been surprised to encounter the nuns and the invalids after so long an absence and in such weather.

Ruth was there too, with Mitchell, but the boy had insisted on being taken as far as possible from the others, out towards the jetties and the few remaining boats.

Jameson was the first to see her and he called to her. She waved back and shouted that she would come to see him later. He saw Mitchell pull her arm, turning her back to him.

Jameson had with him the Aquinas prayers, still unsold. The earlier deal had faltered. A new prospective buyer was coming to inspect the manuscript and Jameson had arranged to meet him at a hotel in the town. There was an hour before the man was due, and so Jameson was able to show the book to Margaret, as he had promised. Elizabeth had suggested going directly to the hotel to wait, out of the cold, but he had insisted on coming to the lake, and it was as they sat there that the nuns and the invalids had arrived.

Eventually, Margaret left the others and came to join them. Jameson showed her the manuscript and she examined it, savouring its feel, its weight and its scent. She read aloud from it, and she and Jameson discussed its unknown provenance. She had seen another like it, twenty years earlier, in a convent in Perugia. This was valuable information to Jameson, and she told him all she could remember. She concluded by remarking that it was more than chance which had led him to meet her before the book was sold, and when he asked her what she meant she flicked her eyes to the sky.

She told them that the unscheduled visit to the town had been her idea. The hospital remained in a state of flux; there was a great deal of uncertainty and confusion. She had spoken to Sinclair, and he had told her that many there now felt as though they were being abandoned. The first of the suspected influenza patients had arrived, and everyone felt further unsettled by this. Lowering her voice, she told them that the patients with her now were having their beds and belongings moved while they were away. She regretted the deception, but had agreed to it; it was why, despite the cold, she had volunteered to bring them into town. 'God forgive me,' she said.

She closed the book and sat with both her palms resting on it, as though she were drawing some sustenance from it. Jameson watched her closely. She reminded him of the padres he had seen in the field dressing-stations walking round with their fingers inserted into Bibles intoning words of cold comfort over wounded and dying men.

'If your man doesn't take it, may I see it again?' she asked, finally handing the book back to him.

'I'll bring it out to the convent.'

'But of course he'll buy it – he'd be a fool not to. Four hundred years of devotion; how could anyone refuse that?'

'And he'll get it at a good price,' Jameson said.

Elizabeth saw by the way Margaret spoke that she did not expect to see the book again.

'Whatever, I'm grateful to you for showing it to me,' she said. 'Do you suppose he will have any idea of its true value?'

Jameson shook his head. 'He'll sell it on to someone else at a profit. That's the way these things work.'

'And how is business in general?'

'What do you care?'

'I don't; but I care for you, and you care for it.'

'In that case, business is very good and I'm thriving on it.'

Elizabeth wondered how much Margaret understood about the source of Jameson's profits, but guessed by the way that she avoided asking him any more directly that she must have known.

Margaret turned away from them to watch the invalids along the walkway. 'They need warmer coats,' she said, 'but none are being sent.'

'Is there a reason?' Elizabeth said.

'No point sending coats to men who might soon be leaving. According to Cox, Mitchell might soon be going, repatriated.'

'Oh?' Jameson sought out the two distant figures. He saw them on one of the jetties amid a group of fishermen sitting around their boats.

'They've moved him into a smaller ward,' Margaret said.

'Why?' There was alarm in Jameson's voice.

'Apparently, he's been behaving badly, arguing, picking fights with some of the others, staff and patients alike. He's growing resentful of his injuries. He wants someone to blame. It's only natural.'

'He blames everyone,' Jameson said. 'And with no just cause.'

'Cox was supposed to come with us, but he told the driver to drop him and a few others off in the town. He's meeting us here later for the journey back.'

Jameson continued to watch Ruth and the boy as Margaret spoke. Ruth stood slightly apart from the fishermen, but Mitchell sat with them. Their laughter and the murmur of their distant voices were audible over the water.

'They've started taking down the orchard,' Margaret announced unexpectedly.

'Taking it down?'

'Chopping down the trees. Uprooting those that are already half fallen. They'll clear the space, burn the wood and plant something else.'

'More trees?' Elizabeth said. She thought of the small graveyard, the true source of Margaret's concern.

'I doubt it. They say they need too much looking after. A winter of storms will see the weakest of them fallen.'

'It seems such a pity.'

'It is. I shall miss them.'

'Will the nuns do the work?' Elizabeth asked.

'Some of it. The clearing up. Dr Armstrong has offered help from the hospital. There are still men there who know about these things.'

'When will they do it?'

'Soon. Some of the trees are in a dangerous condition. Every wind brings down a bough or two.'

The two women sat in silence for a moment, until distracted by Jameson, who suddenly rose, said, 'Look,' and pointed to where Ruth and Mitchell were walking further along the jetty and out over the open, deeper water. Elizabeth recognized the jetty as the one she and Hunter had walked on, the longest of the structures, the one with its floating pontoon rising and falling with the motion of the lake.

At first neither she nor Margaret could see anything wrong.

'She's taking him too far,' Jameson said. 'She's leading him.'

Margaret rose and shielded her eyes to look.

Jameson climbed onto the bench to get a better view. The fishermen remained around their boats; none of them appeared to be paying any attention to the girl and the boy.

'He won't be led anywhere he doesn't want to go,' Margaret said, but she, too, was unable to disguise her concern at what might be happening. She watched the gathering swell of unbroken waves further out over the lake.

'Ought we to go to them?' Elizabeth said.

'Yes. But calmly,' Margaret said. 'Don't alert any of the others; there's nothing wrong in what they're doing.'

Jameson was the first to move. He picked up his parcel and went down the steps to the lower walkway. Elizabeth followed him. Margaret paused to whisper instructions to another of the nuns before walking quickly to join them.

Halfway to the jetty, Jameson saw that Ruth had now pulled free of Mitchell and was walking ahead of him. She spoke to him and held out her arms to him as though beckoning him towards her.

'What does she think she's doing?' Elizabeth said.

They continued walking, quickening their pace.

They reached the fishermen and exchanged greetings with the men.

Out along the jetty, Ruth and Mitchell were no longer moving. She had stopped at the end of the fixed walkway. Beyond her, the floating platform rose and dipped in the swell.

Jameson called out to her, and Mitchell turned and faced him. The boy demanded to know what was happening. Ruth spoke to him, but her voice was low and inaudible. Mitchell moved towards her, his arms out, coming close to the edge of the walkway.

'Tell him to be careful,' Jameson shouted, cupping his hands to his mouth.

But still Ruth said nothing; instead, Mitchell shouted back for them to be left alone. He said he could feel the vibrations of their feet on the wooden slats and he called for them to stay where they were. When neither Jameson nor Elizabeth responded to this, he shouted again, this time stamping his own feet and turning in a circle, as though feeling for the edge of the boards. Throughout all this, Ruth remained silent, watching, and only when Mitchell appeared to be about to step off the jetty into the water did she warn him not to move. The sound of her voice stopped him instantly, and he stood perfectly still, his feet together, facing out over the lake in the direction of the far shore.

Jameson continued forward alone, slowly, ensuring that he could neither be heard nor his footsteps felt by the boy. He still carried the package under his arm.

Margaret joined Elizabeth, and the two women waited behind him as he moved closer to where Ruth and Mitchell stood.

'Don't,' Ruth eventually called out to him. 'Leave us alone, leave him, go back to them, to *her*.'

'You heard her,' Mitchell shouted, his face still turned over the water.

I won't come any closer,' Jameson said. 'Just bring him back towards me. What were you thinking of, bringing him all the way out here in the first place? Ruth?'

'Because I told her to,' Mitchell shouted. 'Because I told her to, that's why. And what I tell her to do, she does. Isn't that right?' He turned his head from side to side.

Jameson knew by the way Ruth responded to this that Mitchell was lying.

'She loves me,' Mitchell went on. 'I told her to bring me somewhere where we could be alone, somewhere *you* wouldn't come sticking your bloody nose in. What business is it of yours? Bugger off back to your own tart.' He laughed, stamping his feet in childish delight and anger; water splashed over the boards.

Jameson watched as Ruth took several silent steps away from the boy. He wished she had not allowed Mitchell to stand between them on the jetty, otherwise he would have risked shouting for her to run back to him.

Almost as though he was aware of these thoughts, Mitchell

suddenly threw up his arms, further blocking her way past him towards the shore. He moved closer to the centre of the jetty and stood with his feet apart, his legs rigid.

'Don't move,' Jameson called to Ruth, sensing that she might now be frightened enough to try and run past Mitchell before he heard her or understood what was happening.

'Don't worry,' Mitchell shouted. 'She isn't going anywhere. I told you – get back and leave her with me. That's what she wants.' He turned to Ruth. 'That's what you want, isn't it? Tell him. Shout and tell him. Tell him that's what you want.'

Ruth remained silent.

'Tell him!' Mitchell shouted.

Jameson saw her flinch at the words and then raise her arm defensively across her chest. The wind which blew over the water wrapped her long skirt around her legs.

Mitchell started to pant where he stood.

'Stay where you are,' Ruth said, eventually.

'Shout louder. Louder. Shout.'

'Stay where you are,' Ruth shouted.

'Tell him to go and leave us.'

'I can hear you,' Jameson called to him. 'I'm going, look. Listen.' He stamped his feet several times on the wood to give the impression he was walking away. The boy looked directly towards him. Jameson moved silently closer to him.

'Is he going?' Mitchell said loudly to Ruth.

Ruth watched Jameson for a moment. 'Yes,' she said.

Mitchell began to laugh. He lowered his arms.

Jameson moved closer. He laid down his package on the wet boards.

Elizabeth and Margaret remained where they stood. The fishermen joined them. Some of the men wanted to go further along the jetty, but Margaret held them back.

Ruth moved closer to where Mitchell stood between her and Jameson.

Behind her, the waves beneath the pontoon had begun to gather, causing the platform to rise and fall more markedly. Jameson could feel the vibrations of this in the fixed boards beneath him.

'Is that far enough back?' he called out, keeping his voice low to suggest to Mitchell that he was further away.

The boy turned to face him. 'You must think I'm bloody stupid,' he said. 'You haven't moved. So don't pretend you can't hear me. You can hear me, all right. What do you think I'm going to do? Do you think I'm going to push her in? You'd like that, wouldn't you? Then you could play the big hero again and dive in and rescue her. Is that it? Is that what you think I'm going to do?'

'Just let me come past you,' Jameson said, now making no pretence to have moved. 'The water's rising; it isn't safe.'

'How would you know? How would you know?'

Ruth said something to the boy which Jameson could not hear.

'Hear that? She said she can't swim. If you'd gone when I told you to go, she'd be back there with you by now. It's your fault she's stuck out here. Yours. Not mine, yours. It wasn't me who made her come out here. It was her idea, not mine. Why do you suppose she wanted me to come out here with her, do you think? Well?'

Jameson refused to answer. He watched Ruth move even closer to the boy, until she stood only a few feet behind him. The water lapped more vigorously over the jetty.

'Feel that,' Mitchell shouted, lifting and shaking one of his legs. 'Getting a bit choppy. You didn't answer my question. Why do you think she wanted to bring me out here in the first place? Answer me.'

'I don't know,' Jameson shouted. 'You tell me.'

'You bloody liar. You know. You all know. You're all bloody liars, the lot of you. You all know. You all know everything. I said tell me.'

But before Jameson could respond to this, he heard footsteps behind him and turned to see Cox running towards him. As he approached, Cox called out to Mitchell, telling him to stay where he was. He stopped beside Jameson's package, stood over it for a moment and then came on.

'You stupid bloody interfering idiot,' he said, arriving beside Jameson, pausing briefly and then pushing past him.

Ahead of them, the jetty shook, and Cox went on more cautiously, all the time talking to Mitchell, trying to calm him, as though the boy were a nervous horse set to bolt.

'Let the girl come past, Johnny boy, don't be stupid. Think about it. Let her come by you and then you can come back yourself. It's me, Cox. You can trust me. It's these others you don't trust. They're the ones who want to trick you. Think about it. What have they ever done for you? It's me, Cox. You trust me.'

'It's her who brought me out here,' Mitchell shouted. 'She's the one who wanted me to walk off the end, her.'

'I believe you, Johnny boy. Like I said – none of this is your fault. They're the ones to blame, not you. Just don't make it any worse for yourself. Come back with me. Come back now. I'll make sure you're all right, that they listen to you.' Cox continued moving forward as he spoke.

Jameson stood silent throughout all this. If he had spoken it would only have confirmed everything Cox said.

The boy's resistance seemed suddenly to flag, and he dropped his arms to his side and bowed his head. But a moment later, just as Cox came within a few feet of him, within reach of grabbing him and holding him, Mitchell shouted out again, half scream, half roar of frustration and anger, then swung his fists wildly in the direction of Ruth and threw himself off the walkway into the water. He went under and then surfaced. Ruth screamed and Jameson ran forward.

Mitchell floundered for a moment, but made no effort to reach out for the jetty and save himself. He shouted again, but this time the water-filled yell was more laughter than scream, and hearing this Cox ran and dived into the water beside him. Ruth ran until she reached Jameson, and he stopped her and held her firmly by her shoulders. She was crying and he pulled her face into his chest. Behind them, Elizabeth, Margaret and the fishermen ran out along the jetty. When Jameson finally loosened his grip on her, Ruth pulled herself free and walked away from him.

Out in the water, Cox had his arm round Mitchell's neck and was paddling to keep them both afloat. He was trying to shout. The boy was laughing again, still making no attempt to save himself. Two of the younger fishermen leapt into the water beside them.

PART 4

39

They saw neither Ruth nor Margaret during the following days. When news of what had happened reached the hospital, all further visits to the town were finally cancelled.

Elizabeth went several times to see Jameson at the studio, but on each occasion he had been elsewhere. She learned from Emil that he had been twice to visit Hunter, and when she inquired why he hadn't asked her to accompany him, Emil said he didn't know and became reluctant to discuss the matter in Jameson's absence. He admitted to knowing as little as she did about these recent visits. She asked him if there had been any developments regarding Hunter's removal and trial and he swore to her that Jameson had said nothing.

They finally met four days after the near-drowning. He was waiting for her in the hotel. Most of the few remaining guests now avoided each other. Some behaved as though they were there by accident, or awaiting a transfer to somewhere more comfortable and accommodating.

'He gave me a copy of his will,' Jameson said.

'A precaution, surely?'

'Of course.'

'Have you read it?'

He shook his head. 'He told me not to. Not unless I was contacted.'

'I suppose he feels the need to prepare for every eventuality,' she said.

'Is that what it is?' he said abruptly.

'What else did he say?'

'Not much. We were each as evasive as the other. Stiff upper lips, you see, neither of us wanting to offend or be forced to face something we didn't want to see, perhaps something we can't see.'

'That's ridiculous. Nothing was said because nothing needed to be said. You understand each other perfectly, so why prolong the agony with all this pointless speculation?'

'I saw Cox,' he said after a long pause.

'And Mitchell?'

'No. Apparently, he's been moved.'

'To another hospital, home?'

'No. To a secure ward. The sooner they send him home now the better for everyone concerned.'

'You think it would be like pulling the fuse out of a bomb.'

'What do you know about fuses and bombs?' he said, equally coldly. 'Nothing.'

'You're right, nothing. Except that without the fuse the bomb is useless. No bang.' She resented having become the victim of his frustration, and wished they had met after so long an interval under different circumstances.

She had already started to pack her belongings, was already

moving towards her departure. It had reassured her to see how quickly and completely she might remove all trace of herself from the room when the time finally came for her to do so; she saw how quickly she would be forgotten, how swiftly she would disappear into whatever lay ahead of her.

'Cox, of course, blames Ruth and Margaret for what happened,' he said.

She wanted to tell him to stop, for them to talk about something else.

'Imagine if the boy had drowned,' she said. 'You can see his point.' She believed his continued concern for Ruth to be misplaced. She herself believed the girl to have been wholly responsible for what had happened.

'I don't want to see his point,' he said.

'Were either Ruth or Margaret at the hospital?'

'No. I asked Sinclair, but he's seen neither of them since it happened.'

'And you think Ruth will have been punished for what she did? By the nuns, by Margaret?'

'For what she allowed to happen. Probably. I'm going out there tomorrow. Not the hospital, the convent. Weather permitting.' He glanced out at the overcast sky with its now constant threat of snow. 'I want to find out.'

'I imagine Margaret has everything under control,' she said. 'She won't let any harm come to Ruth.'

'No, I know.'

'Do you want me to come with you?'

'It might be easier,' he said.

Then she showed him the long letter she was writing to Mary. 'I can't really think of what to say to her. I don't know what she wants to hear. I've sent telegrams to her asking her to write and let me know what she's doing, but so far I've had no reply.'

'Is there anyone else you can contact to find out – some other family member? It might be easier and quicker to learn everything from them. Is she still in hospital?'

'In Oxford, yes.'

'I heard from Osborne,' he said.

'Is he still—'

'Paris. He's in Paris. On his way back. Some other business he's taking care of for me.'

'I see.' She wondered how long he'd known.

He was about to add something, but she raised her hand to stop him.

'I have to get on with my preparations,' she said.

'Of course.' He rose and she stood up beside him. She expected him to embrace her, but instead he held out his hand to her and then left without saying anything more.

She went to the entrance, watched him descend the steps and then turn into the darkness beneath the bare trees. And despite seeing him the following day, and the days after that – and despite the events of those days – she afterwards always thought of that occasion – of his vanishing into the night beneath the trees and of her own puzzled reflection looking back at her from the glass of the hotel door – she always thought of that occasion as being the precise moment of their parting, of their withdrawal from each other, and she could not at the time understand why she felt so little moved or so little hurt by this.

40

They waited in the convent courtyard for Margaret to join them. Leaves lay in mounds against the colonnaded walls; water no longer fell from the simple fountain; the benches and iron tables of the outdoor schoolroom had long since been removed. The gates leading to other yards were all closed, along with most of the shutters on the windows overlooking the courtyard.

She and Jameson had taken the bus from the town, its only passengers for the last half of its journey. The driver complained at the expense of continuing the service; it was his intention to turn back at the convent rather than drive on to the empty glacier hostel. He spoke with more enthusiasm about the possibility of ferrying the departing patients from the hospital to the railway station.

A small tree by the convent entrance had fallen in a storm

two days previously, damaging the wall there; this had since been sawn back to a stump, its sections of trunk lying along the roadside like giant bobbins.

They had come through the building into the yard expecting to meet someone they knew, but they saw no-one. They waited and were eventually seen from inside. A nun came out to them and asked them what they wanted. Neither of them recognized the woman. Jameson explained to her who they were. She told them to wait, then left them, looking over her shoulder at them as she went.

Margaret finally appeared. She embraced Jameson and kissed Elizabeth on the cheek.

'You should have come sooner,' she said.

'I don't think she believed us,' Elizabeth said, indicating the nun, who now stood in the darkness of the gateway and watched them.

Margaret explained that the woman had arrived from Dijon only the previous day. 'New blood,' she said, unable to hide her feelings. 'Some from here are sent elsewhere, and some from elsewhere are sent here. I imagine those who come to us consider themselves to have been given the rawer deal.'

'And those sent elsewhere?' Elizabeth said.

'It varies. Some of them have been here many years. We are accused of complacency. For years and years we work hard in the fields, at our devotions, in maintaining this place, and then every now and then the light of a far greater understanding is shone in upon us from outside and all our failings and weaknesses are revealed and put right. I daresay there is a good reason for all this when viewed within the broader scheme of things.' She raised her hand to the watching woman, who stood for a few moments longer before turning and walking noisily away over the cobbles.

'Has Ruth been sent away?' Jameson asked as the footsteps finally receded.

Margaret shook her head. 'Ruth is still with us.'

'Was she punished for what happened?'

'I'm afraid so.'

'You too?' Elizabeth asked, guessing at what was being left unsaid.

'Who could find it in their hearts to punish an old woman like me?' Margaret said. 'Especially when someone more responsible, someone more deserving of that punishment might easily be found?'

'How?' Jameson said.

'She is made to stay in the convent, all her privileges withdrawn, such as they were. Her classes and instruction have been increased. I did try to explain what happened, but there were many other witnesses.'

'How has she responded?'

'You know Ruth. Of course, there are those who consider this to be no punishment at all. I was with the Mother Superior the following day when Cox came and—'

'Cox came here?'

'He came demanding to know what was going to be done. He accused us of leniency and then of negligence. He accused me of not caring, and Ruth of deliberate provocation. He was concerned for the boy.'

'Concerned? On whose authority did he come?'

Margaret wiped a hand over her face. 'I doubt it matters to know, or even to make the distinction. He was angry. Things have happened to the boy. I believe he, too, is being restrained.'

'You mean physically?' Elizabeth said.

Margaret bowed her head.

'Can we see Ruth?' Jameson asked her.

'I'm afraid not. The withdrawal of her privileges includes having no visitors from outside. I still can't say for certain if she will remain with us. Higher authorities, I'm afraid . . .'

'How long will this go on?'

Margaret shrugged.

'Are you being similarly punished?' Elizabeth said, still guessing.

Margaret hesitated before answering. She looked around them at the shuttered windows and the dark gateways. 'I imagine I was sent out to you because they know you will listen to me. There are so many new faces. There is talk of us withdrawing completely from the hospital. Talk also of it being turned in its entirety into an isolation hospital, a sanatorium.'

They were all distracted by a sudden gust of wind and by the trail of smoke this blew in at them.

'They've started grubbing out the trees,' Margaret said. 'Burning the old wood. A clean start. Apparently, it will take a week, perhaps longer. Everything that might contaminate the soil must be destroyed. It seems very harsh.' She could not hide the sadness in her voice.

'It must be hard for you,' Elizabeth said.

'It is. But I imagine the physical labour involved is the least of it. Perhaps we, too, shall be cleansed by the effort.'

'Is Ruth involved?'

'She is my assistant. We drag away the cut branches and feed the fires.'

Somewhere inside the convent a bell began to toll.

'I have to go,' Margaret said.

'Will you tell Ruth we came?' Jameson said.

'Of course.'

'When can we return?'

'You're always welcome here.'

'I mean when will we be able to see her again, when will *you* be free to talk to us without being watched?'

'Ah,' Margaret said.

The bell stopped tolling. Margaret took hold of each of them. Her hand felt weightless in Elizabeth's own.

'Do you still pray for me?' Jameson said.

'We both do,' Margaret said. And then she released her grip on them and left them.

They waited in the courtyard until she was indoors and then made their way back out to the road.

They passed the hospital gates and looked in: a large part of the lawn alongside the entrance had been rutted and churned to mud by the number of vehicles now coming and going from the place. A heavy chain and two padlocks secured the gates.

Elizabeth stood back from him. She saw the columns of pale smoke rising from beyond the convent, barely clearing the roof before succumbing to the wind.

41

Returning to the hotel, she encountered the Gottliebs in the lobby surrounded by their cases and bags. Herr Gottlieb shouted in German at the harassed clerk, who understood little of what he said. Gerda was the first to see Elizabeth, and she came towards her.

'My father ordered a car,' she said, indicating the luggage.

'You're leaving? Today? I didn't realize.'

'In one hour, from the station.'

Frau Gottlieb came to her daughter and pulled her away from Elizabeth.

'Is there a problem?' Elizabeth asked, watching Herr Gottlieb.

'It does not concern you,' Frau Gottlieb said. 'My husband will deal with the matter.'

At the desk, Herr Gottlieb continued berating the clerk, shouting the word 'taxi' over and over.

'You never came,' Gerda said to Elizabeth.

'Came where?'

'For our conversation.'

'Did we make an arrangement?'

'Come away, Gerda,' Frau Gottlieb said. 'You are only making a nuisance of yourself. Can you not see that Miss Mortlake has far more important things on her mind, perhaps even a more pressing engagement.'

'I misunderstood,' Elizabeth said.

'You misunderstood nothing,' Frau Gottlieb said, and before Elizabeth could respond to this, Herr Gottlieb left the desk and came over to them. He wore a thick coat, a hat, and a scarf which covered his chin.

'Ah, you have come to say your fond farewell,' he said. 'You, too, will no doubt be pleased to see the back of us. Is that the expression?'

'I've just returned from the convent,' Elizabeth said.

'Ah, yes, the stupid girl who tried to drown that pathetic boy. How unfortunate they did not leap into the water together.'

'Father,' Gerda said.

Frau Gottlieb smiled. 'Perhaps they had an agreement,' she said. 'Perhaps the ridiculous girl lost her nerve.'

Elizabeth looked from one to the other.

'I can tell you one thing that is for certain,' Herr Gottlieb said. 'We will not be returning to this place.' He raised his voice so that the clerk might hear. 'Not next year, not the year after, not ever. Next year we shall go to Caux, to the Palace Hotel. Perhaps you have heard of it. A very expensive place to stay, but at least there you get what you pay for and the service is reliable. At least there they do not employ peasants.'

He was about to say more, when the door was pushed open and a man came in. He looked from the luggage to the Gottliebs.

'Gottlieb?' he said. 'Taxi?'

Frau Gottlieb went to him and began to supervise the removal of their belongings.

Herr Gottlieb remained facing Elizabeth, Gerda beside him. 'You see,' he said to his daughter. At first the girl looked puzzled, but then she nodded. 'Everything I told you, everything I warned you against.' He flicked his hand at Elizabeth as he spoke.

Elizabeth said nothing in reply, still uncertain of the true cause of this sudden flaring of animosity. She knew she had disappointed them, that they had had their expectations of her, but now there was something more.

'Give my regards to your sister-in-law,' Gerda said.

'Thank you, I will.' Elizabeth turned to Herr Gottlieb. 'Shall I tell her that you, too, wish her well, *Herr* Gottlieb, that you, too, hope she makes a swift and full recovery? Shall I tell her that you and your charming wife are looking forward to seeing her again when she is healthy and well and back to her normal self?' She stopped abruptly. She was shouting. The clerk, Frau Gottlieb and the taxi driver stood watching her.

'As you wish,' Herr Gottlieb said.

'I wonder who you pity the most,' Elizabeth said to him. 'Her, or me. Tell me.'

He shook his head. 'Come, Gerda.' He turned to his daughter and led her back to her mother.

42

She was woken the next morning, only seven days before her own departure, by Jameson banging on her door and calling to be let in. It was the first time he had come directly to her room. She heard other voices behind him. She called for him to wait, and still barely awake she put on her dressing-gown and let him in.

'They're coming for Hunter. Today.' He stood for a moment to regain his breath.

'Coming? Who?'

'I don't know. Sinclair came to the studio yesterday. He must have been in town while we were at the convent. There was a note from Emil waiting for me when I returned. I don't know where *he* went. Get dressed, quickly.'

'But what can *I* do? What can *you* do?'

'I don't know. I want you to come with me.' He moved

anxiously around the room, almost falling over the mound of her belongings she had gathered together. 'We need to hurry.'

She knew she would do as he wanted, but she wished then that she had the strength of her conviction to tell him that his mission to save Hunter was useless and that she had known this all along. Instead, she started to search through her clothes.

The door to her room was still open. There was a further knock, and Monique came in. There were still others, the few remaining guests, gathered outside.

'They're taking Hunter,' Jameson said to Monique, as though he expected her, too, to share his sense of urgency and distress.

'I saw him come running in,' Monique said to Elizabeth. She went to help her dress. 'I thought something had happened at the studio.' She turned to Jameson. 'The manager knows you're here. You'll have to wait outside until she's ready. Sinclair called yesterday afternoon. Emil's out of town. He won't be back until later today, if then.'

Jameson went, leaving the door ajar, calling in to them, urging Elizabeth to hurry.

'What does he think he can do?' Monique whispered to her.

'I don't know. What has he been able to do so far?'

'Look outside,' Monique said. She went to the window and drew back the curtain. It had snowed again in the night, more heavily than previously, and the road and lakeshore were covered a foot deep. It was not yet fully light, and the few street lights were reflected in the whiteness.

'Will the road be blocked?' Elizabeth said.

'Probably. But I doubt that will stop him.'

'No.'

Monique held Elizabeth's jacket for her.

Jameson shouted to ask if they were ready.

'Tell the manager what's happening, what's happened,' Elizabeth told Monique.

'Why?'

'He'll want to know what all the commotion is about.'

'He'll want someone to blame for it, you mean. He'd do that anyhow, without knowing. Forget it. A month ago it might have mattered, but not now.'

Jameson shouted again and then came back into the room. Monique stood away from Elizabeth.

'I'm ready,' Elizabeth told him.

Jameson went to the window and looked out. Below, one of the horse-drawn carriages had arrived in front of the hotel.

'I sent word for him,' Jameson said.

Elizabeth guessed that it was the gypsy driver, the only one prepared to undertake the uncertain journey.

Jameson grabbed her arm and pulled her with him out of the room. Monique drew the curtains behind them, returning the room to darkness.

The snow had been driven up the hotel steps and lay in a smooth slope against the door. They followed Jameson's footprints down to the street.

The road along the lake was passable, dry where the snow had been blown clear. They passed the casino and left the few early lights of the town behind them.

Jameson continued to speculate on what was happening. Little of what Elizabeth said reassured him, and it was only when she pointed out that if the road to the hospital was blocked ahead then no-one would be going anywhere, that he finally calmed down.

He unfastened the canvas blind and leaned out to look ahead of them. She did the same. There were no marks on the road, only the rocky outcrops and trees on either side to show the line they were following. The snow was deeper here, beyond the buildings, and in places the horse sank up to its belly in the drifts. The driver struck it with his whip and pulled the reins from left to right to encourage the animal to free itself. Beneath them, the lake was discernible only as a limitless darkness bordering the white.

It was mid-morning before they arrived at the hospital. A line of waiting ambulances stood cold and empty along the driveway. Few lights showed in the buildings; the entrance hall was empty.

Jameson leapt down and ran inside without waiting for her.

Looking out, Elizabeth saw that here, too, there were few marks in the snow, and she felt certain they had arrived in time. She saw by the cloud-filled sky that it would soon begin to snow again.

A solitary orderly appeared in the echoing entrance.

'What's he doing?' he asked Elizabeth, indicating Jameson, who was running from door to door calling for Armstrong and Sinclair.

'Have they taken Captain Hunter?' she asked him.

'Who's Hunter? Has who taken him? I've only been on duty an hour. What are you talking about? He can't come in here making all that racket.' He came out from behind a table to stand beside her. Elizabeth stamped the snow from her shoes and legs. The man watched her.

Jameson returned to them.

'Just calm down,' the orderly said.

Jameson grabbed him by the shoulders. 'Where's Sinclair? Where is he? Just tell me.'

The man became hostile and swung his arms against Jameson to release himself.

'Tell me,' Jameson shouted.

'Not until you calm down, mate.' He turned to Elizabeth. 'You'd better tell him.'

If she hadn't been present, the man would have refused him everything.

'He's anxious,' she said. 'It's been a difficult journey. He heard someone might have come to take Captain Hunter away and he wanted to see him before he went. If he won't do it, then I'll apologize for his rudeness.'

The man looked at Jameson. 'That's more like it. All we need to do is to stay calm.'

Elizabeth fixed her gaze on Jameson.

'I'm sorry,' he said. 'Just tell me.'

'Right,' the orderly said. 'For a start, no-one's been out of here at all today. Look at the weather. I doubt if even half those engines will start up in this cold.'

'Last night, then,' Jameson said. 'Yesterday.'

'Couldn't say. People have been coming and going for the past few weeks. There aren't half the patients there were a fortnight ago.' He looked beyond them to the door. 'Ask me, somebody's left it too late. How they going to get the rest of them away in this?'

'See,' Elizabeth said to Jameson. 'He's still here. Wait until someone can find Sinclair or Armstrong and you'll be able to—'

'Sinclair's gone,' the orderly said, shaking his head. 'Went yesterday afternoon. Late on. Him and most of his patch-up jobs. All unexpected. That's why he went with them. Some of them panicked, said they wouldn't go anywhere without him. Bit pathetic, really.'

'That's impossible,' Jameson said.

'Are you sure?' Elizabeth asked the man.

'Positive. They sent two wagons especially. Sinclair had everybody carrying out his records and equipment.'

'To take them where?'

'Don't know. Railway station, I suppose. They came straight through here in a line. It was definitely Sinclair. He's definitely gone.'

The news stunned Jameson and he could think of nothing to say except, 'We were at the convent. He stopped at the studio and I wasn't there.'

'But Dr Armstrong's still here?' Elizabeth said.

The orderly shrugged. 'I suppose so. But I couldn't say for certain, not these days. Whole place is upside down. Worse than a Number One Station.'

'What's worse than a Number One Station?' Cox had arrived, and having come silently into the entrance, he now stood close behind them and made a spectacle of his arrival. They all turned at the sound of his voice. Cox grinned at the surprise he had created, then again at Jameson's anxiety and uncertainty.

'I was just saying – about this place,' the orderly said.

'Just saying *to civilians*,' Cox said.

'They were asking about somebody called Hunter.'

'I didn't tell you to explain yourself,' Cox said. The grin fell from his face.

The orderly took several paces back from him.

'Shouldn't you be at the desk?' Cox said.

The orderly looked back at the table. 'He was running around shouting,' he said, indicating Jameson, wanting to deflect Cox's attention away from himself.

'Was he now? He's very good at that, running about and shouting the odds. You'd think he was still an officer, or something. Not that it ever gets him anywhere.' He turned to Elizabeth. 'And she's seldom far behind him.'

'I told him that Dr Sinclair had—'

'Him and all his little heroes. Gone. Two dozen little

360

monsters, more like, all set loose to wander.' He gestured like a magician performing a trick, further savouring his authority over the proceedings.

'Just tell us about Captain Hunter,' Elizabeth said.

'You,' Cox jabbed a finger at the orderly. 'Desk.'

The man was relieved to go.

'Now ask me again,' Cox said. 'Only this time ask me more politely. Treat me like you might treat one of your fancy friends in your fancy hotel.'

'Of course,' Elizabeth said. She drew off her gloves. 'Could you please tell us if Captain Hunter has been taken away or if his departure is imminent.'

Cox repeated what she said.

'I don't know how to ask any more politely,' she told him.

'How about—'

He was interrupted by Jameson, who said, 'He's gone,' and she saw by the way that Cox seemed to suddenly deflate that he was right.

'I never said he'd gone,' Cox said, his voice betraying the lie even further.

'When?' Jameson said.

Cox looked at him hard for almost a minute. 'There wasn't anything anyone could have done, least of all you. What did you think – that you were going to come running in and convince the Military Police that some big mistake had been made and that Hunter wasn't the traitor and murderer everybody else knows him to be? Is that what you thought? Look at yourself. You're ridiculous. All your sort are.'

'I should have come yesterday,' Jameson said absently. 'We went straight past.'

'He was gone by mid-afternoon,' Cox said. 'We didn't even

know they were coming for him until they arrived and started shouting the odds themselves.'

'*He* must have known,' Jameson said.

'Why must he?'

'He'll have known.'

'Can we go to his room?' Elizabeth said.

'What for?'

'His belongings. He has books belonging to Jameson.'

'Probably gone with him,' Cox said. 'Or packed up and stowed away. They clear the rooms as fast as they're emptied these days.'

Jameson walked away from them. He stood in the doorway, looking out into the barely brightening day.

Elizabeth went to him.

'You wouldn't have prevented him from being taken,' she said. 'And if he'd had warning himself he would have left you a letter or note, he would have contacted you.'

'No he wouldn't,' Jameson said. 'He wanted this to happen, to be sucked back without anyone holding onto him. He needed it. They'll try him and find him guilty and he'll need and accept that too.'

'They won't execute him,' Elizabeth said. 'Not now, not after all this time.'

'Won't they? How reassuring. Whatever they do, it won't be enough for him; he's already more dead than alive.'

'You're wrong,' she said, but with little conviction. 'Otherwise, why would he ask you for books, why would he go on reading, studying?'

'Because he knew it was what I wanted to believe of him. He even wanted me to believe that I was capable of doing him some good. I'd already fooled myself into believing it, so it can't have been too difficult a pretence for him to keep up on my behalf.'

'You're wrong,' she repeated.

'No I'm not. And please, you can't even convince yourself, so stop trying to convince me. You knew all along how useless everything I did was. I deluded myself. Look at me, what am I?' He turned to face her. He held her shoulders and ran his hands down her arms. Then he left her and returned to Cox. 'Is Armstrong still here?'

'Somewhere.'

'And are you going too, Cox? Back to your own dreary little life where no-one pays you any attention or jumps when you snap your fingers?'

'Think what you like,' Cox said.

'And what about that other deluded idiot, the boy who thinks he's blind?'

'What about him?'

'What will he do now that this cosy idyll's about to come to an end, where will *he* go?'

'He'll go home, like the rest of them.'

'And will he suddenly see again, do you think, or will the world stay black and shapeless for him on account of his pension? How old is he, twenty, twenty-one?'

'Nineteen,' Cox said.

'Nineteen.'

Several nurses entered the hospital and stood in the doorway brushing snow from their skirts.

'And what about you, Cox, Corporal Cox, what conclusions do *you* draw from all this?'

'I don't know what you mean. All what?' Cox looked around him, as though the impossible answer stood somewhere revealed in the room.

'Forget it,' Jameson said. He went back to Elizabeth and took her arm.

They went outside.

'You knew it would happen like this,' she said. 'There was no other way. You knew it all along.'

'Perhaps.'

'He won't have gone struggling or screaming,' she said.

'Not like some others, you mean. Struggling and screaming into an Army jail, struggling and screaming into a courtroom, and then struggling and screaming to a post or a chair in a back yard or a quarry or a depot somewhere, struggling and screaming to that.'

'No,' she said.

'I'm over-reacting,' he said. 'I know I am. But look at me. I'll ask you again: what *am* I, what have I allowed myself to become?' He walked away from her back to the waiting cab. Ahead of him, despite being fully risen above the distant peaks, the sun was still lost to them in cloud, and she knew the day would remain dark, a lesser night, leading only to the darker days ahead.

43

That night, and for the first time since her arrival, she dreamed of her dead brother. In the dream she and Michael had been flying above and around their childhood home, and having flown above the house and the garden, above the surrounding countryside, roads, rivers and fields, they had then swooped down and flown into every room in the house, along every passageway and corridor, up and down each staircase, along walls, across floors, around furniture. And the people beneath and beside them – everyone she had ever known as a child – had risen at their approach and applauded them, called out to them and waved, encouraging them to continue. She had seen and heard everything in the smallest, most precise details. The engine of the plane had made no sound. Walls and closed doors, corners, bends, narrow passages – none of these had impeded them in their silent passing, and the pair of them, her and her brother, had laughed uncontrollably throughout every moment of their charmed flight. Michael spoke quietly to her and she heard every word he said. He had only just then learned to fly, it seemed to her, and this was his first time in complete control of the machine. She felt the warm summer air scour her face and blow through her hair. She held out her arms over the sides of the fuselage.

She could not remember what had woken her from this dream, but she had woken with a start, and she tried to remember if there had been some collision, or if she had woken to avoid one, but nothing returned to her. The pleasure of the dream left her slowly, and the harder she tried to cling to it, so the faster it went from her, until all that remained was the memory of her brother's face and his whoops of delight at each complicated manoeuvre so perfectly and effortlessly achieved.

She saw by her watch that it was not yet three. Outside, it was again snowing lightly.

She remembered everything about the previous day, and about the days before it, but for a moment her dream was more real to her than these events, more substantial and sustaining, and before it went from her completely she lost herself in the grief of its vanishing.

She had a framed photograph of the two of them together, and she took it now from one of the cases at the end of her bed. His eager young face smiled out at her. The side of his head, his blond hair, always too long and boyishly unkempt, rested on her cheek. She remembered the occasion on which the photograph had been taken, the garden in which they had been standing. He was about to push her away and she was about to chase him. She, too, was laughing. She remembered the novelty of it all, the feeling that none of this would ever change, and that if it did change, then it could only ever be a change for the better.

She saw herself running from her brother to her father, who held the camera. She remembered her disappointment at being told she would have to wait for the film to be developed.

She put the picture on the empty cabinet beside her bed. Four years had passed since it had been taken. She spoke to him. She told him about Mary, about all these other lost men and women. She told him about herself. She would have flown around the world with him in that same warm and silent vacuum, anything to have remained close to him and to have ensured that he came safely back to her.

44

The manager came to where she sat at the window. It was mid-morning, and with the exception of a group of chambermaids and kitchen staff sitting at a distant table, she was alone in the dining-room. The shutters on the windows remained half closed, blocking off her view of the lake and snow-covered mountains.

'I have your bill already made up,' he said. He sat opposite her. He was unshaven, and with dark rings of sleeplessness around his eyes.

Two days remained until her departure. She picked up the bill and looked at its final figure. She neither knew nor cared what she was expected to pay.

'I'll go to the bank,' she said. 'A money order.'

'Fine.' He, too, seemed unconcerned. Where, previously, there had been an undercurrent of hauteur in all his dealings with her, now there was only the same sense of helplessness and resignation that had settled over the hotel staff as a whole. She felt it too, wherever she went in the town. The small museums and galleries no longer opened, and most of the cafés and restaurants now served only for a few hours at lunchtime or in the evenings; others were already locked and shuttered until the spring.

'There are no forecasts of the railway being blocked,' he said. 'Not in the immediate future. The people who know about these things say another week will pass before the weather really deteriorates. By which time you will be safe at home.'

'And the hotel?'

'Another week. Accommodation will be found elsewhere for those few who wish to remain. They are the same people each year. They pretend to protest, but they know what to expect.'

'And the staff?' She had searched the distant group upon entering, but Monique was not among them.

He shrugged. 'They, too, know the situation.' He pulled open the shutters and studied the distant peaks. 'There have already been some heavy falls to the east,' he said. 'All roads blocked. And what happens there, later happens here, that much is common knowledge.'

In her room, her belongings were largely packed. The clerk had given her labels for the railways and boats. She had studied the timetables. She knew which connections were viable and which were not.

She would go to see Jameson later in the day. It would be her last visit to the studio. She had not seen him since

Hunter's departure, and neither he nor Emil had tried to contact her.

'Tell me,' the manager said, drawing her back to him, and then pausing to consider his question before asking it.

'Tell you what?'

'Do the English despise *all* foreigners?'

'Mostly,' she said. 'At least, most Englishmen despise most foreigners.'

'That's what I thought.'

'I know,' she said.

'*I* don't despise *you*,' he said.

'No?'

'Perhaps at the beginning.'

'Or perhaps you just despise me less now.'

He smiled at the truth of this. 'And do you imagine that once you set foot on your train you will do anything other than run straight back to your safe little life at home in England?' It was the second time he had used the word 'safe'.

'Is that why you despise me?' she said. 'Because you think all this is a game to me, nothing to do with how I really live?'

He was about to answer when a commotion at the distant table attracted his attention. She thought he might rise and shout for silence, but he remained seated, watching her, unwilling to concede this final point.

'I'll go to the bank,' she said again, tapping the bill.

He rose and left her, this one small victory gained in silence.

She looked back over the lake. Its waters were again blue where they mirrored the sky, and she watched as one of the large steamers was towed from its dock by two inadequate-looking tugs, barely moving as it was pulled away from the quayside, but then gathering momentum as it reached deeper water, sounding its whistle every few seconds, and then clearing its smokestack to leave a succession of small black moons floating above it in the still air.

45

Jameson sat slumped at his desk, asleep. A bottle lay on its side by his hand, its contents spilled across the surface, soaking the books and papers scattered there.

'He's been like this since yesterday,' Emil told her.

Downstairs, the shop door opened and then closed. Monique called up to them. Arriving beside them, she announced that she was no longer employed at the hotel. She looked past them to Jameson. 'Again?' she said to Emil.

'Still,' Emil said.

Other books and papers lay strewn on the floor, where they had been thrown or swept from their shelves and cases.

'He was throwing things around before he started drinking,' Emil said. He stood the empty bottle upright and then pointed to others around the room. 'He hasn't eaten since he came back from the hospital. I was going to call and ask you to come, but he stopped me. He stopped me from answering the door to anyone.'

Then Jameson mumbled something, slapping his palm on the desk, and then letting his hand wander, as though it were searching for something of its own accord. The unintelligible remark silenced them.

'These are valuable books and papers,' Emil said, picking them off the desk and the floor. Monique knelt to help him. Those which were ruined beyond salvation, Emil threw back down. He cursed Jameson for what he'd done, but with concern and not malice in his voice.

'You should have ignored him,' Elizabeth said. 'I would have come.'

'I know. But I think this was something he needed to do. He's calmer now than he was last night. Everything's slipped from his grasp. This—' he swept his arm around the room '—this is just the last of what he had to lose. Before he started, he told me to disregard everything that happened, that when it was all over he would be back to whatever he was before.'

'Do you believe him?' Elizabeth said. 'He knew it was coming.'

Emil shook his head. 'No. He'll go. What is there here for him now? He'll leave and settle again somewhere else, discover there is nothing for him there, either, and then he'll go from there.'

Monique lifted Jameson's head from the desk and gently wiped his cheeks and his mouth with her sleeve. She cradled him in her arm for a moment, stroking his hair back from his face.

Emil opened a window, instantly chilling the overheated room and dispelling its fetid odour.

Elizabeth picked up several books from the desk, holding them so that the moisture dripped from their saturated pages.

'Are many of them ruined?' she asked Emil.

'Difficult to say.'

The next volume she picked up fell apart in her hands, its binding destroyed. It was an illustrated work, and the pictures fell out and stuck to the desk and the chair. Others fell and stuck against Jameson's chest, and she peeled these away from him and screwed them up.

Jameson mumbled again. He lifted his head and opened his eyes. He looked around at them, but it was clear to them that he saw nothing, or that if he did see them, he had no idea of what was happening. He wiped a hand across his face. Print from his fingers left lines across his cheek.

'He'll regret all this when he recovers,' Monique said.

'I doubt it,' Emil said. 'This is the only thing keeping him away from his regret.'

Together, they carried Jameson from the desk to the bed. Elizabeth took off his shoes and unfastened his belt. She soaked a cloth and wiped the ink from his face.

Monique fetched towels and the three of them mopped up what remained of the spilled drink.

Jameson continued to groan where he lay, turning away from them to face the wall.

They left him after that and spent the evening together in the studio below, where Emil and Monique were now living, and where a large fire burned. Emil gave Monique money and she went out for food, returning with bread and a joint of hot pork from the nearby butcher. She cut this up and served it to them. Emil opened more wine. They played gramophone records and talked, and when they, too, became drunk they took it in turns to dance with each other. And when Elizabeth danced with Monique, the girl kissed her on her neck and rubbed the small of her back with her fingers.

Later, Emil became maudlin and started to bemoan the fact that he had nothing to occupy him during the coming weeks.

'I'll occupy you,' Monique told him. She sat astride him where he lay on the couch and rolled up her sleeves. She tucked her skirt beneath his legs.

Elizabeth continued dancing alone. She held her arms around herself. When one record finished she replaced it with another; she recognized few of the tunes; voices sang in French and German and Italian. Some of the tunes were solid and dark, funereal almost, and she changed these for lighter, faster ones. The same songs were repeated over and over.

Emil pushed Monique from him and she fell to the floor. He took out a bottle of brandy, and because he was too drunk and impatient to search for clean glasses, he drank from the bottle and handed it to Elizabeth. She did the same and passed it to Monique.

'I ought to be leaving,' Elizabeth said eventually. She stumbled against the table on which the gramophone stood.

'Stay here,' Monique suggested. 'Or you could stay upstairs. Keep an eye on Jameson.' Her words were slurred.

Elizabeth half fell, half dropped into a seat and knew she would be unable to stand again.

Emil remained on the couch, and Monique lay where she had settled in front of the fire. The music ended, and the click of the gradually slowing turntable sounded its own hypnotic retreat into the night.

46

She woke the following morning to the sound of the fire being raked. She was momentarily disoriented. She saw Jameson kneeling at the hearth. Emil and Monique lay together on the couch.

She yawned, and Jameson turned to face her.

'When did you arrive?' he said.

'Yesterday evening.'

'I see.'

'How are you feeling?' she asked him.

'How I deserve to be feeling. I would have come to see you today.'

'Oh?'

'I'm going to the hospital. The road's clear at last. He can't have taken everything with him.'

'And will you see Ruth?'

'Hopefully.' He was clean-shaven and his hair was wet and flat against his head.

She reminded him of the arrangements she'd made for her departure the following day.

He turned back to the fire. 'I hadn't forgotten,' he said.

On the couch, Monique pulled her arm from beneath Emil and rubbed the cramp from it. She pushed herself upright. Even in the dim light of the room she shielded her eyes to look around her, moaning at the small effort this required. The aroma of the brandy and the cooked meat remained. She saw Jameson kneeling at the hearth. 'You all right?' she said.

He held out his hands and looked at them.

'What time is it?' Elizabeth asked.

'Seven.'

'I'll come to the convent with you,' she said.

'There's no need.'

'I'd like to say goodbye to Margaret. And to Ruth.'

He made no further protest.

Monique slid free of Emil's sleeping embrace, half waking him as she rose. She pulled one of the covers from him, a tasselled curtain, and draped it over her shoulders, giving herself the appearance of a Red Indian squaw.

She left them and they heard her preparing coffee in the room along the corridor.

Emil drew the remaining covers around him.

The fire, though still alight, gave out little real warmth, and Jameson crouched with his hands only inches from it.

'Are many of your books ruined?' Elizabeth asked him.

'I doubt it. Some.'

'Is it over?' she said.

He considered the question for a moment and then nodded. 'I think so.'

Monique returned with the coffee and what remained of the bread and meat.

Elizabeth pulled herself upright, held out her hand and then shouted in pain at the heat of the bowl.

Jameson took it from her and sat beside her. She blew into her palm. She saw the line of missed stubble on his shaved jaw and the drop of dried blood where he had caught the cleft of his chin with the razor.

47

A cloud of smoke still hung above the convent, supported and thickened by the columns which rose to feed it. And looking at this gathering cloud, it was clear to both of them that the fires beneath were now being fed and stoked with a new vigour and urgency.

At first, Jameson was reluctant to enter.

'Perhaps we shouldn't have come,' he said, his voice deadened by the scarf he wore.

'We had to,' Elizabeth told him.

They went through the entrance and the courtyard into the open space beyond.

There were several fires, evenly spaced over the cleared ground, some of them low and dying, but most newly-stacked and blazing. The largest of these stood at the far end of the lost orchard, between where the trees had once stood and the wall of the small graveyard. All around lay the chopped and fallen trunks and tangles of branches waiting to be burned. Most of the grass had already been trampled to mud. Pieces of blackened, smouldering wood lay amid this mud and meltwater and the few remaining patches of snow. And here and there stood the brighter piles of sawdust where the felled trunks had been recently sawn.

Elizabeth felt Jameson hesitate again upon encountering this scene, and she guessed he had seen others like it.

Men and women came and went among the fires apparently at random. Some worked at cutting, stacking and throwing the wood; others merely wandered from blaze to blaze. Not a single tree remained properly upright: some had been grubbed out and now rested on their boughs; others lay with their splayed roots rising from water-filled craters.

There were men there from the hospital, orderlies mostly, but a few of whom Elizabeth recognized as patients, passing the days before their own delayed departures. Other men, local farmers and their labourers, did most of the work with the fallen wood. The nuns and girls stood around the fires, mostly in groups, but some standing alone and close to tears at what they were witnessing. An old nun in the small courtyard had sat weeping with her face in her hands, barely looking up as Elizabeth and Jameson had approached and greeted her.

Beside her had stood several of the pregnant girls, some of them now close to bearing the children who would afterwards be taken from them. Elizabeth recognized those girls she had seen in the outdoor classroom. She spoke to these too, but again no-one responded to her. She felt little pity for them, only a vague sense of sympathy or sadness that the natural order of achievement and loss in their young lives had already been destroyed, now forever weighted in favour of the latter and the sudden cold shadows this would continue to cast over them for as long as they lived.

In the orchard they searched for Margaret and Ruth. Elizabeth was the first to see them, and she pointed out to Jameson where the woman and the girl stood together, Margaret with her hands on Ruth's shoulders, beside the gateway leading to the graveyard. She knew immediately that Margaret was protecting the entrance, preventing anyone from passing through into the sacred ground beyond.

They made their way towards them. Fountains of sparks rose all around them. Ash and cooling embers filled the air, and the faces of many were already marked where they had wiped these away. Smaller, untended fires burned where embers had fallen amid the waiting timber and sawdust, kept in check only by the wet ground.

Cox was there too. He saw Elizabeth and Jameson and came towards them. He carried a short piece of wood, one end of which still smoked.

'Come to help?' he said to Jameson. 'Or have you come like you always come, just to watch? There's a name for men like you.'

Jameson ignored him. He raised his hand to Margaret, who had just then seen him and who waved in reply. Ruth took a step away from her, but the nun pulled her gently back.

Cox turned to Elizabeth. 'Surprised you're still here,' he said. 'You going to live here with him? You ought to have gone long since.'

She, too, said nothing.

Cox looked at the smoking brand he held. 'They should have done all this before the snow. That would have been my advice.'

'How's Mitchell?' Jameson said unexpectedly, silencing him.

'How do you think? The little bitch could have killed him.'

'Just tell me.'

'Why? So you can go and tell her everything's all right? That she has nothing to blame herself for? Why should I? He hasn't been right since it happened. He's started ranting and raving. He hasn't been let out of his room since. Christ knows why, but he used to think something of her. Still does. The way he sees it, *he's* the one being punished for what happened. Not her, *him*. Tell her that. Tell her the truth for once. He'd have been long gone by now if it hadn't been for all this, for her. As it is, they won't move him, not the way he is, not yet. Armstrong's even talking about putting him in some kind of institution back home while they work out what to do with him afterwards. And you want me to tell you that he forgives her? Forget it. It's about time she opened her stupid eyes. You too, the pair of you.'

'But he does, doesn't he?' Elizabeth said.

'What? He does what? What are you talking about?'

'He – Mitchell – he does forgive her. It's *you*, not him – you're the one who wants to see her punished. That's the real truth of the matter.'

Cox could think of nothing to say in reply. He raised the smoking wood, waved it in front of her face for a few seconds and then threw it violently to the ground. 'If it's forgiveness she's after, tell her to go and beg it from one of this bloody lot.' He motioned to the nuns. 'I don't want her near me, and I don't want her near him. Never. And I don't want to see *him* near the place, either.' He pointed at Jameson.

They were approached by a group of several other orderlies, attracted by Cox's raised voice, who now stood watching, but who made no attempt to intervene.

'Ask my opinion,' Cox said. 'They ought to burn the bloody lot down and start from scratch. Smash it all down and then think about whether it's worth rebuilding.' Then he left them, drawing the orderlies after him.

Across the fires, Margaret again raised her hand to them.

They continued through the mounds of stacked and burning wood to where the woman and the girl waited, Margaret still with her hands on Ruth's shoulders.

'No lessons,' she said as they arrived. 'Everyone was allowed out to participate or to watch.'

'It's good to see you again,' Jameson said to Ruth.

She held out her hand to him and he took it. Margaret relaxed her own grip on the girl.

'You'll have to start making plans for the spring,' he said to Margaret. 'Give you something to work towards.'

'I daresay.' But she refused to encourage this false hope.

'How's Mitchell?' Ruth said. 'I ask, but they only tell me not to.'

'He's fine. He'll be going home soon.'

'People treat me as though I wanted to drown him. Someone should ask him what *he* wanted.'

'What do you mean?' Jameson said.

She didn't answer him.

Nearby, a length of trunk was thrown into one of the fires by six men working in unison, and a spectacular gush of sparks rose up into the form of the lost tree. All four of them turned to watch.

Ruth whispered something to Margaret, who nodded her assent. The girl then pulled on Jameson's hand and led him a short distance to one side.

Elizabeth stood with Margaret and watched them go.

'She'll be gone herself before the spring,' Margaret said, as much to herself as Elizabeth.

'Oh?'

'It would be stupid to deny it.'

'And you?'

'I don't know. I sometimes feel like a boulder at the centre of a stream, spate or drought, there – here – I stay. Life passes us by. It acknowledges us, it respects us, it makes way for us, but it passes us by all the same. I sometimes wonder if that isn't our true function.'

'You and all the other boulders?' Elizabeth said.

'Me and all the other boulders.'

'I'm sorry – I wasn't being facetious. I do understand what you're saying.'

'I know you do.'

They turned their attention to Jameson and Ruth, who stood in close conversation. Elizabeth saw that the girl had now slid both her hands into his.

'What did she hope for?' she asked Margaret.

'Who knows? Perhaps nothing more than any of us hope for, yourself included.'

'I'm leaving tomorrow.'

Margaret nodded. 'Did you know there'd been talk in the Town Council about reopening the quarry on the far side of the lake?'

'It would be work, I suppose,' Elizabeth said. She tried to remember what she had seen of the abandoned workings during her trip along that shore.

'I know. They want it for headstones. Military cemeteries. The mayor referred to it as "our contribution". They are already speculating on the amount of stone needed, on the cost and the profits to be made. I wonder how many they'll need.'

'Millions,' Elizabeth said.

'A whole mountain, then,' Margaret said. 'I doubt I can

even imagine what one million men looks like. Perhaps there's something in us which prevents us from being able to do so, because if we could imagine it, if we could see them, those million men, they would be too awful for us to contemplate.'

'Perhaps some things only become tolerable when they are reduced to profit and cost,' Elizabeth said.

'Like all this, you mean,' Margaret said, indicating the fires.

The crowd had grown smaller since their arrival. Only three or four of the fires now burned with any real energy, and most of the others were no longer being fed. It would be dark in two hours and the freezing air and whatever fresh snow might fall would quickly extinguish what remained of the blazes.

Elizabeth watched Jameson and Ruth. She wondered if the girl felt betrayed by how he had treated her, neglecting her in favour of Hunter since the incident on the jetty. Beside her, Margaret had fallen silent. She, too, was watching Jameson and Ruth.

'Will you return, do you think?' she asked Elizabeth.

'Here? Of course. Perhaps next year.'

Neither of them spoke for several minutes, neither of them willing to force the other into any further deception, into turning the present and what had passed into the future.

Elizabeth shivered at the growing cold, and she was about to suggest calling to Jameson when she was distracted by a disturbance at the far side of the burning orchard.

Two more orderlies had just then arrived, running, breathless, shouting for Cox, almost frantic in their efforts to locate him.

Jameson saw them too, and he and Ruth came back to where Elizabeth and Margaret stood.

'Something's wrong,' he said.

Ruth released her hold on him and moved closer to Margaret.

The two orderlies ran among the fires, pushing people aside and calling out for Cox, until Cox and those with him finally revealed themselves and the men ran to them.

'Stay out of it,' Elizabeth said to Jameson, but he had already left them and was moving towards the men. As he went, the fire closest to where they stood lost its heart and collapsed into its empty centre, blowing ash and embers all around. Jameson walked through these, kicking them aside to clear his path.

Elizabeth followed him. Margaret and Ruth remained where they stood. Elizabeth had expected at least Margaret to come with her, but the old nun simply put her hands back on Ruth's shoulders and held her against her, at once restraining, protecting and comforting her. It was the last Elizabeth saw of the woman and the girl, the two figures so close they were barely distinguishable one from the other through the warp and drift of the rising smoke and heat.

She, too, kicked aside the embers through which Jameson had walked.

'What's wrong?' she said, arriving beside him.

'Something's happened at the hospital.' He called to Cox, to the men around him, asking them what was happening, but Cox and the men merely looked at him without speaking. Then he and the orderlies ran back through the convent. Jameson followed them, ignoring Elizabeth, who called for him to wait for her.

She finally caught up with him at the hospital gate. She held his arm. 'It's none of your business,' she told him. But he refused to listen to her and he pulled himself free and ran on. She ran after him. Ambulances and lorries came and went again along the hospital drive. She searched for someone she might recognize, someone who might help her, or someone who might at least explain to her the cause of this sudden commotion.

She followed the running men into the hospital.

Somewhere inside the building an alarm bell rang, falling silent as she guessed at its source, creating a sudden and powerful vacuum into which everyone present was then drawn.

She was relieved to see Armstrong emerge from his office ahead of them.

Jameson saw him too and called to him.

'What are you doing here?' Armstrong said.

'We were at the convent.'

'This is nothing to do with you, either of you. You'll have to wait here. We can deal with him.'

'It's Mitchell, isn't it?' Jameson said.

Armstrong held a hand against his chest. 'I said stay here.'

'What's happened?'

'I don't know. Something. That's what I'm going to find out.'

As he spoke, a nurse appeared. She held a hand over her mouth and was at the same time gasping for breath. Her cap and long strands of unpinned hair hung from the side of her head.

'Help her, someone,' Armstrong shouted.

The woman came towards them. She lifted her hand, as though about to say something, but instead she vomited, spraying the floor ahead of her. A second nurse ran to help her. She pulled off her apron and held it to the sick woman's face.

Armstrong took his hand from Jameson's chest. 'I have to

go,' he said, turning from them and walking only a few paces before he, too, started to run.

Jameson followed him.

Elizabeth shouted after him. 'He told us to wait here. There's nothing we can do.'

And again he ignored her.

She went to the two nurses. 'What is it?' she said, looking from one woman to the other in hope of an answer. The woman who had been sick began to retch again and Elizabeth stepped back from them.

She followed Jameson along the corridor and then down a flight of stairs to the basement. She imagined Mitchell had broken free of whatever restraints were being used on him, perhaps broken out of his room, and that in his frustration and rage he had attacked someone, one of the young nurses, someone who reminded him of Ruth, someone, perhaps, who, in whatever confusion or delirium which now fed his rage, he had believed *was* Ruth come to test him or taunt him again.

At the bottom of the stairs she was surprised by the sudden silence and the apparent calm there. There were still shouting voices and the sound of running footsteps, but beyond these there was nothing, as though the tremor of alarm and urgency had spread outward from its centre leaving this inner circle of calm in its wake. She heard Armstrong calling out orders.

The corridor ahead was empty, but turning a corner she saw a small crowd gathered around an open doorway.

An orderly came towards her, his head down, concentrating on something he was carrying. He stopped when he saw her.

'What's happened? Is that Mitchell's room?'

She thought that he, too, was going to ignore her, but

then he held up a bundle of blood-stained bandages for her to see.

'He did this,' he said. 'He's gone mad, he must have.'

The bundle was almost wholly red.

At first she thought the dressing was wrapped around one of his own hands, that Mitchell had attacked him, cut him or bitten him, but then she saw that he was merely carrying the bundled dressing, cupping his palms for want of a bowl, and that his hands beneath were uninjured, coloured only by the blood which dripped through them.

He pushed past her and ran up the stairs.

She joined Jameson at the back of the small gathering.

'Have you found out what's happening?' she asked him.

'Not yet.'

Ahead of them, Armstrong turned at the sound of their voices.

'He's coming out,' someone shouted, and everyone in the crowd took several paces backwards, creating another small panic in the confined space.

She expected Mitchell to emerge, or someone with him, restraining him, but instead Cox came out alone, and he, too, carried a blood-soaked bundle. He spoke briefly to Armstrong and then came on through the crowd, which cleared ahead of him. Then Armstrong and several others went into the room.

Cox stopped in front of Jameson and held up the cloth for him to see more clearly. 'You'll be happy now,' he said.

'What's he done?' Jameson said. 'Who has he attacked? A woman, a girl, who?'

But Cox stood unable to answer him, as though he himself were only just then aware of what had happened, of what he held, unable to take his eyes from the bloody mess in his own cupped palms. And when he did eventually speak, his voice was broken and dry. 'What's he done?' he said. 'What's he done? He's proved us all wrong – proved *you* wrong – that's what he's done. No more guessing now, no more is he or isn't he for poor old Johnny boy Mitchell, none of that, not now, not any more. That's what he's done, that's what he's done.'

Elizabeth watched as blood fell in viscous lines to the floor. She understood then what had happened.

'Tell me,' Jameson said.

'Why don't you go and see for yourself,' Cox told him. 'No danger now of you getting *your* hands dirty. Not now, not when—' He stopped abruptly and looked hard at Elizabeth. 'Ask her,' he said. 'She knows. She's worked it out, ask her.'

'What?' Jameson said. 'Worked what out? Tell me.' He looked from one to the other, but neither of them answered him, and unable to contain his frustration any longer he left them and followed Armstrong into the silent room.

'What was it?' Elizabeth said to Cox.

He was less reluctant to talk now that Jameson had gone. 'A knife,' he said. 'God alone knows where he got it from. You'd never imagine a man could do something like that to himself, not to himself, you wouldn't think it was humanly possible, not something like that.'

'Has he—'

'Everything. Not just his eyes. His lips, his nose, his cheeks. They think he might have been like that for an hour. Blood everywhere, soaked in the stuff. Never made a sound, apparently. They said he was sat laughing to himself when someone finally looked in on him. Laughing, surrounded by all that blood, all that . . . You wouldn't think it possible . . . How could a man do that to himself? Not even a man, a boy . . .' Then he, too, noticed the dripping blood, saw it pooled at his feet, and he left her.

She went slowly to the open doorway, but drew back before reaching it, and stood with her face to the wall, a hand pressed hard over her mouth. There was now no limit to the world in darkness.

48

She returned to the town alone.

An ambulance stopped for her beyond the hospital entrance. At first she didn't hear the driver calling to her, but then turned at the sound of his horn.

She climbed in and sat beside him. He had arrived at the hospital that same morning and had no understanding of what was happening there, relieved only to be leaving the place, and anxious that he might be caught by a further fall of snow and be forced to turn back.

It grew dark as they went.

She asked him if there were any patients in the rear of his vehicle and he told her that he was loaded only with boxes of files and suitcases, which he was taking to the station.

It resumed snowing as they began their descent into the

town, lightly at first, but then more heavily as they reached the outskirts.

Elizabeth said little, absorbed in her thoughts of what had happened. She was finally distracted from these by the driver, who stopped on the lake road and asked her which was her hotel. She looked out, surprised to see that the strings of coloured lights beneath the trees had once again been switched on, creating patterns in the falling snow. She pointed out her hotel and he drove on.

She collected her key and went to her room.

She looked around her at the luggage waiting to be taken down, and as though somehow prompted by the sight of all this, and by the need now to leave, to be moving forward and not to be caught or to be motionless or to feel herself being drawn back, she began to hurriedly gather together the last of her belongings, carelessly stuffing these – clothes, jewellery, books, cosmetics – into her travelling bag, only then to stop a minute later as suddenly and as inexplicably as she had begun, throw down what she held, fall onto the bed and look around her at everything in disarray, knowing that it would all need to be emptied out and repacked in the morning.

The curtains had been drawn, and she pulled these back to look at the snow drifting past the window.

She stepped out onto the small balcony and into the night, allowing the snow to blow into the room behind her, the cold air tugging at the curtains and at her strewn clothes. She stood oblivious to its effect.

Beneath her, the lights remained lit, swaying slightly and still creating their changing patterns in the darkness, their shapes and colours reflected and broken on the settled snow and the surface of the lake.

And then she looked down at her hands and saw that in her haste and confusion she was still wearing her white kid gloves with their mother-of-pearl studs, and she looked closely at these, darkened now by the molten flakes, and for a reason as inexplicable to her as her frantic packing, they seemed suddenly abhorrent to her, and still barely understanding what she was doing, or why, she pulled them off and threw them to the ground below, watching them as they fluttered down through the darkness and the falling snow like nothing more than a pair of shot white doves.